About  the Authors

USA Today bestselling author **Naima Simone** writes romance with heart, humour, and heat. Her books have been featured in *The Washington Post* and *Entertainment Weekly*, and described as balancing 'crackling, electric love scenes with exquisitely rendered characters caught in emotional turmoil.' She is wife to Superman, and mum to the most awesome kids ever. They live in perfect, domestically challenged bliss in the southern US.

Red Garnier has found her passion in penning charged, soul-stirring romances featuring dark, tortured heroes and the heroines they adore. Nothing brings a smile to Red's face faster than a happy ending. Red is married with two children and, though she travels frequently, likes to call Texas home. For more information on Red, visit her website at redgarnier.net/site/

USA Today bestselling author **Michelle Major** loves stories of new beginnings, second chances, and always a happily ever after. An avid hiker and avoider of housework, she lives in the shadow of the Rocky Mountains with her husband, two teenagers, and a menagerie of spoiled furbabies. Connect with her at michellemajor.com

Fake Dating

Fake Dating:
Family Feud

NAIMA SIMONE

RED GARNIER

MICHELLE MAJOR

MILLS & BOON

First Published in Great Britain 2023
by Mills & Boon, an imprint of HarperCollins*Publishers* Ltd,
1 London Bridge Street, London, SE1 9GF

www.harpercollins.co.uk

HarperCollins*Publishers*
Macken House, 39/40 Mayor Street Upper,
Dublin 1, D01 C9W8, Ireland

Fake Dating: Family Feud © 2023 Harlequin Enterprises ULC.

Blame It on the Billionaire © 2020 Naima Simone
Wrong Man, Right Kiss © 2013 Red Garnier
Her Accidental Engagement © 2014 Michelle Major

ISBN: 978-0-263-31976-7

MIX
Paper | Supporting
responsible forestry
FSC™ C007454

This book is produced from independently certified FSC™ paper
to ensure responsible forest management.

For more information visit: www.harpercollins.co.uk/green

Printed and Bound in the UK using 100% Renewable Electricity
at CPI Group (UK) Ltd, Croydon, CR0 4YY

BLAME IT ON THE BILLIONAIRE

NAIMA SIMONE

To Gary. 143.

One

Honor thy mother and father.

Grayson Chandler smothered a sigh. With all due respect to Moses, but if he'd been stuck listening to Grayson's mother nag on and on and about his lack of duty, loyalty and wife, the prophet might've asked God to nail down the specifics on that commandment.

Swearing. Out.

Muzzling. Out.

Faking a coronary episode to avoid her complaining. Gray area.

For a moment, a flicker of guilt wavered in Grayson's chest. But at the moment, he was caught in his mother's crosshairs. Pit bulls with lockjaw had nothing on Cherise Chandler. She didn't let go of something—whether it was a project, a subject or a grudge—until she was done with it.

Which didn't bode well for him.

He was thirty years old and president of KayCee Corp, one of the most successful global tech start-up companies in the country and he hadn't been a child to be controlled long before he left his parents' house. For years, he'd answered only to himself, owed no one else explanations or justifications.

Yet none of that mattered when it came to the crystal blue gaze that could make him feel like the little boy who'd been busted hiding a stray dog under his bed for a week.

Hell.

Parental guilt trips were a bitch.

"Grayson, your stubbornness is becoming ridiculous," his mother said, a note of irritation in her voice. She shifted closer and a small frown marred her brow. "You've proven your point with this little business venture of yours and Gideon Knight's. But your father needs you now, your *family* needs you. It's time to stop playing at CEO, step up and take your place at Chandler International. It's your responsibility. Your duty."

He clenched his jaw, trapping the vitriolic stream of words that scalded his throat. *This little business venture. Time to stop playing.* As if striking out on his own without the emotional or financial support of his Chicago old-money, well-connected family was the equivalent of a rousing game of Monopoly. With those few words, she'd dismissed years of his and Gideon's hard work, relentless determination and resulting success.

He should've been used to this casual disregard. Of his accomplishments. Of him. As the second son, the "oops baby" of Daryl and Cherise Chandler, he'd been an afterthought from birth. But somehow, his skin had never grown that thick.

Another black mark in the "Why Grayson Isn't Jason Chandler" Column. Right under rebellious. Selfish. And disloyal.

Didn't matter that he'd had a hand in founding a tech platform that served major businesses and assisted them in tracking their shares with its unrivaled software. Didn't matter that his business was one of the most successful start-ups to hit the financial scene in the last five years.

None of it mattered because it wasn't Chandler International.

Dammit.

Grayson shoved his hands in his tuxedo pockets and glanced away from his mother's scrutiny. Guilt and shame knotted his gut.

He was throwing a pity party, but at least he was *alive*.

Jason couldn't say the same.

And because his mother had lost her son—her favorite son—Grayson imprisoned the sharp retort that weighed down his tongue.

"I take my position at and ownership of KayCee Corp as seriously as Dad does with Chandler. I also understand my obligation to our family. But as I've told both of you, my company is my legacy just as Chandler is Dad's."

"Don't be deliberately obtuse, Grayson. It's not the same—"

"Mother," he interrupted, voice cold. "Now isn't the place or time for this conversation."

She parted her lips, but after a second snapped them closed. Oh yes. Only proper decorum and being potential fodder for gossip trumped getting in the last word.

"Cherise, it's so wonderful to see you again," a feminine voice intruded.

The pleasant, soft tone shouldn't have scraped him raw, leaving an oily slide of disgust. He didn't need to glance behind him to identify the woman. He'd be able to identify that dulcet tone, that light floral scent anywhere.

Identify it, then crucify it.

"Adalyn," his mother crooned, a smile erasing her frown as she moved toward Adalyn Hayes with outstretched arms. "Don't you look beautiful?"

Grayson shifted to the side, studying his mother as she warmly embraced his ex-girlfriend. The woman who'd almost become Mrs. Grayson Chandler.

The woman who'd stabbed him so deeply in the back he still had phantom pains from the scar a year and a half later.

She hadn't changed at all. Still stunningly beautiful with oval-shaped green eyes, delicate features, pretty mouth and long sleek hair as dark as a raven's wing—or as dark as her heart. A midnight blue gown that glittered as if stars had been sewn into it clung to her small breasts and willowy frame before flowing over slender hips to pool around her feet.

No, she hadn't changed a bit. But he had.

That beauty no longer stirred desire inside him. Those embers had long turned to dust, incapable of being lit ever again.

"Grayson," Adalyn purred, turning to him and linking her arm through his mother's. "I didn't know you would be attending the gala this year. It's wonderful seeing you."

"Hello, Adalyn."

Damn if he'd lie just for the sake of pleasantries.

"I've missed you," she murmured as if his mother had disappeared and just the two of them existed in the crowded ballroom of the North Shore mansion. "We need to get together for dinner and catch up with one another."

"I love that idea," his mother chimed in, patting Adalyn's hand. "We've missed you, too. I was planning a dinner party for next week. You and your parents are invited. I'll call your mother to officially issue the invitation."

The conversation sounded benign, but something seemed...off. Too jovial. Too neat.

Too false.

"Matchmaking, Mother?" he asked, infusing a boredom into his tone that didn't reflect the cacophony of distaste and rage roiling inside him like a noxious cloud. "You don't think this is a little beneath you?"

"Not when you insist on flitting from woman to woman, behaving like a male whore," she snapped, and no, it wasn't the first time he'd heard those words.

Manwhore. Playboy. Embarrassment. But again, that damn not-so-thick skin. The barbed insult pricked him like the cockleburs that would sting his fingers when he visited his grandmother's horse farm as a child. Back then, he'd plucked them off and rubbed away the nip of pain. Now, with his ex a witness to his mother's disdain, those nips drew blood.

Deliberately curling his lips into a mocking smirk, he bowed slightly at the waist. "Thank you, Mother. Now tell me what you really think because I sense you're holding back."

She scoffed, returning her attention to Adalyn who watched him with a gleam in her eyes. A gleam that heralded trouble. For him.

"You're thirty years old and it's time to put away such childish behavior. The future CEO of Chandler International needs a good woman by his side supporting him. The board will not endorse or accept a man whose name and picture ends up on those dirty little gossip websites as often as the business section."

He stiffened. The smile he gave his mother was brittle, felt close to cracking right down the middle.

"Well then I guess it's a good thing I don't intend to be the future CEO of Chandler International. Which makes the board and my love life nonissues. Now, if you'll excuse me, I see several people I need to speak with." Bending his head, he brushed a kiss over his mother's cheek. "Mother. Adalyn."

Without waiting for the diatribe about his rudeness, he pivoted and strode away from the two women, the noose that had slowly been tightening around his neck loosening with each step.

He should've seen this coming. His mother had been less than subtle about her wishes for him to settle down and marry. Especially in the last six months.

Since Jason had died.

The thought of his brother lanced him through the chest, a hot poker that hadn't cooled in the time since his death. With a thirteen-year age difference and the knowledge that Jason was the favorite between them, they hadn't been close. But Grayson had loved his older brother, respected him. And the tragic randomness of a brain aneurysm had only made Jason's death harder to accept.

But Grayson hadn't had time to grieve before his parents had started pressuring him to leave the business he'd created and return to the family company. The Chandlers were American royalty, and with the heir now gone, the spare had to step up and perform his duty. Which meant helming Chandler International and, according to his mother, committing himself to a woman from a respectable background.

The knot that had started to relax around his throat tightened again, and he jerked at his bow tie. God, the thought of being back under his father's thumb, having to answer to Daryl Chandler and the board full of men just like him... Of having his independence stripped from him... Of having to live by the constricting rules that governed being a Chandler, one of Chicago's oldest and wealthiest families...

He was already suffocating.

Fuck, he needed air.

Charging across the ballroom, he didn't stop until he exited the cavernous space filled with the glitterati of Chicago. They were supposed to be his friends, his business contacts, his people.

And all he wanted was to escape.

Escape them all.

Two

The last place Nadia Jordan belonged was this gorgeous North Shore mansion that wouldn't have been out of place in the French countryside. And as the security guard skimmed a glance over her dark brown hair that no doubt looked like she'd been dragging her fingers through it—because she had been—and down her leather jacket and faded jeans to her tennis shoes, he no doubt agreed.

But in her defense, it was a Saturday night, and she'd been on her way back home from one of her brother's travel league baseball games when she'd received the emergency call from her supervisor that had brought her here. As the older sister and guardian to a teenage boy, her idea of an emergency included a hospital, an asthma attack or broken limbs. But obviously she and her boss, the vice president of operations with KayCee Corp, had very different ideas of what constituted a crisis. His involved a high society gala, a white tuxedo shirt and spilled shrimp cocktail.

When she'd received the call, she'd wanted to tell him

she was off the clock. He could button up his jacket for the rest of the night. But being a rural transplant from Tatumville, Georgia—and yes, it was as small as it sounded—she'd been lucky to land the job in Chicago as secretary in one of the country's hottest tech firms. And with a brother who was involved in every extracurricular activity his new high school had to offer, as well as his college tuition bills on the very near horizon, she literally couldn't afford to say no to her supervisor's sometimes wacky requests.

Being a secretary hadn't been her dream job. Nursing held that honor. But leaving for school and entrusting her brother to her mother's seriously lacking maternal care hadn't been an option. Nadia had cared for Ezra since their mother had come home from the hospital with him, even though Nadia had only been seven. Sacrificing for him so he could have a stable home and a chance at a successful future hadn't been a hardship. She would do anything to ensure he had the opportunities she hadn't.

Which explained why she stood in the foyer of an ostentatious mansion, holding a garment bag with a clean dress shirt, waiting for a black-suited security guard to grant her entrance.

"Ma'am, your name isn't on the guest list," he informed her, scanning the screen of the tablet he held.

She fought not to roll her eyes. *No shit, Sherlock.* She belonged in a world with linoleum and mass-produced light fixtures. Definitely not this alternate universe with gold and marble tiles and mammoth crystal chandeliers. "I know. My supervisor, Mr. Terrance Webber, is the guest. I'm his secretary, and he asked me to bring an item by for him." She held up the garment bag, silently explaining the "something."

"He assured me he would leave a note with security so I could bring this to him. I shouldn't be long at all."

"A moment, please."

"Sure." She forced her lips into a smile, when she really wanted to lament the fact that she could be curled up on her living room couch, covered from chin to toe with an afghan, settling in for an evening of campy B horror movies.

Several moments passed as the guard spoke into a headpiece, and she tried not to gawk at the over-the-top evidence of wealth surrounding her. A gilded staircase that could've graced any classic Hollywood movie set curved to a second level. Paintings that appeared old, and therefore expensive, were mounted on the walls and a huge fireplace inlaid with more gold damn near covered a far wall.

So this was how the one percent lived.

Enlightening.

And intimidating as hell.

Finally, the guard ended his conversation and glanced down at her.

"Mr. Webber is currently in the first men's room in the east wing. He instructed you to meet him there." He turned and pointed toward the rear of the foyer and a corridor that branched off to the right. "If you'll follow that hall to the end, make another right. The men's restroom is the last door on the left."

"Thank you."

Relief poured through her as she marched forward, ready to have her errand done so she could return to real life. Which didn't include this uncomfortable tumbling in her stomach.

Well, her life in Chicago didn't include it. In Tatumville, she'd been intimate with this feeling—this sense of not belonging, of not being worthy. When you were the daughter of the town Jezebel, who was also a drunk, people tended to stuff you in the "won't amount to much" box. But when Nadia and Ezra left her hometown and started over in Chicago, she'd vowed never to let anything, or anyone, make her feel that insignificant again.

The music drifted away until she could barely hear it as she traveled down the hall. Her cell phone buzzed in her jeans pocket, and she paused to fish it out. A grimace crossed her face as she read the text.

Terrance Webber: Where are you, Nadia? I need the shirt ASAP. They're about to serve dinner.

Inhaling a deep breath, she held it for several seconds, then slowly released it. Being snippy with the boss was a definite no-no.

Nadia: I just arrived. I'll be at the restroom in a minute.

She typed the reply and started walking, tucking the phone in her back pocket. The sooner she got this over with the bet—

"Oof."

The air barreled out of her lungs as she slammed into the wall that had just sprung up in the middle of the corridor. She stumbled back several steps, and the garment bag tumbled from her fingers. Big, strong hands gripped her forearms, steadying her before she could follow Mr. Webber's shirt to the floor.

"Thank you. I'm sorry about…that…"

Her words dried up on her tongue as she met a unique gaze. Heterochromia, it was called. She'd looked it up soon after starting her job. One vivid, sky blue eye, and one forest green. Startling and beautiful. And only one man she knew possessed it.

Grayson Chandler. President of KayCee Corp. Her employer.

And the man she'd been secretly lusting after for over a year.

Oh, God. Surely You couldn't be so cruel.

But as Grayson cocked his head to the side and skimmed his gaze from her face, down her body and back up, she had to admit that yes, indeed, God might have a mean streak. Otherwise, why else would He allow her to come face-to-face with this beautiful man while she looked like something that had been dragged over home plate a couple of times?

He bent down and snagged the forgotten garment bag from the floor. Standing, he offered it to her, a smile quirking the corner of his mouth. Wow…that mouth. Full, sensual with a deep dip in the center of the top lip. Her fingers itched to trace it, to test the softness. She shivered, and from the narrowing of his eyes, she didn't think he missed it.

"I've heard of Cinderella showing up late to the ball clothed in a beautiful gown. But not with her dress in tow." He held the bag out to her, arching an eyebrow. "I think you need an upgrade in fairy godmothers."

"Yes, well, Cinderella was high-maintenance," she murmured, accepting the luggage.

A sharp bark of laughter escaped him, and from the slight widening of his eyes and the surprise flashing through the blue-and-green depths, it seemed the crack of amusement caught him off guard. Join the club.

"And you're not high-maintenance?" he asked, slipping his hands into his tuxedo pants.

The movement opened his black jacket, offering a glimpse of his pristine white shirt stretched across a broad, powerful chest and flat abdomen. Heat tangled in her belly, and she fought the urge to cover it with her hand. As if that futile gesture could contain it.

"You would be the first, then," he said. Before she could respond to that loaded statement and the hint of bitterness in it, he continued. "I've never met the anti-Cinderella before, and I have to admit I'm curious. After you change, will you allow me to escort you to the ballroom?"

Mortification swelled inside her chest, scorching a path up her throat and pouring into her face. It figured that when she stepped into a fairy tale and met Prince Charming, instead of being the bejeweled, beautifully gowned princess, she was the poor scullery maid. Only thing missing was the ash on her face.

Clutching Mr. Webber's shirt tighter, she hiked up her chin. She might be embarrassed, but damn if she'd show it. "Actually, I'm only here to drop off this shirt for my supervisor. He's the guest, not me."

He frowned. "It's Saturday. Aren't you off the clock?"

She shrugged. "Technically. But when the boss calls…"

"Are you getting paid overtime for this little errand?" he pressed.

She didn't reply. They both knew the answer. And judging by the darkening of his eyes, from irritated to thunderous, he didn't like it. Why did that send a thrill tripping down her spine? Especially when it was *Grayson's* employee who had delivered the order for her to be here? She refused to analyze the first or share the second.

"What's your supervisor's name?" he asked. No, *demanded.* The hard, flat tone brooked no refusal. Again, that trickle of excitement, only this time it sizzled, arousal hardening her nipples, clenching her belly…pooling heavy between her legs.

She didn't do controlling men. Not after the childhood she'd experienced and all the things she'd witnessed between her mother and her "boyfriends." In many ways, Grayson reminded her of those men. Rich. Handsome. Pillars of the community. Respectable. Untouchable. Except for furtive meetings with her mother in the alleys behind bars or in the back seats of expensive cars.

Yes, he bore more than enough resemblance to those

hypocrites that she should shy away from him. But from the first, Nadia had been drawn to his lovely mismatched eyes, the sharp angles of his cheekbones, nose and jaw. The carnal perfection and temptation of his mouth. The tall, elegant frame with wide shoulders and chest, a tapered waist and long, powerful legs.

But unlike those men who'd ignored her mother on Main Street but couldn't get enough of her on back streets, Grayson seemed to possess a core of integrity. The few times they'd run into each other since she'd started working at KayCee Corp, he'd been nothing but respectful, his gaze not dipping to linger on her generous breasts or her equally generous ass. He'd never uttered sly innuendo or propositioned her. It'd been…refreshing. And had only deepened her schoolgirl crush.

Yet none of that justified her reaction to that implacable, disobey-and-bear-the-consequences tone. Or explained why she imagined him clasping her chin in his big hand, holding her still for a hard, hungry kiss while cuffing her arms above her head.

Arousal rippled through her, and she clenched her thighs.

"Cinderella," he said, stepping closer, while she stared up at him like prey caught in the unblinking stare of a predator on the hunt. "His name."

"W-why?" she stammered. *Oh, for God's sake.* She tipped her head up, drawing her shoulders back. "Why do you want to know?"

Why do you care?

"So I can have a very civil conversation with him about taking advantage of his employees and not compensating them for their time. To discuss how not to abuse one's position of power over another, including expecting them to be at one's beck and call."

"There're a lot of 'one's' up in there," she grumbled.

Shaking her head, she ignored the curl at the corner of his mouth, and the warmth it caused to slide through her veins. Like liquid sunshine. And all because she'd made him smile. Somewhat. *Good Lord, woman. Get it together.* "I can't do that. One, I need my job, and two, it's no big deal." Even though it kind of was.

"Oh, but it is," he purred, mirroring her thoughts. "And you don't have to worry about your job, Cinderella. Whoever he is wouldn't dare to fire you."

The arrogance and satisfaction in his assurance shouldn't have been sexy, but damn, it *so* was. Even the fact that he didn't remember her, though they'd met a handful of times, couldn't diminish the desire he stirred in her. Did it sting? Oh yes, and more than a little. But she worked for his company, not for him directly. And if life had taught her anything, it was to be realistic. Men who were constantly photographed with sophisticated, slender, gorgeous social-ites, actresses and models wouldn't notice a small-town, curvy, unassuming secretary.

So yes, him not recognizing her made sense. Still hurt, though. Every woman—even Cinderella—longed to be memorable. Especially to the man who starred in her every dark, sweaty, erotic dream.

"I appreciate your concern, but my lips are sealed, and I really need to—"

"What would it take to unseal them?" he murmured, and she stiffened, shock winging through her as his gaze dropped to her mouth. And stayed there.

Nervous, she sank her teeth into her bottom lip, and something flashed in his eyes. On another man, she would've labeled it lust. But not him. Never *him*.

"Tell me what I need to do. What you need me to give you," he added.

Her apparently filthy mind supplied answer after answer, and none of them had to do with clean shirts, bosses' names or uncompensated time.

She cleared her throat. "I don't—"

The hallway plunged into darkness.

"What the fuck?" Grayson snapped.

Yes. What the fuck indeed.

Three

"Any word yet?"

Grayson glanced down at the woman sitting on the floor of the hallway. The light from his cell phone revealed her back pressed to the wall, her long, entirely-too-gorgeous legs stretched out in front of her and crossed at the ankles. Jesus, what this woman did for denim...

Dragging his attention away from the siren's call of her thighs, he returned it to the cell in his hand. "Citywide blackout," he replied, his voice rougher, more abrasive than usual. Unexpected, and inconvenient, lust clawed at him. "I wasn't able to get any calls out, but I managed a couple of texts. According to my friend, the police are advising everyone to stay where they are. Which won't be a problem for us. It seems the tech guru who owns this mansion installed a state-of-the-art security system that has now malfunctioned, locking us all inside." Grayson shook his head. He'd met the man earlier. The guy epitomized the definition of "book sense but no common sense." As the grandiose house and the money spent on it testified. "So until the blackout is over, and power is restored, we're trapped here."

Quickly, he typed out a text to his parents, but it didn't go through. Damn. But at least he knew they were safe somewhere in this building.

"Shoot," she muttered, thrusting her hand through her thick brown hair.

No, not brown. That was a woefully inadequate description for the beautiful blending of auburn and shades of copper and chestnut.

"Yes, I'm afraid you're stuck with me for the foreseeable future," he drawled, lowering to the floor and setting his cell phone between them, so the flashlight app created a small, dim circle of light. Drawing his legs up and propping his wrists on his knees, he glanced at her. "Look on the bright side. I could be your supervisor."

He chewed up the word *supervisor*, angry still at the thought of the nameless, faceless man. What spoiled, selfish asshole made his employee traipse all the way out to the Gold Coast to bring him a shirt on the weekend? She still hadn't revealed his identity, but he intended to find out. And when he did, Grayson would enjoy throwing around his last name to put the fear of God in the man. No, the fear of a Chandler.

"Good point," she agreed absently. But then a smile lit her face, and a peculiar and *unwelcome* catch snagged in his chest. Forget the light from his phone, the beauty of that smile could illuminate the entire building. Hell, the Chicago skyline. "Oh, thank God. He's safe."

"Who's safe?" he asked, because screw it, he was curious about her. Any woman who showed up to the DuSable City Gala in a leather jacket and skinny jeans was way more interesting than one in a gown and jewels.

At first, he didn't think she'd answer, but after a moment,

she said, "My brother. I left him at his baseball game, but he's at a friend's house instead of on the road."

"Did you try reaching your parents? Just in case he wasn't able to contact them?" Almost as soon as the words exited his mouth, he wanted to snatch them back. Emotions flickered across her face, there and gone before he could decipher them. Well, except for one. Pain.

"It's just my brother Ezra and me," she said, tone flat.

He recognized that particular note. Too well.

"I'm sorry," he murmured, curling his fingers into his palms until the short nails bit into the flesh. It was either that or erase the distance between them and cup her too-lovely face. "I know the pain of losing someone, too."

Her eyes, as dark as espresso, softened. She shook her head. "No, I'm sorry for your loss." If he hadn't been studying her so closely he might've missed the slight shift of her hand from her lap. As if she, too, considered touching him, but decided not to at the last moment. "My parents aren't dead. They're just not...here. I'm my brother's guardian, and we moved to Chicago a little over a year ago. It's just us."

More questions piled into his head, his curiosity about this beautiful woman insatiable. That in itself should've alarmed him. The last woman to elicit even a tenth of this magnetic pull had left his heart and pride battered and bruised.

Still, she'd satisfied a small piece of his curiosity. That honeyed drawl. Definitely not a clipped, flatter Chicago tone. She hadn't mentioned where she'd moved from, but he'd bet his favorite bottle of Glenlivet that she'd lived somewhere hot and south of the Mason-Dixon Line. The slightly exaggerated vowels and soft consonants flowed over his skin like a heated caress. He had the insane urge to strip naked and let it touch every inch of him.

He shook his head as if he could somehow dislodge the

thought. Yet…he couldn't stop his gaze from roaming over her features. When he'd first bumped into her, he'd focused on steadying her and keeping her from falling backward. But when she'd lifted her head, he'd been struck dumb for the first time in his life.

Years ago, he'd started boxing as a way to release aggression and get some exercise. He clearly remembered the first time he'd had his bell rung by a sparring opponent. The other guy's fist had plowed into Grayson's stomach, blasting the air from his lungs, leaving his legs rubbery and his head spinning. When he'd peered into this woman's dark brown eyes and beautiful face, he'd been back kneeling on that mat again.

Long-lashed eyes that turned up at the corners. Regal cheekbones to match the almost patrician slope of her nose with its flared nostrils. Below, her wide, full, utterly perfect mouth had him fighting the urge to press his thumb to it. Just to feel the softness of that slightly heavier bottom lip that formed a natural pout. That mouth would inspire both worshipful poems and dirty limericks.

Then there was her body.

Even the worn leather jacket, simple white T-shirt and ripped skinny jeans couldn't detract from the lushness of her curves. If anything, the plain clothes emphasized the miracle that was her body. Tall, even in gym shoes, the top of her head brushed the underside of his jaw. Strong but slender shoulders. Beautiful, firm breasts that would more than fill his hands—and God, did he want to find out for himself if that were true. A tucked-in waist that accentuated the wide flare of hips that had his palms tingling to cradle her—hell, degenerate that he was, he wanted to dig his fingers into her…leave his prints behind on that flesh. Impossibly long, thick legs and that ass. He briefly closed his eyes. God only gave asses like that to those He really loved… He must love the *hell* out of her. Round. High. Flawless. Made to be adored.

Yes, Grayson's first glimpse of her had pummeled the sense from his head and ignited his body like a struck match tossed in a pool of gasoline. Not even Adalyn had garnered that reaction from him.

And sitting here with this woman in a private world carved out of darkness, he couldn't deny that he wanted her. Wanted to feel her breath on his lips, his skin. Wanted to taste her mouth, taste that golden almond skin, discover its flavor for himself. Wanted to feel those abundant curves pressed to his larger, harder frame, adhered to him by sweat and lust.

The clawing desire also had him mentally scooting back.

Nothing that powerful could be good. Especially for him and his addictive personality. During his teens, it'd been the excess afforded him by his parents' wealth and social status. Later it'd been women. Then he'd poured that intensity and driving need into founding and building KayCee Corp. And then into Adalyn.

Yeah, he sensed that he could become wildly addicted to the woman next to him, whose vanilla and earthy scent— like fresh wind after a summer storm—reached out to him, tempted him. Hell, a woman whose name he didn't even know.

And that scared the hell out of him.

And yet…

"What's your name?" he demanded.

Her hesitation was brief, but he still caught it.

"Nadia," she said.

"Nice to meet you, Nadia," he murmured, stretching his hand out toward her. "Grayson."

Again, she paused. But then, she slid her palm into his. And when an electrical charge sizzled up his arm and straight to his cock, he instantly regretted touching her. Only pride kept him from jerking his hand away.

He shifted his gaze from their clasped hands to her eyes, expecting to see the same shock. Instead he glimpsed resignation. And shadows. His gut clenched. Experience had taught him that secrets lurked in the shadows. Lies lived there.

Slowly, he released her, returning his hand to his knee. Resisting the urge to fist his fingers and ease the residual tingling.

Or capture it.

Turning away from her, he stared straight ahead into the enveloping dark. "Why don't you want me to know your name?" he finally asked, casting aside the socially acceptable tact that had been drilled into him since birth. "Do we know each other?"

Her sharp but low intake of breath glanced off his ears, and he faced her again, openly scrutinizing her face for any telltale signs of deception. But she was good. Aside from that gasp, her expression remained shuttered. Either she had nothing to hide or she was damn good at lying.

He couldn't decide which one to believe.

"No," she whispered. "We don't know each other."

Truth rang in her voice, and the vise squeezing his chest loosened a fraction of an inch.

"And I guess, I didn't see the point of exchanging names. If not for this blackout or you being in this hallway instead of the ballroom, our paths wouldn't have crossed. And when the power is restored, we'll become strangers again. Getting to know each other will pass the time but it's not because we truly want to. It's not…honest."

Her explanation struck him like a punch. It echoed throughout his body, vibrating through skin and bone. *Honest.* What did he know about that?

In the world he moved in, deception was everywhere—

from the social niceties of "It's so good to see you" to the cagey plans to land a business deal. He wasn't used to her brand of frankness, and so he didn't give her platitudes. Her honesty deserved more than that.

"You're right," he said. "And you're wrong." Deliberately, he straightened his legs until they sprawled out in front him, using that moment to force himself to give her the truth. "If not for me needing to get out of that ballroom and bumping into you here, we wouldn't have met. You would be outside, unprotected in the parking lot or on the road. And I would be trapped in the dark with people I wish I didn't know, most likely going out of my mind. So for that alone, I'm glad we did connect. Because Nadia…" He surrendered to the need that had been riding him since looking down into her upturned face, and clasped a lock of her hair, twisting it around his finger. "Nadia, I would rather be out here with you, a complete stranger I've met by serendipity, than surrounded by the familiar strangers I've known for years in that ballroom."

She stared at him, her pretty lips slightly parted, espresso eyes widened in surprise.

"Another thing you're correct and incorrect about. True, when the lights come back on and we leave here, we probably won't see each other again. But in this moment, there's nothing I want more than to discover more about Nadia with the gorgeous mouth, the unholy curves and the underwhelming fairy godmother."

Maybe he shouldn't have pushed it with the comments about her mouth and body, but if they were being truthful, then he refused to hide how attractive he found her. Attractive, hell. Such an anemic description for his hunger to explore every inch of her and be able to write a road map later.

Her lashes fluttered before lowering, hiding her eyes. In her lap, her elegant fingers twisted. He released the strands of her hair and checked the impulse to tip her chin up and order her to look at him.

"Why did you need to escape the ballroom?" she asked softly.

He didn't immediately reply, instead waiting until her gaze rose to meet his.

Only then did he whisper, "To find you."

Four

Nadia struggled to compose her features. To not let the yearning tangling in her to reflect on her face. Especially with Grayson's piercing scrutiny attempting to peel away her carefully constructed protective layers. She'd spent years erecting them and couldn't afford to let him see the insecure woman who raised her brother the best way she could, constantly afraid she would screw him up in some way as their mother had with her.

But *oh God*, did he tempt her to lower her guard. To surrender to the quiet invitation in those amazing eyes.

Still, Grayson Chandler, president of KayCee Corp, one of the most successful tech start-ups to explode onto the financial scene in years, the golden son of the revered Chandler family, *couldn't* want her. Not Nadia Jordan, formerly of Tatumville, Georgia, daughter to Marion Jordan, the town's notorious man-eater and drunk.

It had nothing to do with her self-esteem—or lack of it—regarding her body. If her mother had bequeathed anything to her, it was a confidence in her curves. Because Nadia had inherited her build from Marion.

From the time Nadia had been old enough to understand what was happening, she'd witnessed the lust and appreciation men possessed for Marion's large breasts, wide hips, thick thighs and not-so-small behind. Those rich pillars of the community might ignore her in public when standing next to their wives and daughters, but in the dark, in secret, they couldn't get enough of Marion's brash laugh, her flamboyance, her casual sensuality, and of course, her body.

And when Nadia hit puberty and started to fill out, their dirty leers had transferred to her. Almost everyone in her hometown had expected her to follow in Marion's footsteps. Like mother, like daughter. Earlier than she should've, she'd learned to dodge grasping, searching fingers, to avoid deserted hallways and dark corners where teen boys and older men could trap her.

It was why she'd escaped Tatumville as soon as she could. To move to a place where she wasn't seen as her mother's daughter. To give her brother a chance to grow up out from under that censure.

So no, she didn't have body issues. Still, she'd seen the pictures in society and gossip magazines and blogs capturing Grayson with women who were the anti-her.

And then there was the matter of his wealth.

He might not know all of her background, but from her clothes and the conversation they'd shared, he had to know she was not only from the other side of the tracks, but that those tracks were miles away.

She didn't trust rich men. Too many times had she witnessed her mother not only using those kinds of men for money, favors or gifts, but also allowing them to use her, too. Nothing they gave Marion had been free, and in Nadia's experience, rich men did nothing without expecting something back.

Staring at Grayson with his *"To find you"* ringing in her ears, she forced herself to remember those lessons. She tried to resist the small but insistent whisper in her mind asking what would be the harm in letting go just once in her life? Who would it hurt if she took something for herself?

"You don't strike me as the kind of man to believe in that fated nonsense," she finally said, resenting the rasp in her voice.

"I'm not," he agreed. "I don't believe in ideas like destiny, blind faith or unconditional love. I forge my own path, make my own choices and live by them. And there are always conditions, strings attached to everything. Nothing in this life is free," he said, echoing her own thoughts. "You know what I do believe in, Nadia?" She shook her head, and the intensity in his gaze seemed to deepen. "What I can touch, see…taste. If I can't, then I don't trust it."

"And yet…" She trailed off.

"And yet," he continued. "It might not have been you who dragged me out of that ballroom. But I'm here. And I'm not alone."

Alone.

That one word resonated inside her, expanding until it rang like a struck gong. A man like him shouldn't be alone. It struck her as…wrong.

"It seems to me that someone who attends a gala that even peons like me know about isn't often alone." She cocked her head. "Unless he wants to be."

"You know what they say about assuming, Nadia." He tsked, but she didn't miss the thread of steel in the teasing. As if he were warning her to back off the topic. Which perversely only heightened her desire to pursue it.

"Well then don't let me assume, Grayson. Enlighten me. Tell me something about yourself. Something nobody knows. Something that will stay here in this hallway. Between you and me."

He studied her for a long moment, and Nadia met that blue-and-green gaze, no matter how much she might want to duck her head and avoid it. And, she didn't rescind her request. She waited, her chest tight, hoping he would answer. Even if it was some bullshit that every gossip outlet knew. For this moment, she could pretend it was only for her.

"I hate this pretentious, fake, incestuous fishbowl," he finally murmured, drawing his legs back up and propping his arms on his knees again. Turning from her, he stared straight ahead, but a small muscle ticked along his jaw. "No, not a fishbowl. A shark tank. A tank full of predators waiting for the slightest sign of weakness so they can tear you to pieces. Do you know how exhausting it is to be constantly on guard?"

"Yes," she whispered. God, did she. "But, you know, the thing about sharks? We see them as ruthless, single-minded killers, when they're not. They're important to the ocean's ecosystem. In a way, they're protectors. Smaller fish depend on them for survival. I could make the argument that if they didn't exist, neither would the weaker, more vulnerable species."

He shifted his gaze back to her, and a faint smile played with his lips. Heat rushed into her face. Thank goodness for the dark so he couldn't see the evidence of her mortification. Unfortunately, her mouth wouldn't stop running.

"I watch a lot of Animal Planet," she mumbled. "But maybe, you're in that tank to protect the defenseless so they can thrive."

The smile disappeared. And she regretted whatever she'd said that had caused it to vanish.

"I've been called a lot of things in my life, but protector has never been one of them. You make me sound noble, and I'm not," he said, that vein of harshness entering his voice again. This time, it might've induced her to back away from the subject—if not for the presence of something else there, too, something that tasted of desperation, of…pain.

It drew her to him.

The press painted Gideon Knight and Grayson Chandler as light and dark, the yin and yang of KayCee Corp. Gideon was the intimidating, merciless owner, while Grayson was the golden, charming half. But the glimpses of him she'd received tonight…

Who was Grayson?

Those glimpses promised that more lurked beneath that affable mask. It was the *more* that had her reaching out to him. Had her settling her hand over his.

"In my experience, people who warn you that they aren't noble are the ones with good hearts. It's the ones who brag about being righteous and moral that you need to watch out for."

Grayson's gaze dipped to her hand, then slowly lifted until it met her eyes. A shiver rippled through her, and he didn't miss it.

"My heart isn't good, Nadia. I'm selfish. Greedy. Spoiled. And if you knew the thoughts in my head right now, about you, you would remove your hand from mine," he warned.

She didn't. Even though her heart thudded against her sternum, she didn't heed his warning.

"Go on and ask me," he murmured, and her breath caught in her lungs at the sin in his voice. "You're thinking it. I can see that in those pretty brown eyes. Ask me what thoughts are in my head."

Here in the dark, the caution that ruled her life started to unravel. That small, low whisper encouraging her to take grew in volume, in strength. In this hallway, cut off from the real world, with only the man she'd fantasized about for company, she was Eve reaching for the apple even knowing she shouldn't.

Knowing that traveling down this path with her employer would be one of the biggest mistakes of her life…

She bit the apple.

"What are your thoughts about me?" she asked, the question barely there.

"Are you sure?" he pressed. When she nodded, he did, as well. "You bumped into me earlier, but only because I'd already stopped. I couldn't move. Watching you walk is pure sex. The confident stride of those legs that mesmerize a man. Give him thoughts of how they would clasp him in their strong embrace. The sensual sway of hips I want to dig my fingers into while I press you close and take your mouth that was created to be claimed, corrupted. That's what you are, baby. Corruption. Sin. Desire in flesh. And I want to kneel in front of you and beg you to consign me to your hell. Because I want to burn in you. With you."

Oh God.

Desire, scorching hot and out of control, blazed a path from her belly, up her chest and to every limb of her body. Consuming her. With just words, he caused her nipples to tighten, her sex to spasm in need. Thank God she was sitting, because her trembling legs wouldn't have supported her. Not when the blood in her veins had become liquid lust. Not when the breath in her lungs had evaporated into smoke.

I want to kneel in front of you… Because I want to burn in you. With you.

Now, she could do nothing but picture him on his knees in front of her, that proud head tilted back, his amazing eyes fixed on her. His fingers clasping the tab of her zipper and steadily lowering…

She closed her eyes, not to block out the image but to dwell on it.

"Nadia." Gentle but firm fingers pinched her chin and lifted her head. "Look at me," Grayson ordered, and she did. When she stared into his amazing eyes, he nodded. "Your turn. Tell me something nobody knows. Something that will stay here in this hallway," he said, lobbing her words back at her.

Brave. She'd always prided herself on not backing down from any challenge. Especially because it'd almost always meant going without something—food, rent, money. But here, brave meant being selfish. It meant grabbing ahold and taking for herself...for once.

And God, did she want to take.

Could she do it only for tonight? Slap the time-out button and live brashly, without a thought for the consequences? Who would she hurt?

Maybe just herself once morning dawned or the lights came back on. But she was prepared to walk out of here accepting that when she returned to work on Monday, she would go back to being the nameless, faceless employee on the twentieth floor.

If she could have this slice of time with Grayson, then she'd deal with the hurt of becoming invisible again.

"I like tequila shots," she whispered. "What no one knows is you're like that hit of tequila. Potent as hell, hot and strong like the first punch of alcohol to the stomach— and I'll gladly get drunk on it, on you, even knowing I'll be hungover and remorseful in the morning."

The silence between them thickened and heated. His grip on her chin tightened, and the slight pressure drew a gasp from her. His eyes. They seemed to glow with the same need that snapped inside of her. His skin tautened across his cheekbones, his sensual, full mouth flattening into a firm line.

"Do you understand what you do to a man like me when you say that?" he growled.

"A man like you?" she rasped.

"I told you," he said, voice rough, harsh. His hand shifted

from her face and up into her hair, gripping the strands. "I'm greedy. Selfish. And will take without conscience what you're offering me." He tugged on her hair, and pinpricks of pleasure danced across her scalp. She sank her teeth in her bottom lip to trap a moan. "What are you offering me, Nadia?"

"Me," she breathed. "For tonight. All of me."

As if those words snapped a fraying leash on his control, Grayson swooped down and crushed his mouth to hers. *Oh God.* She hadn't been prepared. Maybe she'd believed she was. But foolish, foolish her—she wasn't.

Not prepared for the intensity, the hunger, the *ravishing.* She felt silly even thinking that antiquated word, but no other could describe how he consumed her. Dragged her under with the thrust of his tongue, the hard but sensual molding of his lips to hers.

His holds in her hair and on her chin tightened. He tugged her head back farther, and his thumb pressed firmer just under her bottom lip. Both helplessly and willingly, she opened wider for him, for the plunging and tangling of his tongue. For his possession. A possession she not only welcomed but craved like her next breath.

He had become that vital.

His mouth abandoned hers, and with a disappointed whimper, she followed him. But he shifted his grip to her jaw and held her still. He trailed a sizzling path from her lips, down her throat and to the crook between neck and shoulder. There, he nuzzled her, and she gasped as a jolt leaped from that spot to her taut nipples, through her knotted belly and down to the already damp and spasming flesh between her thighs.

Reaching for steady purchase to cling to in the erotic maelstrom, she dug her fingernails into his shoulder. And held on.

"Come here," he murmured, his hands dropping to her

hips and drawing her toward him. Over him. In breathless seconds, she straddled his rock-hard thighs. Slowly lowered herself until the long, thick length of his erection pressed against her denim-covered sex. A low, shaky gust pushed out of her lungs. Damn. He was... Screw it. He was big. And for a woman who hadn't had sex in well over a year? Intimidating.

But for a woman who'd never indulged in sex where she didn't need to worry if the man would gossip about her afterward?

Exhilarating.

Liberating.

Rolling her hips, she stroked her sex over him. A full-body shiver worked its way through her, and she groaned at the stunning pleasure. Layers of clothes separated them, but they didn't prevent her from *feeling* him. His width, his hardness, his strength.

Sinking her teeth into her bottom lip, she ground against him, rubbing, rocking over his flesh, getting lost in the swells of desire that threatened to quickly drown her in the release that already loomed wonderfully close. Jesus. She was going to embarrass herself by coming quickly just from some fully clothed dry humping, and she couldn't bring herself to care.

"I like that you're using me for your pleasure, baby," he praised in a silk-and-gravel voice that both slid over and abraded her skin...her nerve endings. "But don't hide from me." He pressed his thumb to her lip and gently tugged it free from her teeth. "I want to hear every sound, every word of your need for me. Don't keep anything from me."

Oh God. He was temptation, a sinful lure enticing her to fall in the most spectacular of ways.

With deft hands that spoke of skill and practice, he removed her jacket and shirt. Seconds later, she sat on his lap, his rigid dick between her thighs and his beautiful, bright gaze on her half-naked body. She resisted the urge to lift one arm over her plain bra and cross the other over her stomach.

No, she might not be ashamed of her body, but that didn't prevent insecurities from creeping in with their sly reminders that she wasn't like the women he'd been pictured with. Though Nadia worked out and ran—not just for health reasons but because it was also a great stress reliever—she would never have a cut six-pack unless she drew it on her abs with a Sharpie. Her flatish, soft belly carried faint stretch marks, and her breasts... Well, they were firm, but their weight would always make them sag a little rather than sit high on her chest like perky B cups.

"Don't even think about it," Grayson snapped, his eyes sparking with blue-and-green fire. Stroking his hands up her arms, he squeezed her shoulders, before continuing his journey south until he cupped her breasts in his big hands. "Maybe I should've been more specific when I told you not to hide from me. Not sounds, not words and definitely not this gorgeous body."

"You're certainly bossy, you know that?" she said, arching an eyebrow but leaving her hands on his shoulders. "Does that usually work for you?"

"Yes," he rumbled, whisking his thumbs over her stiff, aching nipples. "And it does for you, too." He pinched the tips, wringing a low cry from her. "Doesn't it, baby?"

She didn't answer but lowered her head and took his mouth, swallowing his wicked chuckle. He didn't let up playing with her body, tweaking and tugging her nipples until she ripped her lips from his and threw her head back. More than anything, she wanted him flesh to flesh, no barriers. Reaching behind her, she unclipped her bra and yanked it off. An almost feral growl tore from him, and he hefted her breasts, lifting one to his mouth and sucking deep while continuing to toy with the other.

Every flick and circle and suckle agitated the insatiable creature she'd become. She tunneled her fingers through his hair, gripping, caught between clutching him close so he couldn't turn her loose and pushing him from her, unable to bear the brutal sting of pleasure.

Switching to the other mound, he rubbed the wet tip, but slid his free hand down her torso, over her stomach and beneath the band of her jeans. Her audible catch of breath echoed in the hallway, and she stilled as his fingers slipped underneath denim and cotton, resting on top of her sex.

Lifting his head, he met her gaze. "Yes or no?" he asked.

Desire burned in his mismatched eyes, but so did resolve. His stare assured her that he wanted her, but if she said no, he would back away.

"Yes," she said, the answer firm and sure.

She wanted his touch. *Him.* Releasing her hand from his hair, she dipped it under her pants as well, covering his fingers with hers. "Yes," she repeated.

She tilted her hips, and their combined touch glided over her flesh. Twin thick groans saturated the air, and she couldn't contain the cry that slipped from her lips. Together they stroked her, slid through her folds and down to the small, tight entrance to her body. On the tail end of a curse, Grayson abandoned her breast to wrench the button on her jeans free and tug down the zipper, granting them more room.

Fingers tangled, side by side, they caressed her opening. But it was him that pushed inside, stretching her with a familiar but almost-forgotten burn. And now, with his fingers buried deep, she wondered how she would go on without it.

In a duet that was as dirty as it was beautiful, they coaxed a tune from her body.

"Touch yourself," he commanded, and she obeyed, untangling her fingers from his and slipping beneath his palm to slick a caress over the swollen button of nerves. She jolted, whimpered.

He gave a soft chuckle. "Do it again, Nadia. We're going to take you there together."

Shivering, she circled the nub, again and again, his rough praise and encouragement pushing her to rub harder, more, harder, more...

"Oh God," she croaked, then splintered.

She cried out, quaking from the inside out. Grayson replaced her fingers with his, making sure she received every measure of the orgasm rippling through her. She went limp, falling into his body and wanting nothing more than to curl against him, lethargy weighing down her limbs.

Like she was a rag doll, he lifted her from his lap, damn near ripping the tuxedo from his powerful frame. Then he stripped her of her remaining clothes and arranged her on the makeshift pallet he made of his suit. He loomed above her, the dim light from his cell phone still managing to highlight the corded strength in his arms, chest, abs and thighs. His cock. Her lungs locked down all available air in her lungs at the sight of the heavy column of flesh rising from a dark nest of hair. The desire that had settled to a hum low in her belly sparked and crackled, the flames leaping to hot life. He was sexy, perfect...beautiful.

Thank God this wouldn't go beyond tonight. Because she had the unnerving sense he could also very well be heartbreak.

Grayson tore open the small foil packet he'd retrieved from his wallet and rolled on the protection. The virile, erotic sight caused all her unsettling thoughts to scatter. All thoughts except him finally being inside her.

Lifting her arms to him, she murmured, "Grayson."

An invitation. A plea.

"Gray," he rasped, crawling over her and settling between her thighs.

"What?" She moaned as his weight pressed into her.

"Gray," he repeated. "Those close to me call me Gray."

But we're not close, hovered on her tongue and from the sharpening in his blue-and-green gaze, maybe he expected and anticipated her protest. Sex didn't make them close, didn't grant her privileges.

But this was a night for pretend. For fantasy.

Both caused her to whisper, "Gray."

Satisfaction gleamed in his eyes, and he settled more firmly over and against her, every rock-hard, unforgiving plane of his body pressed to her softer, rounded curves.

"What did you say you were willing to give me, Nadia?" he growled, his erection at the entrance to her body.

"All of me," she rasped, then gasped as he surged inside in one long, smooth, powerful thrust. "Take all of me."

And he did.

Not holding back. Not allowing her to hold back.

He slid his hands under her ass, angled her up and, withdrawing in a slow drag that lit up nerve endings like fireworks, he then plunged back inside her. Stealing her breath. Words. Sanity.

Circling her arms and legs around his neck and hips, she clung to him, let him hurl her into the storm he created with each flex, each parry and thrust, each branding kiss.

The man was a sexual act of God.

He powered into her, taking her body, giving her pleasure…breaking every notion of what sex really was. Because she'd had sex before, but as he buried himself in her again and again, riding her until her thighs trembled and her breath stuttered, she could admit to herself that this… this exceeded all of it.

This, she'd never experienced.

And already, even though she'd promised herself there couldn't be a repeat, she craved it again.

"Gray," she cried out, fearing and welcoming the end that swelled dangerously near.

"Let go, baby," he ordered, his voice harsh with the same need that clawed at her. "Let go and give it to me."

As if all she needed was his permission, she did as he commanded. She let go. And ecstasy whipped through her like lightning. Illuminating her, searing her, sending her flying.

Above her, his hoarse shout dimly filled her ears, but she was already falling into the darkness, embracing it.

Knowing in the morning, she would have only memories to hold on to instead of Grayson Chandler.

Five

"Thanks, Pete," Grayson said to his longtime driver as he alighted from the gleaming black Lincoln Town Car. Shivering a little against the cool October Monday morning, he shut the door before the other man could. "I should be finished by six tonight, but if I'm staying later, I'll call a cab."

"Yes, sir," Pete drawled, touching the brim of the black cap that Grayson insisted he didn't need to wear. "But just give me a call when you're ready. Look what happened the last time I wasn't around to drive you. Blackouts. Trapped in locked-down mansions. You're obviously not safe without me."

"Cut it, old man," Grayson rumbled, but grinned at the chauffer.

Pete was more than a driver. When Grayson was a child, the older man had been his best friend, pseudo-uncle and confidante. Hell, it'd been Pete who'd sat Grayson down and explained the more intimate details of sex. Which had been a vast improvement over his father's uninspired "For

God's sake, cover your dick, Grayson, and don't get any gold-digging whores pregnant" speech.

"Have a good day and try to keep Gideon from turning anyone into a statue with that black-eyed stare," Pete teased, rounding the hood of the car. With another mocking touch to his cap, he ducked inside the car and pulled off.

Grayson shook his head, chuckling, but also wishing his friend hadn't mentioned the blackout or being trapped in that damn North Shore mansion. He'd spent all of yesterday and last night attempting to exorcise that evening from his mind. More specifically, trying to remove memories of Nadia and the hottest sex of his life from his mind.

So far, he'd failed. Epically.

Maybe if he hadn't woken up alone, cold and half-hard on a marble floor, with her scent still saturating his clothes, his skin… Maybe if he didn't bear the scratches of her desire on his shoulders and back… Maybe if his dick didn't rise to attention every time a passing thought of those espresso eyes flickered in his head…

Maybe then he could pass off that evening as an unexpected and pleasurable incident.

But today wasn't that day.

As the day before hadn't been. And tomorrow wasn't looking too good, either.

Clenching his jaw, he ignored the low-grade throb in his body. As a boy and then a young man who'd lived most of his life by someone else's rules, he guarded his control like a dragon jealously protecting treasure. Now more than ever, with his parents trying to snatch his life away again and force him back into the world he'd been so desperate to escape.

Waking alone and with no way to contact Nadia, no way to see her again—it had threatened that need to determine his own fate. Because although he'd agreed to one night, he'd lied. After tasting her delectable mouth, caressing that gorgeous body, he wanted more.

Those hours in that hallway had been the most honest, unfiltered interaction he'd had in years. He craved the sincere honesty as much as the hot-as-hell sex. And while the hunger to reinitiate contact with a veritable stranger for conversation should have been an ear-splitting blare of caution, he couldn't deny—at least not to himself—how much he wanted it.

"Good morning, Mr. Chandler," the lobby security guard greeted him from behind the large black desk.

"Good morning, Gerald. And welcome back," Grayson paused in front of the desk. "How's your wife and the new baby?"

The young man beamed, his joy evident in his wide smile. "They're both doing wonderful. Thank you for asking, sir."

"Good. Congratulations to you both." Grayson nodded, then continued toward the bank of elevators, a disquieting emotion sliding under his rib cage.

The guard's obvious delight in his family had Grayson flipping back through his own memories. Had his parents' gazes ever contained that gleaming sheen of pride, of happiness at the mention of him? Not that he could remember. For his brother, yes. Even a couple of times for his sister, Melanie. But not for him.

Just yesterday, disappointment and anger had colored his mother's frosty tone when he'd declined her invitation—order—to attend a family brunch. He'd already been raw from the previous night and sitting down with his mother and father with anything less than full, emotional body armor was foolish. And contrary to what they believed, they hadn't raised a fool.

Resentment, weariness and, yes, pain flickered in his chest, but he ruthlessly smothered them. Feeling *anything* was not only futile, but messy. Refusing people access to your heart, to your soul, prevented them from handling it like fruit in the supermarket bin—squeezing, bruising, then abandoning it.

He jabbed the call button on the elevator a little harder than necessary, willing it to hurry the hell up. As if by getting on the lift and traveling the twenty-five floors to his office, he could leave these morose thoughts in the lobby.

"...a little something, Gerald. Congratulations to you and your wife."

Grayson froze as the soft voice with a hint of a rasp reached him from across the lobby. The elevator finally arrived, but the doors opened and eventually closed without him moving toward it.

That honeyed drawl. New and too damn familiar. He'd heard it in his head last night when he'd jerked awake in his bed, hard and hurting.

It wasn't possible.

Since she'd been on his mind only minutes ago, he was probably having an aural hallucination...

Slowly, he pivoted, his gaze zeroing in on the guard's desk—and the woman standing in front of it handing a small gift bag to Gerald.

Even across the lobby, she appeared tall, the nondescript black heels adding only a couple of inches. Rich chestnut hair was tamed into a painfully neat ponytail. A dark brown suit that seemed a size or two too big hung from her frame, nearly obliterating the curves beneath. From the hair to the wardrobe, nothing about this woman was similar to the woman he'd spent an unforgettable, sex-drenched night with.

Nothing but that melodic accent, which sent all his blood rushing south.

Forgetting everything—the meeting he had scheduled with Gideon, the conference call with a prospective client—he retraced his steps toward the security desk. Before he reached his destination, she turned, a smile curving her lips. Then she lifted her gaze. Met his. And her smile disappeared.

Shock vibrated through him, the echo of it growing louder until only white noise filled his ears.

Nadia. In his building.

His gaze dipped to the familiar green and white badge clipped to the lapel of her jacket. A KayCee Corp employee.

Shock morphed into anger edged with the bitter taste of betrayal.

His employee.

Saturday, she'd pretended not to recognize him, but she'd known who he was all along. Why hadn't she said something? Had she planned to use their night together against him? Blackmail him?

One of his personal codes was never to become involved with employees—ever. Not only was it unprofessional and a legal suit waiting to happen, but with his position of power, no relationship would ever be equal.

But by remaining silent, she'd unwittingly made him violate his own rule. She'd stolen his choice away. That knowledge burned, fueling the already scalding fury at her duplicity.

"Nadia," he greeted, ice coating his voice. Alarm flashed in eyes he'd laughably thought of as honest. Good. She should be worried. He scanned her badge. "Nadia Jordan. What a surprise meeting you here. And with that badge on."

"Mr. Chandler," she said, striding forward and erasing the space separating them. Her chin hiked up, the defiant gesture belied by the crossing of her arms under her breasts. As if protecting herself. "Good morning."

"Good morning," he repeated, arching an eyebrow. "So formal. But then again, it appears you're very good with pretenses," he drawled. "As far as this one goes—" he deliberately scanned her from the top of her scraped-back hair to the tips of her plain shoes "—it's a good one. I almost didn't recognize you."

She dropped her gaze, but a moment later, her shoulders straightened, and she returned her eyes to his. "I didn't—"

"What? Lie? Be very careful how you finish that sentence," he warned, anger slipping into his voice and replacing the mocking tone. "Especially when it isn't a party guest you're talking to now, but your employer."

Something that could've been guilt flashed across her face.

Could've been. Probably wasn't.

"I didn't lie. We didn't—don't—know each other. I've worked for KayCee Corp for a year, have spoken to you a handful of times, and you didn't even know my name."

"So we're going to play semantics?" he growled, leaning closer. Close enough that her fresh, earthy scent filled his nostrils. "Is that your game? Be care—"

"Grayson."

He jerked his head up at the sound of his name spoken in the crisp, cultured voice he'd grown up associating with displeasure and chastisement.

Hell.

He inwardly groaned. Grinding his teeth together, he shifted his glance over Nadia's shoulder.

"Mom."

Cherise Chandler's ice-blue stare swung from him, to Nadia, then back to him, dismissing the other woman. "I've been trying to call you all morning."

Yes, and he'd been ignoring her all morning. In the last few months, his mother had taken to blowing his phone up and always with the same subjects: returning to Chandler International, marriage, duty. He was...tired.

"I'm sorry I missed them," he lied. "I didn't mean for you to come all the way down here, though." Truth.

"Well, how else was I supposed to invite you to lunch with us?" she asked.

Us? For the first time he glanced behind his mother and noticed the petite woman standing with her. Adalyn. *Jesus Christ.* How much worse could this damn Monday get?

"Adalyn." He nodded in his ex's direction.

Adalyn smiled, taking the curt greeting as an invitation to approach him, place a hand on his chest and rise on the tips of her stilettos to brush a kiss across his cheek. Only manners bred into him since birth kept him from stepping back and wiping the imprint from his face. From the glitter in her green eyes, she guessed it. She'd always been fond of games.

He'd never divulged the true reason behind their breakup to his parents. Adalyn hadn't cheated, but in some ways, it would've been less devastating to him if she had. Still, he'd given his parents the old "two different people" excuse, not so much to protect Adalyn's reputation but to shield himself from their scorn. His father would've called him a fool, and his mother would've gifted him with her patented "You're a disappointment" look and the "marriage is about more than love" speech.

No, he'd kept his mouth shut. But now, with Adalyn using this opportunity to wheedle back into his life, he regretted the decision. His father and mother might have scoffed at him, but at least they would have known why he couldn't abide this woman's presence.

"I was so delighted when your mother called and invited me to come see you this morning. Like I said Saturday, it's been such a long time. I would love to catch up with you," she fairly purred.

At one time, that sensual tone and pouty mouth would've had him ready to find a private place. But that had been before he'd discovered her love had been an act. Before he'd discovered he was just a walking, blue-blooded bank account to her. Before she'd shattered whatever he'd had left of his belief in the inherent integrity of people.

She'd been a brutal but effective teacher.

"I'm afraid lunch isn't possible today," he said, switching his attention to his mother and not bothering to address Adalyn. "My schedule is full."

"Nonsense," his mother dismissed his excuse with a wave of her hand. "We're family, and you can move meetings around. I've already made an appointment for twelve at—"

Anger, frustration and, yes, he wasn't too proud to admit it to himself, desperation, coalesced inside him, and before he could question the logic of his decision, he moved forward, closer to Nadia. He slipped an arm around her lower back, his hand resting on the lush, feminine curve of her hip. She stiffened, but he ignored it, silently praying that she didn't pull away from him.

"No, you misunderstand. Lunch isn't a business meeting. I already have plans with Nadia." He paused, then pushed out, "My girlfriend."

A silence filled with "what the hell?" reverberated between all of them. Beneath his hand, Nadia damn near vibrated with tension, fury, shock—most likely all three. And he couldn't blame her. He'd just thrown her under a runaway bus, rendering her the sacrifice on the matchmaking altar. In the deafening seconds that passed, he could've rescinded his announcement, passed it off as a joke, but he stayed silent, hoping she'd go along with him.

"Don't be ridiculous," Cherise snapped.

"You can't be serious," Adalyn spat at the same time, dropping the butter-wouldn't-melt-in-my-mouth act.

Both women glared at him, then switched their glowers to Nadia. The need to protect her surged within him, and he shifted closer, his hold tightening.

"Of course I'm serious," he replied, tone silken and heavy with warning. "Why wouldn't I be?"

Adalyn sputtered, red flooding her face, but she pressed her lips together, wisely remaining silent. His mother had no such compunction.

"She's not exactly your type, is she, Grayson?" she scoffed, her gaze scouring Nadia. Cherise then settled a hand on Adalyn's back. A smirk curved his ex's mouth.

He frowned and parted his lips, a hot retort jumping on his tongue. But Nadia beat him to it.

"*She* isn't a type at all," Nadia said dryly. "But a person who just so happens to be standing here."

"So you are seeing my son?" Cherise demanded, as imperious as a queen speaking to a peasant.

Again, he opened his mouth to warn his mother about her tone, but once more, Nadia beat him to it.

"That's what he said," she said. Then with such sweetness Grayson would need to make an appointment with his dentist, she added, "He's not in the habit of lying, is he?"

He swallowed back the growl that shoved against his throat. She'd thrown his own accusation about lying back in his face. God, he didn't know whether to snarl at her or murmur "well played."

"Grayson, I need to speak with you." Cherise paused and shot a meaningful look at Nadia. "Alone."

"I'm sorry, Mother," he apologized again. "I don't have time right now. Gideon is probably waiting in my office." Leaning forward, he brushed a kiss across his mother's cheek. "I'll call you later. Adalyn." He nodded abruptly at the other woman, then turning, he strode back across the lobby, his arm still around Nadia's waist.

This time when he punched the call button for the elevator, seconds passed before the doors slid open, and he guided her inside. Only when they started to rise, did he drop his arm and shift away.

And tried to ignore that he could still feel her, as if the prolonged contact had branded the sensation of her into his skin.

He wished he could ignore her, forget that the scene downstairs had happened. But he couldn't. As angry as he remained that she'd lied to him—and he still couldn't stop the nagging need to know *why*—he'd dropped her right in the middle of a family issue without her permission.

That made him a desperate asshole, but an asshole nonetheless. He already knew how he looked in her eyes—a hypocrite.

A year ago, he wouldn't have had any problem telling his mother to back off, to stop the matchmaking. But that had been before Jason died. Before Grayson witnessed his stalwart mother fall apart in grief. Causing her any more hurt when she'd lost the son of her heart...

Maybe it made Grayson a coward and a hypocrite, but he couldn't do that to her. But neither could he let her or his father rule his life again. He'd labored and sacrificed for this company, for his freedom.

God. He clenched his fingers into a fist at his side, staring ahead at the sealed doors.

He was so goddamn lonely.

And other than Gideon, trusting in someone had burned him in the past. So Grayson took only what he allowed himself to have. Those few hours of sex, pressed close to someone and pretending they were intimate. Pretending they were sharing more than just pleasure. Pretending that in the morning, he wouldn't escort them from his home with no promises.

He glanced at the silent woman next to him. In that hallway, he hadn't needed to feign anything. And maybe that's why he couldn't eradicate the inane sense of betrayal.

For once, he hadn't been faking it. And she had been.

Focus, he ordered himself.

He had to fix the problem he'd created that now involved her. And unfortunately, he saw only one way out of it.

The elevator drew to a halt on the twenty-fifth floor, and he moved forward, cupping Nadia's elbow.

"This isn't my floor," she objected, stiffening under his hand.

"We have to talk," he said in way of explanation. "I can hit the emergency button on this elevator, and we can do it here and chance the fire department being called, or we can go to my office and have privacy. Your choice."

"That's a choice?" she muttered but moved forward.

"I never claimed you would like either option," he said, not bothering to keep the bite from his tone.

He guided her down the quiet hallway toward his office. Not many people had arrived yet, but those that sat behind their desks threw him and Nadia curious glances. He could just imagine the gossip that would erupt behind them as soon as they passed.

Moments later, he paused next to his assistant's desk. The older woman regarded both of them, but nothing in her expression or voice betrayed any curiosity. Only one of the reasons he valued her. She was the very definition of discretion.

"Mrs. Ross, would you please notify…" He trailed off, frowning. "Who is your supervisor?" he asked Nadia.

She arched an eyebrow, and he swallowed a growl at the not-so-subtle reminder that he didn't know a damn thing about her. "Terrance Webber."

He nodded, familiar with the VP of operations. And now he knew who to have a talk with about requiring their employees to work when they weren't on the clock or financially compensated. Although he would now make sure Nadia would be for Saturday night.

"Would you call Terrance and let him know Ms. Jordan is in a meeting with me and will be a little late arriving?

And also, call Gideon and tell him we need to move our meeting back a half hour."

His friend wouldn't be happy, but the delay couldn't be helped.

"Yes, sir," Mrs. Ross said. "I've updated your calendar. You have a conference call scheduled for ten thirty. Lunch with the Forester Group at twelve thirty and an appointment with legal at two. I've also emailed you the messages you've received so far this morning, listed in order of urgency."

"Thank you." He reached into his briefcase and pulled free a couple of paperbacks. Settling the books on top of the desk, he pushed them toward his assistant. "For Jack. You mentioned he just started the J.D. Robb In Death series. I saw these and picked them up for him."

A warm smile spread across the woman's face, lighting it up. At sixty-three, she should've been readying herself for retirement, not still working. But her husband had been injured on his job five years ago, and even with his insurance, the bills had piled up. Not that she seemed to mind being the breadwinner of the family; the woman was devoted to her husband.

"Thank you, Mr. Chandler," she murmured. "He will love these." Clearing her throat, she gave him another smile. "I'll make sure you aren't disturbed."

Nodding, he headed toward his office, still clasping Nadia's arm. Once he closed the door behind them, he released her. What he had to propose would be unprofessional enough without any more unnecessary touching.

"Please, have a seat," he invited, waving toward the two arm chairs that flanked his wide glass desk.

"If you don't mind, I'd prefer to stand. Since I won't be staying long," she added. "You're either going to fire me for Saturday or order me to pretend the scene downstairs didn't happen. Neither should require much time." She emphasized her point by peering down at the slender watch on her wrist.

Her reminder of the night of the blackout rekindled the fury simmering inside his chest. "That's where you're wrong, Nadia," he snapped. "I can't fire you because I had inappropriate relations with an employee."

Hell, "inappropriate relations." Such an anemic description of the cataclysmic sex they'd had. Even standing here with her, frustration and anger a hum in his blood, he couldn't deny the presence of the third emotion swirling in his body. Lust. For the plush mouth set in a firm, unsmiling line. For the full breasts that had filled his palms to overflowing. For the long, thick legs that her ugly skirt couldn't hide. For the sex that had clutched him like a lover's embrace.

"My actions could be misconstrued as sexual harassment or coercion. It doesn't matter that you hid the fact that you are my employee." He cocked his head, studying her impassive face through narrowed eyes. "Care to explain to me why you didn't enlighten me about our association? Whether I recognized you or not, you damn sure knew me. And you. Said. Nothing. Why?"

She didn't immediately reply. Instead, she mimicked his gesture, tilting her head, as well. "Does it really matter now?" She flicked a hand toward the desk behind him. "Do you need me to sign a contract or affidavit swearing not to sue you or the company for sexual misconduct?"

"No," he snapped. *Yes.* The businessman inside him snarled at the same time. Jesus, she had him arguing with himself. "I want an answer to my question."

"I don't have one to give you, *sir*," she replied evenly. Stubbornly.

"You mean, you don't want to give me one." When she remained silent, continuing to meet his glare, he bit off a curse and dragged a hand through his hair, pivoting. After several seconds, he turned back around, scrutinizing her. So many questions ran through his head. *Who are you? What were your motives? Did you use me? Were you faking?*

No.

Her motives for remaining in that hallway with him might've been self-serving, but those lust-soaked moans, those hoarse whispers… Those had been real.

"About downstairs…" He exhaled a deep breath, focusing on the main reason why he'd escorted her to his office. "I'm sorry I dragged you into the middle of it. But now that I have, I need your help."

For the first time since entering the office, an emotion crossed her face. Surprise. Quickly chased by suspicion. Smart woman.

"My help?" she slowly repeated. "What kind of help could you possibly need from me?"

"For you to be my fiancée. I need you to agree to marry me."

Six

Nadia stared at Grayson Chandler. No, gaped. Because she couldn't have heard him correctly. He hadn't just... proposed to her. Between leaving her house this morning and arriving at work, she must've been in a car wreck and was currently in the hospital, hopped up on morphine and she was dreaming.

Dreaming of coming face-to-face with him in the lobby when that had never happened before.

Dreaming of being an awkward witness to the tension-filled confrontation between him, his mother and the gorgeous woman who obviously had biblical knowledge of him.

Dreaming of him introducing her as his girlfriend.

And now dreaming of him announcing that he wanted her to marry him.

Damn good drugs could be the only explanation for this hallucination.

"Nadia?"

She blinked, and no, Grayson still stood there, and so

did she. The prick of her fingernails against her palm further solidified that all of this was indeed real.

"What did you say?" she whispered.

He sighed and thrust his fingers through his hair, half turning away from her. His profile as sharp as freshly hewn marble and utterly perfect.

And she really shouldn't be admiring the striking angles of his cheekbones, the arrogant blade of his nose and the criminally sensual fullness of his mouth. Not when he'd apparently lost his mind.

"Not for real, Nadia," he said, returning his blue-and-green gaze to her. God, those eyes. She'd somehow convinced herself they couldn't possibly be that vivid, that penetrating and stunning. She couldn't have been more wrong. Though she wanted to glance away from the intensity of his stare, the unique beauty captured her. "I don't need a real fiancée, nor do I want one. I'm asking you to pretend that we are a happily engaged couple for several months. Long enough for my mother to forget this idea of fixing me up with Adalyn Hayes."

"Wait." She threw up a hand, palm out. "Your ex, Adalyn Hayes?"

His gaze sharpened. "Yes. How do you know about her?"

When she first started working at KayCee Corp, she'd inhaled everything she could uncover about him. Still, she doubted announcing *"Because I have a humiliating crush and looked up everything about you"* would go over well. Shoot, it mortified her just to admit it to herself.

"Who doesn't?" She deflected his question with a shake of her head. "So you two are getting back together?"

He frowned. "No. But unfortunately, my mother doesn't seem ready to accept that hell will have a freak blizzard before I marry Adalyn."

She blinked. "Well."

"So will you help me, Nadia?" he pressed, moving forward, and she just managed to check the urge to backpedal, maintaining the space between them.

She needed that distance, *required* it. Otherwise his sandalwood and mint fragrance would wrap around her and influence her to do foolish things. Like bury her face against his chest. She'd fought that same impulse in the longest elevator ride known to mankind. And had barely won the battle. She wasn't pushing her luck in this office.

Again, she shook her head. "I still don't understand. This must be a one-percenter thing, because normal, poor people don't do this. Why not just tell your mother that you're not interested?"

Something flashed in his mismatched eyes. Before he said a flat, blunt and enigmatic "Right now it's not an option," she'd known he wouldn't reveal anything to her.

Turnabout was fair play, she guessed. After all, she'd dodged his question about why she hadn't admitted to knowing him. Maybe if he'd been the flirtatious, warmer man she'd been trapped with, she might have felt safe confessing her reasons. But she couldn't tell this cold, guarded version of Grayson that she'd selfishly wanted a night for herself, that he'd been her fantasy come to vivid life. That for once she hadn't considered the consequences. That she didn't think he would recognize her if their paths crossed again.

No, she couldn't share that with this familiar stranger. Would he use that info against her in some way? Fire her? Or worse…mock her?

"I'm sorry, but I—"

"Don't you want to know what saying yes entails?" he interrupted her, his steady gaze assessing. Analyzing. And she didn't like it at all. "Five hundred thousand dollars. If you agree to be my fiancée for four months, I'll give you half a million dollars. And another two hundred and fifty thousand after a staged breakup."

She gasped, shock pelting her like icy sheets of rain. "Seven hundred and fifty thousand dollars?" she wheezed. "For four months?"

He shrugged a wide shoulder. "Call the extra quarter of a million bonus pay." Studying her, he murmured, "So what is your answer, Nadia?"

Good God, what she could do with all that money. Pay off debt, move to a better neighborhood, splurge a little for both Ezra and herself, have actual savings. To a successful business tycoon and billionaire like Grayson, seven hundred and fifty thousand dollars might be pocket change, but to her? To Ezra? It meant a complete change in circumstances, in lifestyle. Hell, in *life*.

But who would believe you two are a couple? Even his mother refused to accept it.

The soft, scoffing whisper ghosted across her mind, and she felt the lash of truth.

Grayson was a Chandler. They were American royalty, like the Rockefellers or the Kennedys, possibly richer and with a more sterling reputation. A woman from a tiny, obscure Georgia town who was the daughter of the town Jezebel and didn't even know who her father was didn't belong with a man who could date his ancestors back beyond the Mayflower.

He needed someone like his ex—urbane, sophisticated, moneyed, connected, gorgeous…thin. No one looking at Adalyn Hayes would question why they were together. Next to women like Adalyn, Nadia would seem like a deviation, a charity case from the other side of the tracks.

Then, there was the night they'd spent together. Ducking her head, she crossed her arms over her chest. Both to hide the inconvenient puckering of her nipples at the thought of him naked on top of her…inside her…and a feeble gesture to protect herself from his piercing scrutiny. She couldn't deny the unrelenting arousal that his presence ignited. Even when he stared at her, cool and calculating, offering three-quarters of a million dollars. Being in close proximity to him for months spelled *Danger* with a capital *D*.

He would be a menace to her reason, her control and, as much as she loathed admitting it, her heart. That treacherous heart that insisted on forgetting that rich, handsome men expected the world, and when they didn't receive it, left wreckage behind.

She refused to be wreckage for anyone else again. Ever.

"Your offer—" *bribe* "—is generous, but I'm going to turn it down."

Though his expression remained passive, his eyes glinted with anger. "Why?" He slowly perused her from head to toe, and she ordered herself not to fidget as he regarded her thrift store suit made for a woman a little bigger than her own size sixteen and shoes that weren't fashion forward but comfortable. With a growing man-child under her roof and the bills to match, the shoes weren't only all she could afford, but they were also her armor. And damn Grayson Chandler for causing a sliver of embarrassment to slide between her ribs.

"You don't need the money?" he asked.

Bastard. "No, because I'm not a whore," she ground out.

He arched an eyebrow. "I don't believe I mentioned sex being included in our arrangement."

Of course he hadn't. Heat rushed up her neck and poured into her cheeks. The night of the blackout had been an aberration for him. He might have professed to admire—no, adore—her curves then, but today, except for that insulting scan down her body, his gaze hadn't wavered from her face. She hadn't glimpsed so much as a glimmer of desire in his eyes. Frustration, yes. Anger, oh, plenty of it. But not the need that had flared so brightly in his gaze less than two days ago.

Like she'd said, an aberration.

Though mortification singed her face, she hiked her chin. "You're right, you didn't. But there's more than one way a woman can prostitute herself," she said. Her company. Her pride. Her soul. "And sorry, but I'm not willing to do it. So, if that's all…"

"Do you want more money? Is that it?" he pressed.

Fury mingled with her humiliation, and both loosened her tongue. "You're my employer, as you pointed out earlier. When you roped me into that scene downstairs, it wasn't like I could've disagreed with you and not feel like I was jeopardizing my job. But now that you've assured me that you won't fire me, I feel very safe in saying, Hell. No." She pasted a fake, too-bright smile on her face. "Now, if *that's* all…" she repeated.

Not waiting for him to dismiss her, she pivoted on her chunky heels and exited his office. Gratefully, Mr. Webber had meetings for most of the day and didn't ask her about hers with Grayson. And she didn't volunteer any information. By the time she clocked out for the day nine hours later, her head throbbed with a low-grade headache. A couple of aspirin, a glass of wine and a bed with a Netflix series called her name. They were the only things that could possibly salvage this day.

Just as she exited the elevator and stepped into the almost deserted lobby, her cell phone rang. She smiled, already knowing who waited on the other end.

"I'm leaving now," she said to her brother in lieu of a greeting. "And I'm cooking spaghetti and meatballs," she added since one of his favorite questions was "What are we having for dinner?"

Ezra laughed, and she could clearly picture his wide, easygoing grin and sparkling dark eyes. From his laid-back and affable manner, no one would guess they had grown up in the same house with the same neglectful mother. Or that he'd seen things in his seventeen years that no child should.

Though they shared a mother, it was anyone's guess who his father was, just as Nadia would have a better chance of winning the lottery than finding out the identity of hers. She and Ezra had the same brown eyes and facial features from their Caucasian mom. But where Nadia's lighter, caramel skin and loose curls and waves hinted at a father with Spanish or even biracial heritage, Ezra's darker tone and tighter curls that he'd twisted into locs denoted an African-American or Afro-Latino father. Didn't matter to Nadia. He was her brother, bonded by blood and experience.

She loved him as if she'd birthed him herself. And protected him just as fiercely.

"See? I wasn't even calling you about that, but it's good to know." He laughed again, and she grinned. "I couldn't wait until you got home. I had to call you now."

Nadia halted midstride across the lobby, pausing in front of the security desk. Nerves tumbled and tugged in her stomach, her fingers tightening around the phone.

"What is it?" she breathed.

"I got in!" Ezra crowed, his excited shout blasting in her eardrum. "I got into Yale!"

"Oh, my God!" she shouted before quickly remembering where she was. The evening shift guard quirked an eyebrow at her, and she jabbed a finger at the cell she still held at her ear. "He was accepted into Yale!" she explained as way of apology, and at only a slightly lower volume. The guard mouthed congratulations, and she gave him a thumbs-up.

"Who are you talking to?" Ezra teased. "Please tell me you didn't just tell a complete stranger that your little brother was accepted into college?"

"Not a total stranger," she scoffed. Then she chuckled. "Okay, kind of one. But he's happy for you, too. Ezra," she whispered, pride, joy and such an immense surge of love swelling inside her. "I'm so happy for you. So damn proud.

You'll be the first in our family to attend college. And not just any college. *Yale.*"

"You should've been the first, Nadia," he said, loyal to the end. "You're brilliant and could've easily gotten into any school you wanted. But instead you stayed at home. Because of me."

Blinking against the sudden sting of tears, she waved a hand in front of her face and battled back the moisture. She continued out of the building and stopped on the sidewalk. Closing her eyes, she tilted her face up to the gray-and-purple sky that still contained the last rays of sun. Yes, she'd sacrificed her dreams of a degree in nursing for him, but she'd never regretted it.

"And I'd do it again," she murmured. "Now," she cleared her throat of the emotion clogging it. "Spill. Give me everything."

He read the acceptance letter, delight coloring every word, his normally relaxed voice pitched high with exhilaration. "And, Nadia, they awarded me a partial scholarship!"

"That's amazing!" But worry sank its fangs into her delight, poisoning it. Partial scholarship. The annual tuition for Yale was almost fifty thousand dollars. When he'd first applied, they'd been counting on him receiving a full ride. With his grades, it was possible. But even with the help of the aid he was receiving, she still had to come up with twenty-five thousand.

And she couldn't help him. When Nadia had been eighteen, she'd tried to get a car loan only to discover that her mother had been using her name and social security number for everything from bills to credit cards for years. If Nadia applied for loans on his behalf, and on the off chance received them, the interest rate would be so high, she would be repaying that loan even *after* she died. And she hated for Ezra to incur debt even before he graduated college.

Jesus. They were barely making ends meet as it was. And tuition didn't include books, food and other necessities...

"That's okay, sis," Ezra said, as if reading her mind. "It's just an honor to be accepted. I understand if we can't afford for me to go. There are plenty of great colleges here in Chicago. And—"

"Ezra." She broke in on his sweet but heartbreaking speech. "No, stop it. You're going to Yale. I'll come up with the money."

"But how, Nadia?" he demanded, the stubborn nature they both shared making its appearance. "If you'd just let me apply for loans..."

"No," she said, adamant. His young life shouldn't begin choked by debt that would take decades to pay off. "I'll handle it, okay? I don't want you to worry. You should be celebrating right now! So forget spaghetti. When I get home, I'm treating you to a deep dish at Pequod's. Be ready," she ordered. "And I mean it, Ezra. I'm proud of you. Congratulations."

"Thanks, sis." He coughed, cleared his throat. "And I love you."

She gasped even as tears stung her eyes again. This time she let a few tears roll before carefully wiping them away. "Good God! Did the zombie apocalypse hit and nobody told me? You actually said the *L* word!"

He sighed. "And you wonder why you don't have dates. You insist on talking."

She loosed a loud bark of laughter, startling the couple walking past her. Their pace kicked up a notch. "Oh, you're going to pay for that one. Don't be surprised when you wake up one morning eyebrowless."

With his chuckling still traveling through their connection, she hung up. As her arm dropped to her side, her hilarity ebbed, then disappeared, allowing entrance for reality and the dread accompanying it.

Only one option would completely cover Ezra's tuition and expenses.

Dropping her phone in her purse, she turned and headed back inside. All the way to the elevators and then the ride to the twenty-fifth floor, she reminded herself why she couldn't turn tail and run in the opposite direction. She conjured images of Ezra—as a gap-toothed six-year-old with a mess of unruly curls; at eleven, wide-eyed and big for his age on his first day of middle school; at fifteen, when he walked into her bedroom, clutching the ragged piece of notebook paper their mother had left behind explaining how she'd moved on with her new man.

Nadia's little brother had experienced too much—suffered too much—to not receive everything life had to offer.

She stepped off the elevator and retraced the path she'd taken that morning beside Grayson Chandler. His assistant's desk loomed large and empty, so she strode to the closed double doors of his office and knocked. Maybe he'd already left for the day, too. God, she hated the thought of having to do this all over again tomorrow...

"Come in."

The deep, commanding timbre reached her through the doors, and she couldn't contain her shiver. Not fear or revulsion. Far from it. It was a dark, wicked sensation that knotted her belly even as it pooled low beneath her navel.

Oh, for the love of...

She had to get it together before she walked into this office and committed a cardinal sin. Like throw herself at his feet and beg him to touch her, make her explode under his knowing fingers, brand her with his mouth and his...

You're here for one reason alone. Ezra.

With those words ringing in her head, she twisted the knob and entered the lion's den.

Grayson sat behind his desk, his focus on the computer monitor. A small frown creased his brow, but nothing could detract from his almost overwhelming masculine beauty. Trepidation struck her again, full force in the chest. How could she ever hope to pull this off? What made her think she could go through with this or that people would believe it?

He glanced up, noticed her standing in the doorway and the V of his eyebrows deepened. "Nadia?" He rose from his chair. "What's wrong?"

"Wrong? Nothing."

But he'd already circled his desk and stalked across the office toward her. The predatory stride did something totally inappropriate to her lungs and her sex. As if the two were mystically joined, and Grayson's sexual magnetism had flipped the switch to activate the connection.

She shook her head, closing the door behind her. "Really, nothing's wrong. I just…" She exhaled a hard breath, and he drew to a halt inches away, his disconcerting and too-damn-perceptive gaze roaming over her face. "I wanted…"

"You've changed your mind," he finished for her, his stare hooded, full lips absent of the gloating smile she'd expected. Instead, his face remained an inscrutable mask that revealed none of his thoughts.

Again she asked herself, who was Grayson Chandler? And the fact that she couldn't pin the answer down unnerved her.

"Why?" he asked.

"Does it matter?" she replied. Going through with this charade meant giving him access to her time, her personal space and even her body if they were to pretend to be a loving couple. She had to shield some parts of herself from him. And her life with her brother was one of those parts. Grayson couldn't have that. "Is the offer still open?"

He didn't immediately answer but continued to scrutinize her as if she were a column of profits and losses that refused to reconcile. She wasn't, though. She was just a desperate woman willing to sacrifice her pride for the one she loved, but not her soul.

Not her heart.

Never that.

He crossed his arms over his wide chest. "It is. Are you sure you want to do this, Nadia? Are you sure you can handle all it entails?"

"Yes."

No. Hell no.

"I'll pretend to be your fiancée for four months, and at the end we break up. Money exchanged. We resume being employer, employee." Although, how she was supposed to return to being a random secretary instead of "the boss's ex-girlfriend" she had no clue. It seemed unrealistic to think everything could go back to normal, but she'd cross that bridge when she came to it. Maybe while she played fiancée, she would also search for another job. "What wouldn't I be able to 'handle'?"

"Since it's my parents and Adalyn that we're trying to convince, that means attending dinner parties, galas and other social events. It means bearing the brunt of the scrutiny and attention and not wavering. It means..." His voice lowered, and she tightened her thighs against the pull deep inside. "It means not flinching when I put my hands on you. It means moving into my touch, making every photographer and media outlet believe you want it—my touch, my lips. Make them believe you want me. Can you do that?"

Could she do that? Pretending to want him wasn't hard. The most difficult part would be keeping him from knowing how much she craved him.

No, the most difficult part would be guarding her heart so it didn't mistake fiction for fact, desire for affection.

She'd made that mistake once. Had let herself forget that most rich men only crossed the tracks for one thing. Women like Nadia were good for dirty little secrets, but not to openly court, not to marry. For a moment, she believed that rule hadn't applied to her, but she'd been cruelly reminded.

She'd never forget again.

But dammit, why did he have to describe what he expected in detail? Now she couldn't evict the images of him lowering his head to nuzzle her throat or brush her mouth with those beautiful lips.

"I can do it," she said, forcing a firmness into her voice that was more bravado than certainty. "Can you?" She'd asked it in jest, in challenge, but underneath, she truly needed to know.

"Can I convince anyone that I'm hungry for you? Can I make people believe that I might be holding your hand, but I'm five seconds away from dragging you over to the nearest flat surface and making you come until we're both sweating and shaking?" A tight smile barely curved his lips. "Yes, Nadia, I can do it."

Oh. Damn. His words seemed to seep into the air, burrow into the walls, camp out on the furniture of his sitting area. They inhabited the room, inhabited *her*, so she breathed them, wallowed in them, drowned in them.

"Promise me one thing," he murmured, his blue and green eyes shadowed, his jaw like stone. "Don't fall in love with me."

She blinked. Then laughed, the sound hard, strangled. "Well don't you think highly of yourself." Was he serious? Fort Knox had nothing on the fortress hiding her heart. "I don't think that will be a problem."

"Good," he said, still in that soft tone with the underlying thread of steel. "Because I don't want to hurt you. Do you make my dick hard? Yes. But that's where it begins and ends. I don't want a relationship. So don't let me hurt you, Nadia. Protect yourself from me."

Her breath caught in her throat. She made him hard.

That wasn't anything special. He wanted her to remember her place and stay in it. To not have delusions of grandeur where he was concerned. Contrary to the fantasy fairy tales peddled, princes didn't fall for scullery maids.

Fine with her. She didn't believe in princes and their false professions of love anyway.

"Like I said, that won't be a problem," she assured him. "And since we're setting boundaries and rules. I have two." She ticked up a finger. "One. As you mentioned earlier, sex isn't on the table. Which I'm fine with." The low thrum between her legs sent up a plaintive *Are we really, though?* Ignoring her traitorous and greedy body, she continued, "But that means it's off the menu with everyone else, too. I refuse to be a pathetic side piece in the public's eye." Been there, done that. No thank you on a repeat. A scowl darkened Grayson's face, but again, she moved on. "And two, at the end of the four months, *I* break up with *you*." She paused. "That's a deal breaker."

She didn't go into why it was important to her that she be the one to end this relationship, fake or not. Redemption, maybe. Or pride. It was one thing to look like Cinderella with Prince Charming. It was another thing to be dumped by Prince Charming and return to the cinders and ashes.

The scowl eased and something uncomfortably close to understanding darkened his eyes. She fought not to squirm or, worse, explain herself.

Finally, he nodded. "Human Resources has your banking information, so I'll transfer five hundred thousand there from my personal account tomorrow."

"No." She shook her head. "I only want two hundred and fifty thousand." Just enough to cover all four years of Ezra's tuition and a little extra for incidentals.

Once more, displeasure creased his brow. "The agreement was for half a million now and an additional quarter million when the four months were up."

"No, we didn't agree on that because I turned down the original offer. The terms of our new arrangement are two hundred and fifty," she argued.

"Who in the hell turns down that much money for a lesser amount?"

"That would be me. Take it or leave it." When she walked away from this it wouldn't be feeling like a gold digger. She stretched her arm out toward him. "Deal?"

He studied her palm before closing the distance and enfolding his big hand around hers. It was just her hand but, God, she felt...surrounded. That small gesture reminded her of how he'd wrapped his larger frame around her body, holding her tight as he thrust inside her with care and ferocity.

"Deal."

Why did that one word sound like a warning?

A hard squeeze of her fingers shattered her thoughts, and she glanced from their connected hands to his hooded, sensual gaze. "You have secrets, Nadia Jordan. And I'm going to enjoy uncovering each and every one of them."

Now *that* was definitely a warning. She jerked her hand away from his, not caring how he interpreted the action. Pride demanded she deliver some pithy remark and casually stroll out of the office. But self-preservation... Well it screamed louder than pride at the moment.

With a jerky nod of her head, she wheeled around and damn near charged out the doors, not daring to look back.

Best not to tempt fate...or her shaky resolve.

Seven

The ballet.

She was going to the freaking ballet.

Standing in front of her small closet, Nadia squeezed her eyes shut, pinching the bridge of her nose. She counted to ten and once more surveyed the contents. Jeans, shirts, blouses, skirts and a couple of dresses—all clothes suitable for work and casual time outside of the office. But nothing in the cramped mess came within even centimeters of appropriate fashion for the *ballet*.

God, every time she said it aloud or in her head, her stomach rolled and pitched like a ship in a storm. Unless she could count the number of times she'd watched *Fame*— and honestly, did that even count?—she'd never been interested. But apparently not only did the elite of Chicago attend ballets, they hosted parties *before* them.

When Nadia had decided to take part in this relationship charade, she'd figured on having at least a few days to become accustomed to the idea that her life wouldn't be hers for the next four months. But no, Grayson had called the following morning—this morning—to inform her they were attending a pre-ballet cocktail party at his parents' house.

God, what had she been thinking to agree to this?

Ezra needs to go to college debt-free.

Right. If she kept repeating that to herself, maybe she could make it through this evening and the long ones ahead of her.

Sighing, she reached inside the closet and withdrew her black "any-do" dress. The dress that would do for any occasion whether it was a wedding or funeral. Holding it up, she peered at the modest neckline, cap sleeves and knee-length hem. Simple and perfectly respectable.

Perfectly boring.

Well, there wasn't anything she could do about it. Unfortunately, her budget didn't allow for a shopping spree on the Magnificent Mile. Tossing the dress on her bed, she bundled her hair on top of her head and glanced at her watch before slipping it off and setting it onto the bedside dresser.

Five thirty. She had an hour and a half before Grayson picked her up. Between now and then, she had to shower, put on makeup and get dressed. She would definitely be cutting it close, but—

The loud, obnoxious buzz of the doorbell interrupted her thoughts. Frowning, she hesitated before treading out of her bedroom and down the hall. Who could that be? Ezra had travel ball and wouldn't be home until after nine. And other than his friends, no one else would drop by unannounced.

Because she no longer lived in Tatumville, she peeked out the small window bracketing the front door. A beautiful woman in a perfectly tailored forest green pantsuit stood on the doorstep. Confusion and curiosity warred as Nadia opened the door.

"Can I help you?" Nadia asked.

The woman, who appeared to be several years older

than Nadia, smiled, and a sense of familiarity niggled at her. Did she work for KayCee Corp? Is that where Nadia had seen her? Had to be. It was doubtful Nadia would've met this woman of obvious sophistication and wealth at one of Ezra's ball games or at the neighborhood supermarket.

"Nadia Jordan?" she greeted.

"Yes." Nadia nodded, arching an eyebrow. "And you are?"

"Melanie Chandler. Gray's sister." She dipped her head in the direction of the tiny foyer behind Nadia. "May I come in?"

"Oh. Um, sure." Though a barrage of questions pinged off her skull, she stepped back, granting Melanie entrance. "I'm sorry if I forgot that you were coming over. I don't remember Grayson mentioning—"

Melanie arched an elegant eyebrow, and in that moment, she looked so much like Grayson, Nadia wondered how she hadn't immediately guessed her identity. Though Melanie's eyes were sky blue, she and Grayson shared the same strong facial features and confident bearing.

"Why am I not surprised?" Melanie shook her head, then glancing over her shoulder, waved at someone behind her. "In here, Pete."

In moments, an older man with white hair, dressed in a black suit, strode up Nadia's short, narrow walk. He carried several garment bags and a smaller case. With a smile in Nadia's direction, he entered her home and stood next to Melanie. Her small foyer suddenly seemed tinier and shabbier with these two in it.

"Where should I put this, ma'am?" Pete asked Nadia.

"I don't know what 'this' is," she said, flustered and a little annoyed at the sense of being ambushed. "Anyone want to tell me?"

Melanie sighed then crossed her arms. "Let me guess, Gray not only didn't mention my arriving, but also didn't mention that he instructed me to bring over several dresses for you to choose from for tonight?" Nadia's expression must've reflected the icy punch of shock ricocheting through her because Melanie huffed out a bark of laughter. "Well this is…awkward. Why wouldn't he tell you since he asked me to come by?"

"Probably because he knew I would've told him I'm not a paper doll that needs to be dressed since I've been doing it quite well on my own for all these years," Nadia gritted out from between clenched teeth.

Mortification seared her, probably branding her cheeks a neon shade of red. Yes, she wasn't wealthy, but dammit, she wasn't a charity case, either. *He'd* asked *her* to go along with this charade. And now having his own sister show up on her doorstep with clothes because obviously what Nadia had to wear wasn't good enough… He might as well as have said *she* wasn't good enough.

Face still burning, she straightened her shoulders and met the other woman's gaze. "This is really nice, but not necessary."

"Wait, before you toss us out of your house—which you're well within your rights to do," Melanie said, holding up a hand. "I realize my brother's method might bear all the sensitivity of a goat, but his heart is in the right place. You're someone he cares about, and he wants to make sure you're comfortable and confident tonight. While you are a beautiful woman, and I can see why he's so taken with you, a gorgeous dress never hurts. Besides… You haven't seen the shoes, Nadia." Melania smiled, an almost avaricious glint in her gaze. "The. Shoes."

In spite of the lingering hurt and embarrassment, Nadia laughed. Melanie didn't appear to be covered in the same condescending ice as her mother, and she didn't deserve Nadia's anger.

Capitulating, Nadia waved toward the small living room. "These better be some shoes," she muttered.

Pete walked ahead of them carrying the small pile of luggage, and Melanie looped her arm through Nadia's.

"One thing you'll learn about me really quick. I don't kid about stocks, world peace or footwear."

Chuckling, Nadia let herself be led forward.

An hour later, she stood in front of the cheval mirror in her bedroom. And stared.

This can't be me.

She lifted her arm, about to press trembling fingers to the glass, but at the last minute, she aborted the gesture. Sheepish, she glanced over her shoulder to see if Melanie had seen the foolish move, but the other woman was busy packing up her makeup case. Returning her attention to the mirror, Nadia again gaped at the woman gazing back at her.

Though she'd initially been upset with Grayson for his high-handed tactics, now she...

Oh hell, she felt like freaking Cinderella.

Instead of hiding her abundant curves, the deep silver dress accentuated them. The boat neck flowed into a formfitting top that glided over her breasts and stomach. The rich satin skirt gathered at her waist before falling in stunning draping to the floor. Melanie had parted her hair down the middle and then gathered the thick strands into a bun low in the back. The pointed toe of stilettoes sprinkled with twinkling rhinestones peeked out from under the dress's hem. Diamond studs that'd had Nadia nearly hyperventilating graced her ears and an impossibly thin silver necklace with a diamond nestled in the dip of her throat encircled her neck.

Forget Cinderella. She looked like a goddess.

It both delighted and terrified her.

Yes, in this attire she might look like she belonged more

than she would've in her black wedding/funeral dress. But no dress, shoes or jewelry could change the fact that she *didn't*.

A wave of panic blindsided her, and she pressed a palm to her chest. What if she humiliated herself and Grayson? She didn't know how to mingle with people who might as well as be from another planet instead of a different part of town.

From one moment to the next, she was once again standing in her old house in Tatumville with Jared informing her he wouldn't be escorting her to his parents' anniversary party because it was doubling as an engagement celebration for him. To the woman worthy enough to wear his last name. Not her. Not Marion Jordan's daughter. Nadia might be good enough for a secret roll in the sheets, but not to introduce to his family and friends…

Pain, sharp and bright, sliced into her, and she gasped at the agony of it. Even now, almost two years later, that memory still contained the power to bring her to her knees. Of all the lessons she'd been taught in her life, that one had nearly devastated her.

It was also the one she could never afford to forget.

"Nadia?" Melanie's reflection appeared behind her. Gentle hands cupped Nadia's shoulders. "Are you okay?"

"Yes, of course." Nadia forced a smile to her lips, and in the mirror, it looked as strained as it felt. Turning away from the condemning visual, she faced Grayson's sister. "Thank you so much for all your help. I can't believe you worked that much magic in an hour."

"Please," Melanie scoffed, squeezing Nadia's shoulders before releasing her. "Like I had to do much. You're gorgeous, Nadia." Melanie tilted her head to the side, studying her. "I have to confess, when Gray asked me to pick up dresses and shoes he'd chosen and to come over and assist you for tonight, I was curious. It's a first. You're obviously different."

"I know." Nadia waved a hand. "I'm poor. Can't tell a salad fork from a dessert fork. Thick. Come from peasant stock instead of American royalty…"

"Yes," Melanie agreed, but with such a matter-of-factness, Nadia couldn't take offense. "All that is true. But I was thinking, you're different because my brother gives a damn. He's never asked for my help before, and he's never chosen a woman's evening gown to my knowledge. The fact that he cares about you being as comfortable as possible makes you…more." She paused, and the corner of her mouth quirked. "And the salad fork has longer tines but a shorter handle. The dessert fork is the opposite. Shorter tines, longer handle."

"Thanks," Nadia murmured. And not just for the flatware advice. Melanie's words whirled in Nadia's head. *My brother gives a damn. The fact that he cares about you being as comfortable as possible makes you…more.*

The charade. Grayson needed to make the charade as believable as possible. It was all a part of the act.

Silently repeating those reminders, she picked up her purse from the bed. Just as she finished fastening the band, the doorbell rang. The knotting of her stomach belied the words tramping through her head. Nerves because of the evening ahead. Nothing else.

Liar.

"Here's your wrap." Melanie laid a matching length of satin over Nadia's arm. "And I'll see you there." Squeezing Nadia's hand, Melanie disappeared out of the bedroom.

Dimly, Nadia heard Melanie greet Grayson, and though Nadia's mind ordered her to get going, her feet refused to cooperate. Closing her eyes, she inhaled several deep breaths. She could do this. For Ezra, she could do anything, face anything. Even the cliquish, Chicago social elite—and Grayson's mother.

With an image of her brother walking across Yale's illustrious campus planted firmly in her mind, she exited the bedroom and strode down the short hallway toward the front door.

Grayson stood with his hands in the pockets of his pants, his back to her. But maybe he heard her carpet-muffled footsteps or caught the frantic slamming of her heart against her ribcage… Either one, he turned and faced her.

And God, did he look amazing.

The perfect American prince in a tapered black suit that practically worshipped his tall frame. A stark white shirt emphasized the golden tones of his skin, while a light blue-and-gray pinstriped tie that appeared to be silk even to her untrained eye, drew attention to the hard wall of his chest. A pocket square of the same pattern and color as the tie peeped out of his jacket and a gold, black-faced watch adorned his right wrist.

She'd encircled her fingers around that strong wrist as his full mouth had sexed hers. She'd stroked that chest. Brushed her lips across it while he'd plunged into her over and over again. Faint twinges of pleasure echoed deep and high in her body.

Fake fiancée. No sex. Ezra's tuition money.

Drawing in a breath, she halted several feet away from him.

"Well, I'm ready," she needlessly announced, running her palms down her thighs in a nervous gesture she regretted revealing. She raised her gaze to Grayson's and resisted the urge to fidget. She waited as his hooded, blue-and-green inspection swept over her from the middle part of her hair to the jeweled toe of her shoe. After an insurmountable amount of time—okay, seconds—his scrutiny returned to her face. His expression remained as neutral as ever, but his eyes...

The minimal amount of air left in her lungs made a break for it. Driven away by the gleam lighting his stare like flashes of dry heat. That was...good.

Good for the pretense. To help convince people that he did indeed find her attractive.

But, oh God, not so good for her resolve to remain distant. When he looked at her like that—she nervously fingered the small diamond pendant at her throat. When he looked at her like that, he almost made her believe, too.

And that was dangerous.

"You are stunning," he stated, and the flinty tone contradicted the blaze in his eyes that had flames dancing along all her exposed skin. He withdrew his hands from his pocket and approached her. She almost dipped her head. Anything rather than study the careless sensuality in his confident prowl. "Here." He extended his palm toward her, and in the middle sat a small, black box. "I can't have my fiancée showing up at our first public event without her ring." His lips curled in a sardonic twist as he lifted the lid.

She should've been blown away by the huge, multi-carat diamond nestled in the bed of white satin. The thing could've funded a small developing nation. But it left her cold. Probably because *it* seemed cold. A statement piece, not jewelry lovingly and carefully chosen for a woman he planned to spend the rest of his life with. Or shoot, maybe it was the kind of ring he'd bought Adalyn at one time. If so, that was incredibly sad.

"Thank you," she murmured, as he removed the jewelry and slid it on her left ring finger. The rock weighed her hand down, and wasn't that just apropos? This whole sham of a relationship was an albatross around her neck. "It's lovely."

The half smile deepened, as did the hint of a snarl. "Lovely," he repeated, rubbing his thumb over the square-cut gem. "Most women would've been gushing over a five-carat diamond, but I get a 'lovely' from you. Maybe if I told you it was yours to keep after the four months are up, you could manage more enthusiasm," he said.

"That isn't part of our bargain," she replied, stung by the implication in his admonishment. "And I'm so sorry my response didn't meet your standards. Should I throw myself at you and squeal with glee? Or maybe get down on my knees in gratefulness."

Something dark and...hungry flickered in his eyes, and she stiffened against the spark of need igniting deep inside her, tingling in the tips of breasts, clenching between her legs.

He shifted forward until a mere breath separated them. Lifting her hand at the same time he lowered his head, he brushed his mouth across the ring, and she barely stifled a groan at the whisper of those full, soft lips she remembered so well ghosting across her skin.

"When you get down on your knees for me, Nadia, it won't be out of gratitude," he said in a silken tone that caressed her flesh even as it triggered every feminine warning in her body. This wasn't a threat.

It was a promise.

"We should go," she breathed, tugging her hand free.

For a heart-stopping moment, he didn't release her, and in that same moment, she didn't want him to. She wanted him to drag her closer, consume her mouth like he had in that shadowed hallway and possess her, claim her. Mark her.

But then, he did let her go, and she exhaled. Relieved.

Or at least that's what she tried to convince herself she felt as she let him settle her wrap around her shoulders and they headed out of her house.

Relief.

Not disappointment.

Eight

"Prime property, Grayson," Harold Denson boasted. Grayson gritted his teeth as his father's friend droned on and on about a deal that must be invested in. Why the other man thought Grayson cared remained a mystery.

"Ready to be snatched up and developed. I was telling your father about the project, and he told me to talk it over with you since you will soon be stepping up to head Chandler International. I was happy to hear that, and if I must say so, it's about time, too. That tech business you've been fooling around with has been profitable, I'll give you that. But it isn't Chandler. Without your brother—"

"If you'll excuse us," Nadia interrupted from beside him. The hand she settled over his chest stemmed the surge of anger strangling him. Between his father obviously announcing to anyone who would listen that Grayson was returning to the family company and the insensitive mention of Jason, he needed space, air, a drink. And to get away from this ass.

"I'm so sorry to steal Grayson away from you, but he promised me a tour of his childhood home before we leave for the ballet."

"Oh, of course! Grayson, show this young lady how the other half lives. Just don't get lost, you two," he added with a chuckle and a leer over Nadia's breasts and hips that had Grayson's fingers curling into his palm. Older man or not, friend of his father's or not, the man needed a quick lesson in how to respect women. Especially the woman on Grayson's arm.

"Thank you," Nadia said with a smile. She covered his fist with her other hand, squeezing lightly. "How about we start with the library?"

"Sure, baby," Grayson murmured, allowing her to lead him away. The library was in the opposite direction, but at this point, he didn't care. He just needed to be…away.

Focusing on the twist at the back of her head, he imagined loosening it and tunneling his fingers through that wealth of thick strands. Just the thought of wrapping them around his wrists and tugging, hearing that low, hungry moan, diverted his attention from the stranglehold of frustration and sadness he'd felt since stepping foot in his parents' home.

Jason was everywhere. In the pictures mounted on the mantelpiece over the formal living room's fireplace. In the framed degrees hanging prominently in the receiving room.

In the empty space beside their father as he held court with his guests. Everyone knew Jason's spot had been at Daryl Chandler's elbow.

Grayson briefly squeezed his eyes shut, then reopened them, zeroing in on Nadia again as if she were his lodestone. His true north that guided him away from the dark abyss of regrets that just waited for him to slip and plummet into its depths.

"Here." Nadia held out a glass of ruby-red wine, her

knuckles grazing his chest. "You look like you could use this."

"Only if it has a shot of whiskey in it," he growled, but he sipped the alcohol. Grateful for the private corner she'd found and the distraction of doing something with his hands. Because they would either be wrapped around Harold's neck or cupping Nadia's ass. Both would give Grayson immense satisfaction—touching Nadia even more than choking his father's friend—but both actions would also get him into trouble he didn't need.

"Do you really want a tour of the house?"

"No," she said, lifting her own glass to her lips.

He shook his head, raising the wineglass for another sip and studying her over the rim. Part of him desperately wanted—no, needed—to call bullshit. Even Adalyn, who'd been born to a wealthy family had been awed by the Gold Coast greystone mansion. Soaring three stories up, the majestic home had been in his family for four generations. With huge bay and picture windows dotting every floor, stone steps leading up to several entrances and towering peaks, his childhood home resembled a Victorian house deposited in the middle of Chicago.

But Nadia had strolled past the tall iron gates surrounding the property and the gurgling fountain with just a passing glance. Once inside she hadn't gaped at the vaulted cathedral ceilings, the grand foyer with the winding staircase, the priceless art decorating the walls or the cavernous rooms with huge fireplaces, antiques and crystal chandeliers. No, Nadia had only given his family's prosperity and affluence fleeting attention. Just as she'd done with the ring.

Why her obvious lack of enthusiasm for the piece of jewelry still grated, he didn't know. Couldn't explain. It just…did. He peered down at her left hand and the diamond setting that cost more than some people's yearly salary. When he'd bought the ring, his intention had been to ensure everyone who saw it understood his serious intentions. In his circle—or his parents' circle—money spoke much louder than words. But Nadia, it seemed, didn't care about what it said.

Yes, he wanted her awe. For her to be excited. Or hell, just affected. Because if not, that made her different. And he didn't trust "different"—it unnerved him. He couldn't get a handle on it, couldn't analyze and add it up. It meant she wouldn't stay in the neat box he'd created for her.

The last thing he needed was for her to be more than any other woman.

The last thing he needed was for her to be...different.

"You didn't like the ring."

Hell. Where had that come from? And yet, he couldn't stop himself.

"Why?" he pressed.

She studied him, her espresso gaze unwavering. "In my experience, rich people wield their money like a weapon. Protecting themselves and those they deem worthy and waging war on everyone else. They arm themselves with money to bring people to heel. When you've been on the receiving end of that short leash, how many dollars a person spends on their home, car, clothes and even you, doesn't matter much."

Grayson stared at her, each word an indictment against him, his family, his world. They were all guilty—especially him. Wasn't he paying her to lie? To pretend to be someone she wasn't for his benefit?

He shook his head as if the gesture could rid him of the thought and the unsettling pinpricks of guilt. She could've turned him down. Hell, she had, but then had returned to *him*, accepting the bargain. And it was just that—a bargain. One they both profited from. Just like other women in his past, she wanted money from him. Only this time, he was going in with his eyes wide open. No feelings attached. No fervent promises of love. No commitments.

It was the most honest transaction he'd ever entered in his life.

"If money doesn't matter, then what does?" he drawled, mocking her. "Love? I hate to break it to you, Nadia, but the two are mutually exclusive."

"Tell me something," she murmured, and when he didn't reply, she continued, "Was that ring for me...or for you?"

A disdainful response hovered on his tongue, but remained stuck there, something deep inside him refusing to loose the vitriolic words. Instead, he stared down into her upturned face, spying a knowledge in those dark eyes that made him want to remind her of who he was—her employer, the man paying her a quarter of a million dollars, a fucking Chandler...

He wanted to beg her to stop peering inside him and seeing the secrets, the wounds he zealously guarded.

"Grayson," an all-too-familiar voice interrupted his and Nadia's visual showdown.

He tore his gaze away from his fake fiancée to meet the green one of his ex-fiancée. Adalyn smiled, and the sultriness in her eyes stirred nothing in him but irritation.

"I haven't had a chance to speak to you all evening," she said.

"Hello, Adalyn," he replied, nodding.

Objectively, he noted the sleek length of her raven hair and her petite figure encased in an off-the-shoulder cocktail dress. Without conscious thought, he compared her to Nadia with her tall, lush body showcased to perfection in the silver dress that had his hands itching all night to touch her. He'd cupped those hips. Dug his fingers in the soft flesh there as he drove into her.

Because he could—because this charade granted him permission—he slid an arm around Nadia's lower back and rested his fingers against that enticing curve. Pressing his fingertips into it, melding the present with his vivid memories.

"You remember Nadia. Nadia Jordan, this is Adalyn Hayes," he murmured. Turning his attention to his ex, his voice hardened, losing the warmth it'd contained when speaking to Nadia. "Adalyn, Nadia Jordan, my fiancée."

Adalyn flicked a look at Nadia and then down at her hand. Unless Adalyn had gone spontaneously blind she couldn't have missed the diamond on Nadia's finger. Her mouth flattened briefly before regaining the polite society smile that could mean anything.

"Yes, I'd heard the news about your sudden engagement. It's the hot topic of conversation this evening. Congratulations," Adalyn said, the sweetness in her smile nowhere near the dagger-edge sharpness in her eyes. "How exciting." She settled a hand on his chest, and it required every bit of his control not to flinch. "I remember holding that title once, as well. Fiancée to Grayson Chandler. The experience was…thrilling," she added, her tone lowering, as if inviting him to recall the intimate times they'd shared.

Unable to stand her touch another second, especially with Nadia's warm body tucked against his, he stepped back. Adalyn's arm dropped to her side, and he didn't miss the glint of anger in her gaze.

"Nadia, right?" Adalyn asked, swinging her attention away from him. But Grayson stiffened, a surge of protectiveness sweeping through him. He'd witnessed Adalyn's cutting disdain in action. No matter that his and Nadia's relationship wasn't real. He wouldn't allow Adalyn to slice her to pieces with that razor she called a tongue. "I almost didn't recognize you from the last time we met. Your dress is lovely." Adalyn tapped a French-tipped finger against her bottom lip, her eyes narrowed. "Is that Michael Kors?

I'd heard he'd incorporated a few pieces in his collection for...healthier women."

The petty bitch.

Grayson shifted forward, anger blazing his path. "Adalyn..." he growled.

"Actually, I'm not certain who the designer is," Nadia interrupted, wrapping an arm around his back and leaning closer. She chuckled, the sound light, soft and so sweet, he tore his glare away from his ex and glanced down at her. With her head tipped back, she returned his gaze, her lovely mouth curved into a smile that held not just affection, but a sensuality that Adalyn damn sure couldn't miss. Even knowing her expression was feigned for the other woman's benefit, his breath snagged in his lungs and his cock stirred, hardening.

She was—damn, she was dangerous, the smile on that made-for-sex mouth a fully loaded weapon.

"Can I be honest?" she asked, treating Adalyn as if she were a close friend. "I'm not really into fashion. But thank goodness I have a man who knows me so well, he chooses gowns that I'll love. Or more importantly, that he loves to see me in."

Nadia trailed a finger down his chest, and his shirt might as well as have disintegrated under the teasing caress. He forgot about silently applauding how she deftly fielded Adalyn as fire trailed in the wake of her touch. Not caring how it appeared, he grasped her wrist and lifted her hand to his mouth, brushing a kiss across her fingertips. Surprise flared in her eyes. But so did desire. And the sight of it had an electrical current traveling through his veins.

Adalyn's laugh carried an edge, like shattered glass. "Well, isn't that sweet? And, I apologize if I offended you, Nadia. But can I be honest, as well?" She didn't wait for Nadia to reply but dipped her head as if about to confide a secret. Again, Grayson fought the urge to step in front of Nadia, to shield her from Adalyn. "I know tonight has probably been a little overwhelming for you, but you'll have to forgive us our curiosity. This relationship came out of nowhere. Usually, Grayson is constantly in the society columns and gossip sites. But we haven't seen him with you once. Almost as if he's been keeping you under wraps. Hiding you."

Adalyn's implication was clear. That he was ashamed of Nadia. His fury returned tenfold, and he couldn't contain the menacing rumble that rolled out of him. Even Adalyn had the sense to back up a step.

"You're right, Adalyn," he agreed, voice quiet, carrying a warning. "There is nothing 'usual' about Nadia. She's unlike any woman I've been with." He allowed the *including you* to remain unspoken. "I selfishly wanted to keep her to myself before subjecting her to the BS that goes along with being my wife. She's that special to me." Sliding his hand from her hip and up her spine, he cupped her neck, drawing her closer until she rose on her toes. Until her breasts pressed into his side. "Now that you've experienced the other side of my life, are you ready to leave me?"

"Never," Nadia said in that same teasing lilt, but her eyes… Those dark eyes held all the confusion swirling inside of him over how far he was taking this exhibition of affection.

"Good," he murmured. Then brushed his lips over hers.

But it wasn't enough.

That small hit of her taste had him ignoring Adalyn and the roomful of people, including his parents and sister. He returned to Nadia's mouth for more. For a deeper sampling. To thrust his tongue past her parted lips—whether parted in shock or desire, he didn't know—and take what his memories wouldn't let him forget. Reacquaint himself with what his logic assured him couldn't possibly be as good as he remembered.

Logic could go fuck itself.

She was every carnal wish and wicked sin wrapped in beauty and light.

She was the one to break the kiss. The one who retained a modicum of propriety and restraint. Not him.

That quick, she'd gone to his head, and he'd gotten drunk on her.

Goddamn.

He lifted his head, noticed the stares, heard the murmuring. Adalyn had disappeared at some point during the kiss, but he could almost feel the weight of his parents' displeasure. In spite of the playboy reputation he bore, he didn't do this—lose control, make a spectacle of himself—ever.

This woman. She flayed to pieces every resolve, every vow he'd made. He couldn't go there with her. Deliberately, he conjured an image of himself a year ago after he'd ended his relationship with Adalyn. How broken he'd been. How disillusioned he'd been. Adalyn hadn't only cracked his heart down the middle, she'd stolen his ability to trust himself, his judgment.

His ability to trust, period.

And Nadia, though she might desire him, she only wanted from him what every other woman did.

What he could give her.

He could never lose sight of that.

Never.

"Grayson," Nadia whispered.

But he couldn't look at her. Couldn't meet that gaze. Because, despite the reminders of why he had to tread carefully with her—with himself—if he glimpsed desire in those beautiful eyes, he might seek out the nearest room with a door and lock. And damn the consequences, he would lay her out and take everything she would offer him. Then demand more.

"We should get ready to leave for the ballet," he said,

grasping her elbow and leading her toward the living room entrance.

He had to reestablish the grounds of their arrangement. This relationship was fake. It had an expiration date. Nadia Jordan was his end game.

She could be nothing else.

Nine

"Mr. Chandler, your father is here to see you," Mrs. Ross announced on the other end of the line. "He doesn't have an appointment, sir."

A faint spurt of humor echoed through him at his assistant's reminder that was more directed at his father than him. Her disapproval hummed beneath the cool tone, but it would be lost on Daryl Chandler. He was the kind of man people shuffled their schedules for. The kind of man who demanded it.

Leaning back in his office chair, Grayson closed his eyes, pinching the bridge of his nose. Sadly, he wasn't shocked at this visit. Well, correction. He was surprised his father stood on the other side of his office door instead of his mother. After the performance Grayson and Nadia had put on at the cocktail party three nights ago, he'd expected this "intervention."

"You can send him in, Mrs. Ross," he said, setting the phone down.

He rose and rounded the desk, standing in front of it. Preparing himself. That he braced himself as if readying for battle spoke volumes about his relationship with his father.

Seconds later, his office door opened and Daryl Chandler strode through as if his name was engraved on the gold plate instead of Grayson's.

To Grayson, his father had always been bigger than life. He'd inherited his height and big, wide-shouldered frame from Daryl Chandler—a throwback to the ancestors who had worked the railroads instead of owning them—and though his father probably wouldn't easily admit it, Grayson had inherited his business acumen, too. But ever since he'd been born with a defect—his different-colored eyes—Grayson had been flawed and second best with his father.

There'd been a time when Grayson had lived up to his father's opinion. Like when, as a teen, he'd decided to have an impromptu party on his father's yacht. Or when he'd been caught smoking weed on the private school grounds. But those stunts were in the distant past. Over the years, he'd proven he could control not only himself, but his life, and run a successful company.

None of that seemed to matter to his father, though.

When would it cease mattering to Grayson?

"Good morning, Dad. This is a surprise."

His father arched a still-dark eyebrow. "Somehow I doubt that, Grayson." He lifted an arm and waved it toward Grayson's desk. And for the first time, he noticed the manila folder in his father's hand. "I won't make this long."

"Of course." Curiosity and a weighty sense of foreboding expanded inside Grayson's chest. This was the first time since he and Gideon founded KayCee Corp that his father had visited the offices. This one didn't bode well.

He led Daryl to the two armchairs in front of his desk. He lowered into one and waited for his father to settle. A steely pair of green eyes studied him, but Grayson wasn't that rebellious teen anymore. He was a thirty-year-old man who'd matured, carved out his own future and lived on his own terms. If his father waited for him to squirm, he might need to cancel his meetings. Wasn't going to happen.

"I believe you can guess why I'm here," Daryl began, resting the folder on his thigh. Grayson tried not to stare at it, but at this moment, the innocuous light brown file loomed like the real threat in the room. "After that... undignified display the other night, your mother and I thought it best if I paid you a visit."

Undignified display? To what did he refer? His engagement? Or the kiss? "I'm afraid you're going to have to be more specific, Dad. I attended as Mother requested with my fiancée. Which part offended you?"

Daryl scoffed, irritation flashing in his eyes. "Take your pick, Grayson. Showing up with that woman. Springing this joke of an engagement on both of us and making us accessories to it because you knew we wouldn't cause a scene in front of all our friends."

Though anger tightened his gut, Grayson propped his elbows on the arms of his chair and templed his fingers beneath his chin. "An accessory?" He snorted. "You make my relationship sound like a crime. Which, I suppose you see it as one. Still, the time when I had to bring the woman I'm seeing by for approval has long since passed—if it ever existed." He shook his head. "I will apologize for not letting you and Mother know about the engagement in a more private setting, though. It hadn't been my intention to embarrass you."

Just waylay any more matchmaking attempts by his mother.

His father waved aside the apology with a flick of his hand, dismissing it. "Considering the number of women you run through, all captured by those unseemly gossip sites, we're thankful you haven't brought them to our home."

The barb struck true, no doubt as Daryl had intended. But Grayson refused to let him see the effect. "But when you contemplate giving a woman our last name and bringing her into our family, she certainly requires our approval. And this Nadia Jordan does not meet the standards of anyone who will be a Chandler. Not even remotely." His father picked up the envelope and extended it toward him. "Take it, Grayson. Read it."

Though he wanted to tell his father to forget it, Grayson reluctantly accepted it. Knowledge meant power. And though his and Nadia's relationship was fake, he would protect her, shield her from his parents, if need be.

He opened the folder and removed the thin sheaf of papers, scanning the top sheet. An investigative report on one Nadia A. Jordan. Surprise reverberated through him, discordant and ugly. Well, hadn't his parents been busy?

Several minutes later, he lifted his head and met his father's gaze, hardening his expression into a mask that he hoped revealed none of the thoughts whirling through his head. Father unknown. Neglectful mother with a reputation that must've made being her daughter a nightmare. Arrested for shoplifting. No college education. Wrecked credit.

His parents would read this report and see a poor, uneducated woman from nowhere trying to get her greedy hooks into their son.

Grayson saw a woman, who in spite of the kicks and punches life had thrown, had risen every time to not just continue, but to thrive. A life that might have bent her, but from the passion and defiance she'd shown him, hadn't broken her.

He saw a survivor.

"Is this supposed to change my mind?" he asked, tossing the report onto his desk. "So, she wasn't born with a building named after her family? That doesn't make her unworthy to wear the illustrious Chandler name," he drawled.

Red surged into his father's face, the only sign of his rising temper. "You're damn right that makes her unworthy. If you want to screw her, fine. But marry her? A thief? And from that GED, a high school dropout? The daughter of a whore? And God only knows if she falls far from the tree. No, Grayson. Marriage to her is out of the question."

"You want to stop right there, Dad," Grayson said, voice flat. A tone he'd never used with his father before. He had no intention of marrying Nadia, which made this whole discussion moot. But no way in hell would he allow his father to denigrate her. As if she were something on the bottom of his shoe. "You have your opinion of Nadia, but you don't get to talk about her like that to me. Ever." He struggled to remain respectful, but if it'd been anyone else but Daryl Chandler uttering these insults, they would've been picking themselves up off the floor.

Again. His anger made no sense.

But it didn't have to.

"This is what I'm talking about, Grayson," Daryl snapped, shooting to his feet. He paced away from Grayson, who also stood. "I can see why some of her… charms would grab your attention. But stop thinking with your dick," he growled, striding back toward Grayson and halting in front of him. "This is about more than you, it's about family, about loyalty, about living up to the Chandler name and all that it entails instead of dragging it down as you seem intent on doing."

How? By living when Jason didn't?

The question clanged in his head like the rattling of a ghost. A ghost that refused to be exorcised.

"So forget my own happiness, my own future?" he asked quietly, now referring to more than Nadia. To his company, to making his own choices, to living an existence out from under the smothering burden of a legacy he hadn't asked for. "How much do you expect me to sacrifice?"

"Whatever it takes," his father shot back. Inhaling a deep breath, he shoved his hands into the front pockets of his gray suit, visibly calming himself. "We all sacrifice, Grayson. Particularly now that Jason…" He cleared his throat, his gaze briefly shooting to the floor-to-ceiling window behind Grayson. When he returned his regard to Grayson, his eyes reflected none of the emotion that had wrapped around Jason's name. "I can't helm Chandler International forever, nor do I want to. It's a birthright passed down from father to son, and it is now your turn, your privilege, your *destiny* to lead and build it into even more than I have.

"And you need the right woman at your side. The *right* woman, Grayson. And as high-handed as your mother might be, she's right. Adalyn is a perfect choice. She's from an exceptional family, has been educated at the finest schools, is beautiful and knows our world. Also, her father and I are in the middle of discussing a very lucrative business deal. It would mean expanding both Chandler International and The Hayes Group into a power to be reckoned with in the national and global financial markets. I'd prefer not to anger Thad Hayes by having my son rebuff his daughter, which would result in the failure of this venture."

"Now who's the whore, Dad? You want me to pimp myself out for a company expansion," Grayson growled.

"I want you to do what's right," Daryl snapped. "It's not like you and Adalyn aren't compatible. You were engaged before, so there's no need for the theatrics."

"Were," Grayson ground out. "And there's a very good reason why I didn't go through with it."

His father shook his head. Pulling his hand free of his pants pocket, he glanced down at his watch. "I have to go. But get rid of the girl, Grayson. And start courting Adalyn. If you must be photographed like a common reality

TV star, then it should be with her, not a plaything. And," he narrowed his eyes on him, "I expect you to attend the next Chandler board meeting. The directors need to understand that you will be stepping in as CEO and become familiar with you."

With that order, his father turned and strode out of the office, leaving Grayson alone. And angry. Saddened. And so goddamn powerless.

And he resented his father for that.

Hated himself even more.

Family duty and loyalty strangled him, crushing him under its burdensome weight. As the "spare," he hadn't been his parents' first choice.

But now, he was the only one left.

Ten

"Ezra, can you get the door?" Nadia called from her bedroom. She'd just emerged from the shower and answering the doorbell in a short, threadbare towel didn't seem like a great idea. On Saturdays, she tended to go casual, but not *that* casual.

"Yeah, I got it," her brother yelled back. As was their custom, on Saturday mornings she cooked a big breakfast, and he cleaned up afterward. Since her bedroom was off the same hallway that led to the kitchen, she heard him tramp down the hall toward the foyer.

She shimmied into a bra and panties, then tugged on a black, V-neck sweater and her favorite pair of boyfriend jeans that were faded from multiple wears and washings. As she searched for a pair of socks among the endless singles, a knock echoed on her door.

"Come in," she said, triumphantly retrieving a matching pair.

A second later, Ezra opened the door and poked his

head through, his dark locs swinging against his handsome face. His handsome, frowning face. "There's a guy here to see you."

Her heart thumped against her rib cage. She hadn't made many friends in the short time she'd been in Chicago and hadn't dated once. So the "guy" could be only one person.

"Okay, I'll be right out," she said, infusing a calm into her voice that belied the tumble of nerves in her belly.

Still frowning, Ezra backed out of the door. Moments later, she emerged and padded down the hallway toward the front of the house. Though the thin carpet masked her footsteps, Grayson still looked up as she approached, his blue-and-green gaze steady on her. She almost faltered, the power of those eyes like a physical blow.

Though days had passed since the cocktail party, and their contact had been minimal, she still felt his mouth pressed to hers and tasted the hunger in that kiss. She dreamed about that kiss. Even now, she forced her hands to remain by her side so she didn't lift one and press fingers to her lips. As if she could somehow capture it.

In the middle of his parents' living room, she'd yearned to wrap her arms around his neck and demand a deeper touch that would fill her empty places. She'd longed to be burned by the pleasure that had haunted her body, her mind. The desire that had flared so hot between them during the blackout hadn't abated, hadn't dimmed. Before that kiss at the cocktail party she could convince herself that the out-of-the-ordinary circumstances had stirred the combustible heat between them.

The kiss had razed that opinion to ashes.

But it'd also reinforced her emotional walls with steel. If one kiss could level her... As much as she'd believed she'd loved Jared, he hadn't ignited the out-of-control need to surrender herself that Grayson did.

It was...terrifying.

Because Grayson, with his innate sensuality, dark emotions that seemed to seethe just under the surface, had a dominance that could strip away the control she'd fought so hard for. He could render her vow to never lay her heart and soul out for a man to use again to cinders.

She couldn't permit that.

She didn't know if she would survive intact.

No way in hell would she risk finding out.

She repeated that warning in her head as she took in his tall, lean frame in black slacks and a cream-colored sweater that probably cost more than her living room furniture.

"Grayson," she greeted, drawing nearer. His sandalwood and mint scent reached out to her, and she cursed herself for inhaling deeply, savoring it. "This is a surprise." She halted next to her brother. "I don't know if he introduced himself, but this is my brother, Ezra. Ezra," she nudged him with her elbow, "this is Grayson Chandler, my...uh, friend."

"Friend, huh?" Ezra snorted, rolling his eyes, appearing all of his seventeen years. "Okay, we'll go with that." He stuck out a hand toward Grayson. "Nice to meet you, Mr. Chandler."

"You, too, Ezra. And it's Grayson." Grayson shook her brother's hand.

"So what are you two crazy kids up to today?" Ezra questioned, crossing his arms and glancing back and forth between her and Grayson.

"Please," she scoffed, shoving his shoulder. "Get out of here and finish the dishes."

"Fine," he grumbled, then pivoted and headed toward the rear of the house.

Once he'd disappeared, she returned her attention to her "fiancé."

"Grayson, what are you doing here? Did we have something scheduled?"

He shook his head. "No, I stopped by to see if you were free today."

"For?" she pressed. "What's the occasion? A dinner party? A charity event?"

"Neither. I—" His lips snapped shut, and a muscle leaped along his jaw. Several seconds later, he said, "Do you trust me, Nadia?"

"Not even a little bit." Truth, but not all of it.

When it came to him, she trusted herself even less.

A ghost of a smile flirted with his mouth. "I deserve that. And respect it. But will you give me a pass today? Take a chance on me."

Take a chance on me.

The simple words shouldn't have been a temptation. But for her, they were. In the past, when she'd trusted people, they'd either disappointed or devastated her. She didn't go in blind anywhere; she required a map, seven different exits and an escape hatch. Yet...

Yet, as she met his mesmerizing eyes, she wanted to place herself into his hands, let him alleviate the exhaustion of always being in control. Even if just for a little while.

"Okay," she murmured. "Give me a few minutes. I'll be right back."

He nodded, his expression revealing nothing. But she caught the flash of something in his eyes. Something she believed could be relief. That was probably her imagination, though. Her trying to convince herself she wasn't in this confusing place of emotional quicksand alone.

Sighing, she returned to her room and then quickly applied a minimal amount of makeup, tugged on her ankle boots and grabbed her jacket. At the last second, she picked up the ostentatious engagement ring and slid it on her finger. Moments later, she slipped back out of her bedroom into the hallway.

"...says you're a friend, but I can guess what kind of

friend you are." Ezra's voice drifted to her as she treaded closer. Ahead, her brother stood in front of Grayson, his back to her. Though Grayson had him by several inches, Ezra straightened his shoulders and tipped his head back. "I don't know what kind of thing y'all have going on," he continued in his drawl. "But she's my big sister. And she's been through enough for a lifetime. I don't want you adding to it."

Silently, Nadia groaned. Love for her brother and his overprotective streak poured through her, but she also longed to yank him up and shove him back toward the kitchen. She could take care of herself without him threatening would-be boyfriends. Still… Damn, she adored the kid.

"I don't plan on hurting your sister," Grayson promised, his voice solemn, no hint of amusement. He could've easily patronized the teen, but sincerity rang from his words. And part of her believed him. The only problem was, most people usually didn't *plan* on harming other people. They just did.

"Good." Ezra nodded. "She's all I have and she has been taken advantage of and hurt too many times in the past. She needs someone who'll take care of her for once instead of the other way around. Especially after Jared—"

Oh God.

"I'm ready," she called out, moving down the hall at a desperate clip. Jesus, why would Ezra bring up her ex-boyfriend? Both Grayson and Ezra turned to face her, and guilt flashed across her brother's face. But it quickly morphed into a stubbornness she was well acquainted with. "You." She jabbed a finger in his chest. "Dishes. And if you go out tonight, make sure you call and let me know."

"Sure." He kissed her cheek, then glanced back at Grayson, giving him that chin tip that seemed to be a part of the masculine language. "Nice talking to you, Grayson."

When he once more disappeared into the kitchen, she shifted her gaze to Grayson. "I'm sorry about that," she said with a small wince. "He's a little overprotective."

But Grayson shook his head, his stare flicking over her shoulder in the direction her brother had gone. "He loves his sister and is watching out for her. There's nothing to apologize for." Nabbing her jacket from her hand, he held it up, and she slipped her arms through the sleeves. "You're lucky to have one another," he murmured, his large hands settling on her shoulders. His fingers lightly squeezed, before releasing her. "Let's go."

Though questions about his enigmatic statement whirled inside her head, she went.

"I should be annoyed with you right now," Nadia muttered, sinking into the chair that Grayson pulled from the restaurant table.

A delicate glass vase filled with water and floating, lit candles in the shape of lilies cast a warm glow over the white linen. Folded black napkins that reminded her of origami sat next to sparkling silver flatware. A breathtaking view of Lake Michigan through floor-to-ceiling windows, its gently lapping waters gleaming orange, pink and purple from the setting sun, provided a stunning backdrop. Even though other diners and the low hum of conversation surrounded them, their corner table, partially shielded from prying eyes by a wall of lush greenery, exuded the illusion of privacy. And from the curious looks they received upon entering, she clung to that illusion.

By himself, Grayson would draw attention. But with her by his side? The looks seemed sharper, the whispers louder. Part of her wanted to rise from the table and walk out. She'd been on the receiving end of hushed talk behind hands enough to last a couple of lifetimes. But the other half of her—the half that brimmed with defiant anger—

met their furtive glances. Yes, she'd dared to enter their cushy, exclusive turf. But she wouldn't lower her eyes in apology for being there.

Grayson ordered wine for both of them, and as their waiter hurried away, he turned to her. "Annoyed with me?" he repeated, the corner of his mouth quirking as he settled in the chair across from her. "Whatever for? Didn't we just spend a great day together? Buckingham Fountain. The SkyDeck. The Riverwalk. Navy Pier. Fried Twinkies."

"Yeah." She sighed. "Extra points for the fried Twinkies. They're probably the only reason I *should be* annoyed and am not full-blown irritated." He arched an eyebrow, and she sank her teeth into her bottom lip, fiddling with the napkin on the table. "I sound like an ungrateful shrew, and I'm sorry. Thank you for an amazing day I wasn't expecting. Ezra and I have been in Chicago for a little over a year, but between work and his schedule and, well, life, I haven't had the opportunity to explore the city. Today was wonderful. So again, thank you."

"You're welcome, Nadia. It was my pleasure," he murmured. Cocking his head to the side, he studied her. "Now tell me what you're not saying."

She huffed out a ragged laugh that abraded her throat. "It's...this." She leaned back and waved a hand up and down her torso, indicating the royal blue long-sleeved sheath dress that both glided over and clung to her breasts, hips and thighs. Beneath the table, black knee-high stiletto boots of the softest leather embraced her calves and feet. Yes, Grayson had escorted her all over Chicago in a laid-back, surprisingly *fun* tour of his city. He'd gifted her with a day that had made her feel free and special. But... "The dress for the cocktail party, this one—they're not part of our bargain," she finished.

It went deeper than not wanting to be the recipient of his charity. So much deeper.

"But it is part of our bargain, Nadia," Grayson contradicted. "I asked you to play the part of my fiancée. And that includes making you look the role, as well. And that's my responsibility since the arrangement was my idea, not yours. What kind of man would I be if I didn't take care of the needs of the woman I supposedly love? Not just emotional and sexual needs. But her material needs, as well? And not because I owe her anything, but due to it simply being my pleasure."

She didn't have an answer. Couldn't formulate one because her mind had stopped functioning at "emotional and sexual," fogged over by the heated arousal pouring through her. She, more than anyone, comprehended how well he fulfilled a woman's desires, satisfied her body.

"You're still not being completely honest, though," he continued, those piercing eyes glittering like gems in the light of the candles. "Tell me. Is your aversion to receiving gifts a general issue, or is it specific to me?"

She stared at him, the width of the square table seeming to shrink to that of a postage stamp. Suddenly, he was too close, his presence too large, too compelling. Too...tempting. Everything in her screamed to avoid that gaze, to keep silent. That she didn't need to divulge more to him—didn't need to give him more of herself—than what was required to pull off the relationship charade.

But trapped by his enigmatic, fascinating eyes, she couldn't squelch the impulse to confide in him. Even if it was just this little thing.

Because all she could afford with this man was "a little."

Defying the voice that warned that even a small amount was too much, she murmured, "It's both, I suppose."

Their waiter appeared with their wine. She gladly sipped from her filled glass, appreciating not just the sweet flavor of the Riesling but the temporary reprieve it provided. Moments later, the waiter left them again after taking their dinner orders, and she set her wineglass down on the table. Lifting a fingertip, she traced the slender stem, focusing her attention on it instead of Grayson.

"I grew up in a small town in Georgia. The kind where there's still a dime store, a pharmacy that also sells ice cream and a church on every corner. As you can imagine, everyone knows everyone and their business. For some, this could be the perfect place to grow up, but when your mother is…" She paused, the scraps of familial loyalty and respect her mother hadn't destroyed not allowing her to call Marion Jordan a whore. "Popular with men," she substituted, "your life can be hell."

She shifted her regard from the glass to his face, searching for a reaction to learning who her mother was. Surprise? Revulsion? But his stoic expression revealed none of his thoughts. The absence of a reaction gave her the courage to continue.

"My mother didn't work. She was taken care of by the men she 'dated,'" she said, using Marion's term. "Mostly wealthy men. They paid her rent, her bills, and yes, bought her jewelry and clothes. That's how Ezra and I survived— off the gifts of these men. But that's only when my mother decided to share the wealth. When she would remember to buy groceries or clothes for us, when she wasn't spending the money on herself. Once, when I was sixteen, I was so desperate to feed my brother, I stole a loaf of bread and jars of peanut butter and jelly from the store."

Her voice didn't waver as she confessed her one and only crime to him, and she didn't lower her gaze. The store security guard, the gossips in her town, the judge had all informed her she should've been ashamed of herself. But she hadn't been then and wasn't now. She'd done what needed to be done so her little brother didn't go to bed hungry, his stomach cramping with pains because he hadn't eaten in two days. Their mother had vanished on one of her many disappearing acts, probably with some man at a hotel where she ate while her children starved.

No, Nadia had accepted the probation and the town's scorn and the whispers of "the apple doesn't fall far from the tree," and apologized to Mr. Carol, the grocery store owner, but she'd never bowed her head in shame.

She wouldn't start with Grayson.

"I learned those gifts came at the price of my pride in taking dirty money, knowing what my mother did to earn it. The price was our sense of security, our independence. As soon as I was old enough—and as soon as I could find someone willing to hire me—I got a job at a gas station convenience store in the next town over. It meant spending time begging for rides or biking it the thirty minutes there and back, it meant less time with my brother so I could provide for us, it meant not finishing high school and graduating with a GED, it meant passing on college. But it also meant not depending on another rich man's 'gifts and generosity.'"

Silence reigned between them for precious seconds. Her heart thumped against her rib cage, the pulse ponderous in her ears. In this instant, staring into his unique eyes, she tried not to cringe under the vulnerability clawing at her. She felt more exposed than she had when he'd stripped her clothes from her body in that dark hallway.

Not only had she confessed that her mother had been the town whore, but Nadia had also admitted that she had a criminal record and was a high school dropout. Not exactly fiancée material compared to the women he dated.

"What did you want to go to college for?" he asked quietly, taking her aback with the question.

"Nursing," she said. "Maybe because I've always been the caretaker in my family." She lifted a shoulder in a half shrug. "It just wasn't meant to be. And besides, Ezra is the genius in our family. He's—" She bit off the rest of the sentence, almost spilling about him being accepted to Yale.

Though she'd shared some of her past, she still didn't trust him with her family. "He's brilliant. Special," she added.

"And you aren't?" he challenged, a snap in his voice. She frowned at the scowl that creased his brow, at the flash of anger in his narrowed gaze. He propped an arm on the table and leaned closer. "Baby, from what you've told me, you practically raised yourself and your brother. You sacrificed your childhood so he could have what little security a teenager could manage to give him when his real parent couldn't be bothered. You packed up from the only home you ever knew to move thousands of miles away to a strange city. You're a fighter, a survivor. A GED doesn't make you any less brilliant, any less special. Not going to college doesn't mean you're not as smart, not as driven or successful as other people. In my eyes, it requires more intelligence, more grit to carve out the living you've made for both yourself and Ezra than to just accept all the advantages of being born with wealth and opportunities as your due. One takes character, determination and strength, the other the Russian Roulette of birth and luck."

She couldn't speak. Could only *feel*. Surprise. Delight. Gratitude. Sadness. They all swirled and tumbled in her chest, swelling in her throat.

No one—absolutely *no one*—had ever called her smart, strong or a survivor. And for this man to say those words…

She dodged that intense stare, instead ducking her gaze to the pale gold contents of her wineglass. God, she wanted a sip. Anything to distract her from the weight of his scrutiny, from the almost terrifying depth and power of her own emotions. But she didn't dare attempt to lift the glass with her trembling hands.

"Nadia," he said, and though she avoided his eyes, the vein of steel threading through the tone brooked no disobedience.

She lifted her regard back to him, immediately becoming ensnared in the blue-and-emerald depths.

"I'm going to continue to give you gifts. Not because I owe you or as a debt I expect you to repay." He reached across the table and wrapped his long fingers around hers so they both held the glass stem. The warmth and strength of his grip was an embrace that enfolded her entire body, not just her hand. "I'm not going to stop because you deserve them. The girl you were, the teen who grew up too soon and the woman who bears all the responsibility of the world on her shoulders but too little of the beauty. That's what I want to give you. It's my honor to give you. Some of that beauty. Let me."

Again, she couldn't speak. Didn't dare nod. No matter how much she longed to. God, the temptation to relinquish control just for once and let someone—no, not someone, *Grayson*—carry the burden and care for her swept through her like the sweet warmth of a spring day. It lulled her, coaxed her to lie down, to let go.

Who would it hurt?

Her.

In the long run, it would devastate her. Because she could so easily come to rely on him. And the day would come—four months from now to be exact—when he would be a non-factor in her life. When he would disappear, leaving her aching for him—yearning for his shoulder to rest her head on, his chest to burrow her face against—instead of facing the world.

No. Grayson might not be Jared, but he was still a handsome, wealthy man who could make her believe in fairy tales.

Patching up the chinks in her armor that his words and her longing had created, she sat back in her chair, placing much-needed distance between them. Picking up her wine, she sipped, wishing the alcohol would transform into something stronger.

Their waiter chose that moment to return with their plates of steaming food. Thank God. Several minutes passed while they dug into their entrées. In spite of the emotional storm brewing inside her, she moaned at the first bite of tender, perfectly cooked medium-rare sirloin.

"Oh, my God." She closed her eyes, savoring the blend of spices and loosed another near orgasmic groan. She lifted her lashes. "This is so good it should be criminal…"

Her voice trailed off. How could she speak when her lungs refused to release any air?

Grayson stared at her, and the heat in that gaze seared her, sent flames licking over her, engulfing her. His hooded contemplation dipped to her mouth, and she sank her teeth in her bottom lip to trap her gasp. As if he'd heard it, his scrutiny rose to hers.

She wanted to rear back from the intensity and heat—and also tip her face toward it as if his desire was the sun, and she longed to bask in it.

Jerking her attention back to her meal, she concentrated on cutting, chewing and swallowing. Ignoring the tingle in her nipples, the twisting of her belly and the yawning ache between her thighs.

"Can I ask you a question?" she murmured as their plates were cleared away.

He nodded. "Of course."

Though he'd granted her permission, she still hesitated. "Why are you going through this whole charade? In your office, you told me telling your mother you weren't interested in her matchmaking wasn't an option. But why? I know we don't know each other that well, but you just don't strike me as the kind of man who would…" God, how to finish that sentence without offending him?

A slight smirk curled the corner of his mouth. "What? Allow others to manipulate me?"

"Yes."

He chuckled, but the sound was dark, sharp and humorless. "I'm not. Usually." He grasped his glass of wine and raised it, but instead of drinking from it, he stared into the golden depths. "What do you know about me, Nadia?"

She lifted her hands, palms up. "Like I said, not much."

"Really?" He arched an eyebrow. "You haven't looked me up at all?"

"Not really." It wasn't a lie—exactly. She'd obsessively followed any online item about him before the night of the blackout. Now, it seemed almost as if she were betraying him. Which was utterly ridiculous.

"My family is well known. They're a part of Chicago history and trailblazers in the financial industry. First steel, then railroads, then real estate, then they diversified in everything from insurance to media. Chandler International was—is—a powerhouse in the corporate world. And since my great-great-grandfather started the company over one hundred years ago, a Chandler has always sat in the CEO office. And until six months ago, my brother Jason would've continued the tradition."

A shadow crept over his face, dimming his eyes. Guilt for bringing up the subject and an overwhelming need to comfort him crashed into Nadia. Before she could check the impulse, she reached across the table and wrapped her hand around his larger fingers, mimicking his earlier actions. After a slight hesitation, he reversed the hold and his hand gripped hers. As if holding on.

"My older brother died six months ago from a brain aneurysm. It was sudden and so damn unexpected. One moment, he was healthy and strong, the next…" Grayson shook his head, not finishing the thought, though he squeezed Nadia's fingers tight. "My parents, they took his death hard, as you can imagine. Jason was their firstborn, the heir, their favorite. And he should've been. We were thirteen years apart and weren't close, but I still admired him—loved him. He was a good man. Smart. Respectable. Commanding. Perfect."

"No one's perfect, Grayson," she whispered.

"In my parents' eyes, he was," he said. "They adored him. And when they lost him…" His full lips firmed into a harsh, straight line. "I've never seen them so broken. They'd not only lost their child, but their favorite."

Again, she countered him, leaning forward across the table. "Not their favorite. Maybe they had the most in common with him since he was the oldest. Or spent the most time with him since he would one day take over the business. But parents love their children equally. Even my mom did, although that's not saying much. They would've been just as devastated if, God forbid, it'd been you who'd died. Or your sister. Their love is the same."

A grim smile curved his lips even as he lifted a hand, and after a pause, cupped her jaw. He rubbed the pad of his thumb just under her bottom lip, and she fought to contain the sigh that tried to escape. Her lashes fluttered, her body liquefying. It was the first time he'd touched her outside of their charade. And other than when they'd been stuck in that dark hall. If she were thinking, if she were smart, she'd pull back. Instead, she leaned into it, turned her head slightly so her mouth brushed the heel of his palm.

Even across the distance of the table, she caught his ragged inhale. His gaze lowered to her mouth, studying it as if he would receive a PhD on every curve and dip. She trembled under his inspection, and when his eyes lifted to hers again, she shivered harder from the flash of fire there. That stare promised things—things she knew damn well he could deliver on.

"How is it possible that you, who has every reason in the

world not to see the best in people, still believes in things like a parent's love and fairness?" he murmured. With one more caress over her skin, he released her, dropping his hand to his glass of wine. He raised it, sipping, but his scrutiny never wavered from her.

She didn't have an answer for him. But then again, he didn't seem to expect one.

"But to answer your initial question, at this point, I can't tell my mother to back off because no matter our history, I have to be gentle with her. She's been through enough these past months. And other than those first couple of weeks, I don't believe she's allowed herself to fully grieve. Instead, she's focused all her rather formidable attention on other endeavors—one of which happens to be finding me a wife. I think if Jason had married, if he'd had children before he died, her desire to see me settled with someone wouldn't be this...passionate. She would've had a piece of him to hold on to, to cherish. I can only imagine she doesn't want history to repeat itself. And it might be selfish, but I'll suffer through her annoying attempts rather than see her broken again."

Selfish? There were several words she could use to describe him—arrogant, demanding, high-handed, sexy as hell—but selfish? No. Not when he would create an elaborate fake relationship just so his mother wouldn't sink back into dark grief.

Grayson Chandler was...complicated. Playboy. Gentleman. Sometimes asshole. Seducer. Selfless son. Enigmatic stranger.

And with every layer he exposed, she wanted to peel away another. And then another. She longed to find the core of this man, see who lay beneath. See the truth she suspected he revealed to no one.

In other words, damn her, she wanted to be special to him.

Maybe she was more of her mother's daughter than she acknowledged.

"Sir. Ma'am. Can I interest you in dessert or an after-dinner coffee or drink?" Their waiter appeared next to the table, saving her from more enlightening and terrible revelations about herself.

"I'm fine. Nadia?" Grayson asked.

She summoned a small, brittle smile. "I'm through, as well."

Minutes later, table cleared and check paid, Grayson escorted her from the restaurant, a hand placed on the small of her back.

Warmth from his palm penetrated her dress to the skin below. The clothing between them might as well have been invisible, because her imagination convinced her she could feel every hard curve and plane of that hand. Lust, bright and ravenous, curled low in her belly, and every step forward, every brush of her thighs against each other, cranked up that need until she shivered with it.

Oh yes. She'd fallen so far down this rabbit hole. But did she want to climb out?

She didn't know. And that indecisiveness spelled one thing.

Trouble.

Eleven

Grayson curled his fingers tighter around the steering wheel as he guided his black BMW i8 toward Nadia's blue-collar Bridgeport neighborhood. Within the interior of the car, he couldn't elude her wind and rain scent. Couldn't block out the memories of how that scent was denser, richer on her skin—between her thighs.

Sometimes he woke up at night imagining that so-damn-addictive flavor on his tongue. And his hand wrapped around an erection.

Chaining down the growl rumbling in his chest, he kept all his focus on the road in front of him. Because glancing over and glimpsing the long, lush legs molded by her dress might be his undoing.

When he'd purchased the clothing, he'd imagined how it would slide over the full mounds of her breasts, skim over the wide, feminine flare of her hips and cling to the thick perfection of her thighs. Both regal and sensual. Powerful and sexy. But he'd underestimated how the material would caress every dip, arc and curve like a lover's hand. How the dress would have him desperate to peel it from her and expose the walking wet dream of her body that he'd had the pleasure of only once.

Given her mother's history with men, the truth of why Nadia most likely dressed in drab, ill-fitting suits had struck him like a fist to the gut. Finances undoubtedly played a part, but a woman with her looks, her siren's body, had probably deflected more than her fair share of advances. Especially if the opinion in her town had been—how had his own father put it?—that she didn't fall far from the maternal tree.

Yet, he'd harbored no regrets for buying her the dress or the new wardrobe crowding his trunk. As he'd told her, she deserved it all.

Dinner had been a test of how long he could pretend to be civilized when all he hungered to do was climb over her like a stalking, starving beast and consume every goddamn inch of her.

Yes, it'd been a trial, but one he'd passed, and not because of his own strength. She'd successfully kept him in his chair with her vulnerability.

God, she humbled him. With that sliver of trust and with who she was.

His father's report might have included all the bullet points of her history, but it hadn't captured her determination, her fire, her fighter's spirit, her loyalty to family.

Something grimy slid through him. How would Nadia, who'd sacrificed her education, her time and own comfort for family, feel about his refusal to sacrifice for his own family? Had it been his fear of seeing disdain etched on her lovely face that had trapped his confession about leaving KayCee Corp for Chandler? This woman had placed everything on the line for her brother. But Grayson refused to do the same for his father and mother. For Jason.

"Thank you for dinner," Nadia said into the silence that suffused the car. "It was the loveliest anyone's ever taken me to."

"You're welcome," he replied quietly. Then, because an unhealthy curiosity to learn more about her rode him hard, he added, "You're a beautiful woman, Nadia." And sexy as hell. "So while I understand that you came from a small town, I don't comprehend how there weren't any men who didn't want you, shower you with dates to fine restaurants, offer you the world." He risked a glance over at her. Noted the delicate but strong line of her profile. The proud tilt of her shoulders. The thrust of her gorgeous breasts. "Were they all blind?"

"No." The word, though soft, held such an aching note that he battled the urge to jerk the car to the side of the road and look into those deep chocolate eyes. To demand she tell him what lay behind that bleak tone. "They weren't blind."

She didn't say anything more, but Grayson didn't miss how she also hadn't replied to his first comment about whether or not there had been anyone who wanted her. The omission grated, burrowed under his skin.

He wanted all her answers. Her truth.

He wanted her naked in the way he refused to be for anyone else.

He was a hypocrite, and he didn't care.

Minutes later, he pulled the car to the curb outside her humble home. Dark windows stared at them. He should turn off the car and walk her to the door. Make sure at least one of those windows was glowing with light before he drove away.

Instead, he continued to sit behind the wheel, engine idling. Beside him, Nadia didn't make a move to exit the car, either. The silence that had joined them for the ride from the restaurant settled between them again, but this time tension, thick and alive, vibrated within it.

"Is your brother home?" he asked. The thought of leaving her inside the empty house unsettled him. She hadn't mentioned a lack of safety in the neighborhood, but still…

"No," she said. "He texted me earlier. He's staying with a friend tonight."

On edge, Grayson removed his hands from the steering wheel and settled them on his thighs, digging his fingers into the muscle. Reminding himself to keep them there and not reach across the console and touch the soft flesh on the other side.

"Is it sad that the most real relationship I've had is this pretend one with you?" Nadia rasped into the dark. "I've built this…this wall around myself because I've had to. I've learned to. It's how I've survived. But other than Ezra, it's also kept me from getting close to people. The only time I've lowered my guard in years was the night of the blackout. With you. And it felt so *good*. Such a relief to, for once, not have to protect myself because, even though we worked at the same place, I didn't think we'd come into any meaningful contact again. I felt…free. You asked me once if I ever wanted to just let go. Hand over my control and let someone else take care of me for a little while. I did in that hallway, and I want to again. Tonight." She turned to him, and frozen by her admission, he met her gaze. "I don't want to be alone tonight."

Need—a deep, hungry yearning—stretched inside him. It expanded, twisting and tangling until he breathed it, became it. And all because of the woman across from him and seven words: *I don't want to be alone tonight*.

He understood loneliness. Often battled it. But was it him she wanted to keep her company? Or would anyone do? Was he just convenient?

I don't care.

The confession pounded against his skull, the truth reverberating in his chest.

He wanted her—no, *craved* her. Had since first seeing
her in that mansion's hallway. If she wanted to use him to
push back the isolation, the dark, then he wouldn't question why or who he was a temporary replacement for. He'd
give her that. And take some for himself.

Because, damn him, he wanted to take.

"If you go home with me, I can't promise I'll be able
to keep my hands off you. Right now, it's requiring every
bit of self-control I have not to stroke my hand under that
dress and reacquaint my fingers with the wet warmth my
dick wakes up hard for," he ground out as a warning. The
only one she'd get tonight.

"I didn't ask for your promise," she whispered. Her lips
parted, and her gaze dropped to his thighs. To the unmistakable imprint of his erection. When she returned her eyes
to his, they gleamed with the same arousal that coursed
through him. "I don't want your promise."

With that husky avowal echoing in his head, he eased the
car back into Drive and pulled away from the curb. Neither
of them spoke, not for the entire journey to his downtown
condominium. They didn't exchange words as he parked
the car in his reserved space under the seventy-story building or on the swift elevator ride to the penthouse apartment.
The doors opened into his large living room, and, cradling
her elbow, he led her inside.

Sweeping a glance around his home, he attempted to
see the place through her eyes. Vaulted ceilings, floor-to-
ceiling windows that encompassed three walls, an open
plan where each room flowed seamlessly from one to the
other. The Chicago skyline, Millennium Park and Grant
Park seemed to crowd into his place, a beautiful vista of
lights and shadow.

It'd been this view that had convinced him to purchase
the property. Not the paneled library with its stone fireplace, or the chef's wet dream of a kitchen with top-of-the-

line appliances. Not the three luxurious bedrooms with en suite bathrooms or the twenty-four-hour doorman service or exclusive rooftop club.

None of that could compare to the panorama of the city he loved. The city that had welcomed him with open arms, offering him the chance to prove he was more than just the Chandler spare.

Dragging his attention from the glittering skyline, he focused all of it on Nadia. On her face. Her body. Studying her for any hint that she'd changed her mind. That she regretted accompanying him here. From their conversation over dinner, he'd detected her opinion about men with money. They were users. Opportunists. Selfish. Her experiences with rich men hadn't been positive, and with him waving three-quarters of a million in front of her for her "services," she'd no doubt lumped him in the same category as those men who'd exploited her mother.

But maybe she hadn't painted him with the same brush.

Because she stood here in his home, and as she shifted her espresso eyes to him, they didn't hold contempt or remorse.

Just desire.

A groan rolled up his chest and throat, but he trapped it at the last minute, tamping it down. One more chance. He'd give her one last chance to opt out of this before he touched her. Because once he put his hands on her, all bets would be off.

"Are you sure, Nadia?" he rumbled, voice like a poorly maintained engine. "If you've changed your mind, I'll take you back home, no questions, no pressure, no anger. This is your choice, and yours alone." God, those words scraped his throat raw as he uttered them, but they needed to be said. She needed to know he didn't expect more from her than she was willing to give. "Another thing." He allowed himself to cup her jaw even though that small caress sent a jagged bolt of lust ripping through him. "This has nothing to do with our agreement. Whatever happens here—whatever doesn't happen here—is between us alone. Understand, baby?"

She nodded, and as she'd done in the restaurant, slightly turned her head and brushed her lips across his palm. And like then, his body turned to stone, his erection pounding like a primal drum.

"Tell me something nobody knows. Something that will stay here," she whispered, the moist heat of her breath bathing his skin. Her gaze flicked up to meet his as she pressed a sweet and sexy open-mouth kiss to his palm.

Through the almost painful grip of arousal, he recognized the request. They'd asked it of each other the night of the blackout. The past collided with the present. On a dark growl, he lifted his other hand to her face, caging her in, holding her steady as he lowered his head until just a bare breath separated their mouths.

"No one knows that I haven't been able to erase you from my mind since that night in the hallway. You were supposed to be a one-night distraction. But instead, you haunt me. You, this fucking need that grinds my gut to dust, won't leave me alone. And I resent and want you in equal measure."

Her hands clutched the waistband of his pants, holding on to him.

"Your turn," he damn near snarled, a little angry with himself for admitting all he had. "Tell me something nobody knows and that will stay here."

She encircled his wrists, rose on her toes and crushed her mouth to his. With a groan, he parted his lips, welcomed the thrust of her tongue, sucked on the silken invader and dragged an answering moan from her. Jesus, she tasted like his happiest memories and his darkest moments. Like

every decadent treat he'd luxuriated in and every indul-
gence he'd denied himself.

Like addiction and temperance.

Like everything.

The alarming thought whispered through his head, and
he mentally scrambled back from it. This—his mouth on
hers, her tongue tangling with his—was physical and so
goddamn good. But still temporary and simple.

There was nothing simpler than sex.

"Tell me, baby." He ground out the order against her lips.

"You're American royalty, one of our princes," she whispered, her nails biting into the thin, sensitive skin on the
inside of his wrists. "And you make me feel like the Cinderella you called me." She paused, bowing her head until
his lips pressed to her forehead. "More, I want to be your
Cinderella. Just for a little while."

"You dream of being a princess, Nadia?" He thrust his
fingers through her hair, fisting it and tilting her head back
so she had no choice but to meet his gaze. He needed to see
her eyes. "Is that who you'd like to pretend to be?"

"No." Shadows shifted in her brown gaze, but so did the
truth. "I want to pretend to be wanted."

The groan he'd imprisoned before barreled out of him,
and he claimed her mouth. Took it. Voracious for it. For her.
He thrust his tongue past her parted lips, conquering. No,
not conquering, because she opened wider for him, laying
down every defense and surrendering.

Pleasure quaked through him. Pleasure and acceptance
of her gift.

Bending his knees, he dropped his arms and gripped
the undersides of her thighs. With a swift movement, he
hiked her in his arms. Her short, sharp cry reverberated
in his ears, but she encircled him with her arms and legs.

Damn. All that soft flesh and strong muscle pressed
against him, embracing him. Her position shoved her dress

up her thighs, and the material bunched high. He glanced down between them, catching a glimpse of black lace. Clenching his teeth against a curse, he swiftly strode forward toward his bedroom. But each step rubbed her exposed, panty-clad sex against his hard-as-steel dick, and he fought not to stumble and slam them back against the wall.

"I can feel you, baby," he muttered against her lips. "Soaking me through my pants. Already telling me how much you want me. Good," he damn near snarled. That's how much his control had deteriorated. "Because I need you. I haven't stopped since you let me inside this sweet, hot body."

In response, she opened her mouth over his throat, licking a path up the column and sucking the skin right under his jaw. Pleasure charged from that spot directly to his erection, hardening it even more. He inhaled a sharp breath, his grip on her tightening.

"Go on and play," he warned her. "Because when I get you naked on my bed, I fully intend to." She stiffened in his arms, and he gently nuzzled her hair, though he didn't bother to prevent his irritation from leaking into his voice. "No, Nadia," he snapped. "Whatever thoughts just crowded into your head, get rid of them. They don't belong here."

He carefully set her down on her feet in front of him. Once more he burrowed his hands into her hair, cradling her head between his palms and tilting it back.

No hiding from him. Not tonight.

"They don't belong here at all." He gently tapped her temple. "Every curve—" he slipped his hand down her shoulder, brushing the backs of his knuckles over the mound of her beast "—every valley—" he swept a caress over the dip of her waist, the slightly rounded swell of her stomach "—every inch—" he slid his hand between her thighs, cupping her drenched, warm sex "—deserves to be seen. To be worshipped."

A whimper escaped her and in the sexiest, earthiest show of abandon, she grabbed onto his shoulders, threw her head back and ground herself against his palm.

He growled. "Do it again. I want you to do just that again. But on my mouth."

With hands that should've been gentler, less hurried, he quickly stripped her of her dress, her boots and underwear. He refused to leave a scrap of clothing on her.

In moments, he jerked back the dark gray bedspread and laid her out on his silver silk sheets. In the place where he'd woken up sweaty, straining with his throbbing, aching erection in his hand—dreaming about her. But now he wasn't fantasizing. This was vivid reality. And so much better.

Unable to tear his gaze from her, he crossed his arms in front, gripped the bottom of his sweater and tugged it over his head. Toeing off his shoes and peeling off his socks, he stalked forward, not stopping until his knee dented the mattress between her thighs and his hands bracketed her hips.

She tried to close her legs, but his knee prevented the action.

"Open for me," he encouraged. "I need to see you."

He smoothed his hands up her thighs, his thumbs meeting at the juncture. Exerting easy pressure, he waited until her muscles relaxed, then she opened her legs for him. His flesh pulsed behind his zipper, and he groaned at the sight of her glistening, swollen sex. He hadn't even touched her yet, and he was ready to come.

"Damn, Nadia. You're so pretty. So beautiful. I want to…"

He didn't finish the statement. He couldn't with his mouth covering her flesh. With her heady, delicious taste filling his senses. On a growl, he licked a path through her folds, hungry for more. Beneath his hands, her thighs tensed, tightening around his head. A long, high cry erupted from above him, and it only spurred him on. That, and the insatiable appetite her decadent flavor stirred in him.

He feasted on her. Like a man starved who sat before the most sumptuous of feasts. He discovered and tongued, sipped and worshipped every part of her sex. The plump folds, the small, fluttering entrance, the hard little button of nerves at the crest. Wet, open-mouthed kisses; lush, greedy licks; tight, pointed thrusts. He didn't let up, didn't stop until a litany of cries poured from her, and the legs he'd hooked over his shoulders shook.

Focusing on the engorged, quivering nub at the top of her sex, he circled it, sucked on it. And below, he slowly drove his fingers into her soaked, clenching core. He moaned into her flesh, his dick flexing and aching as it remembered the perfect clasp. The clawing need to feel her sex pierced him. He pulled his fingers free and drove them harder.

She exploded.

Satisfaction roared inside him, and he didn't stop pleasuring her until the last tremble rippled through her body. Only when she went limp did he withdraw, jackknifing off the bed and ridding himself of the remainder of his clothes. He retained enough control to yank open his bedside table drawer and remove a condom. In seconds, he sheathed himself and returned to the welcoming haven of her body.

Nadia's eyes, slumberous and deep, met his as he crouched over her, his arms braced on either side of her head. He lowered his head, captured her mouth, and she didn't flinch away from tasting herself on his lips. Giving him one of those whimpers he loved—the ones he counted and hoarded—she slipped her tongue between his lips, dueling with him. She curled a hand behind his neck, holding him to her, and trailed the other over his shoulder, his chest, across his abs and down. He hissed into her mouth as she wrapped her slender fingers around the base and guided him to her entrance.

He jerked his head back, his eyes closing at the first brush of her wet heat against the swollen head. Letting her take control, he followed her lead. Allowed her to feed him inside her, inch by inch. Claiming him with each tiny pulse and arch of her hips. And when she slid around to his ass, cupping him, pressing against him, he sank fully inside heaven.

Curses, praises, prayers—they scrambled up his throat. But he clenched his jaw, locking them behind his teeth. Bowing his head, he blinked against the sweat rolling from his brow and stinging his eyes. He stared, captivated by the view of her folds spread around his staff, hugging him as her silken, tight flesh sucked him deep.

"Grayson," she breathed, lowering one hand and lifting the other until both gripped his shoulders, her short nails biting into his skin.

God, please let her mark him. He wanted to glimpse those little half-moons denting him in the morning.

"Gray," he corrected, lust and his almost nonexistent restraint roughening his voice to the consistency of churned, broken gravel. "Say it, baby. Gray."

He'd ordered her to say the shortened version of his name before in the hallway. And she hadn't uttered it since that night. Hearing her say the name only those close to him used—he didn't analyze why it was damn near vital for him to hear it. He just did.

"Please... Gray," she whispered, levering up and brushing her lips across his damp shoulder. "You feel so..." She rolled her hips, her tight core spasming around him. "I can't take..."

"Yes, you can, baby," he ground out, battling the lust threatening to tear him to shreds. Wrapping his arms around her, he held her close, pulled free of her body, then thrust back inside to the hilt. "You are taking it. Taking me."

Any more words were beyond him. He reverted to that caveman who'd preceded all of his blue-blooded ancestors. Claim. Brand. Possess. Those were the defaults he flipped to, and he lived only to ride her body, plunge into her, mark her as his own. If he wasn't consumed by pleasure, that thought might scare him. And later, maybe it would. But now, with her cries blanketing his ears, her nails marring his skin, her sex pulling at him, urging him to drive deeper, pound harder...

He was an utterly sexual being created to pursue ecstasy.

Nadia clung to him, chanting his name—Gray—again and again, sharper, higher. He couldn't hold out much longer. Not when electrical pulses crackled and raced down his spine, sizzling in his lower back, his balls and even the soles of his feet. He was alive, so much more alive than he'd ever been in his life—except for the last time he'd been balls-deep inside her.

"Give it to me, Nadia." He reached down between their sweaty, twisting bodies and rubbed a firm caress over the stiff nub that peeked out from between her folds. Once, twice...

A keening wail erupted from Nadia, and she bowed so tautly in his arms he almost feared she would snap in half. Her sex clamped down on him like a vise, squeezing hard, milking him, coaxing his pleasure.

And damn, he surrendered to it. To her.

Release barreled down on him, and with a hoarse, ragged growl, he slammed into her, riding it out, at the same time giving her every bit of the orgasm still rippling through her. His senses winked out, leaving him in a space where nothing existed but her and the pleasure she gave him.

Air rasped out of his lungs as he fell over her, at the last second tumbling to her side so he wouldn't crush her with his weight. He curled around her, still connected, still buried deep inside her.

And for this moment, there was no other place he wanted to be.

Twelve

"Why am I feeling a sudden affinity to the poor lamb about to meet his Maker?" Nadia grumbled under her breath as Grayson opened the passenger's side car door and extended a hand to her.

Grayson snorted. Apparently, she hadn't been as quiet as she'd thought. She smothered a sigh and slipped her palm over his. With the other hand, she gathered the skirt of her dress—another gift from him—and stepped from the car. Grayson didn't release his hold on her as the valet drove the vehicle away, instead intertwining their fingers.

It's pretense. Act 2 of the Grayson and Nadia Show.

The cool but frustrated voice of reason whispered the reminder inside her head, and she heeded it. Even repeated it. But it didn't stop her heart from thudding or the slow heat from pooling low in her belly at the casual sign of affection.

Of connection.

Walking into this glittering lakefront mansion where the guests ranged from senators to billionaires like Grayson to celebrities, she needed that connection. This anniversary party thrown in honor of his parents by a family friend was a whole different animal from the smaller cocktail parties and dinners she'd attended by Grayson's side. There'd already been mentions of them in a few society columns, blogs and sites. And while some had been kind toward her and others hadn't been as charitable, the same thought had echoed through each—what was the Chandler heir doing with an unknown like her?

Unknown. That had been the nicer name. The not-so-nice names had included "nobody," "the wide-hipped ingenue," and the ever popular "gold digger."

She didn't like Grayson's world. It was beautiful, but cold, petty and cruel. Her mother, who had perfected the art of "nice nasty," had nothing on Chicago's social elite. In the month since they'd started this charade, Nadia had lost count of how many times she'd chanted "It's for Ezra. It's for Ezra..." to herself. Her brother's future was the only thing keeping her from bailing, returning to her plainer, poorer but kinder world.

Well, Ezra...and Grayson.

She glanced at him as he guided her up the marble steps and past the stone arches soaring high above them. Mounted sconces and strategically placed lamps lit the porch—if that's what rich people called it—illuminating the majestic beauty of the foyer beyond the grand front door that wouldn't have been out of place on a palace.

Grayson fit this place. With his regal male beauty and sexy confidence that he wore as naturally as his perfectly tailored Italian tuxedo, he belonged in this place of wealth and prestige. In this moment, she felt like a girl dressing up in a costume gown. She was a fraud, while he was the real thing.

And yet... Yet, she continued the charade.

Because as unbelievable and impossible as it might

seem, Grayson needed her. And not just to avoid his mother's matchmaking schemes. But in the weeks they'd been spending time together, she noticed he showed people the playboy or the charming businessman. But not *him*. Not the broody, sometimes dark, sharp-minded-and-tongued man who existed beneath the veneer. He granted her peeks, though. Glimpses she suspected he didn't allow anyone else to see. He needed someone with whom he could shed the personas. Even if only for a little while.

And she would be a liar if she didn't admit, if only to herself, that she hungered for those moments.

Stupid. Stupid to want more. Have you learned nothing?

"Are you okay?" Grayson murmured in her ear as they entered the mansion.

"Yes." She pasted a smile on her face that she hoped appeared serene. Or at least normal. "Why do you ask?"

"Because you have my fingers in a stranglehold," he drawled, arching a dark eyebrow.

Immediately, she loosened her grip. "Sorry," she murmured. "I didn't realize."

A tall man in a black suit complete with a bow tie approached them. "Can I show you to the ballroom?" he said, extending an arm toward the rear of the foyer.

"Give us a minute, please." Grayson didn't wait for the staff member's agreement, but cupped Nadia's elbow and guided her toward the fireplace on the far side of the room. A fireplace in a foyer. Jesus, she really had entered another world.

"Nadia." Grayson's fingers pinched her chin, raising her head so she had to meet his blue-and-green gaze. "Tell me what you're thinking."

She tried to quell the tingle that zipped from her face down to her breasts and lower still. Tried. And failed. It'd been two weeks since they'd had sex at his penthouse. In that time, he hadn't touched her more than their pretense required. Part of her understood why. After their discussion that night at the restaurant and what she'd revealed to him about her past, he probably didn't want her to feel as if she were pressured to make sex part of their bargain. He was respecting her boundaries.

But the other part of her... That half wondered if he no longer wanted her. If the novelty of sex with her had worn off. If he didn't find her desirable...

She shook her head, trying to dislodge those destructive words from her head. But the movement inadvertently removed his hand from her. Grayson frowned. And didn't return his hand.

"I'm thinking that I'll be lucky to not embarrass either one of us. This night is on a much larger scale than a dinner party," she said. Not a lie. Those *had* been her thoughts earlier.

His frown eased, and his gaze softened. Once more, he touched her, this time cradling the nape of her neck. A charge sizzled down her spine, and she barely smothered a groan.

"You have the prettiest eyes," she blurted out, desperate to distract herself from her short-circuiting body. But then, her own eyes rounded as what she'd uttered rebounded against her skull. *Oh. Hell.*

Surprise flickered in his stare, before it became shuttered. "What?"

She waved a hand in front of her head as if she could shoo away her words. "Don't mind me. I told you I was nervous. Let this be a forewarning of what I will be like once I enter that ballroom. If I have the chance to meet Cookie or Lucious from *Empire*, I'm just letting you know right now to expect more spouting of random crap."

He didn't chuckle. Not even the corner of his mouth quirked in amusement. "So the comment about my eyes was just...crap," he stated, voice flat.

Now, she frowned. "No, I meant it. Your eyes are gorgeous." She studied the carefully bland expression, heard the monotone timbre. "You don't believe me," she concluded.

When he didn't reply, but just continued to peer down at her, she wavered between being curious and offended. Hell, no one said the two had to be mutually exclusive.

"Present situation aside, I'm not in the habit of lying. Care to tell me why you don't believe me?" She thrust up a hand, palm out, when his lips parted. "And don't you dare say you don't know what I'm talking about."

His mouth firmed into a straight line, and his eyes narrowed. Silence beat between them, but she was raising a teenager; she could out-stubborn him any day.

"My eyes are weird, not pretty. You should save the meaningless compliments for when we have an audience. They're wasted when the two of us are alone," he stated in that same aloof tone.

He'd meant to shut her down. Hurt her feelings and force her into dropping the subject. And oh, goal almost accomplished. Her chest throbbed where that cold arrow had taken a direct hit. Maybe if she hadn't caught the thread of hurt beneath the steel, she might have let it go.

"Ouch," she drawled. And something that could've been regret flickered in his eyes before the shadows shielded it. Risking more rejection, she shifted closer and clasped his head between her hands, tilting it down so this time she was the one forcing him to meet her gaze. "You listen to me. I don't know what asshole put it into your head that your eyes are weird or anything less than unique and beautiful but screw them. No," she snapped, when he covered her hands with his and tried to remove them from his face. "They are beautiful. Gorgeous. Intelligent. Different. Bold. *You*. In this pretentious world of yours where conformity is mistaken for perfection, you are utterly *perfect*. And any-one who says differently can get fucked."

His eyes flared with shock, a heartbreaking and madden-ing uncertainty and...delight. Joy that should've terrified her—and God, it did—swelled behind her ribcage. Afraid of what her face might reveal, she dropped her arms and turned away, taking a step in the direction the staff mem-ber had indicated.

But a muscled arm wrapping around her waist drew her up short. A hard chest pressed against her back, tuxedo jacket lapels brushing the skin bared by her backless gown.

"When you greet my father, I'd suggest you not tell him to get fucked," he drawled. Before it could fully sink in that it'd been his own parent who'd criticized him, Gray-son tightened his hold on her and pressed his lips against her hair. "Thank you," he whispered.

He released her, took her hand in his and guided her forward.

Silently, she exhaled a deep, slow breath.

Okay. Still feeling the imprint of his arm and the caress of his mouth, she straightened her shoulders and hiked her chin. Tendrils of hope cautiously bloomed within her.

Maybe this night wouldn't be as bad as she'd assumed.

You know what they say about assuming.

The taunt floated through her head as she stood near the huge balcony doors of the ornate ballroom. Massive crys-tal chandeliers provided more than enough light for her to glimpse the elaborate gardens beyond the spotless glass.

Sighing, she turned from the temptation of the great out-doors and surveyed the grand room filled with Chicago's wealthiest, most famous and celebrated. For the first hour after she and Grayson arrived, he'd stayed by her side, re-fusing to leave her alone. And she'd appreciated his solid presence. It'd been easier to maneuver these choppy society waters with him.

But ten minutes ago, his father had cornered him and practically yanked him away to speak to business associates. Since then, she'd smiled and murmured hellos to those who didn't stare right through her, floating through the crowd like a ghost.

She strolled to one of the many framed photographs of Grayson's parents and family that were mounted throughout the ballroom. Pausing before the one that included all three Chandler children as well as Daryl and Cherise, she studied it. Grayson's parents sat on a white settee, while Grayson, Jason and Melanie formed a semicircle behind them, Jason in the middle, standing a couple of inches taller than a younger Grayson.

Her attention, almost of its own will, focused on Grayson's older brother. In this picture, he appeared to be in his late twenties. Handsome, refined, a little reserved. But he was the only one who touched his parents. One hand settled on his father's shoulder and the other on his mother's. Cherise had one arm lifted, her bejeweled, slim fingers covering her son's.

That the only sign of warmth in the picture was between the oldest son and his parents was…telling.

And sad.

"We make quite a spectacle, don't we?" a cultured voice laced with amusement and a hint of deprecation said.

Nadia glanced away from the photograph to Melanie, who stood beside her. Nadia had been so caught up in her scrutiny of the image, she hadn't heard Grayson's sister approach. The older woman had been the only person to warmly greet Nadia this evening, and a rush of relief washed over her.

"It's very dignified," Nadia said, opting for diplomacy.

Melanie snorted, a favorite sign of disdain she shared

with her brother. "Stuffy as hell is what I think you mean."
She smiled, her blue eyes gleaming. "What you can't see is
Gray goosing Jason, trying to make him break his austere
demeanor. Only by sheer force of will did Jason maintain
that expression. Dad and Mother had no idea what was
going on behind them."

Nadia laughed, seeing the picture with new eyes now
in light of the story. She picked up the twinkle in Jason's
eyes, the barest of bare smiles on Grayson's mouth. And
the slightest hunch of Melanie's shoulders as if she were
silently midlaugh.

"You remind me of my brother and me," she mused,
smiling with real warmth for the first time that evening.
"We are always teasing one another, too."

The light in Melanie's gaze dimmed, but the love as she
stared at the picture remained. "Jason, Gray and I, we had
a…complicated relationship. But we did love one another.
And there were times like this one where we enjoyed one
another. In those moments you realize there's nothing more
important than family."

"I couldn't agree more," Cherise Chandler interjected,
appearing on the other side of her daughter. She glanced
at the photograph, and for an instant, grief flashed in her
eyes. But in the next moment, the emotion disappeared;
her blue gaze, so like her daughter's, was hard like dia-
monds as she turned to Nadia. "Family is the most important thing in this life."

Did she refer to life, in the abstract, or "this life," as
in the world of Chicago's elite? Since this was Grayson's
mother, Nadia was going with the latter.

"I missed the opportunity to wish you a happy anniversary earlier when I arrived, Mrs. Chandler. Congratulations," Nadia said, offering the other woman a smile.

And as she'd expected, it wasn't returned. "Thank you."
Cherise nodded. Once more, she glanced at the picture of

her family, but this time resolve hardened her features. "Forty-five years of not just marriage, but family, shared experiences, commonality. Yes, loss but also strength and loyalty. Above all loyalty."

"Mom," Melanie murmured, but her mother shot her daughter a sharp glance.

"This needs to be said, Melanie," Cherise replied before returning her attention to Nadia. "Six months ago, this... dalliance Grayson has with you wouldn't have mattered to me. You would've been one of many. But now you're like that company of his—a lark, a distraction from what's important. While he should be focusing on what's best for this family's legacy, he's playing CEO with a business that won't be around in another few years. While he should be considering his own future with a wife who will benefit him both socially and financially, he's wasting time with you. You and that company of his are amusements, diversions for a man who doesn't have responsibilities, who doesn't have a duty to his family. Amusements and diversions none of us can afford."

Each word struck Nadia like well-aimed, poison-tipped darts, and she nearly shrank away in pain and humiliation.

But damn if she would allow Cherise Chandler to witness her wounds. Later, she would curl up around her battered pride and try to regroup. But right now? She would never give the other woman the satisfaction of watching her crumble.

"That's enough, Mother," Melanie bit out, anger vibrating through the frosty reprimand. "Nadia is Gray's choice and guest. This disrespect is beneath all of us."

"You're wrong," Nadia interrupted Melanie, her gaze meeting Cherise's without flinching. And though, inside, Nadia still trembled from Cherise's verbal slap, her voice didn't waver. "Grayson isn't *playing* at CEO—he *is* one. And his brilliance and boldness have propelled the company into success. They've already changed the landscape of technology and finance. And KayCee Corp will continue to do so—years from now."

The passion that swelled inside her and throbbed in her voice was disproportionate for a fake fiancée, but she didn't care. Everything she stated was true. And it was a damn shame his mother didn't recognize his accomplishments.

"And you very well could be right about me. Maybe I'm not the woman who will—how did you put it?—benefit him socially and financially. But who do you believe that woman to be? Adalyn?"

"She belongs here. In our world. Unlike you," Cherise snapped. "They are the same."

Nadia shook her head. "There's so much more to him than how many generations back he can trace his family tree, the blue of his blood or the number of zeroes in his net worth. He's a man, flesh and blood. He needs someone who understands him, who sees beyond the social masks, who will support and love him unconditionally."

"And you actually believe you're that woman?" Cherise scoffed.

"I don't know," Nadia answered honestly. "But he doesn't think Adalyn is. And my heart breaks for him, because it doesn't seem like you are, either." She stepped back, glancing at Melanie. She reached for a smile and failed. "It was nice seeing you again, Melanie. If you'll both excuse me."

She walked off, not glancing back, her hands trembling in the folds of her dress.

When she'd made that bargain with Grayson, she should've asked for hazard pay.

Grayson charged down the hall. Away from the study where he'd allowed his father to lure him with the promise of "It'll only be a couple of minutes." A couple of minutes had turned into damn near thirty. His father had ambushed him, arranging for several board members to join them, where he'd come just short of announcing that Grayson would be returning to the Chandler International fold.

Only respect had locked down his vitriolic tirade. Respect and the ever-present guilt that Chandler International was his duty. That he owed his father and mother this because the son they'd wanted, the son they truly loved, had been snatched from them. No, it wasn't his fault that Jason had died so suddenly, so nonsensically. But still, his parents had lost their *son*. Even if Grayson was the booby prize, didn't he owe them this?

A Chandler to replace a Chandler. A son for a son.

Rage, powerlessness and grief churned in his gut, surging to his chest and up his throat until he had to swallow convulsively against the bellow of fury that clawed at him, demanding to be loosed.

The noose of obligation, duty and love tightened around his neck, choking him even as it dragged him inexorably closer to a future that had been meant for Jason, not him.

"Grayson?"

He didn't contain his growl at the sound of the soft, feminine voice calling his name. Drawing to an abrupt halt, he slowly pivoted, facing Adalyn. Any other man would look at his ex and see a beautiful, confident woman of class and sophistication. Any other man would notice the lovely green eyes, the delicate facial features and the slender body exquisitely showcased in a gown that undoubtedly bore a label from a coveted designer.

What they might miss would be the calculating gleam in those emerald depths or the smile that carried the barest hint of cruelty. When Grayson had been in love with her, he hadn't caught those details, blinded by loveliness and charm. But now, as she neared him with a sultry stride, they were all he saw.

"What do you want, Adalyn?" he demanded. "And let's skip the part where we pretend this meeting is by chance."

Anger glinted in her gaze for a second before her thick lashes fluttered down, hiding the emotion. Hiding the truth. "I don't mind admitting I've been waiting all evening for the opportunity to have you to myself. You've been so—" her mouth twisted, that cruelty making more of an appearance before her smile returned "—occupied of late that we haven't had time alone to talk."

He sighed, thrusting his hands into his pants pockets. "Because we have nothing to talk about," he ground out. "We broke up over a year ago. Anything you deemed important enough to converse about could've been accomplished in that time. Since you didn't search me out, and I damn sure didn't go looking for you, I'm going to assume whatever it is you suddenly have to say can't be vital."

"I've missed you," she whispered, shifting closer to him.

If not for the two years he'd spent as the star pupil in the School of Adalyn Hayes, he might've fallen for the soft longing in her voice. For the lovely pleading in her eyes. But not only had he walked away with a degree in disillusionment and pain when their relationship ended, he'd left with a heart made of stone. And it pumped mistrust and scorn rather than blood. Rather than love.

Obviously, taking his disdainful silence as encouragement, she moved nearer until her floral fragrance filled his nose, and she laid a hand on his chest. Over the heart she'd betrayed.

"We had good times together, Grayson. I wish you would let yourself remember them. I do," she said, tilting her head back. "I remember how we laughed. How we were nearly inseparable. How you treated me like a queen. How you touched me, giving me more pleasure than any man ever had before or since." Her breath quickened, and she trailed a fingertip over his jaw. "We were so good together. You can't deny that. And you can't deny that you loved me."

No, he couldn't deny it. But then, he hadn't been aware that sex had just been another tool in her arsenal. A way to make him fall in line.

"And this return of memories has nothing to do with the business deal between your father and mine?" He arched an eyebrow. "The timing is just a coincidence?"

She shrugged a shoulder. "Our families have always been business associates. At one time, you didn't see anything wrong with making that bond even stronger with marriage."

"You're right. At one time, I didn't," he agreed. "But that was then, and right now I'm thankful that I didn't marry a woman who found me—and my bank account—interchangeable with any other man."

He stepped back, allowing her hand to fall away from him.

Fury tightened her features, hardening them. "So do you think that *cow* out there is better than me? Everyone is laughing at you, at her. She's a joke, and you're the punch line."

"And here's the real Adalyn. I was wondering how long it would be before she made an appearance," he drawled, then shifting forward, eliminating the space he'd inserted, he quietly snarled, "And you go on believing you're untouchable. That because of your face and your father's name that you're beyond reproach. But I'm more than willing to be the one to show you differently. And if you insult Nadia one more time, if I hear you even utter her name with anything less than delight, I'll take you down. Strip you of the so-called friends you surround yourself with. Destroy that sterling reputation you hold so dear. I'll take the gilded cage of your world apart bar by bar and, Adalyn? I'll enjoy the hell out of it."

Leaving her staring at him in shock, he pivoted and stalked away from her. With every step, weariness slowly replaced the anger, the gratification.

God, he was just…tired. Tired of the machinations. The games. The agendas.

He needed to escape this hallway. Get away from Adalyn.

From the reminder of how false beautiful faces could be. How relationships weren't based on love, trust or respect but were barter systems, founded in how much one party could cull from the other. All he had to do was examine the evidence in his own life.

His relationship with his parents.

With Adalyn.

With Nadia.

They were lies built upon a foundation of greed.

And he wanted to raze it all to the ground.

Thirteen

Nadia glanced at Grayson, the shadows from passing streetlamps whispering over his sharp features like ebbing waves. When he'd returned to the ballroom and located her over an hour ago, something had changed in his demeanor. Oh, he was still polite and charming, the playboy and charismatic businessman both making appearances, but he'd been…colder. More distant. Tension seemed to vibrate within him, and it set her on edge.

What had happened between the time his father had asked to speak with him and his reappearance? Even now, tucked in his town car and nearing her house, the question lodged in her throat. As if part of her were too afraid to ask. Afraid of the answer.

Turning from him, she gazed sightlessly out her window. Though it'd only taken a little over a half hour for them to leave the lakefront and reach her Bridgeport neighborhood, the change in worlds might as well have been light-years apart. No majestic mansions, huge iron gates or long private drives. Just weathered storefronts, parks abandoned for the night, brick greystones and bungalows and quiet streets caught between its industrial past and its rejuvenating, diverse present. It'd been her home for only a little over a year, but it felt more welcoming than the town where she'd spent most of her life. And definitely more welcoming than the entitled world she'd just left.

The world Grayson belonged in.

You and that company of his are amusements and diversions for a man who doesn't have responsibilities, who doesn't have a duty to his family. Amusements and diversions none of us can afford.

Cherise's words rang in her head, reverberating in her soul, rattling loose the ghosts she'd convinced herself had been exorcised. She'd been an amusement, a diversion for Jared. This engagement to Grayson might be a sham, but his parents didn't know that. His friends didn't. Those columnists and bloggers didn't. So to the world, she'd once more become what she'd promised herself she wouldn't ever again.

Someone's "for now." Because she wasn't worthy enough to be his "forever."

She sucked in a shaky breath, clinging to the tattered remnants of her pride and wrapping them around her like Cinderella's ash-stained rags. Only this didn't end in a fairy tale. When this pretense with Grayson concluded, she would be two hundred and fifty thousand dollars richer, but she would still be on her side of the tracks, and he would return to his glittering, privileged tower.

The car slowed to a stop, and she blinked, glimpsing the familiar houses on her street. Grayson exited the car, rounded the hood and pulled her door open. He extended a hand to her like he'd done when they'd arrived at the mansion hours ago. Like then, she placed her palm over his and let him help her stand on the curb bordering her house.

"I'll walk you up," he said.

"That's not necessary. Ezra's home," she objected, suddenly needing this night to end. She had wounds to lick, emotional armor to reinforce.

"I'll walk you up," he repeated in a tone that brooked no argument.

"Fine," she murmured, and led the way up the short walk to her porch. She removed the key from her clutch purse and slid it into the lock. As she turned it and grasped the doorknob, a hard chest pressed into her. She gasped. Even through the layers of their clothes, Grayson's heat burned into her, warming her against the cold November night air. He pressed his forehead against the back of her head, and with her hair swept over her shoulder, his breath bathed the nape of her neck. "Gray?"

"Let me come in," he rasped. Except for his forehead and his chest, he didn't touch her, but the quiet desperation in his voice grasped her as tightly as if he'd wrapped his arms around her. "I…" He paused, audibly swallowing. "I need you."

The ragged tone, the harshness that seemed heavy with loneliness didn't speak of physical desire—well, not only that. It was thick with more. With a hunger that exceeded sex. A hunger for connection, for…her.

"Please."

The entreaty shuddered through her. She squeezed her eyes shut and twisted the knob. And pushed the door open.

They walked through together, and she reached behind her, blindly searching for his hand. Locating it, she twined their fingers together and led him to her bedroom. For a moment, nervousness over how he would view her tiny room with its secondhand, scratched furniture, queen-sized bed and threadbare rug washed over her. But then Grayson's hands were cupping her shoulders, turning her and pressing her against the wall next to the closed door.

His big body curved into her smaller one, and he surrounded her. Covered her. And then his mouth crashed to hers, consumed her.

She moaned under his lips, and he crooned, "Shh." Warning her to keep quiet, not to disturb Ezra.

Nodding, she tilted her head, opened her mouth wider to his voracious kiss. He was…ravenous. Barely granting her time to breathe. But, God, every lick, every draw on her tongue, every pull on her lips… She didn't need air. Not when he fed her his.

Greedy hands shoved her coat from her shoulders, jerked down the zipper at her side, dragged the dress off her. He didn't even leave the scrap of thong on her body, leaving her bare and vulnerable. Trembling.

With equally quick movements, he rid himself of his clothes, removing his wallet before casting his pants aside. Hauling her into his arms again, he backed her toward the bed, but enough of her senses remained unclouded by lust to shake her head.

"Not there. The bed squeaks," she warned on a pant.

On a growl, he yanked the bedspread off the mattress and threw it on the floor. Then, he sank to it, taking her with him. Once more, he covered her, notching his hips between her legs. She encircled his shoulders with her arms, holding him so close she swore she could feel every muscle, tendon and beat of his pulse against her. They kissed, tongues tangling, breaths mating. He nipped at her lips, chin, throat. And she fought down a whimper when he levered off her. But he only left to sheathe himself, returning, bringing his heavy, delicious weight back to her. Again, she wrapped herself around him, her legs joining the embrace.

"Please, Gray," she pleaded. Unashamedly. This might have started with him needing something from her, but she was just as desperate for him. Craving those moments where she didn't feel so empty. Only Grayson had given her that.

She buried her face in his neck, drowning in the physical pleasure and refusing to dwell on why Grayson could give her the peace and sense of safety she'd never found with anyone else.

He slipped a hand behind her neck, cradling her as he pushed inside.

She waited, breath suspended, expecting him to destroy her with the fierceness of his passion like the two previous times they'd come together. Like his kiss and touch since they'd entered her house.

But instead, he held still above her, his big body balanced on his forearms, his face hovering over hers. Slowly, so slowly time seemed to stutter, he dipped his head. Brushed his lips over the corner of her mouth. Swept another barely-there kiss to the other side.

He was still set on destroying her. But with tenderness instead of fury.

Give me the storm, her mind railed. She could get lost in the storm. Could be tossed and plundered by it. But this gentle rain... This she wanted to let bathe her, creep beneath skin and bone to quench a thirst born of a neglected girl, a rejected woman. A thirst she could usually deny existed.

Except when he kissed her with rain.

"What are you offering me, Nadia?" he asked, taking her back to that night of the blackout when he'd asked her the same thing. When their time had been limited to a few short hours of pleasure. Before she'd known this beautiful, powerful, flawed man.

"Me," she whispered. "All of me."

Her answer was the same—but different. Then she'd added, "for tonight." This time she didn't add boundaries, an expiration date, although they had one. And from the narrowing of his eyes and the harsh rasp of his breath, he'd noticed the omission.

He withdrew from her, slow, deliberate. And thrust back into her with enough power to yank a gasp from her throat.

"Quiet, baby," he murmured, covering her mouth with his palm. Bending his head so his lips grazed her ear, he whispered, "I need you to keep quiet for me."

Then he consumed her.

She strained beneath each plunge, taking each piston of his hips as if it were her due, her reward. He rode her, branding her flesh with his cock, marking her.

And God help her, she let him. She welcomed it.

And when pleasure crashed over her like a wave determined to drag her under, she welcomed it, too.

Because he came with her.

"You're doing this because of your brother, aren't you?" Grayson murmured.

Nadia stilled in tracing random patterns over Grayson's bare chest. They hadn't moved from the floor, and with her limbs weighted down with satisfaction and lethargy, she didn't want to. Not with his large body under hers, his warmth radiating against her, and the sheet he'd dragged from the bed covering them.

He didn't expound on his question, but he didn't need to. She understood what he meant by "this." Her mind waged a battle against her heart over answering. He'd seen her naked, had touched and kissed every inch of her, but somehow admitting this would bare her even more. And she wrestled with giving that to him. What if he used the information against her? Did she trust him?

In the end, her heart made the decision. And won.

"Yes," she said. "How did you know?"

"I didn't at first," he admitted. "But I never stopped

wondering why you would agree to my offer when you first turned it down. Given what I've discovered about you, money in itself wouldn't be enough to motivate you. Not when you have an issue accepting even a dress from me. But for your brother? You've sacrificed so much for him already. You would do anything for Ezra. Including pretending to be my fiancée. And enduring everything that comes with it."

She hesitated, but then nodded against his chest. "Ezra was accepted into Yale. I found out the afternoon after I left your office. He was awarded a partial scholarship, but without going into debt, we couldn't afford to send him."

"The two hundred and fifty thousand," he said softly.

"The amount of tuition for four years," she confirmed.

Silence fell between them, only the hushed sounds of their breaths filling the room. But he didn't doze off beneath her. Though his fingers sifted through her hair, tension stiffened his body. The urge to comfort, to soothe whatever bothered him rode her. Gathering her courage, she pushed herself up on her elbow. But before she could question him, Grayson lifted his other hand to her jaw and lightly traced the line of it.

"I'm ashamed when I look at you," he said, and she flinched at the disgust in that confession. Disgust that wasn't directed at her, but at himself. Even in the shadowed confines of the bedroom, she glimpsed the glitter of anger in his eyes. "You awe me, humble me. And I feel guilty for touching you, for taking what you give without reservation, without holding back, when I'm not worthy of it."

Stunned, she sat up, uncaring of her nudity. She stared down at him, blinking. Shock, like an ice-cold slap to the face, sent her reeling. "What?" she rasped. "Why would you say that? Think that?"

That familiar shuttered expression settled on his face as

he, too, rose, the sheet pooling around his hips. Anger, sadness and frustration welled within her. She wanted to take a hammer to that mask. Splinter it to pieces so he could never hide from her again.

Why do you care? Three more months left, and it doesn't matter.

It mattered, dammit. It. Mattered.

"You would give—and have given—everything for your family. Even your mother. You raised your brother, provided for him, and never left either one of them. You forfeited your own education so your brother could have his. You put your dreams on hold to make sure he could pursue his. Putting his needs above your own. That is you. It isn't me." He bit off the last words, a muscle ticking along his clenched jaw.

"When Jason died," he began again after several seconds, "it became my responsibility to take up where he left off. Chandler International isn't just a family business—it's a legacy. A heritage. And a Chandler has always headed it, leading it into the next generation. Without Jason, that falls to me. Even though I've received this birthright by default. Even though I'm considered second-best. Loyalty, duty—they come before personal needs. I should be honored to helm this company. But I'm not. I don't want it. I'm not selfless like you, Nadia."

"What do you want, Gray?" she whispered, finding no pleasure in his compliment since he meant it to condemn himself.

"To be free."

She understood the desperation in that quiet statement. How many times had she prayed, begged God to liberate her of her mother's tainted shadow, of people's low expectations, of the chains of responsibility?

"Gray, I love Ezra with all my heart. But I wasn't ready to be mother and sister to him. I wasn't ready to drop out of high school to get a job and provide for him. I wasn't ready to leave childhood—such as it was—behind and enter adulthood way too early. If I'd had a choice, I wouldn't have. And there's no guilt or shame in admitting that. Given the same circumstances that I faced, if I had to do it all over again, I would. Because he was more defenseless than me, more vulnerable. But if I'd been offered a different existence, a kinder one, I would've chosen that for both Ezra and me. One where our futures were our own to shape and forge." She lifted a hand, and it hovered above his thigh before she settled it on him. "You have a choice. That's power—your power. And you shouldn't let anyone steal it away from you with their expectations and demands. They can have them, but you don't have to live by them."

A humorless half smile ghosted across his lips. "You make it sound so simple."

She released an impatient sound that was something between a scoff and a curse. "Of course it's not simple. Disappointing those we love and respect is never easy. But..." She squeezed the thick muscle of his thigh. "What are you afraid of?"

He shook his head, a slight sneer curling the corner of his mouth. "I'm not—"

"You are," she insisted, interrupting him. She slashed her other hand through the air. "Forget that macho, masculine bullshit. What are you afraid of?"

An internal battled waged over his face, in his eyes. Though part of her braced for his rejection, she curled her fingers around his. And only long moments later, when he flipped his hand around and gripped hers, did she exhale.

"Killing what little pride in me my parents have left," he finally rasped. The harsh timbre of his confession rubbed over her skin like sandpaper. And she cherished it. "Losing their love. Losing them." His eyes closed, and the dense fringe of almost absurdly long lashes created deeper shadows. "But just as much, I fear who I will become if I give in and return to Chandler." He lifted his lashes, and his blue-and-green gaze bore into hers. She met his stare, though the stark pain in it was almost too hard to glimpse. "I fear being trapped."

"Gray," she breathed. On impulse, she climbed onto his lap, straddling him. Cupping his face in her palms, she leaned forward, pressing her chest to his, her fore-head against his. "Oh, Gray." She sighed. Easing back just enough so she could peer down into his eyes, she mur-mured. "You are..." *Everything.* "So worthy of your par-ents' unconditional love and acceptance. Just because you are their son. But also because you're beautiful, brilliant, a testament to the same pioneer spirit that started Chan-dler International, and devoted. Not surrendering to their demands doesn't make you disloyal. It makes you the man they raised you to be. A man who thinks for himself. Who is successful. Who thrives in difficult situations. Who stands by his commitments, his dreams and his decisions. And if they can't see that... If they can't be proud of the person you are, *their son*, then that's their issue, not yours. Never yours."

She wrapped her arms around his neck, ordered herself to stay quiet. That she'd said enough. Any more and she might reveal more than she intended. More than she could afford. But then she smoothed her thumbs over his sharp cheekbones. Swept them over his full, heart-stopping lips. Gazed into his beautiful eyes.

And she couldn't stop the last words from slipping free.

"I've only known you—truly known you—for weeks. And, Gray, I'm proud to know you," she whispered in his ear. "I'm proud of you. If no one else tells you, I will."

She brushed a kiss over the soft patch of skin beneath his earlobe. Another to the bridge of his nose. One more to his chin. And one to the center of his mouth.

As if the last caress snapped a tether to his control, his arms whipped around her, hugging her so tightly her ribs twinged in protest, but she didn't ask him to release her. Instead, she clasped him closer, as well. And when his mouth took hers, she opened to him. Surrendering. Giving.

Falling.

Fourteen

Nadia stepped off the elevator onto her floor Monday morning. Greeting several early arrivals like herself, she made her way to her desk.

You can't just walk around smiling like a ninny. Jeesh.

The exasperated admonishment echoing in her head didn't dim the wattage of her soft grin at all. Not when the most nonsensical, bright joy glowed in her chest like a lamp on the highest setting.

All because she'd woken up next to the man she loved Sunday morning.

Yes, she loved Grayson Chandler.

More than a little panic simmered beneath her happiness. Somewhere in the last few weeks, she'd ignored every warning to herself. Had broken every promise, disregarded every cautionary tale and fallen for the man she'd sworn would remain off-limits. The last time this sense of excitement, fear and hope had trembled in her heart over a man, the demise of the relationship had nearly destroyed her.

But Grayson wasn't Jared.

Yes, Grayson had initially thrown money at her to get his way, but his motives had been altruistic, to avoid causing further grief to someone he loved. Yes, he was arrogant and domineering, but he was also selfless, generous, a little broken but possessing a beauty even he didn't recognize.

So, yes, she'd fallen for him.

And she couldn't decide if she was foolish as hell...or taking a wondrous leap of faith.

She could still feel the phantom press of his body as she dozed after making love—

She rolled the phrase around in her mind. Had they made love? On her part? Yes. On his...

Her belly knotted, pulling taut. She didn't know. Grayson certainly enjoyed sex with her, but did he see her as more than his fake fiancée and occasional bed partner?

Could he love her?

That damn, flighty hope shivered inside her again, and she dumped her purse on her desk with one hand and rubbed a spot on her chest with the other. Directly underneath her fingers, her heart beat out a nervous tattoo.

"Good morning, Ms. Jordan," Mr. Webber greeted, stopping in front of her desk.

His gaze dropped to the big rock on her ring finger before lifting back to her face. Ever since it'd become office gossip that she and Grayson were "engaged," her supervisor had been a little guarded with her. As if unsure how to treat her—a regular employee or *his* future employer. Either way, there hadn't been any more requests for weekend work.

"Morning, Mr. Webber," she replied with a smile, opening her bottom drawer and storing her bag in it. She reached for her computer and booted it up. "Is there anything I can get you?"

"Could you email today's schedule to me?" he asked.

She fought not to roll her eyes. Because she sent him

the next day's schedule every evening before she left. He'd had it sitting in his inbox since Friday night. But instead of telling him to check his mail, she nodded and murmured, "Sure thing."

Her boss entered his office, and she lowered into her chair, ready to get the day started. Speaking of today's schedule, she needed to check her phone to see if Grayson had added anything for them to attend tonight. Weeks ago, he'd synched their calendars so if he added an event, the notification would pop up. But first...

Swallowing an irritated sigh, she opened her email and composed a new message, attached Mr. Webber's schedule and sent it off. She moved the mouse to the minimize button when a bold message in her inbox from an address she didn't recognize snagged her attention. Curious, she clicked on it.

Then frowned. Not understanding what she read. But if the words took moments to sink in, the pictures that populated the email did not.

Her heart pummeled her sternum so hard it hurt her chest. Air that had moved in and out of her lungs so easily just seconds ago jammed in her throat. Thank God. Because it blocked the pained whimper from escaping.

She scrolled through image after image.

Grayson and Adalyn standing close in a hallway, her hand curled into his tuxedo jacket.

Adalyn touching Grayson's jaw in a lover's caress, wearing a sensual smile.

Grayson with his head bent low over Adalyn, their faces so close their mouths nearly brushed.

There were ten in all, revealing a couple caught in an intimate moment.

From the clothing, the pictures were taken at the Chandlers' anniversary party. Where had Nadia been while Grayson and Adalyn met? Had she been defending herself against his mother while he cuddled up with his supposedly hated ex? Had Cherise been a distraction while those two arranged to meet?

Question after question bombarded her, and she wanted to cry out with the onslaught. She shoved to her feet, her chair rolling back to hit the wall behind her. Ignoring the curious glances thrown her way, she flattened her palms to the desk, unable to tear her gaze from the images. With trembling fingers and humiliation blazing a path through her, she moved the mouse, scrolling up to the message above the pictures.

I didn't want to have to resort to such measures, but you didn't leave me another choice. If you won't believe my words, then maybe you will believe pictures since they're supposed to be worth a thousand of them. Grayson has never stopped loving me, as you can very well see. Whatever you think you have with him, it's not real. You're doing nothing but making a fool of yourself. Find your dignity and walk away with at least some of your pride intact.

There wasn't a signature, but one didn't need to be included. Adalyn. She'd discovered Nadia's email address and blindsided her at work with proof of the unresolved feelings between her and Grayson.

Wait, wait. Grayson had been adamant, when they first struck their bargain, that he'd never reunite with Adalyn. If something had happened between then and now to change his mind, he would've told her... Wouldn't he?

Yes.

The part of her that stubbornly clung to belief in his integrity hissed out the agreement. There had to be an explanation for the pictures. For the emotion and intensity that seemed to vibrate from them.

Before she could reconsider her decision, she hit Print on the email. Moments later, she snatched up the still-warm papers and headed toward the elevators. Though Mr. Webber would probably reprimand her if he exited his office to find her gone, she was willing to risk it.

She needed answers.

Minutes later, she stepped out on the executive floor of KayCee Corp and strode towards Grayson's office. Mrs. Ross, his administrative assistant, glanced up as she neared, a polite but welcoming smile curving her mouth. Nadia forced herself to return the gesture, even if it felt brittle on her lips.

"Good morning, Mrs. Ross," she said, surprised by how even her voice sounded. "Is Grayson, I mean, Mr. Chandler in?"

"He had to step out of his office for a moment." The older woman swept a hand toward the closed double doors. "But I'm sure he wouldn't mind if you went in and waited for him. He should return shortly."

"Thank you," she murmured, heading toward his office. Once inside, she closed the doors behind her and exhaled, leaning against the wood.

Just ask him. I'll just ask him. He'll explain and everything will be fine.

She nodded as if someone else had offered the advice and pushed off the door. There had to be an explanation. She'd encountered Adalyn Hayes only a handful of times, but they'd been enough to tell the woman was manipulative and wouldn't be above trickery to get what she wanted. Which, in this case, was Grayson.

The cool logic of the argument blew on the flames of hurt and humiliation burning inside her. She crossed to Grayson's desk to sit in one of the visitor chairs to wait on him.

"What the hell?" she breathed.

She stared down at the manila envelope with her name typed across the label. The email printout floated from her numb fingers to the top of Grayson's desk. The thought of respecting his privacy and not opening the file didn't occur to her. And before she could convince herself it wasn't a good idea to snoop, she already had the flap opened and the thin sheaf of papers freed.

Stunned, she read the private investigator's report.

Marion Jordan, town drunk and whore. Children by two different men.

Nadia Jordan's arrest record.

High school dropout.

Everything about her past—about her—in black-and-white. In startling, stark detail.

Anger. Pain. Shame. They all seared her, rendering her to a pile of ash. She couldn't breathe, couldn't think, couldn't... Oh God, she just *couldn't*.

"Nadia."

The papers fluttered to the floor as she slowly pivoted at the sound of the deep voice that she adored...and now resented.

Grayson watched her, his unique eyes hooded. Examining. He knew what she'd discovered, what she'd been reading.

"You had me investigated," she stated, amazed at the flat tone. Shouldn't her voice be a pitted, ragged mess from all the internal screaming? First his ex's email, then this report. Both of them had emotionally flayed her, and she should at least sound like it. "You pretended not to know about me, about my mother, my life in Georgia, when you knew all along."

"I didn't order that report. My father did," he said, that inscrutable, aloof mask firmly in place. Except for his eyes. They remained alert, bright.

"But you didn't tell me about it, either," she accused. Releasing a chuckle that abraded her throat, she shook her head. "And all the way here, I was telling myself that you wouldn't lie to me. That if you had something to tell me, you would be upfront about it. Not hide anything from me. Then I find that."

Like a movie reel cut to the slowest speed, she replayed all the moments she'd shared with him. How she'd showed him her heart. And the whole time, he'd already known. Had already been judging…

"What are you talking about, Nadia?" he demanded, eyes narrowing as he advanced on her. "I haven't lied to you. That thing," he flicked a hand toward the report scattered on the floor, "doesn't mean anything to me. My father had you investigated to prove a meaningless point. I don't care where you were born or who your mother is. I care about the woman standing in front of me. You should know that by now."

"Then about this?" she whispered, picking up the pictures from where she'd dropped them and thrusting them toward him.

He didn't remove his eyes from her until his fingers closed around the papers. As he read the email and studied the pictures, his features darkened until his scowl could've incinerated the whole office. Finally, he lifted his head and fury lit his blue and green gaze.

"Where did you get these?"

She shivered at the barely leashed rage vibrating in the question. "An email from Adalyn, I'm guessing. It was waiting for me when I arrived at work this morning."

"This is BS," he growled, tossing the email to the seat of the visitor's chair. "I don't know how Adalyn arranged for those pictures to be taken, but they're misleading and false." He thrust a hand through his hair, disheveling the thick strands. "She cornered me at my parents' party, and we argued. She did get close to me, touch me, but what those pictures don't show is me pushing her away. They don't contain an audio file of me telling her there's no way in hell there could ever be an 'us' again. Of me threatening her about insulting you again. She's a vindictive bitch who's seeing dollar signs in her future and refuses to take no for an answer."

Nadia couldn't speak, the hurt from the email and the report too fresh. She'd arrived at work hopeful, cautiously happy. But now, she'd curled back into her protective shell, too afraid to place her bruised heart on the line.

"Nadia." He sighed, again running his fingers through his hair, gripping it before dropping his arm to his side. "Do you know why I ended my relationship with Adalyn?" He glanced away for a brief moment, before returning his focus to her, shadows darkening his eyes. "The night of the anniversary party, Adalyn told me that I loved her. And she was right. I did. With everything in me. When I thought of my future, I couldn't picture it without her in it. Did I know she wasn't perfect? Yes, but who was? She was everything to me. Until she wasn't."

He stalked across the room toward the floor-to-ceiling window behind his desk. She stared at his back, the tense set of his shoulders. A part of her wanted to urge him to continue. But a greater, more fearful part, didn't want to hear it.

"Just after we were engaged, we attended her friend's engagement party. I stepped outside to take a phone call, and when I finished, I heard Adalyn and her friend on the far side of the balcony. I headed in their direction, but then I heard snatches of the conversation. It was about me. And Jason. She told her friend that she'd managed to catch me, but only because my brother turned her down. She'd tried to seduce him, but he hadn't been interested. So she pursued me and won me. In her words, one Chandler brother was as good as another just as long as she landed one of them. The man didn't matter—the inheritance did. I loved her, but she loved my money and the lifestyle it would afford her."

"Gray," she breathed, pain for the man he'd been weakening her legs. Reaching out, she steadied herself on the edge of his desk. "I'm so sorry. No one deserves that kind of betrayal. Especially you."

"It's over with. In the past," he said, his tone abrupt as he spun to face her with his hands stuffed into his pockets. "The only reason I'm going into it is so you can understand that however those pictures might appear, there will never be anything between Adalyn and me again. I haven't lied to you."

She believed him. But that didn't beat back the sadness, the foreboding and the buckling sense of loss that swept over her, threatening to drag her under. Because while she accepted the truth about Adalyn, she also couldn't deny another certainty.

He couldn't love her.

She would never be more than a buffer between him, his mother and ex-fiancée.

The death of that resurrected hope stabbed her, and she sucked in a breath, willing the pain to recede. But it wouldn't. She'd been a fool twice. And this time, it was much worse. At least with Jared, she hadn't known he was using her. With Grayson, she'd entered their bargain with eyes wide open. He'd even warned her against falling in love with him.

...I don't want to hurt you... Protect yourself from me...

And now she understood. He could never trust another woman with his heart. Not after Adalyn had betrayed him so deeply. Yes, he'd been upfront about what he'd expected from Nadia and their bargain. She'd been the one to forget the consequences of dreaming, of hoping...

She forced herself to straighten away from the desk. Though agony seemed to pulse through each of her limbs, she would face this like she hadn't faced Jared.

Head held high.

With pride.

And walking away.

"You told me once that your greatest desire was to be free," she reminded him softly. "But as long as you're holding on to the past, you will never be completely free."

He frowned at her. "I'm not holding on to the past. After everything I've just said, you still think I want Adalyn?" he demanded, removing his hands from his pants pockets and splaying them wide. "Nadia—"

"No." She shook her head. "I believe you. But that doesn't mean you're not still trapped there, locked to her." If she were smart, if she possessed even an inch of self-preservation, she would leave now. But she couldn't. Not until she'd laid herself out there. She'd walk away, but it would be with no regrets. "You shared with me, so I'll do the same. I have an Adalyn in my past, too. His name was Jared. He was a couple of years older than my twenty-two, the son of a town councilman, rich, handsome. And he said he loved me. I believed him. I *wanted* to believe him. That someone like him could find me beautiful, desirable…"

"You are beautiful and desirable," Grayson snapped.

She smiled and didn't try to mask the sadness in it. "He was the first man to make me see it in myself. Until, like you with Adalyn, I discovered the truth. I was his dirty little secret. Stupid me had thought we were in a real relationship, that he didn't care about who my mother was, about my past, that he just loved me. I found out way too late that he'd been dating the daughter of his father's buddy and planned on marrying her. But I shouldn't have worried," Nadia continued with a bitter crack of laughter. "He still intended to keep me, even though another woman would be his wife. In his eyes, I was supposed to be flattered that I would be his side piece."

"He was a bastard, Nadia," Grayson growled. "A little boy masquerading as a man. You didn't deserve that kind of disrespect or pain. That speaks more about him than it does your worth."

"I couldn't agree more," she said quietly. "I promised myself then that I would learn my lesson. That I would guard my heart, demand better for myself and never give my body or my soul away to someone who didn't earn it. Who wasn't worthy of it. In the last few weeks, I've broken my vow. Jared might have betrayed me years ago, but I've betrayed myself now."

He stepped toward her, his frown deepening. "Nadia. What are you saying?"

She dragged in a breath, and it sounded ragged and painful in the room. "I'm saying that I've fallen in love with you. Against my better judgment, I have. And the man you are…" She pressed her palm to her chest, over her heart. "God, Gray, you're so worthy. But so am I. I deserve to be honored, cherished, valued…loved."

He stared at her, his face etched out of stone, carefully aloof. "Nadia, you don't mean that."

"Oh, but I do," she countered, pain lacing every word. She didn't have the strength to mask it. "I also realize you can't give me what you don't have. And maybe, a few years ago, I would've been okay with that. Taking crumbs. I'd like to think I wouldn't have been. But then again, I've never met a man like you, Grayson Chandler. You've made me believe in love again." A wistful smile curled her lips. "But being by your side these last few weeks has shown me what I could have. What I dream of obtaining one day. And I'm not willing to settle for less than that. For so long I've settled for half a life, desperately trying not to become my mother while raising Ezra. And though I have zero regrets about my brother, I've never focused on who I am. Who I want to be. I want more. I deserve more. In who I am and who I'm with."

"Goddamn it, Nadia," he snarled, advancing on her a

step, before drawing up short. "What do you expect me to say? That I love you, too? I've been honest with you about what I want from the beginning. Is this bait and switch supposed to be some kind of guilt trip?"

His accusation slapped at her. But instead of flinching and cowering away from the impact, she hiked her chin higher. "I never asked for your heart or your love, Grayson," she said, purposefully using his full name. "I'm not even offering you mine, because you can't care for my heart. You can't protect it. And I can no longer afford to put myself—or my heart—in the care of someone who doesn't value it like it deserves. Not again."

She turned then, and though it cost her, she strode away from him toward his office door. Only when she grasped the knob and paused, did she speak again.

"The night of the blackout, I didn't tell you my identity or that I knew you because I wanted to have that night for myself. Ever since I started work here, I've been attracted to you. Crushed on you, as silly and immature as that sounds. You were always a gift to me. And for one night at least, I let myself have that gift. But that'll teach me to reach too high. The fall, the breaking, isn't worth it."

She opened his office door, and without glancing back, walked out on him.

But not on herself. For the first time ever, she was walking toward herself.

Fifteen

Grayson jerked his tie loose then off as he strode into his living room. He paused long enough to fix a Scotch at the bar before striding to the window. Before, the view of the Chicago skyline always soothed him. The strength, beauty and grit of the city with the soothing calm of Lake Michigan's waters. They balanced each other, and they balanced him.

Usually.

That was before Nadia had walked out of his office a week ago after announcing she loved him. But didn't trust him with her heart.

His fingers tightened around the squat tumbler.

Not that he'd asked for her heart. Or wanted it. Because he didn't. He'd been down that road and had no interest in traveling it again. Only an idiot or a masochist would eagerly court that kind of disaster. That kind of pain.

And he was neither.

But when Nadia had said she loved him… He sipped the

alcohol and relished the burn as it slid down his esophagus. The path of liquid fire distracted him from the precious second when a flame of joy had flickered in his chest when she'd admitted her love for him. Then, he could deny its existence. And in the long, brutal hours he'd put in at the office since she'd left, he could pretend he hadn't felt that second of incandescent delight. Before he ruthlessly snuffed it out.

While recounting the ending of his relationship with Adalyn, he'd relived that moment when he'd overheard her lies, her careless disregard for his love. Reexperienced the pain. The humiliation. Feeling that again...and with Nadia...

He threw back the rest of the drink, closing his eyes. Adalyn had damn near destroyed him. Nadia would finish the job, if he let her.

And he couldn't.

The intercom near the elevator doors buzzed. Shaking his head, he strode over to the entrance and pressed a button.

"Yes?"

"Mr. Chandler," the lobby security guard said. "There's a Mr. Ezra Jordan here to see you. Should I send him up?"

Nadia's brother? Grayson's heart thudded against his rib cage. He should say no. Nadia had left his office, then quit her job, walking away from not just him but his company. She'd ended their association, so what could he and Ezra possibly have to talk about?

"Send him up, please."

He was a glutton for punishment.

And yet, he waited next to the doors and stood there to greet Ezra when he stepped from the elevator a minute later. Grayson didn't say anything, just watched the teen stalk toward him, anger tightening his handsome features and vibrating off his frame. Ezra stopped directly in front of Grayson, shoving his locs out of his face as he glared at him.

"You hurt her," he barked, fury gleaming in his dark eyes. "You promised me you wouldn't, and you did. She won't tell me what happened between you two, but she's not the same. She quit her job, man. So something must've gone down. You should've left her alone if you—"

"She left me." Grayson interrupted Ezra's tirade, impatience brimming inside him. He needed this boy with Nadia's eyes to leave so he could return to his obsessive brooding.

"But you must've done something to make her do it," Ezra snapped in return. "You're the first man she's opened up to since that asshole Jared. She doesn't trust easy, and she damn sure doesn't love easy. And I'm not blind. She loves you. But you just threw it, and her, away."

"I understand you want to defend your sister, Ezra. And if I was in your place, I would do the same for mine. But you don't know all the details about what happened between your sister and me," Grayson said.

"I don't care," the seventeen-year-old snapped at him. Admiration swelled in Grayson for Ezra. Due to Grayson's power, position and wealth, most men wouldn't dare speak to him like Ezra was doing. But Ezra didn't give a damn. Just like his sister. "I don't need to know the details. The only thing that matters is Nadia has been through a lot— too much. She's given up too much. She deserves the world. And if your head is too far up your ass, then it's your loss. And that's what I came over here to tell you. She's the best thing that ever happened to you. If you're too stupid to hold on to her, then that's your bad. Not hers."

Jerking his chin up, he pinned Grayson with one last glare then spun around and marched back to the elevator. Grayson didn't move as he disappeared behind the doors.

Didn't move as the minutes ticked by and the teen's adamant and proud words echoed in his head.

She's the best thing that ever happened to you. If you're too stupid to hold on to her, then that's your bad. Not hers.

How long he stood there, he didn't know. He couldn't move as the truth bombarded him, pummeling him and rendering him frozen.

Frozen except for the rapid beat of his heart.

Images of the past few weeks passed before him at light speed, and he locked his knees against the dizzy sensation that almost pushed him to his knees.

From the moment they met in that hallway, locked for the night in the blackout, she'd seen him—*really seen him*—like no one else. Not even his family. She'd challenged him, gone toe to toe with him, shielded him, teased him, encouraged him...loved him.

Gray, I'm proud to know you... I'm proud of you. If no one else tells you, I will.

In this pretentious world of yours where conformity is mistaken for perfection, you are utterly perfect.

I've never met a man like you, Grayson Chandler. You've made me believe in love again.

Oh God. What had he done?

What in the *hell* had he done?

He loved Nadia.

It'd been there all along, but he'd been so busy guarding his heart that he hadn't recognized it. When the truth was, she'd captured his heart the night of the blackout. The night she'd called him a protector and offered herself to him, trusting him.

She'd called him noble, and then he'd been too much of a coward to strip away his fear and tell her she didn't have to ask for his heart. She already had it.

But he still wasn't worthy of it. That didn't mean he

wouldn't move hell, heaven and earth to earn her heart, her belief that he would protect it, cherish it.

Where once he'd been afraid to risk his pride and heart, that fear no longer trapped him.

For Nadia, he would risk it all.

Sixteen

Grayson entered his parents' home, a sense of urgency tingling under his skin. Weeks ago, he would've been riddled with guilt, his shoulders weighed down by the heaviness of disappointment or even failure. But now, as he strode to the informal living room where his family often gathered, only determination and impatience flowed through him. This was a task he needed to get over with so he could move on to the more important business ahead of him: Nadia.

The scene that awaited him was one he'd pictured in his mind. His father seated in his armchair near the fireplace, a book opened in his hands, flames dancing behind the iron screen. His mother, a planner splayed wide on her lap, settled on the love seat. And his sister sitting on the opposite end of the small couch, her laptop perched on her thighs. Yes, the scene was expected—and a little sad. They all sat in the same room as a family, but no one interacted, no one laughed or even lovingly argued. If he just replaced his father and mother with him and Adalyn, this would be their future.

And he wanted none of it.

His father glanced up from his book, noting Grayson in the living room entrance. "Grayson," he said, a faint frown creasing his forehead. "This is a surprise. What brings you by?"

His mother and sister looked up from their work, and Melanie stood, setting the laptop on the coffee table. She came over and planted a kiss on his cheek. "Good to see you, little brother."

He smiled, squeezing her shoulders. "Thanks. I came by to talk with all of you for a moment." Not willing to beat around the bush, he leaped in. "It's about assuming the CEO position of Chandler International."

At the announcement, he'd won his parents' complete attention. A hint of satisfaction gleamed in his father's eyes and slightly curved his mouth. His mother nodded, as if his decision to helm the family company had been a foregone conclusion.

"I'm not returning to be CEO or take over when you retire, Dad."

A deafening silence filled the room, and his father blinked, staring at him. Seconds later, red mottled his father's face, and he pushed to his feet, his eyes narrowing on Grayson. His mother also rose, her hand pressed to her chest. Beside him, Melanie touched his elbow, and that small show of support beat back the force of their disappointment and anger.

"I know this isn't what you wanted to hear, but it's my final decision. I know the history and importance of Chandler International, and I respect it. And you may not see it this way, but I'm honoring that history by creating my own legacy with my company. The same hard work, spirit and determination that went into creating and building Chandler is going into KayCee Corp. It's mine. It's something I can leave my children along with Chandler International. This is my path, and I won't abandon it out of guilt or a misplaced sense of loyalty."

"This is unacceptable, Grayson," his father snapped. "Completely unacceptable. And I won't hear of it."

"You're going to have to, Dad," he murmured. "And it might be unacceptable to you, but you must accept it. I'm not Jason," he added quietly. "Heading Chandler was his dream, not mine. And I won't be—I can't be—a substitute for him."

His mother's gasp echoed in the quiet.

"That's not what we were trying to do," she objected, voice hoarse. "We just needed to impress on you the importance of this family's tradition. It's our strength, our power."

"No," Grayson contradicted, shaking his head. "The people in this room are the strength and power of Chandler. All of us. Dad—" he turned his attention back to his father "—you've been so focused on me taking over the company that you overlooked the one Chandler who has worked hard by your side for years. Who knows the company just as well as Jason, and most importantly, wants to be there. Who enjoys being there, but hasn't received any recognition." He glanced down at Melanie, and his sister's eyes widened as his meaning sank in. "Yes." He nodded. "Melanie deserves to helm Chandler International, not me. And if you don't announce her as the incoming CEO to the board, then I promise you I will do everything in my power to persuade her to leave Chandler and come over to KayCee Corp."

His father sputtered in outrage, but Grayson wasn't finished. He pinned his mother with a steady gaze.

"And Mother, I love you. I freely admit, I haven't confronted you about quitting all the matchmaking attempts because I didn't want to hurt your feelings or cause you more pain. But, no more. Not with Adalyn or any other woman. It ends here. I'm in love with Nadia Jordan. She is everything to me, and I won't stand for any more disrespect thrown her way by you, Father or Adalyn. You need to accept this decision and her. Because if you don't—if you do anything more to hurt or malign her—then you'll lose a son. Like I said, I love you, but when it comes to Nadia, there isn't any divided loyalty. She's my first and only choice."

"She's a lovely, good woman, and I'm happy for you, Gray," Melanie said, taking his hand and squeezing it. "We'll welcome her, won't we?" she said, studying their parents.

Neither his mother nor father answered, but the disappointment, the shame he'd anticipated, didn't appear.

"Well, it seems you've made your decisions, and we have to live with them," his mother said, ice dripping from the words.

"You do," he agreed. Kissing his sister's temple, he nodded at his parents. "One day, I hope you'll understand my choices. In the meantime, I need to go win back the woman I love."

Seventeen

Nadia stared at the numbered buttons in the elevator as they lit then dimmed as floor after floor slid by. Finally, they arrived on the fifteenth floor, and she stepped free of the elevator. She'd been on this level only a couple of times. And both had been in her early days at KayCee Corp. But what could Human Resources possibly want to see her about now as it'd been almost two weeks since she'd quit and walked out?

Nerves plagued her belly, and she surreptitiously glanced around. As if Grayson would appear around every corner or stride out of a closed office door. Which was ridiculous. The president of the company did not just hang around the HR floor. Still… She'd gone nine days without seeing him, hearing his voice, inhaling his sandalwood and mint scent. In time, she hoped to stop dreaming about him, waking up hurting in her heart and body over the loss of him.

But today was not that day. And glimpsing him, even

from far away, might break her into too many pieces to recover.

No, distance was her friend now. Distance and denial.

Not that she regretted her decision to end their "relationship." She didn't. Yes, every breath seemed edged in an ache, but for once, she'd chosen herself. She'd placed her well-being, her heart, her worth first. She deserved to be valued. To be loved.

And she refused to settle.

Inhaling a deep breath, she approached the executive assistant's desk for Marsha Fowler, the head of Human Resources. Another mystery. Why the head of HR would ask her to come in and talk. How many employees who quit without notice were invited back? Not that Nadia intended on working for KayCee Corp again. The company was phenomenal, but she just…couldn't.

"Hello," she greeted the young blonde on the other side of the desk. "Nadia Jordan. I have a nine o'clock appointment with Ms. Fowler."

"Yes." The assistant smiled and rose from her chair. She rounded the desk and gestured for Nadia to follow her. "They're waiting for you, Ms. Jordan."

They? Unease twisted and knotted her stomach as she trailed the other woman down a hall. Who…? She didn't have long to wait to find out the answer. The assistant knocked on a closed door, then opened it.

"Ms. Jordan is here." Smiling at Nadia, the blonde stepped aside so she could enter.

"Thank you," Nadia murmured and moved into the large office. And drew to an abrupt halt. Shock. Confusion. Anger. And God, so much love, slammed into her with the force of a flying hammer.

Marsha Fowler sat behind a wide desk. Melanie Chandler sat in one of the chairs in front of it. And Grayson stood next to the other.

Though it pained her to look at him, to soak in the beauty of his chiseled face, lovely eyes and firm, sensual mouth, she couldn't tear her gaze away. She was a starving woman plopped down at a table overflowing with the most succulent food and drink.

Leave. Self-preservation kicked in moments too late, and just as the words "setup" whispered through her head, Ms. Fowler waved her inside. "Ms. Jordan, please come in. And thank you for coming by on such short notice."

"Hello, Nadia," Melanie greeted with a warm smile. "I can imagine you have a ton of questions. I promise we won't hold you up long."

"Hello, Nadia."

That deep voice of velvet night wrapped around her name had her nearly closing her eyes to luxuriate in it. But she forced herself to meet his gaze and nod.

"Grayson."

His blue and green eyes burned into hers, and in them she saw her broken hopes and foolish dreams. Unable to bear them, she glanced away and silently ordered herself to focus on the two women in the room. That had to be the game plan if she intended to make it through this meeting and leave unscathed.

"Please have a seat." Ms. Fowler waved to the empty chair. Nadia obeyed, sinking down into the seat. "Well, Ms. Jordan, I know you left the employ of KayCee Corp almost two weeks ago, but I also understand the circumstances were…unusual." She cleared her throat, briefly glancing at Grayson. "Mr. and Ms. Chandler asked that I call you in so they can present you with a counteroffer."

"I appreciate this, Ms. Fowler. But I'm afraid my mind is made up—" Nadia said, preparing to stand once more, when Melanie laid a hand over hers.

"You're under no obligation to accept, but please, just hear me out," Melanie requested. Nadia hesitated, but nodded. "It's come to my attention that you have an interest in nursing."

Nadia jerked her head toward Grayson, who hadn't uttered a word after greeting her. His steady contemplation of her didn't waver, didn't flicker to his sister or the HR director. Heat flooded her face, and she couldn't determine whether it was anger or embarrassment. Both. Definitely both. And the fault rested firmly on the wide shoulders of the man several feet away from her.

"Yes, Gray shared that info with me," Melanie continued, drawing Nadia's attention back to her. "In the spirit of transparency, he's also told me why you were working here instead of pursuing a degree in your preferred field. Several nonemergency urgent care chains fall under the Chandler International conglomerate. I would like to offer you a position at one of the centers as a receptionist while you enroll in a nursing program. Chandler will cover the expenses for those classes, of course. That way, you're pursuing your degree while actively working in the field and gaining experience."

Stunned, Nadia stared at Grayson's sister. Shock barreled through her, and she couldn't speak. Could barely comprehend what she'd said. Going to school? An entry job in her chosen field? Paid tuition?

What the hell was happening here?

Bewildered, she once more disobeyed her own instructions and yanked her attention from Melanie to Grayson.

"Marsha, Melanie," Grayson finally spoke. "Could we borrow the office for a few minutes?"

Both women stood, and in moments, only Nadia and Grayson remained. Seconds ago, the office had been large, but now, with only him there, it seemed to shrink, his presence filling it to overflowing. Unable to remain sitting, Nadia rose. But the sense of vulnerability didn't dissipate.

Suddenly, she felt naked, bared to him. And she hated it. Resented the effect he still had on her.

Feared that it, too, would never disappear.

"Why?" she asked, her voice stronger than the whirl-wind of emotions whipping inside her. "I know you're be-hind this. What is this supposed to prove?"

"What is it supposed to prove?" he repeated, shoving his hands in his pockets and cocking his head to the side. "Nothing. No, I take that back," he added. "It's supposed to prove to you that you're not only worthy of good op-portunities but deserving of them. That you shouldn't al-ways have to be the provider, protector and sacrificial lamb. Someone should do the same for you. Cover you. Shield you. Give everything to you. This isn't a handout, Nadia. Because there's no one in this world who has earned those things more than you."

She choked back an inconvenient sob, refusing to shed one more tear over this man. At least not in front of him.

"That sounds pretty. But we're over, remember? I don't need those sentiments. Especially since no one's here to witness them."

His eyes briefly closed, and if her own hurt wasn't col-oring her judgment, she might believe pain spasmed across his face. "You want to lash out at me? Fine. I can take it. You're more than justified. Not only was I an ass for reject-ing the most beautiful gift you could ever offer me, but I was a willfully blind ass. Which makes my crime worse." He blew out a breath, then his mouth firmed into a straight, grim line. "You told me that as long as I'm holding on to the past, I'll never be completely free. At the time, I didn't want to hear that. Didn't believe it. But you were right. I might have been over Adalyn, but I hadn't let go of the anger, the pain, the fear. I was in a prison of my own mak-ing. And rather than escape it, I just locked more chains on the bars. Keeping myself in…and you out."

He took a step toward her, removing his hands from his pockets. He raised them, bowing his head, as if studying the palms. But, moments later, he dropped his arms to his sides. Then he lifted his head, and... *God*. Her breath stuttered in her lungs, and her heart slammed against her chest, as if trying to break free and fling itself at his feet.

Gone was the inscrutable, aloof mask. Gone was the shuttered gaze that hid his thoughts and emotions. Gone was the charming, affable smile that had been his playboy persona.

Loneliness. Pain. And love. They all creased the bold lines of his face. There for her to see, his shield completely torn down. For her.

Tears stung her eyes, clogged her throat. She balled her fingers into fists and held them over her chest, caught between wanting to—needing to—protect herself and reaching out to him.

"Nadia, you told me that you couldn't offer me your heart because I couldn't care for it or protect it. And again, you were right. Then. But now..." He moved forward, those big hands palm up again in supplication. "Now, I can. I will. I don't have the right to ask you to trust me with the most precious gift you have, but I am. I'm begging you to believe in me one last time, and give me your heart, your dreams, your future. I'll guard it with my life, keep it from harm. I love you, baby. With you here—" he pressed a fist to his chest "—I don't have room for fear or bitterness. If given the choice between living in the past or walking toward a future with you, there isn't a choice. It will always be you, first and only. Please, Nadia." His voice roughened, and he stretched a hand toward her, his fingers stopping just shy of her chin and jaw. "I don't want to be in prison any longer."

On a gasp and cry that erupted from her, she took the last couple of steps that brought her into contact with his hand. She clasped his with both of hers and turned her face into it, pressing her lips to the palm. And because she was touching him again after being starved of him for nearly two weeks, she kissed him again. Then cupped his hand over her cheek.

"My love—my heart—is yours," she breathed against his skin. "It always has been. And there's no one else I'd rather have keeping it safe."

"You'll never spend another moment of your life doubting if you're loved, baby," he whispered, lifting his other hand to cradle her face. In seconds, his lips molded to hers. Then he shifted them to her jaw, the bridge of her nose, her forehead. "I love you."

"I love you," she whispered.

Hope, it turned out, wasn't foolish.

Or only relegated to fairy tales.

Epilogue

One year later

"Now there's a sight I imagine no one would believe they'd ever see," Shay Knight mused.

Nadia followed the direction of the other woman's gaze. But besides the couples crowding the DuSable City Gala's dance floor, she didn't notice anything different.

"What?" Gideon asked, slipping his arm around his wife. Grayson's business partner and Nadia's former employer appeared as impassive and intimidating as ever, but she'd spent a lot of time around him and his wife. The man might scare the hell out of other people, but not her. She'd witnessed how much he adored Shay, and that kind of scaled down his scary factor from a ten to a three and a half. Okay, four.

"Darius King and Isobel Hughes together. And the Wells family, too, all in the same room, and no open warfare," Shay teased. Catching Nadia's confused frown, she grinned. "Oh, Nadia, I have to bring you up to speed on all the gossip you've missed out on. That group used to make the Hatfields and McCoys look like bosom buddies. Now, Darius and Isobel have two children together, and the Wells are doting grandparents."

"Speaking of grandparents..." Gideon dipped his head in the direction of the back of the ballroom. "Mom and Olivia just arrived. Since Shay told them she's pregnant, Mom has been a helicopter grandmother," he drawled. But his affection for the women in his life shone brighter than the light from the crystal chandeliers.

"We'll catch up with you," Grayson said, clapping a hand on Gideon's shoulder. "You know your mother loves me best, so if I don't come say hello, she's going to be crushed."

Gideon slid him a cutting glance, but the smile playing about his lips ruined the threat in the look. Grayson laughed, and Nadia snorted.

"So, Cinderella," he said, turning to Nadia and lifting her hand that he held clasped in his. The laughter in his eyes warmed her, as did everything about her husband. They'd been married for nine months, and she still lost her breath around him. Still pinched herself that she could call her longtime crush her spouse. The name he'd once called her in this same place a year ago fit. She was Cinderella come to wonderful life and had the most beautiful man as her Prince Charming. "Will you honor me with a dance?"

She scrunched her nose, pretending to think it over. "Depends. Do I get to lead?"

"Always." And with a grin and a heart-melting kiss to her ring finger, and the smaller, princess-cut pink diamond in an antique setting that replaced its ostentatious predecessor, he led her among the swaying couples. "Just in case I haven't told you tonight," he murmured, drawing her close into his arms, "you look amazing."

"Thank you." She cupped the nape of his neck. "But

since you picked this dress out, I think you're really just giving yourself a backhanded compliment."

He chuckled. "Possibly. But in my defense, you did tell me to pick whatever. I love when you're neck-deep in work. It allows me to get away with so damn much."

"Something tells me after I graduate, it's going to be hard as hell to rein you in," she grumbled, but the words ended on a bark of laughter. "Between you and Ezra, I'm going to have my hands full."

Ezra, in his freshman year at Yale, still called her regularly to compare class schedules, homework and tests. He also checked in with Grayson almost daily. Those two had become as close as brothers, and she couldn't be happier that the two men she adored most also loved one another. Between work at the urgent care clinic, school, her husband and her brother, her life had never been as full.

Or as blessed.

As perfect.

"Just think," she said, tangling her fingers in the shorter hair above his neck. "This time last year we were trapped in a hallway—"

"Having sex," Grayson interjected with a wicked grin.

She playfully slapped his shoulder. "And yes, having sex." She laughed. "A lot has changed since then," she said.

"In the best ways, though," he murmured, placing a kiss on her lips. "I've found the love of my life. I'm happier than I could've ever imagined. Melanie is already growing Chandler. And my mother actually smiled at you last week."

Nadia grinned. "Cherise is coming around." Okay, so she was being generous, but Grayson's parents were thawing toward her. But their acceptance of her didn't matter when their son stared down at her as if she were the most precious jewel he'd ever seen. It wasn't just enough—it was everything. "After all we've been through, we're definitely going to have stories to tell our kids about this gala… And we can start in about seven months."

For a moment, Grayson's face blanked. Then, seconds later, joy so bright suffused his face, it was almost hard to gaze upon.

"You're pregnant," he confirmed, voice hoarse and thick with the blinding love that gleamed out of his mismatched and beautiful eyes.

"I'm pregnant," she said, grinning.

With a shout, he lifted her in the air, twirling her around, heedless of the people around them. "She's pregnant!" he shouted.

Heat poured into her face as applause broke out, but she threw back her head, laughing. And when his mouth covered hers, she lost herself in it. In him.

Out of the darkness of a blackout, she'd found the shining light of love.

Happily ever after wasn't just for Cinderella.

It was for her, too.

* * * * *

WRONG MAN,
RIGHT KISS

RED GARNIER

As always, with my deepest thanks to everyone at Mills & Boon Desire – who make the best team of editors I've ever come across! Thank you for making this book shine.

This book is dedicated to my flesh-and-blood hero and our two little ones, who it turns out are not so little anymore.

One

Molly Devaney needed a hero.

She could think of no other way to solve her dilemma.

She'd been tossing and turning at night for the past two weeks, obsessing over what she'd done, wishing and praying and hoping she could figure out how to fix things and fix them fast.

It had taken fifteen days and fifteen hellish nights to come to the conclusion that she needed some help—and pronto—and there was only one man who could save the day, just like he'd previously saved her on plenty of other days.

Her hero of all times, ever since she was three and he was six, and Molly and her sister, Kate, recently orphaned, had ended up living with his rich and wonderful family in their San Antonio mansion.

Julian John Gage.

Okay. The guy was definitely no saint. He was a ladies' man down to his very sexy bones. He could have any woman he wanted, in any way he preferred, at any time he felt like, and the stupid meathead *knew* this. Which meant he was determined to sample them *all*.

It really rankled her sometimes.

But while he was an incorrigible rake with the ladies, a handful to the press due to his position as head of PR for the *San Antonio Daily,* a problem to his brothers and a bane to his own mother, to Molly, Julian John Gage was nothing short of the bomb. He was her greatest friend, the reason she'd never really found a man until now and the only person on this earth who would be honest enough to tell her how to seduce his hardheaded, annoying older brother.

The problem now was that Molly could've found a better time to expose her wicked plans to him. Bursting into his apartment on a Sunday morning was not her brightest idea. But then she was losing precious time and urgently needed Garrett, his older brother, to realize he loved her before she all but died from the misery of it all.

Now, if only Julian would stop staring at her as if she'd lost it big-time—which he'd been doing for the past couple of minutes, ever since she'd blurted out her plans.

The guy just stood there, easily the most magnificent work of art in his flawless contemporary apartment, his feet braced apart and his steely jaw hanging slightly ajar.

"I can't have heard right." When at last he spoke, his husky morning voice was laden with incredulousness. "Did you just ask me to help you seduce my own brother?"

Molly stopped pacing around the coffee table and, all of a sudden, she felt very much like a tramp. "Well…I didn't actually say *seduce*. Did I?"

An awkward silence followed as they both thought back to five minutes ago. Julian lifted a lone eyebrow. "You didn't?"

Molly sighed. She couldn't remember, either. She'd been a little tongue-tied when the living sculpture—aka Julian—had opened the door, gloriously bare-chested and wearing only a pair of low-slung drawstring linen pajama pants. The pants were so low-slung and sheer, in fact, that Molly could clearly make out the dark V of hair starting just under Julian's flat, bronzed navel, a tidbit which was playing havoc with her mind since she'd never seen a man partly naked before.

Plus, Julian was not just any man. He looked more like David Beckham's younger brother.

The hotter one.

Good thing their friendship made Molly immune.

"Okay, maybe I did say that, I can't remember." Molly shook her head and fought to get back on track. "It's only that I've just realized I need to do something drastic before some bimbo steals him from me for good. I need to get him, Julian. And you're the expert seducer, so I need *you* to tell me what to do."

His eyes—green like the leaves of the oaks outside—flared slightly in concern. "Look, Molls. I don't quite know how to explain this to you, so let me just get it out there." He started pacing. "We all grew up together. My brothers and I saw you in diapers. There's no way Garrett will ever look at you and see anything else but a little sister, the key words here being *little* and *sister.*"

"All right, so it's too late to do anything about the Pampers issue, I get it, but I have solid reasons to believe Garrett's feelings toward me have changed! I mean, has he ever even said he only thinks of me as a little sister, Julian? I'm already twenty-three. He may actually think I've grown up to be quite a sophisticated and sexy lady." *With really nice breasts that he quite happily fondled at the masquerade,* she thought smugly.

But Julian regarded her attire—certainly not one of her best outfits, she'd grant him that—with a look that was the opposite of thrilled.

"Your sister, Kate, is sophisticated and sexy. But you?" He stared pointedly at her boho skirt and paint-splattered tank top, then plunged his hand through his sun-streaked hair as though supremely frustrated. "God, Molls, have you stopped by a mirror recently? You look like you've been smacked, kicked, then put for a spin inside a blender."

"Julian John Gage!" Molly gasped, so genuinely hurt her heart constricted. "My next New York solo exhibit happens to be in four weeks—I don't have time to care about how I look! Plus I can't believe you're giving me crap about my work clothes when you stand there half nak—"

A door slammed shut in the depths of the apartment, and Molly whirled around with a scowl, ready to keep shouting. But she spotted someone approaching out of the corner of her eye and in that instant, she lost all power of speech. That someone was, of course, a woman.

The leggiest, blondest blonde Molly had ever seen was currently stepping out of Julian's bedroom. She was carrying a gold clutch purse and wearing a pair of crimson stilettos and one of Julian's button-down shirts, which seemed to barely contain what was easily a set of enormous breasts that made Molly's girls suddenly shrink before her eyes.

Now *that* woman looked as if she'd been inside a blender. But at a really marvelous speed. Molly wished she could pull off that tumbled look so well.

"I have to go," the mystery woman told Julian sultrily from afar. "I left my number on your pillow, so…" She made the universal call-me sign and puckered her lips. "It was really nice meeting you last night. I hope you don't mind me borrowing a shirt? My dress didn't seem to fare as well as I did." She released a soft giggle, and when Julian remained unmoved by her sexiness and Molly only gaped, she gracefully crossed the room to leave.

The instant the elevator doors shut behind her, Molly's gaze jerked back to Julian. "Seriously?" Annoyance flared through her with such force that she stalked forward and shoved his rigid shoulder. That *womanizer!* "Seriously, Julian? Do you have to sleep with every woman you meet?"

She shoved him again, but his shoulder budged as much as a concrete building would.

With a rumbling chuckle, Julian grabbed her hand and forced her fingers into a fist. "We aren't talking about my love life. We're talking about yours." He frowned down at their fisted hands and briskly released her. "And the fact that you have paint on your nose, in your hair and on your shoes, and this starving-artist look is not going to do anything for my brother."

Molly shot him a harsh glare, then shoved past him and stormed down the hall. "Oh, just let me grab one of your shirts! I'm sure that will do wonders for my pitifully *un-*sexy and *un*sophisticated looks."

"Aw, heck. Molly! Come on, Molls. Moo, baby. Get back here and just let me wrap my head around all this, all right? You know you've always been pretty, and I know that's why you don't give a damn."

Julian reached her in three long strides, promptly snatched her arm and dragged her back to the living room. Molly glared at him at first, but when she heard the low, deep sigh that worked its way up his chest, the sigh that said he just didn't know what to do with her anymore, her anger vanished.

It was just too hard to stay angry with Julian John.

Molly knew he'd do anything for her—and maybe that was why she was here. On a Sunday morning. And why she continued to be a pain in his great-looking butt. Because nobody had ever done the things that Julian John had done to make sure she was safe and protected, except maybe her sister, who had practically assumed the role of a mother when they were orphaned.

Kate had put her through school, coddled her, raised her and loved her every second of growing up without a mom and a dad. So the fact that Julian had been there for her almost as much as Kate said a lot about a man who insisted on pretending he was nothing but a playboy.

Which he first and foremost was.

But that was precisely why Molly was happy that he was just her friend and *not* the man she had set her romantic sights on.

"Look," she said as he released her, feeling herself blush as she remembered her and Garrett's stolen kiss. "I know you might not understand this. But I love your brother so much, I—"

"Since freaking when, Molls? He's always annoyed the crap out of both of us."

She stiffened defensively. "True, okay. But that was when he was so rigid, you know. Before."

"Before what?"

"Before…before I realized that he…" *Wants me. Before he said the things he said to me when he kissed me.* Her stomach wrenched at the painful memory. Anxiously, she pushed her red tresses back behind her shoulders and tried again. "I—I really can't explain it, but something has monumentally changed. And I just know he loves me back, I just know it in my soul, Julian—please don't laugh."

She couldn't bring herself to look him in the eyes for some inexplicable reason, so she spun around and slumped down on the leather sofa. The silence ticked by, and within seconds, she became aware of some extremely strange vibes coming from the vicinity of where Julian stood.

The laugh that broke the silence was worst of all. It was anything but mirthful. "I can't freaking believe this."

Molly held her breath and peered up at him, finding that a harsh frown had settled on his strong, tanned face. She had never seen Julian truly mad, but if that black scowl was a good indicator, he was getting there, and fast.

Her stomach clenched when she once again took a peek at his flat, muscled navel, the dark V dipping into those superloose drawstring pants and leading into— Okay, enough of that. She had to focus on getting Garrett. *Now.*

"Julian…" She really had to say something. Sighing, she signaled at that perfectly tanned, perfectly perfect torso. "Look. While we discuss this, can you put on one of your remaining shirts? The chest and the six-pack and all that you've got going on are just… Let's just say it makes me want to go take a peek at Garrett."

Julian scoffed and flexed seriously impressive biceps. "You know damned well my brother doesn't have these guns."

"He does, too."

He flexed his other biceps. "I may be his baby brother, but I can take the guy down in five seconds flat with these."

"Oh, puleeze. The only thing you're probably better at doing than him is screwing around—and you *deserve* that after saying I look like I live in a blender."

"Ahh. So once again, you missed the part where I said you were pretty." Julian fell down on a chair and for a long moment, they sat there, both staring pensively into space.

When he at last spoke, Molly was relieved to hear that his voice had regained its usual playful note. "Yeah. You're right. I am better at screwing around than both my brothers put together. Not that Landon would ever look at another woman now that he's married."

He leaned back and watched her with the beginnings of a smile that carried a hint of danger while he linked his hands behind his head in a deceptively relaxed pose.

"So let's screw around with Garrett. Why not? He's always been ridiculously protective of you and Kate. He'd go Donkey Kong if he ever found out you were dating someone. Especially someone with a bad reputation. You don't even really have to date the guy, just make him agree to play your doting lover for a while, ask him to be convincing enough to yank ole Garrett's chain."

Delighted that Julian was at last addressing her predicament, Molly almost jumped out of her seat and found herself clapping twice. "Yes! Yes! He sounds charming. But the question is, do I actually know such a man?"

Julian's smile was perfectly wolfish. "Baby, you're looking right at him."

His words appeared to strike Molly like an electric shock, and Julian wondered if that was a good thing, a bad thing or totally irrelevant to his newly hatched plan.

"Excuse me?" She jerked upright on his couch and gripped the leather cushions with such force that it looked as if she was on a roller-coaster ride. "I'm sure I heard wrong. Did you just offer to be my boyfriend or something?"

"Or something," Julian agreed, his lips curling upward.

He knew he looked calm. Collected. But inside his head, the wheels were turning with particularly inspiring ideas. Ideas he might later regret. But they were still damned good.

"Wh-what do you mean 'or something'?" she asked him.

Julian could hardly get over how adorable she looked

sitting there, shocked and disbelieving as if she'd just won the Megabucks.

Her eyes were just so wide and so damned blue you'd have to be made of freaking stone not to be willing to move mountains for her. Honestly, he'd never seen such expressive, genuinely innocent eyes in his life. It was a guarantee that Molly would lose every poker game she ever played, her expressions were so real and so clear. Hell, just the way she *looked* at him with those eyes made him feel like some sort of superhero. Not even his own mother gazed at him like Molly did.

With an amused smile, one he sometimes found himself wearing when he was with her, he explained, "'Or something' means I don't have girlfriends, Molly. I have lovers. And I'd be happy to pretend to be yours."

He'd meant to emphasize the word *pretend,* but somehow when he spoke, the only word he seemed to be able to emphasize was *yours.*

Because obviously he would only ever do this kind of stuff for Molly.

"You're kidding me, Jules," she said as she somberly scanned his face. She was not even moving, had practically become a statue on the couch.

He might have laughed at that, except to his own disbelief and amazement, he was dead serious. Dead. As *heck.* Serious. And now he needed to know if *she* was, too. "I may like to kid around, Molls, but I wouldn't kid you with this."

"So you're prepared to pretend to be in love with me?"

He nodded, and his hands itched to wipe away a green smudge of paint from her forehead and a red one from her cheek. "I figure I've probably done worse, Moo. Like that girl who just left…not really prime in the head, if you get me."

He tapped his forehead, but she wasn't even paying attention.

As though in a trance, Molly rose to her feet, all five feet of chaotic red hair and heavy turquoise necklaces and creamy paint-streaked skin, her eyes shining as his proposal finally seemed to dawn on her. "And Garrett will see us together and be madly jealous! Oh, my God, yes, yes, this is brilliant, Julian! How long do you think it will take to get him to realize he loves me? A couple of days? A week?"

Julian stared at her in silence. She really sounded… enamored. Didn't she?

He thought about it for a bit, and with each passing second, he grew more and more baffled. Suddenly all he wanted was for somebody to please tell him what in the *hell* was going on here. Was this some sort of lame-ass *joke?* Molly? Dreaming about his older brother? For real?

If the ten-year age difference wasn't an issue, the fact that the Gages had grown up with strict codes of conduct regarding the Devaney girls should matter. And tons. Especially to Garrett, who never, ever broke a rule. Had his brother done something to give Molly the impression of being interested?

Dammit, this just struck him as so, so wrong, he didn't even know where to begin.

His brother Garrett was ridiculously overprotective of the Devaney girls. The reason they'd become orphans in the first place was because their only living parent, who had been the Gages' bodyguard, had died in the line of duty protecting Julian's father and Garrett from an armed gang hired by the Mexican mafia to murder Julian's father for newspaper coverage disclosing their names and operations. But the Gages' bodyguard had died protecting Garrett, too. Though the gang members had been sentenced to life in prison, as the lone survivor of that bloody night two decades ago, Garrett had been sentenced to a life in hell.

Now he lived with a boatload of guilt and regret. When their widowed mother had taken the girls under their wing, Garrett had been rabid to protect them, even, apparently, from Julian—who had liked to tickle the hell out of Molly and make her giggle… Well, Garrett had always ridden Julian's goddamn back about the rules where the Devaney sisters were concerned. This annoyed not only Julian but also Molly—who loved being tickled by him.

So now, after Molly had complained a thousand times that Garrett never let Julian and her have any fun, it was damned hard to believe that she suddenly had the hots for Garrett.

What in the hell was that about?

Julian and Molly were friends. Honest-to-God, die-for-you, chase-a-killer-for-you and do-all-kinds-of-strange-stuff-for-you friends.

Julian was Molly's one, two and three on her freaking speed dial. The first number was for his office, the second for his cell phone and the third for his home. Molly even frequently admitted that their friendship was better than a romantic relationship, and it sure as hell had lasted longer than any marriage these days.

But after hearing her profess her love for Garrett several times today, Julian had realized that if she was serious—and apparently she was—he would have to help her.

He was going to "help" her realize that she was not in love with Garrett Gage. *Period.*

"I think we can get Garrett where we want him in about a month," he finally assured her, gazing deeply into her eyes in an attempt to gauge how deeply in love she believed herself to be. Knowing what a romantic Molly was, he actually dreaded the answer.

Hell, she was probably already hearing wedding bells; she looked positively love-struck. Which just hit the wrong chord with him. Oh, boy, did it ever.

"Do you really think he'll go for it? He's so difficult to read most of the time," Molly said in a dubious tone.

"Molly, no man in his right mind would stand by and watch his brother put his paws on his girl."

Blushing in excitement, Molly leaped forward and hugged him tight, kissing his stubbled cheek. "You'd really do this just for me? You're the best, Jules. Thank you so much."

As her slim, warm arms tightened around his narrow waist, Julian's entire frame stiffened as if she'd just zapped him. He was naked from the waist up, and he suddenly could feel Molly everywhere he didn't want to. Warm and smelling of sweet things.

Worst of all was that she snuggled in comfortably, turned her face into his neck and whispered, "You're the best part of my life, you know that, Jules? I never know how to thank you properly for everything you do."

Was she for real?

Because the ideas those words put into his head were so, so wrong, Julian could've shot himself.

He tried remembering his past lovers' names, in alphabetical order, but still could not relax a single inch until Molly extracted herself.

Letting go a long, long breath, he avoided her inquisitive gaze and grumbled, "Don't thank me yet, Molls. Let's just see how it goes, all right?"

"It'll go splendidly, Julian, I just know it. Before the month ends, I'll probably be wearing an engagement ring."

He rolled his eyes because he still could not even believe this was happening. "Well, let's not call the wedding planner yet, all right? Just remember that for this month, you're with me, and heads up, baby, the rest of my family isn't going to be too happy about it."

She frowned in puzzlement and planted her hands on her hips. "Why on earth not? Am I not good enough for you?"

"No, Molls. It's me." He turned to gaze sightlessly out the window as a heaviness settled painfully atop his chest. "They think I'm no good for you."

Two

"You're jerking me around, toad, I just know it!"

Julian leaned back in his swivel chair and suppressed a smile as he watched his brother pace across the state-of-the-art conference room on the top floor of the *San Antonio Daily,* a thriving business the Gage family had run since the 1930s.

"Brother," Julian tsked, "I realize I'm younger than you, but don't forget I *am* stronger and I *will* take you down if you keep pissing me off."

"So you're basically admitting that you're sleeping with our little Molls?"

"I never said that. I said we're dating and she's moving in with me." This last was something Julian hadn't discussed with Molly before, but it had suddenly seemed like a good idea. And when Garrett's complexion turned the color of a ripe cherry tomato, Julian knew he'd struck the jackpot.

Garrett was livid.

Julian and Molly had discussed some basic rules yesterday—like no dating anyone else, a good dose of PDA for show when around family and strangers, and how neither would ever, ever disclose to anyone that their romantic liaison had been fake. This seemed especially important to Molly, who seemed to think it of utmost importance to be convincing in their new "relationship."

Julian was right on board with that.

Hell, he was on board with anything that meant pushing Garrett's buttons.

Not that he had anything against the guy, except the fact that he was maybe too honorable for his own damned good, and ever since Landon, the eldest brother, had embarked on a much deserved sixty-day honeymoon, Garrett seemed to think he carried the weight of the world on his shoulders. Or at least, of the family business.

There was plenty of love among the three, yeah, but Julian had been planning to exact a special brotherly revenge on Garrett for a long. Long. Time.

A revenge made all the sweeter by the fact that Molly suddenly had it in her pretty head to get Garrett's *personal attention.*

Hell, Julian hadn't had a wink of sleep last night just thinking about it.

Now he took a moment to enjoy the fact that his brother's face was taut with displeasure, his knuckles jutting out as he gripped his coffee cup. He stopped his pacing and stood across from Julian at the conference table, where they'd just wrapped up a meeting with their top executives. "Since when are you two interested in each other?" Garrett demanded.

"Since we started sexting," Julian returned, unflinching. Then, before Garrett could ask more, Julian lifted his cell phone and read a message. "Damn, this girl turns me on." He pretended to text Molly back and took his sweet, sweet time about it. Though in reality he was just telling her:

He knows. Guy's going bananas. Tell you about it @ dinner.

Garrett shot him a murderous glare. "Does Kate know about this sexting/moving-in…relationship?"

"Probably, unless she's too busy catering for her next event. She is Molly's sister, after all."

Just then, Molly's response popped up:

No wonder Kate and Garrett get along so well.

Julian quickly typed in:

I suppose Kate no longer worships the ground I tread on?

Molly replied:

Affirmative. Be careful, lover. She has a spatula and she's not afraid to use it as a weapon.

Julian's lips curled in amusement. Ahh, Molly. Light of his life.

"So which part was it?"

Julian gazed blankly up at Garrett, who almost had steam coming out of his ears. "Which part was what?" he asked.

"Which part of what Mother, Landon and I have been telling you for, oh…say, two decades, did you not *get*? The part that Molly Devaney was *hands-off*? The part that you could be *disowned* if you harmed her in any way?"

Julian nodded to placate him. "I heard you all. I heard you the first time, the tenth time, the hundredth time and I hear you now. Now hear this, bro." He leaned forward across the conference table and scowled. "I don't. Freaking. Care. Do *you*...get *that*?"

Garrett clenched his jaw and drew in a breath that inflated his chest. The guy was so rankled, he was probably about a step away from banging his chest like Tarzan. "I'm going to have words with Molly, as I am sure it is in her best interests to reconsider this stupidity. Just know this, Julian...if you hurt her, if you so much as harm a hair on her head..."

He didn't know if it was the threat, or the possessive way Garrett was acting toward Molly or the simple fact that Molly fancied herself in love with the guy. Worse, he feared it might be due to the fact that Garrett wanted Molly for himself. But Julian's cool began to fade, and it took an inhuman effort to keep the mask on his face.

Suddenly transported back to his teenage years, he too easily remembered all those damned times he and Molly tried to get close. The special bond you forged with someone, one that is rare and precious and you'd be lucky to find in your lifetime—Julian had always had that with her. But every time their friendship threatened to develop into something more romantic, his family would panic and they'd swoop down like vultures to emotionally blackmail, harass and coerce him to keep them apart. More than once, he'd even been sent abroad for months, the first time apparently because Julian had been "looking" at Molly in a way that neither Kate, Landon, nor their mother—and especially not Garrett—had liked.

Julian had told himself time and again that he didn't care. And once he was an adult, they'd made him believe he was a playboy until he had no other choice but to play the part. He could have any woman—they always told him—except Kate or Molly. That was the rule.

And every year of his life, that single, simple rule had made him feel tied up, caged like a lion, and as unhappy as a penned-up bull.

Now the command from his brother to stay away from the only woman who truly knew him made a fresh surge of anger rise up from within him. No matter what Molly thought now, or what Garrett planned to do, this was Julian's future on the line—and he had been planning it for years. No one was going to mess with that future. Or with his red-haired, paint-streaked little gypsy girl. Or with him.

Especially when he intended to use this fake relationship with Molly to explore his very real feelings for her.

Quietly and with deliberate slowness, Julian rose to his feet, came around the table and set a hand on his brother's shoulder. Then he whispered, very mildly, but with an edge, "Stay out of this, Garrett. I don't want to hurt you, man, and I definitely don't want to hurt her. So just stay the hell out of this."

Then he grabbed his jacket, reclaimed his cool and stalked out of his office.

"I can't believe it. I really can't. I just know you're pulling my leg, Molly."

Propped up on a stool by the granite island in the Devaneys' kitchen while her sister decorated newly baked cookies, Molly focused on filing her nails, her stomach fluttering with excitement over this being her first night as Julian's fake girlfriend. She could hardly wait to see the expression on Garrett's dark, riveting face when he eventually saw them together. Hopefully, Julian would drape his arm around her shoulders in that aloof, sexy manner he had, in a way that said *she's my girl and aren't I the hottest ticket around?*

"I'm not pulling anything, I swear," Molly assured her. "You can totally call Julian and ask him."

Kate held up her spatula in the air, her auburn-red hair—the same shade as Molly's—haphazardly knotted atop her beautiful face. She exuded such raw sexiness while wearing that frilly white apron that Molly could've hated her if she didn't love her sister so utterly.

If there was one word to describe Kate Devaney, it would be *alive*. Kate thrived doing everything and anything, which explained the rocking success of her catering business; she was a killer cook with killer curves, tall and tanned and confident and fun.

The only thing Molly truly had that might surpass Kate in the looks department was her really nice bust, but then she went through so much effort to hide it, in the end it didn't amount to much of an advantage.

"Julian and *you?* Together? I just can't give credit to this. His girls are always so—"

"Don't say it or I'll hate you," Molly grumbled, smacking her nail file down.

Kate sighed, scooped up cookies from the baking sheet and began packaging them in single decorative cellophane wraps. "Fine. I won't say it. But you know what I mean, don't you?"

Molly stood and went to look at herself in the mirror by the foyer, trying not to remember how Julian's words had hurt her yesterday morning. "You're right, I know they don't look like me," she said as she ambled back with an expression of total displeasure on her face. "They're tall and sexy and sophisticated." *But I don't care because I don't want Julian, I want Garrett,* she reminded herself.

Her lips still burned with the memory of his scorching

kiss, the incredibly sexy rumble of him growling against her mouth, as if Molly's lips were something to suckle on and bite on and feast on...

Everything inside her turned hot, and Molly shook the images aside.

Kate looked at Molly and burst out laughing. "You've really fallen for him, haven't you? I love Julian, Molls, but even I admit that whoever marries him is a fool. And I don't want *you* to be that fool, Moo."

Molly was about to assure her she would never be so stupid as to fall for Julian John. She had never seen a man so determined to sleep with so many women in her life. It was as if he had an itch he needed to get scratched and none of them seemed to cut it for him. She was about to express all of this to Kate, but then she remembered she was *supposed* to be his girlfriend already—or yeah, his *lover,* since Julian was too worldly to have girlfriends— so she clamped her mouth shut and privately thanked her lucky stars that she truly had better sense than to become notch number 1,000,340 on the mysterious and uncatch-able Julian John Gage's bedpost.

Kate paused in her cookie wrapping and lifted two winged eyebrows in question. "So how did it happen? Did he just suddenly—?"

"Did I realize what a fool I've been not to finally admit little Molls is the one for me? Yeah. Exactly like that." The deep baritone that interrupted them startled Molly so much that her arms broke out in goose bumps.

She spun around as Julian shut the front door after him, and her stomach sank in mortification when she realized that once again he would find her in paint-splattered work clothes. Then she remembered she didn't care. This was Julian John and she didn't need to impress him. He already thought she looked like a by-product of a blender. Why ruin it for him?

But it seemed wholly unfair that she would be wearing paint marks up to her hair and he would look so clean and male and good. Black jacket slung over his shoulder, his burgundy Gucci tie almost undone, he looked sexily tousled and delicious. Not that Molly wanted a bite of him or anything, but she supposed another woman would. Hell, they all did.

But Molly had common sense in regards to him.

She mentally patted herself on the back once more while Julian stalked forward as if he owned the place, wearing that playful grin he'd given her ever since they were kids.

"Whatever Kate has said about me, Mopey, don't believe her. It's all due to the fact that she wanted me first." His strong arms coiled like a steel vise around her waist while that Beckham-blond head dipped toward hers.

Molly didn't see it coming. He moved too fast and had incredible strength, and she was only five feet tall and easily handled. Before she could even realize what was happening, Julian had already reeled her in, crushing her breasts against his rock-hard pecs as his mouth settled firmly over hers, expertly, perfectly, oh so hotly.

And ooh. *Oooh.* A tiny working part of her mind frantically screamed at her to push him away. The only one she should be kissing now was Garrett! But the fact was, Julian kissed like his brother. Except Julian tasted clean and minty and not of wine, and he kissed her as if he had all the time in the world.

Those silken playboy's lips pressed with painstaking gentleness against hers and moved so languorously that all her senses began to spin out of control. Molly became magnetized. *Hypnotized.* Almost transported to the night her entire world had flipped upside down, and she'd glanced down to find her heart had been stolen from her chest.

She wasn't even sure she was standing anymore, but trusted that Julian would always catch her fall. The sudden desperate urge to press closer to him flitted through her, burned through her being as he lingered in his kiss for a thrilling, electrifying second, and then he was gone. Leaving her dazed and surprised and scatterbrained as he set her away—thankfully keeping a steady hand on her elbow until she found her ground.

He said something once it was over. She thought it was hello.

Molly pushed her hair back, feeling dazed. "Uh—hi."

He asked her something, his voice huskier than usual, his eyes at half-mast, and she stared at his mouth. His soft yet strong lips became the center of her attention, for she wondered what exactly it was about those lips that had felt so incredibly good when he'd put them on hers.

Even her knees had taken a hit.

She fought to calm down, but remained so shaken she ended up snapping at him for catching her unaware. "What are you doing here, JJ?" she asked, glaring, using his old kiddie nickname just to punish him.

Julian remained aloof and calmly popped a cookie straight from the baking sheet into his mouth. "Nothing, pumpkin buns. Just wanted to check in on my girl." He strode over and squeezed her butt, whispering only for her ears, "JJ? You're going to pay for that, Molls."

She fake giggled so Kate wouldn't notice anything strange and pulled away, her buttocks aflame from his touch. How to get back at him? She said the first thing that came to mind when she caught Kate's confused expression. "JJ loves for me to call him all sorts of pet names when we're...you know," she told her.

"JJ?" Kate turned to Julian, hands on hips, spatula held like a sword. "I thought you absolutely loathed that nickname."

Julian shot Molly a warning look. "I do," he said, jaw square as a cutting board. "But little Molls calls me JJ exclusively when she wants me to spank her."

Molly's satisfaction in getting back at him vanished.

Her cheeks burst into flames. She wanted to die of embarrassment, for now her sister would forever believe her to be into that kind of kinky stuff.

"Baby, its barely afternoon and I still need to make myself sexy and sophisticated for you," she told him as she went around the kitchen and shot him a scowl from behind Kate's shoulders. "Not all of us come by it naturally. Now you'll have to wait for me a bit. I'm sure Kate and her spatula would love to keep you company, though."

He moved fluidly, nonplussed. "I have a better idea, bun-buns. Why don't I help you get dressed, hmm?" Before Molly could deny him, he'd followed her into her bedroom and locked them inside while Kate remained in the kitchen, no doubt still wide-eyed.

"Will you *puleeze* stop provoking me," Molly hissed, pushing him against the door. "Stop calling me bun-buns."

He leaned forward with gritted teeth. "Who's provoking who? You know I freaking hate JJ!"

"And don't you dare kiss me again without warning like you just did!"

"If you ever call me JJ again, I'm going to kiss you—with tongue. So *don't,* otherwise I'll think you *want* my tongue inside your mouth!"

He glared at her and she glared back, wishing that a stream of butterflies hadn't just migrated to her stomach. She couldn't help but wonder what Julian did with his loathed tongue that drove all women crazy, crazy, *crazy*....

"Are we clear about this, Molls?" he demanded, using his thumb and forefinger to tip her head back and force her to meet his gaze. She was appalled to realize she had apparently been staring dumbly at his mouth.

She nodded so that he would release her and swallowed, some rebel inside her wanting to test him and say: *Yes, JJ.*

Then she groaned and thrust him away. "Why, oh, why did you have to tell her you spanked me?" She shook her head and rubbed her temples in complete mortification.

"Because sometimes I swear to God you want me to." He swatted her butt and strolled to the closet, leaving her to grapple with incredibly strange and powerful emotions and an uncomfortably stinging butt.

"So." He yanked out a huge suitcase, turned back and cocked a devilish eyebrow at her. "I told the love of your life that you were moving in with me. What do you say about that, my little Picasso?"

"Was he jealous?"

That smile again. "About as close to banging his head on a wall as I've seen him."

Molly yanked her panty drawer open. "Then I'd be delighted."

Three

"So what else did the love of my life say?" Molly asked as they made a pit stop for food on their way back to Julian's place. He was always hungry. It seemed that his muscles needed a lot of glucose, all the time. The man had a friends group for every sport he participated in: soccer, basketball, kayaks, zip-lining, even the more extreme hang-gliding gigs.

Those hard, taut muscles on his arms and legs and abs and the magnificent golden hue of his skin obviously didn't come from being in an office all day.

He was so lean, he could probably tackle a decathlon as easily as he tackled women in bed…. Hmm, she wondered if Garrett would soon tackle *her* in bed.

"Wait here," he said as he slid his silver Aston Martin into the only vacant parking slot in front of a frozen yogurt chain.

"Hey will you get me an Oreo milk shake with—"

"Three cherries on top—one for chewing, one for sucking and one to leave at the bottom?"

Molly grinned and nodded, and she could still hear his rumbling chuckle even after he'd closed the door.

Minutes later, he returned, and she found herself scowling down at her milk shake. "Why is there a phone number written on my milk shake cup?"

With an easy flick of his wrist, he turned the key and his car engine roared back to life.

"Julian!"

He flung his hands up in exasperation. "I didn't ask for it, Molls."

She shook her head in distaste. But then, could she blame the cashier or whoever had scrambled to write her hopes on Molly's milk shake? Julian was graced with both a face and body that made women gape, stammer and stutter—then behave like twits. That was a fact. And there was nothing Molly—or even Julian—could do about it.

Still, it rankled, and Molly kept shaking her head. "Honestly. I have no idea who in their right mind would hook up with you."

He shifted sideways and put the car in Reverse, then reached out and chucked her chin. "Apparently *you*."

Molly laughed and started chewing her first cherry. "You haven't told me what the love of my life has to say about me—his one true love—hanging out with the likes of you."

Julian turned the wheel, shifted gears and sped onto the highway. "He mentioned guns. At dawn."

Molly sucked on her second cherry. "Just please don't make me a widow before I even marry him."

"*Marry.* Whoa. Now there's a big word."

"There's nothing wrong with the word *marriage*."

"I said it was a big word."

She stopped sucking on her cherry and stared at him in suspicion, pushing the cherry to one side of her mouth as she talked. "And please don't tell me when you said guns you were talking about your biceps again?"

He just smiled that sexy smile. As if he knew a secret Molly didn't. Or as if he'd seen her naked without her knowledge. *Oops, where did that thought come from?*

Her stomach jittered all of a sudden, and she figured she might be cold. It had started raining when they loaded up her suitcases, and now her clothes were soaked and clinging to her skin. Which was unfortunate, because she'd changed into something Julian might even consider sexy and sophisticated. Not because she cared what he thought, but just to prove to him that Molly Devaney had money of her own, had success on her own and only dressed comfortably because she believed inner beauty was more important than material stuff.

Now as she contemplated her soggy outfit, she didn't know if her goose bumps were due to her wet tank or the cold milk shake or excitement.

Julian became pensive as he drove, but that was fine with her. Molly chattered on in her excitement about how she was going to get Garrett, how she could use one of Julian's spare bedrooms if she felt suddenly inspired and had to paint… She *did* have an exhibition soon and needed to finish two more pieces within the next month.

When they arrived at his apartment building, he asked her if he could show her something and Molly nodded eagerly. Eduardo, one of the doormen, took charge of delivering her bags to the twelfth floor while Julian guided her to another elevator and pressed P. They were carried up to the penthouse.

What greeted them when the elevator doors opened was an enormous white space, with floor-to-ceiling win-

dows in every corner and the smell of fresh paint lingering in the air.

"Wow. What is this?"

He met her gaze, and she was mesmerized by the proud
gleam in his eyes, could even hear the pride in his gruff
voice. "These just so happen to be my future offices."

Molly's eyes rounded in surprise. "You—what do you
mean? Is the *Daily* moving from downtown?"

The Gage family owned the most thriving and successful newspaper conglomerate in all of Texas, which included several print publications, internet news sites and
some cable-TV channels, all working under the umbrella
of their first paper, the *San Antonio Daily*. It was a business of three generations and one that gave the family immense wealth and untold power. Their offices occupied an
entire block downtown, so Molly couldn't quite believe the
move would be so easy.

A second passed before Julian answered, and it was as
though he was selecting his words carefully. "No. I'm the
only one moving out, Molls."

Molly stared at his somber expression, loud warning
bells chiming in her head. She immediately sensed this
development was not a positive thing for the family. "Do
your brothers know about this, Jules?" she asked, treading cautiously.

"They will."

Molly took a couple of minutes to digest this shock-
ing news. Her stomach did weird things at the thought
of drama within the family, which had always seemed
to revolve around Julian and his rebel ways. She still remembered each one of the times he'd been sent abroad for
who knew what kinds of wrongdoing. Molly had missed
her friend terribly, like she'd miss a thumb or an arm or

a crucial and important part of her. All she remembered about those wretched months was that she'd cried. A lot.

Now she watched him move lithely across his new office area, easily stepping over plastic tarps while he surveyed the electrical wires that stuck out from the scattered pillars, and she wondered why he'd want to bail out on the family's extremely successful newspaper and publishing business.

As the head of PR and chief of advertising for the company, Julian had the best part of the pie, in her humble opinion. He had the same whopping salary, just as many shares in the company as his brothers but the fewest responsibilities, which allowed him to have the most fun, the most women and the most time for hobbies like flying that Cessna plane he so loved and doing all the sports he enjoyed. Why would he leave the *San Antonio Daily?*

"I had no idea you were unhappy where you were," she said as she caught up with him, searching his face.

He stared out the wide windows and the sunlight caught a dozen golden flecks in his green eyes. "I'm dissatisfied with my life, though not necessarily unhappy. A change was in order."

Her heart clenched with a strange emotion; she supposed it might be disappointment, for she'd believed they were close enough for him to share this important information with her sooner. As in, before he signed the lease for the penthouse. But then Julian was very reserved with his emotions, which was why people thought he had none. "So…" She walked through the space with him, taking in each new desk waiting for its worker. "How long have you been planning this?"

She wanted to know more but also knew Julian disliked being pushed too far, and she sensed that this was all she would get for now.

"A couple of years. Maybe my whole life."

He smiled down at her, a truly honest and content smile, and captivated by it, she returned it in kind, was helpless not to. But while a part of her wanted to clap and say *good for you!* there was another part, the one that was also loyal to the entire Gage family, that wished he'd reconsider. For Molly's entire life, she'd sided with Julian about everything, anytime and anywhere, yet now she felt torn. Because she'd given her heart to Garrett two weeks ago and knew for certain that she'd never get it back. And she knew Garrett would fight tooth and claw to keep Julian in the business.

He was one of their greatest assets and the only Gage brother cocky enough to neither worry nor care about appearances. His suave manner and mysterious ways seemed to both annoy and charm the competition, and made him the best PR person in the state. Molly doubted the *Daily* would have even half the amount of advertisers it did when Julian no longer had a hand in reeling them in. Maybe he would reconsider in due time?

Continuing their stroll with a sigh, she nearly bumped into a blank wall. "All this white space could use something, you know," she suddenly said aloud.

From a few feet away, Julian chuckled, and the husky sound created a compelling echo in the wide-open room. "Now, why did I know you were going to say that?" he asked as he came over.

She grinned and wrinkled her nose at him. "Maybe because I don't like blank walls and you've known this for twenty years or more."

Stopping just an arm's length away, he smoothed the wrinkle in her nose with one lone fingertip. "Then make a mural for me. This entire wall—make it yours."

Molly held his penetrating stare, her nose itching where

he'd touched it. As the wheels in her head started spinning, she turned to the wall and found that her muse had already jumped with an idea. "Are you high? My individual paintings already command five-figure prices. A mural would run at least 150,000 and it would take me months. I need to talk to my gallerist."

Her gallerist had once represented Warhol and he was the savviest art dealer around, selling the craziest, most daring and contemporary art in the world. He was also Julian's friend.

"Leave Blackstone out of it. A hundred and fifty it is."

She gasped. "Jules, I can't charge you that, it feels like I'm robbing my best friend."

"Then it should be fun. A hundred-fifty K, Molls, but make it real pretty for me. As pretty as you." His smile flashed charmingly, and a bucket of excitement settled in Molly's stomach until she could hardly stand it. She didn't know if it was due to the fabulous deal she'd just closed or to being called pretty for once without it being accompanied by an insult to her clothes attached. Perhaps it was both.

"Of course, Jules!" Pulling herself up by grabbing onto the collar of his shirt, she quickly kissed his hard jaw, then wished she hadn't, because he totally stiffened. "Thanks. When can I start?"

He spun for the elevator and cranked his neck as though it had cramped on him. "Tomorrow if you'd like," he said.

Molly floated in a cloud of bliss as she followed him. Had she really just landed an enormous work space just upstairs for the time being?

Had she just been commissioned for her first *mural?*

She could hardly believe her good fortune, although she'd always enjoyed a certain share of luck when it came to her art. The sudden interest from a top New York gallery a couple of years before had placed her works in several important collectors' homes, and before she knew it her name was being piled up next to contemporary artists like David Salle and Sean Scully; big, big, *big* names in the art world. Now for the first time in her twenty-three years, maybe some of that creative luck would rub off on her sadly lacking love life. Maybe she was close to getting what she wanted with Garrett.

Thanks to Julian, for sure.

Because she'd suddenly realized that, just as her canvases did not miraculously paint themselves, her love life wouldn't happen without some encouragement. And that was where Julian's help making Garrett jealous fit in.

Once back in Julian's spacious apartment, Molly chose the guest bedroom to the left of his room, a space done in a pastel blue-and-green palette that she'd always found soothing. She retrieved her night creams, day creams, moisturizing creams, shampoos and toothbrush and aligned them all on the sink, then peeled out of her still-damp clothes, showered and slipped into her sleep shirt, which was actually an old T-shirt Julian had used in high school and his mother had sent to the Donation Station. Nobody knew Molly had fished this shirt out of the garbage bag for being the softest and most worn, and Julian would hardly remember he'd ever owned it.

Once ready for bed, she went out in the hall to look for him and hoped to propose they watch a movie, but his bedroom door was closed. Disappointment crept in, so then she went to bed and lay there, gazing at the walls, the curtains and the ceiling fan for hours.

Sleep eluded her, and her thoughts kept drifting toward Garrett. His black hair, those onyx eyes with the sooty lashes, and *oh, God,* the way he'd kissed her two weeks ago. She remembered that kiss so perfectly that she'd been reliving it nightly, in bed, as she futilely tried to fall asleep.

"I think I'd like to be a spinster," Molly had told Kate that evening as they stood out on the terrace of the Gage mansion, gazing into the brightly lit masquerade party transpiring inside the sprawling 10,000-square-foot home.

Kate had obviously laughed. "Molls. Why on earth would you say that?" She'd lovingly tousled her hair, which Molly had worn loose for the evening. "You're beautiful and sweet and any man would be lucky to have you."

"It's just that no man seems to live up to my expectations."

With a dreary sigh, Molly showed Kate the picture of the three Gage brothers she carried in her iPhone. It featured the gray-eyed, responsible Landon, the dark-haired, honorable Garrett and of course the sex god playboy, Julian. As her favorite Gage brother, Julian was everything that a good husband was *not*.

"I know what you mean," Kate said softly, staring longingly at the picture.

It couldn't have been easy for her to play both mother and father to Molly while she herself had been barely a teen. Although Eleanor Gage had been a stand-in mother for both of them, she was a stern woman, and as one did when running on survival instincts, both girls had tried to put on their best behavior and their whitest smiles with the person who'd given them food and shelter. But when alone, Molly would seek out Kate's warmth and support like she'd seek out a pillow and blanket. Especially during those lonely times when Julian had been sent away. Sometimes Molly even wondered if she wasn't to blame for Kate's lack of a love life, a husband and a family of her own. The thought made her stomach feel heavy.

"You deserve someone, too," Molly whispered.

Kate smiled brightly and winked at her. "Then let's go find one," she teased and rushed for the double doors that led inside, but Molly groaned and stayed back, loathing her stupid costume.

She had been dared by Julian to dress as a tavern wench tonight. And of course he knew Molly could never ignore a dare that he delivered. Alas, now here she was. In an outfit so tight she was barely able to breathe, which showcased her breasts in a way that made her feel as if she'd just stepped out of a porn magazine.

She had never felt so exposed in her life, and as soon as she saw Julian, probably dressed like some evil creature, for sure, Molly was going to tell him off for being such a cad. "I'll catch up in a sec," she lied to Kate before her sister disappeared inside.

Instead of following, she edged farther out on the terrace, where it was dark and the air was fresh from the gardens and nobody would see her in her corseted wench costume.

A silhouette by the banister caught her attention.

Someone was coming toward her. Zorro? she wondered. Or was it the Phantom of the Opera? Or maybe it was Westley, the dangerously sexy man from Molly's favorite movie, *The Princess Bride.*

Whoever he was, he was hot. Clad all in black: black cape, a cloth mask covering both his hair and the upper part of his face. Black boots. And that smile. It just had to be Julian. Nobody smiled like Julian. He smiled like a wolf and made you want to be the lamb he was going to eat; it was very, very bizarre how he pulled that off.

She suddenly caught his glimmering eyes straying to her prominent cleavage and she felt something hot coil inside her belly.

"Well, well, well..." he murmured as he continued to approach.

His voice was thick and slurred, and she wondered how much he'd drunk tonight. He didn't sound like himself at all.

He smiled again and her stomach tightened under his appreciation.

He had a drink in his hand, and when he raised it to his lips, watching her with those eerily sparkling eyes, she noticed that his glass was empty. He cursed under his breath, shook his head and swung around to leave, murmuring something about being crazy.

She frowned when she realized she would not be getting to tell him off just yet. "You're going to leave me all alone out here?" she playfully called after him.

He paused for a moment, then turned, set the cup aside, and started for her with sudden purpose. With each long, determined stride, he dived deeper into the shadows Molly had been trying to hide herself in.

He was not smiling now. Something in his approach, in the tension in his shoulders, made her heart begin to pound. And pound faster. Faster. The way he moved, the way he frightened her...

It couldn't possibly, possibly, be Julian. She began, "What—?"

He pulled her up against him, so fast that her lips flew open and she sucked in a shocked mouthful of air. In one fluid move, he pinned her hands at her sides, then bent his face to hers, mask to mask. Molly had stopped breathing.

It was too dark to make out this stranger's eye color, but she could still sense that gaze like a laser beam boring into her being. Her heart faltered when he made a sound, low and completely unrecognizable—a rumbling groan that was so hot and so male her toes curled.

His lips touched hers. The lightest of touches. Just a graze. Like the tiny spark that sets loose a wildfire. And Molly exploded with a rush of wanting so powerful it scorched every inch of her insides, infusing every particle of her being with heat.

Her lips opened as though on their own, and her body melted under his as a strange, embarrassing little moan escaped her. He seemed to like it, for his answering growl vibrated in her mouth as his lips latched firmly over hers.

He kissed her so possessively, a tornado of pleasure shot through her veins and her heartbeat skyrocketed to the ozone layer. His fingers bit into her buttocks as he dragged her up against him. Closer. Closest. Thrusting his tongue into her mouth with a groan of pleasure.

She tasted wine and immediately felt drunk on him. High on him. Wild for him. She was lost to a staggering rush of sensations as their mouths devoured each other with wet, greedy licks and suckles, her skin screaming with delicious agony as his hand stroked up her arms, caressing her. She had never felt so alive, so connected to another human being, as though her body were an extension of his larger, stronger one.

It was like being caught in a deluge of rain, and now she could feel his desire pour over her. Swimming in sensations, she felt the warm metal of a ring sliding up as he stroked her shoulders, and her eyes jerked open when she realized this man kissing her, this man was…

Garrett?

How could it be?

He rarely put so much as a finger on her, he was so protective. Julian was always pawing her and she loved the little ways his touch made her feel. But while Garrett rarely reached out for her, when he did, Molly always felt this thick, smooth ring anywhere he put his hand. When

he grasped her hand in his—ring. When he petted the top
of her head—ring. When he secured her elbow to keep her
from falling—aha. Ring.

Now Garrett was kissing her as if he was eating her
alive, his ring almost like a brand across her skin as his
hand greedily stroked her shoulders, then suddenly her
throat, down her collarbone, to the top swell of her breast,
tracing the shape of her.

He mumbled something, but she could hardly hear him
through the roaring of her own heartbeat, his voice sounding alien and lust-roughened as he fiercely bent down to
lick the exposed skin.

Rocked with the realization that this man, untouchable
to her like all the Gages had been for her entire life, had
thrown all caution to the wind and was kissing her as if
his life depended on it left her knees in such a weakened
state that she clung to him even while she tried to edge
back to steal a quick peek at his ring.

The platinum band glinted in the shadows as he fondled
her breasts, and yes, it was the same one-of-a-kind ring
Garrett always wore, with a blue diamond at its center.

It *was* Garrett fondling her shamelessly.

And it felt so good, his touch so arousing, a rush of
liquid heat flooded her between her thighs.

He groaned in misery when she went still with shock,
yet he pulled her tighter against him anyway, as though
her lips were powerful magnets for his. "Shh," she heard
him say, cooing to her, calming her as if she were both
precious and wild. "Shh…"

When he edged his knee between her legs to part them,
the skirt of her dress rose, and he expertly eased his hand
through the layers of fabric to cup her between her legs,
right where she'd grown wet for him. The heat of his palm
burned through her panties, and her bones seemed to dis-

integrate into nothing. Nothing but heat and pleasure and sensation.

"Oh," she gasped, body tensing as his fingers began stroking in slow, lazy circles, her head exploding in disbelief and excitement as a rush of hot lightning coursed through her.

His touch consumed her.

He touched her as if he owned her. As if he *knew* and *cherished* everything about her.

She'd never known she could respond like this to another human being.

She'd tried never to feel anything romantic for any of these Gage men—because they were her protectors and Kate said they were like their brothers and were therefore unavailable. But this one…this one wanted her and clearly didn't give one whit about what Kate said. What anyone said. And Molly hadn't realized she wanted him back so much until this very moment, when she was melting in his arms in a way she had never, ever imagined.

Needy sounds bubbled up in her throat as she rocked her hips against him, helpless to stop herself, her body a puppet to masterful hands that continued expertly stroking her. The sensations were so powerful she whimpered in mingled fear and longing, her insides coiling tightly like springs.

He groaned and bent his head to her ear, biting the lobe hungrily, desperately, those gut-wrenchingly sexy noises from his throat shooting arrows of heat to her nerve endings. His hungry mouth traveled all over her neck, leaving a wet path that sizzled as he pressed the heel of his palm seductively between her legs, rubbing and stroking exactly the parts that most ached and hurt and burned.

And then the worst part was that, with one more expert touch, one firm press with the heel of his hand, she'd exploded.

Molly still remembered the way she had trembled with that touch alone, and then she had wanted to cry, because she'd never had an orgasm before. Embarrassed to her core, she'd pushed him away as soon as she was able and gritted, "Don't touch me. Don't even talk to me! This never happened—never!"

And she'd yanked off her stupid mask, flung it aside and left.

The next day, Garrett had pretended that nothing happened, just as she'd told him to. And when she'd gone to talk to Julian about it, he'd been too hung over to focus and in a pissy mood. So she'd kept it to herself for over a dozen nights, her sexual siren having been awakened, now hungry for more and determined to do something about it. Once again, Molly wanted to weep in her bed in silence.

She wished she hadn't kissed him.

She wished she hadn't stopped.

She wished she hadn't pushed him away.

She wished she'd had the courage to face the music, so that he would have done the same.

But more than anything, she wished to feel again like she'd felt that night.

Garrett had broken down and revealed his feelings for her in an unmistakable way, and though Molly had gloried in his intimate touch and his incredible kiss, she'd gotten scared in the end.

She wished she hadn't given out the message that she wasn't receptive to more of his delicious kisses and touches. Because the more she thought of and relived that kiss, the more she was convinced that unique connection wasn't typical and that she'd just found her *soul mate*.

Without words, she'd been able to feel his love so powerfully that her own heart had sung inside her chest, and she ached desperately to be with him again.

Swallowing back a lump in her throat, she pounded the pillow and shifted to lie facedown on the bed. *Go to sleep, Molly, and tomorrow you can show Garrett what he's missing.*

But rather than give her comfort, the thought only made her realize that the one person who had been missing out on the best things in life was Molly.

Julian knew exactly why he couldn't sleep, why he was feeling so cranky and why everything felt like crap lately.

It was all Molly Devaney's fault.

She was driving him crazy in every possible way he could imagine.

First with the Garrett thing. And now just thinking about her sleeping next door made him toss restlessly in bed, frustrated beyond measure.

Tonight, it had been raining outside when they loaded up her suitcases. By the time Molly had stepped into his apartment, she'd looked so…wet. God, he'd really tried not to look at the way she needed to peel her shirt back from her breasts, but he lacked the willpower.

Lying back in his bed, he tried to cool down his roiling blood, his head swimming with the sight of her breasts, perfectly round, with those pointy nipples straining against the fabric of her top.

And when she'd kissed him upstairs, so happy to be painting the mural for him, it had taken all his willpower not to turn his face and capture that kiss with his lips, kiss her long and hard as if he'd wanted to back in her apartment—where she'd been flushed and gasping for breath after the silly little peck he'd given her. And those cherries. Goddamn the sounds she made as she ate those miserable cherries!

It had been a miracle Julian hadn't lunged across the seat of his car, taken her face between his hands and suckled each and every cherry from her cool and sassy mouth.

Hell, this is the worst idea I've ever had in my life.

For years, Julian had grown up with rules that he'd tried to follow, knowing the only girl he'd ever respected and admired was out of his reach. Molly was the one woman Julian would want to be locked in a closet with. Stranded on a deserted island with. She was the only good and pure thing in his life, and despite some failed efforts, he'd tried to keep it that way. Unsullied and unsoiled, happy and protected.

Growing up, he'd always imagined they would have each other. Molly had never liked to date, and she'd always needed Julian. Julian had kept his hands off her and *on* just about anyone else in his efforts to keep busy, stay focused and more importantly, stay away from Molly.

But now—she wanted Garrett.

A Gage.

Julian's stomach roiled with nausea at the reminder. God. He'd never imagined this could ever happen.

At first, he'd thought she was pulling his leg, or trying to make *him* jealous. In the back of his mind, he'd always imagined that if Molly ever fell in love with one of the Gage brothers, it would be…him. Dammit, him and *only* him. Because she sure as hell never seemed to look at anyone else.

Even his family had thought Molly wanted him, which was why every time he got close to Molly, all hell would break loose. His mother, Landon, Garrett, even Kate would pounce. Julian had suffered endless lectures from them all about being good to Molly, staying away from Molly, respecting Molly or finding another home. For the most part, he had been good. Really good.

But now, years and what felt like aeons later, the fact that Molly wanted his brother was a game changer. Julian had been living in this hell long enough, and he could no longer kid himself that the magic, the pull, the impossible chemistry between Molly and him was only due to friendship. He knew full well that when she made his groin throb with her smiles, they were not friendly feelings. Much less brotherly ones.

He'd been dreaming about her for *years*. Powerful dreams. Sexual dreams. Dreams that left him drenched in sweat and groaning in pain and reaching for the first pair of female legs that passed him.

Yeah, he'd thought if he'd had sex more often, his powerful reactions to her would diminish. But all it did was make him want her more—because none of those women were Molly.

No. *No one* could ever even compare to that effervescent little bombshell—no one.

Now he just needed to play his game right. Julian might have a long comfortable fuse where his temper was concerned, but when it came to Molly, his fuse had run damn short. If she kept this up he was going to do something reckless and stupid.

And he didn't want to be reckless and stupid.

He'd been moving his pieces all in the direction of one goal so he could stake his claim on her once and for all.

Now he'd prove to his family that he did not need them, and that he would never hurt a single hair on Molly's beautiful head. He needed them to see that he was worthy of her, that he wanted her for real and not just for sex—though of course when that happened, it was going to be damned amazing, too. But more importantly, he needed to show them that he would do whatever it took to have her. Even cut his ties with them *all*.

If Molly was ever going to settle down with a guy, she was settling down with Julian. Whether they liked it or not.

And as for Molly...

He had to make her see that *he* was the man for her and always had been—and once and for all, he had to finish what he'd started the night he'd kissed her heart out at the masquerade party.

Four

Something about sleeping in Julian's apartment made Molly restless.

Well past midnight, still tortured by the memory of Garrett's kiss, she found herself tiptoeing down the hall toward the kitchen in the hopes of finding some sort of sleep aid in his cupboards. She had her heart set on Sleepytime Tea, but valerian root or chamomile would do, too. Hey, at this point, she'd take anything as long as it meant quieting her troubled brain and getting some rest.

But what she found on her way to the cupboards was a beautifully sculpted, seminaked man instead—and the sight of him was sure to give her permanent insomnia.

Wearing only a pair of white cotton briefs that hugged his buttocks perfectly, he leaned against the open refrigerator door, his head stuck inside as he surveyed the food.

Molly stopped in her tracks, her heart flying to her throat.

The warm fridge light silhouetted Julian's magnificent form, shamelessly caressing every dent, every shadow and every sharp rise of lean, ripped muscle. Her breasts pricked unexpectedly. And suddenly he was not just Julian.

He was every inch…Julian John Gage.

Sexy playboy, dangerous male.

Not a hero, not harmless and definitely not just a friend.

A tremor rushed down her legs as her eyes helplessly drank up what was so blatantly on display, aided by the moonlight that filtered through the windows; she took in the sinewy arm folded above his head as he leaned forward, the broad muscled back, the lean hips and…the rest. His long, muscled calves and hamstrings, his hard buttocks under that snug white cotton.

Her temperature skyrocketed. Not because he was utterly sexy in a way that made her want to swim in ice right now, but because she was here. With him. At midnight. And he was about 90 percent *naked*. When it should be Garrett here, Garrett almost naked, Garrett in her head.

Her hormones clearly knew nothing of reason. They burst into action until she could feel the hot little pinpricks all over her body, to her utter confusion and despair.

Even her fingers tingled at her sides with a painful itch to trace the muscles on his back, determine the texture, the hardness, paint the thick ropes straining in his forearms. For a wild moment she kidded herself that it was the artist in her; it had to be. For she felt the same fever she did when she was gripped with the need to paint.

Except now she was gripped with the need to trace the length of Julian John.

With finger paint. All of him. She thought wildly that if he were a canvas, she would not leave an inch of him unpainted except his lips. He was just too masculine to wear them any way but bare.

But she could still trace them with her fingertips and find out what sort of power they held when they kissed her. She could explore the thick bottom one and then the top one and she might even kiss them again just to be sure her memory wasn't failing her...

Molly, you love Garrett, you tramp!

Shocked by the untoward thoughts, she snapped back to the present and swallowed a lump in her throat. An awful guilt surfaced inside her. Had she actually been thinking of accosting Julian in his own kitchen? What was wrong with her?

Ever since that evening at the masquerade, it felt as if her entire life had been flipped over as easily as a pancake.

Now she could not stop thinking about kissing, touching, tasting, wanting. Garrett had awakened the desperate needs of a woman inside her, and Molly felt so hyperaware of her body now, even her reactions to Julian were uncommonly, embarrassingly...unsettling.

See what you've done to me, Garrett? Apparently I'm a nymphomaniac now.

"Um. Did you forget you have a guest here?" she blurted out from her spot a few feet away.

Julian's shoulders stiffened almost imperceptibly. His head dropped an inch or so, that gorgeous mane with sun-streaked strands that were lighter than the others. "Damn—you're supposed to be asleep, Molls." He pulled his head out of the fridge, his chin dropping an inch or so as he faced her, his hair catching the light just right.

"People with insomnia don't sleep, Jules."

Molly should go back to her bedroom, she supposed, but being squeamish about a man's near-nakedness did not go with her artistic persona. She had to treat it as a natural state of being, or at least that was what she told herself as she woodenly walked over and opened and shut cabinet doors in search of her tea.

"Here, have some milk, always works for me." He shoved the carton he'd just drunk from in her direction.

Molly took it and set her lips over the place his mouth had been, trying not to get too hooked on that discomforting detail as she downed a big gulp. Swallowing, she said, "Ah, it's cold," and handed it back, all her efforts focused solely on not noticing how velvety smooth and hairless his massive chest was.

She had never felt five feet tall when she was with Julian until today. When he seemed to hulk over her, appearing for the first time in her life almost…threatening. Extremely male.

"I'm going back to bed," he said, shoving the milk back into the fridge and shutting the door.

"Can I come sleep with you?" Molly blurted out to his retreating back.

Suddenly she just knew if she went back to sleep alone in her room, she would be haunted. By her masked man. And by Julian in sexy white cotton briefs. She desperately wanted to watch a movie with him and snuggle and sleep and get her best friend back. She ached for him to make her feel…safe. Like when they were kids.

"No," he answered without a single backward glance.

"Don't be a jackass, Jules."

"I don't sleep with women I can't take to bed," he yelled back.

"I'm not women. I'm just *me*."

"Precisely."

She scowled and said, "Just put some pants on and I'll bring my pillow. Come on, don't be mean."

She heard silence, then receding footsteps down the hall.

"Julian?" she called back tentatively.

His laugh made her hope for a moment, but then he spoke. "Good night, Molls!"

And so Molly cursed him all the way to her room, climbed alone into her bed and didn't sleep a wink.

She didn't fare so well on the second night, or on the third, either. Even though she tried every night to get him to invite her for a sleepover, the man's will was iron. She was surprised she couldn't bend him to her plea at all, but she was more surprised by the amount of effort Garrett had been putting into stopping her from getting into a "relationship" with Julian. Which amounted to zero so far.

That was not the approach of a man in love!

Then again, Garrett had always been the most hard-headed of the three, so he'd probably need extra incentives in order to react to her provocations.

Molly fantasized about the sexy clothing she could wear to catch his attention. She was growing so desperate, she even imagined pulling out that stupid wench costume again—but what sane person wore that? Nobody, that was who. Only Molly Devaney on a *dare* from *Julian*.

By the sixth night and seventh morning at Julian's, Molly decided she was being tortured. Cranky from lack of sleep and out of sorts from painting all night, she began to wonder if she might have taken too deep of a plunge into this whole "relationship." She'd barely even seen Garrett, much less talked to him, yet oh, boy, she'd been seeing plenty of Julian John.

Of course seeing him seminaked in the kitchen that first night took the gold.

But the close silver went to the times when he had breakfast in those linen drawstring pants that drove her crazy. He had several in different colors, and when the sunlight hit them at just the right angle, she could almost see through them. It was torture trying *not* to.

Like having an open chocolate bar stare back at you for hours and trying not to eat it. It was *crazy.*

And then watching all those bare shoulders and biceps and triceps and lats and traps and pecs and all that hairless tanned skin moving and flexing as he had breakfast nearly catapulted her to internal combustion. He was just too…defined. His virility too overwhelming to endure when she'd had no sleep.

But on the other hand, the bantering between them was wonderful.

Julian usually read the paper while Molly eyed all the junk mail, and this morning he'd accused her of being the only person he knew who actually enjoyed reading it. They'd laughed about that, among other stuff. And yet there were also moments that felt…serious. Too serious.

Every time Molly rose for more coffee, she caught Julian staring at her bare legs that peeked from under her long T-shirt. She had never in her life been more self-conscious of her walk until she came back to the table with his smooth green eyes admiring her every step. To cover up her awkwardness, she'd blurt out a silly question and Julian would jerk his gaze back to her face, asking a distracted, "What?" as if he had not even heard her.

It was not like him at all; he was usually as sharp as a tack.

Today, his teasing had continued as he drove her to her old place. Once again he mentioned her clothes. But this time his remarks had felt strangely…intimate.

He didn't exactly say her flowered sundress came from her "blender" collection, he merely said, eyes glinting in mirth, "You almost look naked without a single paint mark on you."

Naked.

Molly still wondered why her stomach had twisted like a pretzel at the word, but just the prospect of him seeing her naked made her head spin wildly. Now she waved goodbye to Julian from her front door as his Aston Martin rolled around the curve, a dazed smile lingering on her lips.

She'd promised to catch a ride home with Kate later today, once she managed to pack more of her paint supplies and found herself a dress to wear to tonight's event, a small housewarming for Landon and his wife, Beth. Although the couple had been married for two years, they'd never really taken the time to honeymoon until now. At first, they'd married because it suited Landon's business purposes and would help Beth could regain custody of her son, David. But soon they'd fallen madly in love. Now their turbulent waters had calmed and they had one of the most loving marriages Molly had ever seen.

This was the first time Julian and Molly would face all the Gages at once.

The first time they would face Garrett and make him realize he was an *idiot* for letting Molly go.

And suddenly, sexy and sophisticated wouldn't do.

Suddenly it was *crucial* that Molly look *stunning*.

Using the key neatly hidden in the potted fern outside her door, she quickly entered the apartment to the aroma of baking: cinnamon, cardamom and every scent she associated with home.

Her heart swelled at the sight of their nice, tidy place looking cozy as usual. It was prime-time girly, scattered with lacy pillows and throws on the couches and colorful accessories. Even Molly's old teddy bear sat contentedly under a Tiffany lamp.

After sequestering herself for days in an ultramasculine bachelor pad, the feminine vibe in their small one-story home appealed to her. Right then, she decided to take some of her pink pillows to Julian's place. She needed to make herself more at home if she was going to be there for a while, plus she definitely planned to stock up his cupboards with her beloved Sleepytime Tea.

"Okay, what is going on with you?"

Molly spun around to find Kate standing in the kitchen archway, her red hair tied in a ponytail, a frilly apron around her waist and a what-in-the-world expression on her face.

People used to say Kate had so much energy the sun would burn out before she did. They were right; she was always doing something.

"I just came for some more clothes. Julian's car is so impractical a kid can fit more stuff in a bike basket, I swear," Molly said.

When Kate's expression didn't soften, Molly went to the kitchen to give her a hug, which might have been easier if Kate wasn't holding a bowl.

"I can smell something's cooking, Molly. I'm like your mother and sister and father all in one."

"And *I* smell cinnamon."

Molly peeked at all the yummy offerings on the kitchen island and selected several muffins to take to Julian. She shoved them into a brown paper bag and rolled it closed with a lot of noise.

"Aww, you always do this to me," Kate said, exasperated, setting down her bowl with a plunk. "Those muffins happen to be for Landon and Beth's welcome-back party, Moo. I'll bake some for you tomorrow, okay?"

"Fine," Molly grumbled. Already halfway to her room, she retraced her path to where her sister stood and handed her the paper bag. Instead of leaving, though, she stared into eyes that were clear and blue and almost identical to hers.

Her chest felt so heavy today, she just ached to be truthful with her sister.

They'd always been close with each other. As tight as two people who were left alone in the world could possibly be. But both of them were creatively inclined and tended to disappear into their own private bubbles of imagination half the time. Molly had been known to spend months locked away, painting away her restlessness. Kate cooked her heart out as well so that by the end of the day they were both too tired to even remember that they had lives outside their jobs, jobs which also happened to be their hobbies.

Kate had always been there for Molly, a shoulder to lean on, always supportive but not suffocating. But rarely in all these years had they actually discussed men. Or the strange feelings a woman might have toward them.

It was as though they both tried to pretend men did not exist in their lives. Or maybe just pretend that, other than their wonderful relationship with the Gages, they didn't need any man *at all*.

Molly had been perfectly content with that pretense because she had Julian John's friendship. And he counted for a hundred men. So she'd never felt she lacked any male attention at all.

Until that one night, when *his brother* had made her feel *wanted*.

Until that one night when she'd been kissed and fondled until she'd burst. Literally.

Now Molly couldn't seem to stop craving that extra spark in her life. That wonderful feeling she'd felt as those hot lips, those expert hands, had reminded her she was a living, breathing woman who deserved a man's love. Because why the hell not?

But how to inform Kate of her masquerade escapade with one brother when she was now supposed to be the other's lover?

Molly just couldn't talk about Garrett yet. It was still impossible to mention that kiss that had flipped her whole life upside down. But at least she could mention something else that was gnawing at her.

"Julian hates my wardrobe," she blurted at last. She hated how her stomach cramped at the admission. And she loathed remembering how cockily Julian had assured her that this "starving artist look" would not do anything for Garrett. Damn him anyway for making her feel insecure.

Kate's eyes widened, then she cocked an I-told-you-so brow. "Now, why am I not surprised to hear that?"

"Because you've said the same. There. Does it please you, Kay? That he thinks I dress bad? Because the last thing it gives me is pleasure."

Suddenly, just remembering the sexiness of that woman she'd seen in Julian's apartment made Molly flush in anger all over again. She had to look better than *her*. She had *so* many other looks in her wardrobe, not just the "blender" ones. Jules would see.

Eyebrows joining over a nose that was dotted with freckles, Kate took a step to scrutinize Molly more closely. "Molly, I don't get you. You haven't called in days and when I text you, you tell me you're flying in Julian's airplane over to South Padre Island to get an hour of suntanning with him? Your last two unfinished paintings for the exhibit sit all alone down the hall in your studio with your deadline looming…and after years of listening to me beg you to let me give you a makeover, you finally decide to do it because of what *he* said? What is going on with you two? I couldn't sleep last night—I had to call Garrett. I'm worried sick!"

"*Garrett?* Well, what did he say?"

Looking genuinely mortified, Kate shook her ponytail and rubbed her temples. "He said to relax, that he'll talk to you. I just don't understand how this could come on so suddenly without me noticing what you two were up to. I thought this would happen later, when you were more experienced and mature."

"Forget that! Tell me what tone Garrett used. Was he angry? Concerned? Kind of possessive?"

Maybe the idiot was so arrogantly certain of Molly and her feelings for him, he thought he still had her in his grasp. Well! She'd just have to set the man straight, wouldn't she? And play harder to get with him than ever. In fact, Julian would know just how to take care of that tonight.

"I don't remember exactly what else he said, but I'm truly mortified over this. Moo, I thought you were a virgin until now?"

Kate seized her shoulders, and as her wide blue eyes searched deep into her own, Molly dropped her gaze to the floor, feeling suddenly transparent. "I *am* a virgin," she whispered, then she realized what she'd admitted to, and that the truth, right now, wouldn't do. "I mean I *was* before Jules…"

"Were you hurt your first time, Molly? Did he hurt you?"

That soft question, full of caring and concern, sent Molly for a loop. Suddenly she felt like the very red center spot of the Target sign. That was what liars felt like when they were put on the spot. So now she was going to have to draw on her imagination.

"He didn't mean to hurt me, but you know…" She trailed off and hoped to leave Kate to her own conclusion.

Which, judging by her struck expression, wasn't all that good. "I could kill him!"

"No! No! It was amazing, he was..." Helplessly hooked into an image of Julian John making love to her, Molly trailed off. Or was it Garrett she was fantasizing about? Her mouth felt so moist all of a sudden, she had to swallow. "It was actually perfect," she finished in a whisper.

"But anyway, my pride is smarting like crazy after he insulted my dress choice," she continued after a moment. "I'm truly torn, Kate. I want to show him that I can look fantastic but don't care what he thinks, either. I know you're catering for our event tonight, but do you think you can take an hour off to help make me look good?"

"Good enough to make Jules eat his words?"

"Yes!" Molly laughed, grabbing a frilly pink pillow and playfully smacking Kate with it.

She pictured Julian's face when he saw her walk through those elevator doors. Oooooh, it would be priceless. He'd look stunned and shocked and he would definitely no longer think Molly needed a new mirror.

And Garrett? He would regret every hour of these days they had been spending apart when they could have spent them together. Necking.

Kate slapped the pillow back at Molly, laughing. "Yes, I'll give you a makeover. But Molls?"

"Hmm?" Molly was already storming into her bedroom, rummaging through her closet in search of options that would make a man's mouth water. She didn't have a lot. But she still found a very nice dress in Kate's closet. She extended it to her sister, loving how the sapphire silk fabric shimmered in the light. "It has the tag on," Molly said aloud.

"Take it off," Kate said excitedly, and pulled on the plastic.

Molly shook her head. "But it's new. I can't wear this."

"Yes, you can. I was saving it for a rainy day. You'd look so lovely, Moo."

"I wish you'd stop calling me Moo. I feel like a cow." Molly hung the dress back up with a sigh, and her heart clenched for her sister. "I'll borrow this one day, but only after *you* wear it. When it rains."

They shared a smile, and minutes later, Molly found another dress in her sister's closet. It was black, fitted, and had an open back that was to die for. Molly tried it on backward and loved it so much, she decided she was doing things her own special way and cut off the label. She'd wear it this way and show plenty of cleavage tonight.

By that evening, after spending a wonderful day with Kate, getting her makeover and even helping her sister finish loading some of tonight's munchies into the catering van, Molly arrived at Julian's posh apartment building, her heart pounding in anticipation.

Her hair was held loosely by a shimmering crystal butterfly clasp, with a few soft tendrils escaping along her temples. She wasn't used to pulling her hair back, but it seemed to emphasize her features this way. Her round cheekbones, her plump lips.

Her insecurities flickered to the forefront as she asked the bellhop to hold her canvases and paints below until she rang for them. He kept staring at her as if he'd never seen her before, and she wanted to run back home and put on a boho skirt, let her hair down and grab a huge pair of earrings.

But no. This was not the time to feel insecure.

She would show Julian sexy and confident if it killed her.

She crossed the marble lobby with purpose, aware of her hips swaying, the material clinging to her skin. Garrett was going to like what she was wearing; if he'd liked the wench costume, then he would love this one for sure. And if Julian didn't like it? Her stomach did a twist inside her, and she wondered what that meant. Hopefully it meant *screw him*.

She wasn't wearing this for him. *At all*.

Taking in a deep breath, she waved at the receptionist and pushed the elevator's up button.

All right. Here goes nothing....

The elevator chimed, and Julian glanced up from the bar and almost dropped the bottle of wine he'd been examining. It was a Penfolds Grange Hermitage 1951—so rare and prized, only twenty bottles were left in the entire world, with the last having sold at auction for almost fifty thousand dollars.

But who cared about that now?

Because an exotic-looking creature resembling Molly had just stepped off the elevator, and something that felt like a paddle struck him in the chest, the gut and right between his straining eyeballs.

Holy mama.

He'd though this morning had been tough, watching that redheaded little package prance around in an old T-shirt of his with those curvy bare legs begging to be stroked.

And now...

He was certain that never in his life, after dating models, actresses and even a pampered princess, had he been as fired up by the sight of a woman as he was this instant, watching Molly Devaney and her pinup body walk toward him in that minuscule black dress.

She looked like a sexpot. A sex goddess. A sex *bomb*. Awakening every Neanderthal instinct inside of him.

Julian could hardly take her all in with one long sweep of his eyes, he was so dumbstruck.

Her titian hair was drawn back into some sort of careless knot, but several soft wisps escaped to frame her lovely face, the overall look enhancing the delicacy of her doll-like features. Her lovely, heart-shaped lips shone with a peach-colored gloss, and whatever silver-gray shade of eye shadow she'd worn made her eyes look even rounder and bluer than usual. Her earrings were small pearly dots, unlike her usual flashy chandelier style, and they made her look so elegant he wanted to fly her to Monaco on his jet right now and seat her next to him at a baccarat table.

Then the dress. Ahh, the dress. The satiny black fabric fell from her nape to drape over a pair of beautiful round breasts he'd kill to taste while the plunging neckline revealed inches and inches of smooth porcelain skin in the cleavage between. The skirt was barely a couple of inches long, and it hugged her rounded hips like Lycra. Suddenly he wanted to be that skirt. That dress. That cloth that molded to her and felt her and hugged her and practically rode those curves all over the place.

Molly had always been the funniest baby, the happiest baby he'd ever seen in his life. She cackled all the time. Especially with him. Now she was entirely, 100 percent, take-me-serious woman. And Julian was primed to stop mucking around with her and ready to do some serious, serious things with her. Aww, *crap!*

This was going to be a long night.

Schooling his expression, he set the wine bottle down and noticed his hand wasn't so steady. Not while his heart was doing vaults and backflips. "Is something wrong with your usual clothes, Molls?" He was amazed his voice made it past his dry throat.

"As a matter of fact, yes." She planted her hands on her

hips, thrusting her chin up in a silent dare. "They're not sophisticated and sexy, according to you."

He cocked a brow and remained silent, mentally deliberating what in the world to do now. A part of him wanted to escort this impostor out the door and demand to know where his red-haired, paint-streaked imp was. And another part was just thinking of how good this woman would look in his bedroom. Splayed open on his bed...where he would give her a goddamned hickey that would sting like hell tomorrow...

Okay, no.

No.

He was not doing any of that.

Not so soon and not like this.

But hell, had she actually picked this dress for *Garrett?*

His jaw locked in wordless jealousy, his eyes so starved they felt like Ping-Pong balls as they went from her prominent cleavage to her narrow waist to her sexy stilettos and back to the enticing swell of her breasts and to her slim, sleek arms. A torch blazed inside his chest and the heat quickly spread to every corner of his tense body. "You call that sophisticated and sexy?" he asked gruffly.

Yeah. It was definitely sophisticated and it was so damned sexy his eyes were about to burst. But it was also practically nonexistent. And he told her so.

She stuck her little pink tongue out at him. "Eat your heart out, Jules. I look good."

He was not even going to think of all the places he wanted to feel that little tongue. Really. "*Good* is not the word I'd use."

"All right. I look amazing," Molly countered.

"Says who? You?"

"Come on, I can see you struggling, Jules. Be the better man and admit it," Molly teased, clearly enjoying this.

"I'm the only man here, Molls, and I'd gladly admit it if I wasn't so busy looking for the rest of the dress. So? Where's the rest of the goddamned dress?"

Her smile wavered. "You don't like it? Fine. I'm not wearing this to impress you." With a stiff shrug, she breezed past him to her bedroom, where she began shoving her things into a small clutch purse.

Julian followed her to the threshold of her room and watched her buttocks wiggle as she bent over. His mouth watered. She looked so sweet and so delicious he was salivating like a dog.

He'd had mile-long legs wrapped around his body, centerfold lips around his privates and breasts the size of melons in his hands. And he had never, ever, been so turned on.

He wanted Molly so bad he'd die for it.

He wanted to cup her breasts and suckle her until his jaw ached. He wanted to unpin her hair and watch as every fiery-red strand fell to caress the lovely curve of her nape and shoulders. He wanted to take a plunge into her cleavage and lick his way downward until he found the very center of her being—and he wanted to stay there, all night, drinking and feasting and adoring every prized and special inch of her.

He knew this girl like he knew himself. And he still wanted to know her *more*.

He knew he only had Lucky Charms for breakfast when she did, so he could eat her marshmallows. He knew she had her cereal with almond milk. He knew when she got painting fever she would disappear into her studio for months and not care whether the world kept spinning or fell apart, except for taking a moment each day to see him and Kate. He knew she'd secretly donated the first million she'd made to an orphanage and that when she was younger she'd watched *The Princess Bride* about twenty times, rewinding and replaying the part when the hero tells the princess, "As you wish," rather than, "I love you."

He knew that she wanted his praise tonight.

He had seen the uncertainty underneath the confidence in those striking blue eyes of hers, could see the eager rise and fall of her pretty breasts.

More than anything, he wanted to shower her with the praise she wanted. He wanted to take off that slinky black dress with his teeth so she knew how badly he craved her. Then he wanted to take his teeth from her tiny toes and drag them up her shapely ankles, her firm calves, her slim beautiful thighs, and roam his hands up her tiny waist and her beautiful breasts while he buried his lips between her legs and drowned in the intoxicating taste of her. He wanted to take her to heaven, because that was the place where angels live, and he wanted her to ask something of him—anything—so that he could look into her eyes and tell her, "As you wish."

But he did none of that.

Could not do it. Not yet.

Because she'd worn this dress tonight for another man. And the thought of that alone made him feel like kicking a kitten.

"I can feel your eyes on my back, Jules." Molly broke into his thoughts, probably sensing his overwhelming testosterone encircling her.

He leaned on the door frame with his wide shoulders, still struggling to process this new feeling of complete and utter jealousy. "You're showing off so much skin I'm concerned you're contracting pneumonia as you stand there," he said.

She swung around in surprise. Her mouth hung open, and then she tossed her head back and laughed. "Really?

You're concerned about my health? Or about your ego and the fact that you can't even admit to me for one night in my life that I don't look like I came out of a fistfight and a blender?"

His fingers curled into his palms and his lips clamped shut. So…she thought he'd insulted her?

"If you don't want to be mauled the entire evening, I suggest you at least find a sweater," he instructed. He was trying to sound friendly. Like a good friend. A best friend would make such a suggestion, wouldn't he?

"It's a hundred degrees outside. Why would I need a sweater?"

He stared down pointedly at her breasts—yes, so that she noticed—then back up at her until she squirmed under his stare. "Need I remind you you're my lover for the time being? You're like a property of mine and I won't have any of those bastards…staring at your…your *assets*."

"I'm like five feet tall and almost invisible, Jules. Nobody's going to stare except, hopefully, Garrett. And then he'll propose and we'll have babies together."

Over my dead, rotting body, you will!

He was a hair from hyperventilating by now. "I didn't sign up to play the part of the freaking fool, Molls. What am I supposed to do while you hold court at the family gathering? You're supposed to be *my* girl!"

Her eyes sparkled in mirth, because she'd probably never seen him worked up to a lather before. "Well, at least you can give your big 'guns' a good workout as you fend off my unwanted suitors, huh."

He stalked over and grabbed her shoulders, not amused and very freaking jealous about all this. "Damned right I will, and you know why?"

"Enlighten me."

"All the guys in attendance, from Landon's friends to

business associates, are going to swarm you like a pack of starving beasts. They always have, and you don't even notice. You're so damned different, Molly..." She had no idea, no idea what she did to him or anyone else. She was not only blind to him, she was blind to all men. The looks she received while she was staring off into space, thinking of a painting, were never even noticed.

Had she forgotten all the invitations she'd had to prom? She hadn't even attended, but she goddamned well had been asked.

"You really think I'm different, Jules? You know, maybe that's because of my special relationship with my Oster!"

He laughed and wondered when the hell he would hear the last of that. *Never,* he thought, then growled in frustration and clenched her shoulders. "You don't need to change one whit about you to catch a man. If you need to change your identity to make him see something great about you, then Garrett doesn't deserve you. None of those bastards do."

Something he said struck a chord. Molly stopped fiddling with the bag and clutched it firmly to her abdomen. She surveyed him in curious speculation and tilted her head a notch, those sky-blue eyes wide with innocent expectation.

"So basically," she said, her lips lifting at the corners, those same lips he wanted to kiss more than anything until they were red and swollen and only his. "So what you're saying is—I *do* look good?"

Julian stood ramrod stiff as he struggled to reply, not wanting her to be seen like this by anyone. Anyone. But he owed her the truth and he had to shove his jealousy aside if it killed him.

And it was. Killing him.

Looking at her like this. Killing him.

Wanting her and having to wait. *Killing him.*

He twirled his finger in the air and thickly commanded, "Give a little spin for me."

She spun, slowly. Yep, killing him. Her butt was so perky and round he could already feel it in his hands. Needing to do something—touch her, anywhere—he reached out to tuck a loose tendril of red hair behind her ear, then his lips curled ever so slightly on one side as he inclined his head just a fraction, and said in a gruff voice, "Yeah, baby. You look good." And he gave that rump a little playful pat because he'd been aching to. "Too damned good."

Five

"So do you think Garrett will like my dress, too?"

Molly's question irritated Julian like a painful snakebite as they drove to Landon and Beth's gated home. He hesitated before at last answering her with a tender squeeze of her hands, which she'd been nervously wringing on her lap. "No doubt about it, Mopey. Just relax, you look stunning."

But now it was he, Julian John Gage, who needed to relax.

He felt like drinking hard, but he wasn't stupid enough to get drunk like the night of the masquerade party, when he'd lost control and acted like some sixteen-year-old dweeb with his first girlfriend.

Oh, no. Tonight he needed all five senses and then some.

Tonight Molly needed him to put on a show and damned if he wasn't aching to give it to her.

To *all* of his family.

But he felt like he had a bomb strapped to his rib cage

and he wondered if he'd be able to keep his usual cool. His success might depend on it. Keeping cool, biding his time, being patient. Logically, that was what he must do. But Molly was in love with his brother, dammit, and both his head and his cool had left him a week ago when he'd learned of it.

Things he had planned to do his whole life were happening, and precipitously. Regrettably, not in the manner he had intended them to.

Never had he imagined he would experience this much jealousy over the girl he'd always planned to have for himself falling in love with his brother.

God, he still couldn't believe this was true.

Still, he was trying very hard to screw his head back on and focus on enjoying the parts of the evening he knew would bring him pleasure.

Like showing off his new "girlfriend" to his family. "Mother, have you met Molly?" he could ask while the unspoken words that floated between them would be, *The woman you warned me never to touch? I'm tumbling her all night now, and she loves it. We both do. Hey, will you excuse us for a moment? We're going to go ahead and have sex out by the bushes....*

But sadly, not even that thought brought him comfort as he handed his keys over to the valet and strode over to help Molly out of the car.

Her scent dizzied him as she stood up from the low seat.

Creamy legs...silken red hair...the sexy-as-hell curve of her neck just begging to be bitten...

He wasn't going to think about that now. In silence, he focused on how warm and calm the night breeze was as he led her up the staircase, her hand unsteady in his.

"Molls?"

"Mmm?"

He wanted to tell her she had never looked more beautiful to him. Instead, he lifted her hand and placed a soft kiss on the back of it, tipping her chin encouragingly with his other hand. "We've got this," he murmured, and her instant smile wrapped around his heart.

Hand in hand, they entered the gleaming foyer of the two-story mansion, where a harpist welcomed them with a slow, haunting tune. The gathering consisted of a small group of friends and family and of course Landon's enormous mastiffs, who were plopped on the rug at the far end of the living room.

Molly had told Julian earlier that Kate and Beth's business, Catering, Canapés and Curry, was handling tonight's party.

So at least the food would be good.

As soon as Julian and Molly were spotted, they were split apart. Kate and Beth sequestered Molly for interrogation while his mother, in an evening dress and a pair of bed slippers, flew over to Julian before he could even find a server with a wine selection. "My dear son! My dear, dear son!" she called from afar, crossing the room toward him. "What's this I hear about you and Molly, JJ?"

"Mother, why did you give me two names if you did not plan to use them?" he said, exasperated.

"All right then, Julian John—answer me now and don't test me. My nerves are frazzled as it is without any help from you these days!"

A fond smile played on his lips as his mother stopped an arm's length away, regal and elegant even in slippers and panting for her breath—something only a matron like Eleanor Gage could pull off.

Julian could already taste the satisfaction of watching the "news" affect and disgruntle his overprotective mother. She, who had sent him to Spain, France, Russia and Africa to separate him from his best friend. She, who had warned him if he ever touched the only girl he'd ever truly cared for, he might as well not consider himself a part of the Gage family anymore.

Yeah, it gave him pleasure, perverse pleasure, to see if she would make good on her threats. A part of him savored the fight with her even though he loved her. It had hurt him, incredibly, to be judged and condemned by his entire family for a sin he hadn't yet committed.

He'd been punished since he was just an adolescent, and he'd been suffering ever since.

Yes. It felt good to rebel against them. To give them the exact thing they were afraid of. Because soon they would see how wrong they'd been about him. Dead. *Wrong.*

So now that she was narrow-eyed and thrusting her chin out in warning, Julian ducked his head to her height and kissed her cheek smoothly, unperturbed by her bravado. "If you heard that Molly is with me, then you heard the truth, Mother. Now you can finally make good on your threat and disown me."

Eleanor drew back with a shocked little breath, genuinely traumatized by his suggestion.

Julian wanted to assure her he didn't need the trust his father had left anymore. He could live lavishly with his savings alone, plus he already had a promising business ready to launch, with several billion-dollar companies lined up as clients for his PR services. Instead, he smiled at her to defuse the tension and tucked a wisp of ebony hair behind her ear.

"You knew this would happen, Mother," he said softly. "Just as I knew someday I'd have to prove to you how much I want her and how far I'm willing to go."

Her eyes, the only ones in the family that were green like his own, flared wide with accusation. Julian waited for her comeback, but words seemed to be failing her at the moment.

He really wished that if his mother was staring at him as if he were a monster, it was because sweet, lovely Molly was crazy about him, couldn't keep her hands off him and was letting him have his way with her in bed, in the shower, in the car, in the kitchen and in every place he could think of. And not because of this idiotic little lie.

He needed her to be his.

He didn't know how much longer he could wait, or what it would take for her to realize she and Garrett weren't compatible in any single way that she and Julian were.

"If you think I'm going to let you use that girl like all those Janes you go out with, you're sorely mistaken, Julian John. I'm like that girl's *mother*."

He nodded in agreement. He had definitely understood the position his mother had been placed in two decades ago when the Devaneys had been brought to the house. She had been a recent widow with three young sons, feeling responsible for the death of an employee who left two young daughters orphaned. His mother, always stern but nonetheless a loving woman, had taken them in, but hardened her position with her sons in the process.

It was too much on her nerves to ever think the boys would harm the girls in any way; after all, they owed them their father. And yet nobody had ever understood that Julian did not want to hurt Molly. Just as he did not want to hurt his mother now. It just was what it was.

He wanted Molly. And no one was going to stop him from having her anymore.

In feigned aloofness, he grasped one of her jeweled hands and indolently patted it between both of his. "Why don't you have a little more faith in me as well, Mother? And let us be happy together, for once." Before he left to greet Landon and his wife, he grumbled, "I'd never hurt Molly. *Ever.* And it hurts me that you even think I would."

Molly stood at the other end of the living room with Kate and Beth, who was being brought up to speed on all the excitement.

"I can't believe this. Landon and I leave for two months, we come back and you and Julian are *dating?*"

Molly waved a hand excitedly. "We're actually way past that, Beth. I've moved in already." She nodded proudly, then added, "But you know, that's exactly how shocked I felt when I emerged from a long creative streak in my studio to find out Landon had remarried. I didn't even have a clue he'd met someone. Julian should've kept me up-to-date all those nights he brought Chinese food!"

Looking past Beth, Molly spotted Landon, another gorgeous Gage specimen. He kept glancing in their direction as he addressed Julian, and although Landon was not a man easily perturbed, even *he* appeared slightly confused as he spoke to his youngest brother this evening. Garrett joined them within seconds, and Molly could just sigh at the sight of his broad back. She could imagine their next kiss and already knew it would be as hot as the first....

With a wistful smile, she watched the three men, all of whom she adored. The chandelier lights caught on Julian's streaked golden hair, which sharply contrasted with both of his older brothers' dark coloring, and she melted with tenderness for him. Just to think Julian might be taking crap from his brothers because he was supposedly dating her only endeared him to her more. Would Garrett do something like this for her?

While Julian lounged around effortlessly, seemingly careless to everything they said, Garrett stood sterner, more tense and, hopefully, already jealous. Landon, however, had never looked so utterly relaxed. Like a man completely satisfied with the state of his life and thoroughly in love, as was evident from the frequent looks he stole in Beth's direction.

"Landon said he always knew this would happen," Bethany offered in a private whisper, oblivious to her husband's attention across the room as she leaned closer to Molly. "When our plane landed, he called his office and heard about you two from Garrett. He wasn't even surprised about it. He said it was inevitable."

"He did?"

It was a shock to Molly.

Because who on earth would ever think Julian and Molly could be more than friends?

It was ridiculous. Molly didn't even like to date. And Julian was a playboy.

Plus, the Gage family still viewed her as a child, except for Garrett, who seemed to be the only one who'd realized she was now a full-grown woman. A *kissable* grown woman.

Still reeling at the idea, she looked back at the group of men, intending to admire Garrett from afar and remind herself why she was so in love with him, but her gaze snagged on Julian as he calmly explained something to his brothers.

Already having disposed of both his black jacket and his silver tie, Jules exuded powerful masculinity and self-assurance as he stood there, the cuffs of his shirt rolled up to his elbows to expose his tanned, thick forearms. His stance was so wide and confident, it seemed to say, *Yeah, baby, I own me, I own this and I own you.*

Before Molly could force her gaze back to the man she loved, Julian seemed to sense her scrutiny, for suddenly, his head turned. The smile he wore gradually vanished.

With the glittering lights overhead, his eyes, those eyes that changed from gray-green to gold-green in a moment, right now looked as green as Colombian emeralds. And they blazed at her from across the room—almost proprietarily, as if he *also* thought he owned the little black dress she wore and the pair of black panties underneath.

Molly! You did not just think of your panties!

Mortified, she jerked her gaze away, her stomach clenching, and then she had to look back at Julian. Because...surely she had hallucinated that he was giving her the Wolf vs. Red Riding Hood stare?

He said something to Garrett and started in her direction, and before Molly could understand why her insides spun in turmoil, she realized he must be putting on a show. A show so that Garrett could see that she was desirable to him. And he would get terribly jealous and feel forced to tear them apart and stake his claim on Molly once and for all.

Yes, of course. It was all part of the plan. And it was brilliant.

But as Julian walked toward her with that slow tiger prowl-walk and his stare held her captive, her legs liquefied. She hadn't felt this desirable since the night Garrett had kissed her. The way he stared at her made her feel... wanted. Womanly. So, so, womanly.

Wow, this guy was so good at this.

And he was hot.

And tonight, everyone in this room thought he was *hers*.

"Get over here and dance with me," he prodded as he reached for her with a strong, long-fingered hand.

Molly grinned. "There's no dance floor, you dope."

"Come on, Mo-Mo. There's music and that's all we need."

She smiled and took his hand, and a surprising bolt of

electricity shot through her as he clasped her fingers. He spun her into his arms and yanked her effortlessly against him, almost dizzying her with his strength.

She swallowed a small curse, unprepared to feel his powerful body aligning so perfectly with hers. And suddenly Julian had erased all the distance between them. And Molly had seen him in his *briefs*. And he was so close.

His body warmth enveloped her, causing her muscles to relax while at the same time an odd hyperawareness built inside her midsection. It…disconcerted her.

"You're so good at this, it's almost annoying," she told him with a smile.

And she hardly believed *how* good he was as she wrapped her arms around his strong nape, trying not to think of how utterly helpless she would feel if Julian was to turn on the charm with her like he did with all of his flings. Not that it would ever happen, or even that it would work. Because there could only be one man for her, and he'd *better* be watching them.

"Is Garrett looking?" she whispered, desperate to get this fake-lover charade over with. It was becoming dangerous…playing house with Julian. It was too fun and too easy. "Is he looking this way, Jules?"

"I don't know, Molls, I'm looking at you."

It was the tone he used, deep and husky as a country love song, that made her insides move in a way that made her supremely uncomfortable. Or maybe the sensation was due to the fact that Garrett must be watching them dance. It had to be. For it felt as if the Earth had stopped and not only Garrett, but the entire world, was watching them dance—or at least sway to the harp tune in the middle of Landon's living room.

"I'm pretty sure he's watching," she whispered, moving closer to Julian's ear. There, she leaned against his chest and whispered, "I'm thinking we could just stroll off somewhere and return a little disheveled, you know. Or go lock ourselves in a closet for fifteen minutes and let his imagination run wild."

She could feel the coiled tension in the muscles underneath his shirt as he dropped his head to whisper back into her ear, his lips grazing the lobe. "As you wish."

Fireflies exploded in her stomach, the words were so unexpected, as unexpected as the caressing bump of his lips against her earlobe. Molly drew back with a start, trying to calm her racing heart, telling herself he couldn't possibly know what those words did to her. Or how deeply they spoke to her. "Really?" she whispered, shaking her reaction aside. "It's a good idea?"

He arrested her gaze with tender, heavy-lidded eyes that threatened her equilibrium. All she knew was that in her favorite movie of all time, Westley looked at Buttercup in *just* this manner.

And this was just the way Garrett had to look at her by the end of the evening.

"Yeah." Julian lightly chucked her chin, then with painstakingly slowness, smoothed his calloused thumb across her lower lip in a way that made her shiver. "I've always enjoyed a little closet fun. Let's get lost."

Molly didn't remember moving so fast in her entire life—even though she had to stop several times because she was laughing so hard—than when Julian dragged her down the long hallway. She felt intoxicated with an incredible sense of freedom and mischief and fun—and when she caught a glimpse of Julian's sexy, curvy smile, she wanted to fling herself into his arms and kiss him from the excitement alone.

Within seconds he came to an abrupt stop and efficiently shoved her inside a small downstairs office.

The instant the door closed after him, Molly's heart stopped.

Darkness enveloped them. Silence and seclusion spread between them, around them, like a cloak of velvet. But in this closed space, nearly entirely occupied by a big mahogany desk, Julian's scent suddenly stormed around her like a tornado, and it made her lungs burn. He smelled clean and of spices and within seconds Molly couldn't seem to stand still. Her mouth watered, and she swallowed.

"Do you have lipstick in your purse?" he asked in a voice roughened with exertion.

Her eyes adjusted to the shadows, and she realized with a start that Julian was undoing the top buttons of his white shirt. Molly could barely organize her thoughts at the sight of his tanned throat being exposed, then the hollow between his collarbones, then a part of his pectorals.

She licked her lips and, without even thinking, she lunged at him.

Going straight for the dirty business, she coiled her arms firmly around his neck and kissed his square jaw, pressing her body against his marble-hard one. Next she trailed her lips down the length of his throat. She'd surprised him, she supposed. For he stood utterly still, maybe not even alive.

Oh, no, but he was definitely alive, very much so. His warmth seeped through his clothes and spread heat all the way to her bone marrow. Intoxicated by the incredible feel of his taut, warm skin under her roaming lips, Molly trailed a path of kisses down to his collarbone, where she crazily wondered if she should just go ahead and trace it with her tongue.

"Molly?"

Julian's voice was a thick rasp.

"Mmm," she answered, placing a gentle kiss in that hollow at the base of his throat.

"You could've used your lipstick straight on me, baby. You didn't have to kiss me."

It took a moment for that guttural whisper to register. She had been happily—maybe too happily—dragging her lips along the thick tendons of his throat so that they ended up smeared peach and no one doubted, not even Julian and especially not Garrett, that Molly had kissed him.

She stopped abruptly and backed off in sudden confusion, all of her body heat concentrating on her cheeks. "What do you mean…? I don't even remember where I left my purse, I think Beth has it."

He must have heard the utter embarrassment in her voice, for he gathered her back against him, his voice even thicker and rougher than before. "Shh. Go on then. This works, too."

But she hesitated, her cheeks now scalding. As though encouraging her, Julian undid another button of his shirt, so leisurely that as she watched she began to focus on details she had never thought of before. How gracefully his fingers moved. How both their breaths ricocheted off the walls of the small space.

How she could feel his eyes burn like lasers through the top of her head as she watched him undo another button.

How a hot little tingle spread across every inch of her skin.

And how this would all be so easy to dismiss if she hadn't seen him almost *naked*…

"Now try kissing me a little lower."

He spread his shirt open, fully open, and Molly's windpipe clamped shut. Her knees wobbled in place. Jules could be a sculpture, he was so defined and so lean. At such a short distance, he looked even *more* ripped, like a top athlete. Molly could see every square indentation of his wash-board abs, every sharp rise and fall of muscle.

A tremor rushed through her, and when she didn't move, he slipped his hands onto the back of her head and gently urged her toward him. His fingers were long and felt gentle on her scalp, and as she set her palms on his rib cage and bent her head to his collarbone, she felt his fingertips work on her butterfly clasp and undo her hair.

A hot little shiver rushed from the top of her scalp to the tips of her toes as her hair tumbled to her shoulders. Trembling, she lowered her head and set a dry kiss on the V of his neck. Gingerly at first, holding her breath, trying to suppress another tremor building inside her body. Julian stood utterly still, and she wondered if he held his breath, too. Then she heard him softly say, "Go lower."

Her eyes drifted shut and she set down another kiss, pressing her lips lightly against the tautly stretched skin above his six-pack. She felt the muscles contract under her fingerprints, and her tummy clenched in response. Why did she feel so shaky? Why was her mind spinning inside her cranium? She felt like a teenager stealing a first kiss, like a bad girl misbehaving, which she'd never been before. Of course it was all due to the excitement of making Garrett jealous. She had to remind herself all these emotions were due to the fact that her and Julian's plan was so good, it was going to *work*.

"Lower, baby," he murmured in a thick, raspy voice.

She was so trusting of Julian that she almost automatically obeyed, following his instructions without hesitation, while in the back of her mind she started to wonder how he would get Garrett to see that Molly had kissed his washboard abs, too. Daydreaming of Garrett's jealous face while a strange liquid fire simmered through her veins, she let her lips wander lower, Julian's skin hot and silky under her lips…her heart thundering in her ears as she heard him once again rasp, "Lower." Feeling like she was dreaming, she went lower, her eyes feeling heavy as a strange tremor tingled along her nerve endings, until she heard him unzip his pants.

Startled, she lifted her head in confusion. He was laughing down at her, his eyes sparkling in the shadows, those sensual lips curled at the corners as he zipped back up.

"You're so innocent, Molls. I was wondering when you'd catch on," he said.

She smacked his elbow and straightened, already feeling a rush of color climb up her cheekbones. "You jerk!"

She tried pushing him aside but he seized her wrists and yanked her back to him, his laughter lingering in his voice. "No, no, no, not yet, baby. We need to work on you now."

He rumpled her hair with those long-fingered hands and Molly felt herself clam up, her throat closing with an unnameable emotion. She felt…unsteady. Vulnerable and open to him. Even those feathery touches on her scalp felt special. Electric. Rushing from the roots of her hair to her brain, charging her with inexplicable adrenaline.

As he worked on her hair, the mist of his breath fanned, warm and minty, across her forehead, and she had to use all her effort to fight the impossible flames flicking through her body. His smell was killing her. Dizzying her.

What was happening to her?

This was Julian, not Garrett. *Julian.*

She sucked in an unsteady breath, and his hands went still on the crown of her head. Their eyes locked in the dark as his hands slid down to her nape as he slowly ducked toward her. Closer. Closer.

She was frozen in place, her voice a breathless whisper. "Julian…what are you doing…?"

"Shh. I just want some of your lipstick on my mouth.

Just a little." His breathing changed as he secured her cheeks between his big hands, and she became aware of the bite of something incredibly large and rigid against her stomach.

"Julian..." she said, turning her head to the side. Their noses brushed accidentally, but rather than pull back, Julian dipped his head even farther and scraped his mouth purposely across hers.

The contact singed.

Her mouth parted on a gasp.

Julian pulled back, his eyes gleaming in the darkness. Then he lowered his head and repeated the motion, scraping his mouth across hers. Her legs went rubbery, her core melting like lava.

A little quiver rippled through her, followed by a surge of desire so sharp and powerful, her world tilted on its axis. Not even Garrett's kiss had done this to her. Nothing on this earth had *ever* done this to her. She shouldn't feel such blazing need swimming through her veins, shouldn't want to feel more, feel everything.

But she did, goodness, she did.

His nearness intoxicated her, the brush of his sensual lips fascinated her beyond measure, and she felt weak with wanting, had never wanted anything so much as she wanted to be kissed by him. Right now, in this tiny lightless room, this very instant. Kissed thoroughly and deeply by this sex god everyone wanted but no one could ever have. Least of all Molly.

But Julian did not kiss her. Only teased her with the possibility of it. The delicious scent of his body enveloped and dizzied her. It was incredible; this feeling of flying. He was so familiar and at the same time totally new. As if discovering your body could do something you never expected it to. This was how it felt to awaken to Julian John. And that was the only word she could think of. *Awaken*.

To Julian John.

He just had to kiss her.

Please kiss me.

Her breathing escalated and her lips parted as he scraped his mouth across hers for the third time. She heard a sound come out of herself and almost collapsed in a puddle on the floor when he released her.

"There. I'm probably wearing more lipstick than you are now. Come on, Mo-Mo. Let's get out of here."

He went to open the office door, and light from the corridor spilled in, silhouetting his magnificent form. Their eyes met across the gloom while he waited for her to get her bearings. But her knees felt like soup.

Her legs like noodles.

She blinked but couldn't focus.

She couldn't even breathe.

She didn't know what was wrong with her, but her mind was screaming for him to come back, for him to kiss her, for her to kiss him, for her to do anything to be kissed by Julian John. And suddenly when he swung around to leave, she blurted out, "JJ, wait!"

Her heart stopped when he froze, and for a wild instant, all that was audible in the dark room was both their uneven breathing. Their eyes met again—and something electrifying pulsed between them.

He closed the door so slowly her heart almost disintegrated, and then she heard a click as it hit the doorjamb. Darkness swallowed them again, darkness and something wild and untamable. An unbearable intensity charged the air as he took a step forward.

Molly was not thinking right, felt drunk with sensations. With expectation. *Anticipation*.

"What did you just say?" Julian asked. His voice was very, very soft. Dangerously soft.

Molly held her breath, her lungs near bursting. "I said *JJ*."

His eyes shimmered like lanterns in the night, and her heart rattled in her chest and the blood roared in her ears as he took that last step closer.

With slow, deliberate precision, he placed his hands on either side of her head against the back wall and caged her between his arms as he leaned forward. A gravelly sound stole into his voice as he slid his fingers through her loose hair and encircled the back of her head. "Say it to my face, Molly. Say it one more time to my face. I dare you."

Longing burst open inside her. Hunger. Want. *Everything*.

She knew this was crazy and wrong and yet she couldn't help herself, couldn't stop. Her body was trembling, head-to-toe, trembling. He had been playing a game with her and perhaps she wanted to play back, but this was more than a game.

Maybe?

Was it?

She didn't know anything anymore, except that maybe she should apologize for calling him by his most loathed nickname and just leave.

Maybe she didn't really want to be kissed by Julian John, because she wanted Garrett. Or maybe she'd truly lost her head tonight, because as she met his gaze in the shadows, she heard herself speak between panting breaths.

"I said *JJ*, JJ."

The silence was deafening.

Julian's eyes widened, for he was sure that he hadn't

heard right the first time. But this second time, he just couldn't believe it.

Molly had called him JJ, and he was going to have to make her pay for that. Stat.

In a whiplash move, he yanked her up against him and hoarsely demanded, in a voice as jagged as torn paper, "Do you remember what I told you I would do if you ever, ever called me JJ again?"

Smiling a smile that was all mischief, Molly tilted her back, her breasts rising and falling fast. She nodded slowly, provocatively—tauntingly.

The little she-cat wanted this!

Almost drugged with the thought of exacting his punishment, Julian caressed his hands up her slender arms, savoring the feel of her smooth skin against his calloused palms. "Well, then, I'm going to have to kiss you now," he purred, the words acting like foreplay as he leaned closer. He could almost taste the gloss on her lips already.

"O-okay, Jules," she said, almost a squeak as she gripped the rolled-up sleeves at his elbows as though hanging on to him for dear life.

Swamped with every single emotion in the world and close to exploding with wanting her, he cupped her face between his large hands and lowered his head, his heart going a powerful *baboom baboom baboom*. "'Okay, Jules'? Is that all you have to say? All right, then, you asked for it, Moo…now you're getting it good…"

He started easy, her face framed in his grasp as he lightly set his lips on hers, but with that whisper touch alone, lightning streaked across his veins and seared their mouths like fire. Suddenly, that single, wholly erotic fusion of their bodies lit his entire being on fire. He grabbed her closer, and she slid her hands up his bulging arms, their mouths parting hungrily in unison.

Groaning as her plush lips opened for him, he plowed his tongue into her mouth in a thirsty search for hers. Her soft moan tumbled down his throat as she shyly licked him back.

She tasted like peaches. And he *loved* peaches.

Deepening their kiss, he trailed his open palms down to the small of her back and conformed her curvy body to his. Her breasts softly pressed against his diaphragm, and it drove him crazy when she rubbed the tips of her nipples up against the wall of his chest.

Her nails bit into his shoulders while her mouth eagerly explored his, and when her hips began rocking against his, too, his senses swam with both pain and euphoria. The pain came from his pulsing length pressing against his pants zipper, aching to grind against those luscious hips she taunted him with.

His fingertips dug into her waist as he crushed her tighter to him, and plunged deeper into her mouth, stealing dozens of incredibly sweet and wet tastes of her. Ten. Eleven. Twelve. She tasted pure. And he desperately wanted to make love to her.

Undone by her wildness, he grappled with her hands and lifted them above her head, pinning her against the back wall. This surprised her, and she gasped. He caught the sound and kissed her harder. Wetter. Longer.

His body exploded in chaos as she responded in kind, pulling her arms free and rubbing her hands up his biceps, through his hair, making soft purring sounds against his mouth.

She felt incredible. *Incredible.*

He had never wanted anything or anyone more in his life. Molly. His tiny, sweet little gypsy. He wanted to hear her come undone for him, to lose control like she made him lose his.

But did she really want this? Did she have any idea how serious he was about this, about *her?*

"Molly," he murmured tenderly, then he dived down her neck and twirled a wet path to her delicate collarbone.

"Don't stop yet," she mewed in a little helpless plea, her fingertips sliding back into his hair. "Please let me pretend for a little bit."

His insides twisted with foreboding. "Don't you *dare—*" he came back up and shoved his tongue into her mouth, taking all of her taste, taking all that she could give "—pretend that I'm my brother."

But that tormenting thought now held him back like an iron chain, and he had to rest his forehead against hers with a groan, his breaths jerking in and out as he fought to get a grip. Suddenly, the reminder that Molly was making out with him to make his brother jealous gnawed a hole the size of Texas into his gut.

But her slim arms still clung to him. Her face was still tilted up to his in offering. And he could hardly think straight while she looked up at him as if she adored him.

"You look thoroughly kissed, Molly," he rasped. He cradled her beautiful face with his big hands, drinking up the dewy desire that softened her features.

She licked her lips, her pupils dilating as her gaze darted from his eyes to his mouth, up and down, up and down. He could barely speak, his voice roughened with painful, dizzying arousal.

"Should we just go out there so my brother gets to see what I've been doing to you? He'll probably think I've had my hands all over you this evening."

She made a little choking sound and dropped her face. "Jules, stop. Please don't tease."

Julian's thighs trembled as he fought for control, fought

to keep from doing more, doing everything to her. With her. "I'd just like to know if this kiss was just for Garrett—or because you want me, Molly?"

She kept her head bent, intoxicating him with the smell of raspberry shampoo that wafted to his nostrils. "Everybody wants you, Julian. Everybody. I just can't believe this. What did we do? This was so insane, so stupid!"

"Shh." He pinned her against him when she squirmed, his hands firmly curled around her shoulders as he kissed the top of her head and tried to ease her. "If you can't do this sort of stupid thing with your best friend, then I don't know who the hell you can do it with."

She shook her head but nonetheless buried her nose in the crook of his neck. "I didn't mean for this to happen. All this is your fault! For being such an expert seducer—please don't let go yet. I just want you to hold me. Jules, you smell so good...."

One two three four five six seven eight nine ten eleven twelve...

Not enough. He could count to a million and it was not. Enough. Not enough of her. Not enough time. To hold her. Be with her. Drown in her.

A groan of pent-up desire rumbled up from deep within his throat as his fingers clenched around her waist. "I wasn't seducing you, Molly—but you shouldn't have tempted me to kiss you." Unable to stop himself, he recklessly slid his hands upward to engulf her breasts as he heatedly nibbled on her earlobe. "Now I want to kiss you until you're weak and pliant in my arms. Until you tell me what it is that you really want, because I don't think you even know what you're asking for—"

"*So!* Are you two finished in here—or do we have to call the fire department?"

* * *

The baritone voice that cut through Julian's delicious, seductive words yanked Molly to full wakefulness. She jerked in Julian's arms as if she'd just been dumped into the frigid waters off Alaska and straightened to see Garrett—the man she wanted to marry—standing just outside the open door. Landon stood next to him, and while Landon's expression verged on amusement, Garrett did not look pleased.

And now he'll think I'm a whore.

The sudden thought popped into her mind and she almost wanted to groan in self-pity.

Her cheeks glowed hot as Julian pushed her behind him in a stance that reeked of protectiveness, and she was grateful for that. Taking advantage, she hid against his back and frantically struggled to rearrange her dress and hair.

"We'll be done as soon as you two dopes leave us alone."

How Julian could sound so calm and collected, she didn't know, because panic had gripped Molly by the throat and she could hardly even breathe now.

She'd wanted Garrett to imagine she and Julian had shared a little romp this evening. But she had never, ever expected to be caught while doing it.

What had she been thinking? She had clearly been undone by the strange, tantalizing complexity of Julian's male scent, the desperate desires his mouth evoked, his kisses always somehow bringing the heartbreaking reminder of her night with Garrett at the masquerade. Every time she kissed Julian, her chest began to *ache,* and not in a good way.

"We apologize, but Mother sent us," she heard Landon explain to Jules almost apologetically. "Not a task I was looking forward to."

"I'm surprised she didn't summon the whole party to

come stop us," Julian grumbled, and with one of his powerful arms, he slammed the door back shut.

Cursing low in his throat once they were alone, he extended an arm to keep the door closed and glanced past his shoulder.

"You okay?"

"Yes," she said as she arranged herself frantically, wanting the small room to develop an appetite and suddenly swallow her whole. She couldn't believe Julian had touched her *breasts* just now.

"The point was to look disheveled, Molls. And you do."

He sounded calm, almost too calm. When he reached into his pants pocket and handed over her butterfly clasp, Molly reached for it and clipped her hair back as best she could, her hands still trembling when she finished.

She sighed dejectedly.

What Julian had said made sense, of course. But she felt incredibly guilty and maybe still a little aroused. The things he had been saying to her before they were interrupted? The things he had been saying while he was cupping her breasts?

That was major, major stuff he'd been whispering in her ear!

"You're right," she said, avoiding his gaze, his all-knowing gaze that would intuitively pick up on just how far past her comfort zone they had gone. "This is perfect, couldn't be more perfect. You're a master, Jules. Master of disaster." She gave him a quick peck on the cheek and tried to sound businesslike. "Thank you."

Ducking under his arm, she yanked the door open and swept outside. Determinedly, she walked past both the Gage men, who stood like sentinels down the hall, with their black suits and matching impassive expressions on their faces.

She shot each of them a smile, smiling with her inflamed mouth that had just been kissed like a hussy's.

She even pretended she was proud of it.

But she could feel Julian's eyes on her back, sensed he hadn't moved from the office doorway yet, and as she rounded the corner to the busy and crowded living room, all she wanted was to find a nice spot where she could collapse safely and sort out her out-of-whack emotions.

She heard footsteps and suddenly Garrett loomed at her side, his fingers curling around her elbow. "I'd like to talk to you in private, Molly," he said. "Do you have time tomorrow?"

Surprised, she looked into her beloved's eyes while an avalanche of emotions buffeted her from the inside.

He seemed concerned, intense, his obsidian eyes peering into hers so fiercely, she feared he'd be able to see how aroused and guilty she was.

"Of course," she said with a shaky nod, her voice husky for all the wrong reasons. "I'll stop by your office at noon, Garrett."

"Thank you," he said softly, and placed a kiss on her forehead, his hands lingering on her cheeks for a second.

She was so numb that she couldn't even enjoy his caress that she'd fantasized about feeling again for days and nights.

She could hardly believe that she'd finally caught his attention.

In a daze, she crossed the living room toward Kate and Beth, her thoughts scattered and unfocused. She should be celebrating, she knew. Garrett wanted to talk to her in private tomorrow, and he was, at the very least, concerned. Maybe he was even hiding his jealousy with grave effort. By all appearances, her plan was succeeding. Wasn't that what she'd been dreaming of accomplishing?

But no. She couldn't enjoy her victory because she was too rattled by what she'd done.

What on earth had gotten into her, to tempt Julian the way she had? Were those the actions of a woman in love with another man?

And what if things became awkward with Julian now? What if this stupid charade affected the one relationship in her life she cherished above anything?

"What on earth happened to you?" Kate cried with one startled look at her.

Molly decided she was going to own up to it.

Whatever her sins, whatever her mistake, she was going to *own up to it* if it killed her.

"Julian and I made out in the dark. You should try it sometime, Kate. It was actually fun before those two idiots interrupted."

She glared in the direction of Garrett and Landon, then saw Julian stroll from around the corner of the hall, his hands in his pockets, his blond hair mussed. *Sexy* didn't begin to describe the man. He looked tousled. Delish. Thoroughly kissed, as he'd put it—and there was no question about it. Streaks of what looked like Molly's peach lipstick slashed all over his tan skin. Marking his thick throat, up along his jaw, across the side of his plush lips. He looked so rumpled he could've just battled a Siberian tiger in a cage, and for some reason, knowing the tiger had been *her* caused a pool of liquid heat to rush between her thighs.

"Julian, what happened to you?" Beth asked as he approached.

Julian's green gaze tracked and zeroed in on Molly, and her swollen mouth began to burn under the intimacy of his stare. Between her legs, she burned. Her breasts, the very breasts he had cradled in his enormous hands, pricked hotly in remembrance. Quite simply, and too damn easily, he set her ablaze with his gaze, reminding her of his blatantly sexual words, almost causing her to combust.

"Molls and I had a little fun in the downstairs office. You okay, baby?"

His voice, still husky enough to resemble the timbre he'd used in the dark, did wild things to her overstimulated senses. Awareness had quickly skyrocketed to hyperawareness in that empty office, and now she was frantic to power these sensations off.

While the other women processed his words in stunned silence, Julian made a thorough assessment of Molly's face with a measured expression on his own.

Was he worried they'd gone too far, too?

Trying to offer some reassurance, Molly let her lips curl upward, loathing this awkwardness between them. But thankfully, a playful light kindled to life in his eyes. When he gave her his wolfish smile, Molly almost sagged in relief.

Visibly relaxing, too, Julian put his arms around her and dragged her to his side, and Molly knew as she snuggled against him that whatever happened, it was all going to be all right.

As long as she had Julian.

"You know I love you, don't you?" she whispered up at him once again, kissing his hard cheek. It was not the first time she'd said it, not at all. But this time, he drew back and met her gaze, his smile fading. Then he planted a long, hard kiss on her temple, his voice gruff as he told her, in her ear, so nobody else could hear, "So do I."

Six

So here we are now, Molly thought as she rode the elevator up to the top floor of the *San Antonio Daily* building the next day.

At last Garrett seemed to be ready to do something about her situation with Julian. The question was: What was he going to do?

And how was Molly going to react to it?

She honestly didn't know. Whatever happened today, though, she wore her largest earrings and her thickest bangles and her sassiest attitude to the meeting. It was a trick she used when she needed the extra security boost. There was just something about big jewelry that made her feel better no matter how dreary things looked or how anxious she felt. So now it was one minute until noon, and she was every bit the confident lady as she marched down the long hall that led to the executive offices.

"Molly!" Julian's assistant exclaimed with obvious

warmth, glancing up at her through her spectacles from behind an enormous desk. "I didn't know you were paying a visit! He went out to lunch...."

Smiling, Molly greeted the older woman with an affectionate hug. Ms. Watts had been with Jules forever and sometimes conspired with Molly to pull Julian out of important meetings. Just for fun.

"I'm actually here for Garrett today, Ms. Watts." But her stomach felt queasy, and suddenly she very much wished she was having lunch with Julian instead.

She was led directly into his office by Garrett's assistant, a younger woman who sat at an identically enormous desk not too far away. Molly couldn't help but straighten her spine when she was announced. "Miss Devaney to see you, Mr. Gage," the assistant intoned, and then quickly shut the doors behind her.

Over six feet tall, with dark hair and broad shoulders, Garrett stood by the window with his hands in his jacket pockets, radiating intimidation. Her knees felt knobby as she walked forward, somehow expecting to catch a glimpse of something telling in his expression. But his face revealed nothing at all when he turned around and gave her a brief, almost businesslike smile.

"Molly, I don't think I need to tell you why you're here? Or why Kate—" he signaled to her sister, whom Molly just now noticed sitting behind Garrett's desk, pretty as you please "—and I want to talk to you today."

Molly sat down across the desk from Kate, still absorbing the fact that he had not meant to have a "private" conversation with her at all. Private had merely meant without Julian present.

The realization made her scowl at him, her blackest, angriest scowl.

She couldn't help noticing Garrett seemed so detached

today, unlike the passionate lover of that magical evening. Of course, the man had excellent control, so you never knew with him. That night, he'd sure as hell surprised her, too. Now Molly looked into his eyes but try as she might, she detected no special heat as he looked at her.

Had she completely misread him? Had he been so drunk that just…any "wench" would have done? How could he stand there, so lamplike, after he'd caught her in a dark room with Julian? Even Julian, who was known to be the cool and aloof brother, looked at her with much more… Actually, Julian's looks set her on fire. But enough of that.

They were just different, the two men—and she had to stop comparing them.

She had to get it through her thick skull, once and for all, that those kisses with Julian last night had been pure error. She'd gotten carried away and she wasn't even certain why she'd done something so reckless as to tempt a lion like Julian. Except maybe she knew that he would never take things too far with her.

Or *would he?*

Because last night in bed, she'd been so tormented and confused. The things he'd whispered, the things he'd made her feel as he'd kissed her had been the most intense she'd ever felt in her life, even more than on the night—

No. It couldn't be.

How could anything top what she'd felt that night at the masquerade? Was it right to feel all this excitement and passion when just *any* guy kissed her? No. She knew it was impossible, it was too overpowering, too special.

So then what was the matter with her?

"Can you please explain to us what's going on between you and Julian?" Garrett queried, breaking into her reflections.

Completely disbelieving his tone, Molly leaned back

in her chair and crossed her arms, her bangles making a clanking noise.

Wow.

She'd really made up that whole masquerade soul-mate kiss, hadn't she?

Garrett didn't seem jealous *at all,* and now her silly thoughts of marrying him were quickly being dashed. She'd thought she was luring him in with her plan and now she wondered if he was even hungry for the hook she'd tossed him. Apparently, Garrett only had a weakness for Molly in a *wench* costume and while he was inebriated out of his ever-loving mind.

Wow. Really. She was such a dope.

"Are you two seriously going to pretend you don't know? Or do I need to spell it out to you?" Molly asked him, getting supremely irritated by all this. Where was the man who'd kissed her at the masquerade? Where was the hunger that awakened hers? The passion that had ignited hers? Had it all been a joke? A dream? A ruse?

When neither Kate nor Garrett answered and her masquerade man refused to make an appearance, her irritation increased tenfold. So they were going to drill her and intimidate her. Did they interrogate Julian like this, too?

"We're together, Garrett," Molly suddenly said, thrusting her chin out defiantly and sounding damned proud. "I moved in with him. I'm his gi—lover. And I've never been so happy." The last was true. She'd always had the most fun with Jules, had loved him beyond loving anyone else, protected him beyond anyone else. They covered for each other, laughed with each other, fought with each other....

This morning they'd had breakfast together, and they'd laughed. Even after the debacle of last night. They'd laughed.

"Did you know," Garrett said softly, his eyes kind, "this

is exactly what we feared would happen all these years. My mother, Kate, Landon and I. We feared Julian and you would dive headfirst into each other and one of you, especially you, Molly, might not make it out."

With a painful frown, Molly wondered why Garrett didn't just drop the mask already and step into his sexy black masquerade boots. He'd had *guts* that night, taking what he wanted, which had clearly been *her*. Today? He merely seemed concerned, like a brother would be, and that had definitely not been Molly's plan from the start. "Why would you think that about me and Julian?" she challenged, wanting to scoff at the accusation.

His dark eyes widened in surprise, as though Molly were lacking in brainpower to have overlooked something so obvious. Kate stepped in to explain, "Because when you were teens you were infatuated with each other, Molls. You cried when I told you he was like your brother. You cried for days and when I demanded to know why, you told me it was because of what I'd said. Because you wouldn't be able to marry him now."

Molly groaned and rolled her eyes. "I must have been ten, Kate."

"You never cry, Molly. Never. The only times I've seen you cry in your life have been all about Jules."

"Because they sent him away and it sucked!"

"There you go," Garrett said.

She scowled. "I just don't see how our relationship concerns any of you. We've had a bond since the beginning."

In fact, Molly knew the story by heart, for it had been related to her not only by Eleanor Gage, his mother, but later by Landon, Kate, Garrett, even Julian himself.

On the day the Devaney sisters had come to live at the Gage mansion, Molly had been a mere three years old.

She'd been introduced, along with Kate, to all the family members and staff, but she'd hardly paid any attention because she had a lollipop stuck in her mouth and she was gladly sucking it. Embarrassed by this, Kate had tried to convince her to hand over the lollipop, since she'd been the one who'd given it to her in the first place, but it was all to no avail. And yet while they proceeded to do the introductions, Molly's attention had fixated on the blond, green-eyed boy who looked at her in amusement. She toddled over to him, took her lollipop out of her mouth, and graciously offered it to him with a cheeky grin.

Julian had been six at the time, and even when his mother had beamed a silent command at him to refuse the germ-filled offering, Julian had shoved it into his mouth and smiled down at Molly. Just like that, they'd been instant friends.

Now Molly looked pointedly at Garrett and cocked a brow, wondering if he even remembered that story. They'd only told it about twenty times or so, if she recalled correctly. The family laughed about it, joking that what the other brothers accomplished with force, the younger brother accomplished with a grin.

"Molly." Kate clasped her hands before her in a silent plea. "I just need you to assure me that you know what you're doing. Julian's relationships don't last. In fact, he's never even had one, only one-night stands and weekend flings. You're in way over your head here, Moo!"

"I'm not his weekend fling, Kate," she defended, suddenly fierce, determined to show them she was at no risk and meant more to Julian than that, even though what she was defending was a fake liaison intended to make Garrett jealous. "What makes you think Jules would ever hurt me? He's the only guy I know that would give me a kidney if I needed one! In fact, he's so good to me I'll bet he'd even give me two!"

The worry creases on Kate's forehead only seemed to double. "You've really fallen for him, haven't you?"

It killed Molly not to be able to tell her sister the truth, so she could at least wipe that worry off her pretty face, but then how could she assure her what a lie her relationship with Julian was, when she herself couldn't understand why she'd even kissed him yesterday?

Since she'd moved in with him, she'd been bombarded with strange feelings and emotions, hardly getting any sleep as she lay in her bed, wondering about all the *what-if*s and *could be*s in her life.

Saying good morning to him in his sexy pajamas with his six-pack abs showing was torture. Bantering with him, wanting to be close to him...

She didn't even know what she felt anymore.

She'd wanted to find love in her life, because she'd already found success in her profession. Wasn't it normal to always want something? But this time she sensed that what she wanted was nearby, but she couldn't put a name to it, and that frustrated her out of her mind.

She'd been counting on Garrett to reignite the spark in her today, not leave her feeling cold and empty. She'd been counting on this meeting where he could help her straighten out her head, and more importantly, her emotions.

Instead, she and Julian were being attacked, and it made her want to stick her claws out for him. For them. For what they had, which nobody had ever really understood in the first place.

"Julian would never hurt me," she said as she rose, fighting to keep from shouting. "I promise you if you ever see me cry because of him, I give you permission to shoot me."

"I'd actually prefer to shoot *him*," Garrett said drily.

Whipping around to face him, Molly stared at this large,

handsome man, thinking he'd always been a great influence in her life. He'd always felt responsible for her father's death. Even though the Devaney sisters had never blamed him for what had happened, it seemed as if Garrett would never forgive himself.

Which sometimes made his smiles seem sad. And made him try too hard to make things right for Kate and Molly, protect them. But…protect Molly from Julian? *Oh, puleeze!* Julian had been as crucial as sunshine to her since she was a toddler. He'd been her hero before she even heard of the word or understood its meaning.

Garrett was a good man, a great man, in fact, and Molly knew he would be a faithful and giving husband if he could only give himself a chance. But did he need to be drunk to let go the way he had at the masquerade?

Whatever the reason, she feared that the man who'd kissed her that night was an illusion. And if she'd ever, ever doubted whether she would have to choose between Garrett and Julian, it was an easy choice now that she was faced with it.

Her hero won outright.

"What is your problem with Julian anyway?" Molly asked, aghast and affronted. "Both of you—you're always riding him about something. If I were him, I'd…never talk to you again."

She pivoted for the door, but Garrett's voice stopped her.

"That little toad is my brother. Of course I love him. We merely feel responsible to protect you."

She grabbed the knob and turned. "If I need protecting from anything, I will tell you, but the last person on this earth I need protecting from is Julian." She yanked the door open and then added, "And if you love your brother so much, then I suggest you try to make things work around here before he leaves the *Daily* for good—Lord knows *I* would! Who the hell can even work in peace with this sort of constant criticism? I'm glad he's ready to move on!"

"Excuse me?"

"You heard me!" she shot back.

She gave Kate a look that said *don't do this to me again,* and with that, she stormed outside.

"Molly!" Garrett followed her, stopping her a couple of feet from where his secretary was busily tapping her computer keypad. "Where's my brother going? Is he leaving the *Daily?*"

"I want to go now, Garrett," she grumbled, trying to pull her arm free.

He drew her closer. "He's leaving the *Daily,* isn't he?"

Hating herself for having spoken so rashly, Molly dropped her face. "I think you misunderstood," she hedged.

"No, I didn't. I know he's not happy here, Molly. I've been suspecting for a time now. But if you aren't telling me when he's leaving or where, then at least answer me this. Do you love him?" he asked.

Molly stared up at the man she'd once thought she loved and wondered why her throat closed up in a tight little ball. Why she wanted to wail her heart out to him over that question alone.

Because of course the answer was yes, a thousand times *yes.*

She loved Julian in so many ways, she hadn't even begun to discover them all. And she feared that loving him as a friend was only one of them.

Halting just a few feet from his own office door, Julian saw them. Molly and the "love of her life," together at last.

He saw them say goodbye. Saw his brother pat her back. Saw her take a little sob and drop her face into his jacket. Saw him put his arm around her.

His blood simmered. His heart caved in on itself. And suddenly red-hot anger coursed through his veins and his eyes blurred with the force of his fury. Maybe this was what Molly had wanted all along. She had practiced with Julian last night so she could get out here and make Garrett jealous, make him see her as the lovely, sexy, grown woman that she was.

Perhaps Julian should've stepped back and let his best friend be coddled by the man she wanted to be coddled by.

He should laugh it off, not care. But it mattered very much. *Too* much.

Body shaking, he was amazed he could speak so calmly, so softly, as he walked up to them. "I hate to break up your tête-à-tête, but if you don't take your hands off Molly, I'm going to beat your face until our own mother won't recognize you."

Garrett stiffened, but his arms instantly dropped as his head whipped toward his. "What the hell is wrong with you, Jules?"

Julian gritted his teeth as Molly swung around in surprise. Ignoring Garrett, he stretched out his hand to her, palm up, and gazed intently into her red-rimmed eyes. She'd been crying, or about to cry. Dammit, why? He pursed his lips in anger. At her, at himself, at this entire mess he'd gotten himself into.

He'd wanted time to let things unfold naturally.

He didn't want to pull all the stops he used with other women and seduce the hell out of her. Because this was the only girl who knew him, respected him, admired him— he was *real* with her. He wanted it to be perfectly natural with her. No bull. And it just wasn't happening that way, dammit. "What day is today, Molly?"

She sniffled, then wiped the corner of her eye with one fingertip. "Um?"

"What day is it?"

She told him the date, and he nodded gravely and bent to whisper in her ear so that nobody would hear his words but *Molly*. "Exactly. You're still my girl. Aren't you? We said a month. Didn't we?"

She blinked as he drew back to survey her reaction, and when her gaze strayed to Garrett, Julian's chest tightened with rage.

Garrett, his brother.

Whom he suddenly, profoundly abhorred.

Her tear-streaked blue eyes came back to him, and she nodded and mumbled, "Of course. Take me home, all right?" And to Garrett, she said almost placatingly, "Thanks for the chat. Think about what I told you before I...stepped out, okay?"

Garrett nodded before Julian led Molly by the elbow toward his assistant's desk. He barked a dozen orders, then led Molly with him to the elevators.

Neither spoke on the drive home.

"So tell me," Julian finally said as they entered his apartment, his emotions having fermented during the drive. He was close to exploding now. "Tell me what he did to make you cry like this."

Molly stared at him with wide, shining eyes that made him want to wrap her up in his arms and keep the world from so much as looking at her, she looked so damn lost and so damn vulnerable. Her voice was a soft, puzzled whisper. "What's wrong with you today?"

He drew a deep breath, then let it all out. "He doesn't deserve you, Molly! I know a guy who's so crazy about you, he would do anything to be with you—*anything*. He'd lie for you, cheat for you, steal for you—"

She scoffed, everything sounding more ludicrous to her

by the second. "Are you getting high on my paint supply? Who are you talking about? Who would do such a thing?"

"Take a wild guess, Molls."

"I have no clue what you're talking about!"

"I could kill him for making you cry like this." Julian sat down on the living room sofa and threw his shoes off with a bang. "This obsession with my brother just pisses me the hell off, Molly. Like nothing in my life has ever pissed me off before."

She crossed her arms, suddenly glaring. He might have been pissed off, but he had no idea what was wrong with her. That she cried because she realized the entire masquerade night had been a stupid illusion in the first place. That the man she'd thought she loved…just wasn't the Garrett she knew. And like all the other men she'd ever met in her life, he would end up paling to Julian in every possible way she could imagine.

But how could she admit to this man, whose respect she craved and wanted above all others, that she just might have screwed it all up and was not really in love with Garrett? That the man she wanted was…unattainable. And that his brother and her sister had been warning her away from him because he would hurt her?

Oh, how she'd wanted to tear their eyes out when she heard them! Even if they might be right.

She gnawed on her lower lip and said nothing, focusing instead on getting ready to vent her frustrations on the only person she could vent with.

Julian.

"Just tell me what you see in him all of a sudden that you find so irresistible. Tell me why you'd go cry on his shoulder and not with *me*."

Oh, God, what was happening to her?

Her legs went flaccid with a mere look into those stormy

green eyes. He was so handsome, his jaw square and rigid, his eyebrows two sharp, bleak slashes. He was more enraged than she'd ever seen him before. She could even think he was *jealous,* and the thought summoned a deep, dark stirring in her that she'd been feeling more and more frequently lately—at the most inconvenient times. A powerful little ache in her body that craved for him to wrap his arms around her and... She didn't know what she wanted him to do.

She ached for closeness with him, almost trembled with the need. She wanted to smell his scent all around her and to feel his hands everywhere and enjoy the hardness of those big, big biceps bulge as he held her imprisoned against his body. She wanted him so close, closer, closest. As if mere friendship was no longer enough with him. As if revealing every intimate detail of her life to him, her fears, her desires...

Was. Not. Enough.

Anymore.

"Are you planning to answer me, Molly?"

Molly's throat seemed to be working extra hard to get the words out. She didn't know why her nipples were beaded under her cotton turquoise sundress, why the way Jules was shooting fire at her with his eyes made her breathless and shaky and strange. She fought against the sensations, struggling to focus on his question.

She threw her hands up in the air in frustration. "I don't know, Jules! All right? Maybe I hated when he was overly protective of us, the way he took it upon himself to chaperone you and me. He never let us have fun together, like we were doing something wrong, and we *weren't*. You may be hot for anything that walks but he never realized that we were always just friends. But I truly don't think he was being deliberately mean. Maybe he was just trying to do the noble thing out of caring and respect for me and out of respect for my father, who protected him." She softened her voice as she tried to save the last remains of her hope.

Julian's glare could have melted all the ice in Alaska. "Garrett pulled you away from me because he knew that— He knew I—" His face darkened, and Molly's nipples pricked with wanting as she watched his fingers curl into fists at his sides. An image of those fingers clutching her breasts when he'd whispered sexy confessions into her ear returned to her, and she swallowed. This was *so* not the time to get worked up about that.

Jumping to his feet, he plunged a frustrated hand through his hair and thoroughly ruffled it. "And what about him and Kate? Hell, Molls, have you not seen the way your sister looks at him? You're both pining away for the same man."

Molly blinked in stupefaction, her eyebrows pulling low when she registered what he'd said. "You're lying. You—you can't mean that— Kate doesn't feel that way about him."

"Kate is like a sister to me. I know lust when I see it, Molls."

Horrified, Molly gaped at the thought of her sister loving Garrett. So quietly? And for how long? It couldn't be.

Fiddling with one enormous hoop earring, she shook her head several times. "Jules—you don't understand. Garrett and I have *done* things. We kissed one night and it was... magical, like it was meant to be."

Freezing in place as though she'd said something monumental, Julian openly gawked at her until his expression emptied into such a blank look that it might have been comical if she didn't find it thoroughly alarming. "He *kissed* you?"

Molly offered him an embarrassed little nod, then

groaned in self-pity and buried her face in her hands. "I've never felt such a connection in my life except with you. What I felt that night seemed so real, it was like we recognized each other, like we knew we were soul mates…"

But it was all an illusion, and I can't understand it and I'm so confused.

Julian stalked a short distance away as though he didn't know what do with himself, and then he returned, his jaw muscles working restlessly. "You're kidding me, Molly. Say it now, Molls. Right. Now. Tell me you're kidding me, Moo."

She could only imagine how it looked to him, the guy she had been devouring with her lips yesterday, that she'd let his brother do that, too. What was wrong with her? Why had she felt nothing when she'd looked at Garrett today?

But it *had* happened.

Hadn't it?

"I'm not even sure it was real anymore," she admitted as she fell on the couch and covered her face with her hands. "It all happened at that loathsome masquerade, when I was wearing that stupid wench costume you dared me to wear! He…he was wearing all black. I was outside and thought it was you, and then he kissed me, and we did some intimate things, and I noticed the ring he was wearing as he held me, and I knew that it must be him."

The deafening, tomblike silence that followed stretched so long and taut, she sat up in confusion and studied Julian in growing alarm.

Suddenly, he stormed down the hallway like a man possessed, and Molly sighed and rubbed her temples to ward off a headache. She just hoped he hadn't gone to fetch a gun or something, for what was she going to do now? She was usually the impulsive one and always counted on *Jules* being the one with a cool head.

She considered following him, talking some reason into him, explaining that it was just a kiss and all that, but then he returned less than a minute later and produced something shiny from his pants pocket.

He sounded livid now. Livid.

"You mean this ring, Molly?"

Seven

As Molly stared at the ring he was holding between his two fingers, a horrific sensation crawled up her stomach like a tarantula.

She blinked several times, and her jaw fell open. "Wh-what are you doing with that?"

Garrett used to wear it all day, every day. The platinum was scratched and dented with age, for it had been in the family for generations, boasting at its center a rare blue diamond that was supposed to be worth millions.

"It's my ring. *Mine*. I won it from him. Over a month ago. He bet me that it was worth more than my autographed Mark McGwire seventieth-home-run baseball when he was *really* freaking drunk. He was off by several hundred thousand and lost the bet." Julian smiled at her, a sharp, angry smile that cut through her skin like the clean, expert slice of a dagger. "I just wear the ring to piss him off sometimes when I know I'll be seeing him."

All the color drained from her face, as though all the blood in her body was going straight to her heart, which was racing in her breast like a mad thing. If her ears were hearing correctly and her dazed brain processing correctly, it seemed that he was basically admitting to owning that ring on the night of the masquerade. The night that a stranger had kissed her ever-loving heart out.

Oh. My. God.

The conclusion she'd come up with terrified her. Julian…had been the one wearing that ring? Julian had whispered…those sexy words in his raspy voice while his big, long-fingered hands had touched her so provocatively…?

Julian. Her hero. Her protector. Her best friend. Her young crush. Her lifetime love.

It had been Julian who'd kissed her and made her have an orgasm while he'd fondled her? How he must have laughed! Laughed at her naïveté, at her stupidity, at her…

"I can't believe," he breathed softly, his eyes glowing like golden moons, "that you wouldn't know that I was the one who kissed you that night."

Grief and unexpected humiliation cut through her like a thousand knives. Julian had known all this time.

Her chest constricted so tightly she thought she would break apart, but she still stubbornly shook her head from side to side. "I don't understand."

His kisses. Oh, dear, his kisses. Three total. Each one so different. One, passionate and drunk. The next, cocky and trying to show off in front of Kate. And the last one, in a dark room, where it was just him and her, supposedly playing a game.…

Please no, I can't be that stupid.

"I don't understand," she repeated, more frantic now.

In three steps, he closed the distance between them, and

when his fingers curled around her arm, Molly could feel the leashed power in his hold, see how he visibly fought for control. "I think I do. You thought I was Garrett that night—when I kissed you hard enough to make your mouth swell under mine. You let me put my hands between your legs, touch your breasts, maul you like a—"

"Stop it, Julian. *Stop it!*"

She leaped away and backed off, hardly able to look into those fiercely jealous green eyes, which were only reminding her that he—he who was her *everything*—had done all that. Every bit of what he'd said, and more.

Julian had kissed her, had turned her life upside down with his touch. He'd made her shatter in his arms, and then he'd acted as if it had meant nothing. *Nothing.*

He was her best friend, and yet he'd kept her in the dark all this time. He'd been intimate with her, had made her feel as if he wanted her, cherished her, but instead he'd been happily helping her seduce his own *brother!*

"How *dare* you!" she exploded at that. "How dare you do that to me and then say nothing!"

His eyes flashed, and he threw his arms up in the air. "What did you want me to say? That it was a mistake? That I got carried away by your pretty blue eyes and the way you looked in that scrap of a dress?" he shot back. "You *told me* not to mention it, and since I was drunk and clearly screwed up, I thought it was a damned good idea. You pretended nothing happened the next day, and I *went* with it. At least it gave me time to get it right."

"Get *what* right, you idiot? You just shot our friendship to hell!" She pushed him aside and stormed away to her bedroom, adding as she went, "Now excuse me if I go pack, you…you jerk! How could you even agree to help me seduce Garrett after you touched me like you did, you… Oh! *I can't even think of a word for you!*"

She slammed the door with a bang.

Her lungs burning for air, she fell back weakly against the door and stared at the bed with blurry eyes. She glanced at the walk-in closet, tempted to leave this very second. She would leave. Of course she would. But she needed him to drive her, or Kate to come get her, and she'd die before she made that request of either of them right now.

A desolate sensation weighed heavy on her chest as she thought of the mural waiting upstairs, a safe haven for her to get lost in a sea of color. She had never left a work unfinished and she was not going to start now because of that…that douche!

She would finish it tonight, or at least try to, and then she'd leave tomorrow.

She still couldn't believe it. He had known…all along, all this time. The bastard had already kissed her, fondled her, known how easy it was to make her explode.

What mockery.

That beautiful masquerade kiss now mocked her. Her best friendship in the world—her entire life—mocked her.

One after another, memories flashed before her eyes, and there wasn't a single happy memory that she could remember not featuring Julian. She saw him smiling down at her like a lone wolf, tweaking her nose, rumpling her hair, driving her back home. She saw him snarling at her and teasing her and tickling her, and calling her Mo-Po, Mopey, Moo, Molls, Mo-Mo, Moo-Moo….

Nausea rose up her throat, and she shakily sat down on the edge of the bed, held a pillow to her chest and drew in deep breaths. But she didn't seem capable of filling her lungs. She'd just never felt so empty. So stupid. So used. Nothing in her life had ever hurt this much, not even when Jules had left her all those times.

But he won't make me cry anymore, she thought angrily, remembering Kate's recent words.

Teeth gritted, she curled up into a rigid little ball with the pillow firmly grasped to her core, and something very deep inside her clenched tight as the images of that night bombarded her once more.

His mouth, firm and urgent, the roughened sound he made as he kissed the tops of her breasts, as if he'd just entered heaven and they had been made just for him.

The way he'd groaned and bent his head to her ear, biting the lobe hungrily, desperately, and then how he'd soothingly murmured to her, "Shh…shh…"

Her eyes stung with unshed tears. How could she not have known?

She'd been so sure it was him at first, that wolfish smile so familiar to her, but then the way he'd fiercely kissed her had been so completely unlike her cocky best friend. Why did it have to be him? The man couldn't keep his hands to himself and just had to have a piece of her, too?

She'd promised herself when she was a thirteen-year-old girl that she would not shed any more tears for Julian John. He meant too much to her, was too special to her, made her feel like a princess being rescued by a hero. She'd promised herself she would get rid of the infatuation she had with him, her silly crush, because everyone told her he would hurt her and they couldn't all be wrong.

But it was no use because now the truth stared her in the face, and yes, yes, yes, it mocked her, too.

The man she'd felt she'd die if she didn't kiss again…

The man she knew in her gut was her soul mate…

That man was the only man in the world who could really, truly break her heart into such tiny particles she would never be able to piece herself back together.

And now even their friendship, the one golden and steady thing in her life, was gone.

Julian wanted to punch something.

He paced his room for hours, restless, his emotions gone berserk. Jealousy coursed through his veins like some sort of acrid poison as he remembered Molly's moans, the way she'd responded to him the night of their first kiss, like her body was a harp only his fingers knew how to pluck and tune and play...

And all while she'd thought he was Garrett.

His brother.

The guy who'd been holding her when she was in tears today.

The guy who'd owned every one of her desires for weeks.

The guy whom he very much wanted to kill right now.

He replayed the scenes over and over in his mind, recalling the hurt in Molly's eyes when he'd set her little head straight this evening. When he'd told her that he was the man who had kissed her that night, touched her so intimately and made her go off like a hot, beautiful firework in his arms. Goddammit, she'd almost seemed disappointed he hadn't been Garrett!

He gritted his teeth at the thought, deeply regretting not confronting her about it the day after the masquerade. All this time she'd been hunting for his brother thinking of *Julian's kiss*. To hell with whether she wanted to talk about it or not! If he'd done things right, he might have been holding her in his arms all this time—and not under false pretenses—and kept her from noticing Garrett. All these sleepless nights. Nights she'd wanted to have a friendly sleepover with him—yeah, right. As if he could stand being in the same bed with her without turning into some ravenous, sex-starved maniac.

Did she not *see* he'd been crazy about her for twenty years?

He had thought he could screw Molly out of his head, but clearly that had not worked. Okay, so he'd kissed her when he was drunk and hadn't talked to her afterward. Not suave. She'd expected better of him? Yeah, well, that made two of them. He wasn't too pleased to find out that she'd thought all along that it was his brother who'd kissed her.

Now they both felt like fools.

Groaning in despair, he plopped down on the bed, full of rage and agony and disgust. He couldn't stand the impotence he felt. Restless, he changed into his pajama pants and yanked back his bedcovers, but all he did was toss and turn restlessly on the bed.

So maybe he should've talked to her about that evening. Except he'd thought it best to forget about one drunken night's kiss and continue with his plans until he could do things the right way.

Well, he sure as hell was mucking it up right now, wasn't he?

No way was he going to stand for it. Suave Julian, they used to call him. How he was so cool, aloof. Yeah, right. Clearly not where Molly was concerned. His Achilles' heel. But also his greatest strength. If he had become someone and done something with himself, it was all because of that incredible redhead in his life and his desperation to show his family that he was worthy of her.

Shoving the covers aside, he stalked across his bedroom and out to the hall, where moonlight streamed through the living room windows and across his apartment.

He found the door to her bedroom ajar. He rapped his

knuckles on the wood, waited a second, then pushed the door open wider.

Her bed sat empty. It hadn't been slept in.

Scowling, he stalked the entire apartment, every square foot, and found it empty.

Heart pounding seriously hard now, hard enough to crack one of his ribs, he jammed the elevator buttons and rode up to the penthouse, his mind racing with a thousand thoughts per minute, shouting out its conclusion: *she left, she left, she left, you idiot!*

But when the elevator doors opened, he saw her.

She lay on the marble floor of his new offices, dressed in nothing but a giant button-down shirt, her hair a pool of red fanning behind her as she slept with her hands tucked under her left cheek. He drank up her image as he approached her, drinking up her image, the perfect image of this woman he'd loved since they'd first met.

She should not be sleeping on the floor. God, never on the floor.

She deserved a bed, pillows, satin sheets and a man to love her with all the passion that she unfailingly conveyed in each of her artworks.

His eyes glued to her moonlit face, he knelt at her side— she was just so damned beautiful his eyes hurt. A streak of green paint crossed her forearm to her elbow, and he ached to trace it with his fingers, then with his lips. He noticed the empty paint tubes scattered around her sleeping form and glanced up at the colorful wall before him. His heart wrenched with regret when he realized she'd been trying to finish the mural.

So she could leave.

Leave him for good.

Now, when JJG Enterprises was almost ready for his final walk-through and just days away from opening to its employees. Now, when he had grown accustomed to her being here as he met with contractors, architects, painting her heart away on a wall that had been empty before she'd made it come to life with little playful flicks of her dainty hands.

She wanted to leave now, when Julian was days away from fulfilling one of his dreams and ready to focus on the next one—the possibility of sharing the rest of his life with her.

Throat dense with emotion, he stroked the curve of her cheek with the back of one fingertip.

She sighed contentedly at that, relaxed in her sleep. Shoving aside his hesitation, he reached out, gently scooped her up and carried her back to the elevator. She was as light as a feather and as warm as a little chicken, and his chest swelled when she sought out his heat and snuggled closer. But when the audible chime signaled their arrival on his apartment floor, Molly grew heavy in his arms, and he saw her spiky titian lashes flutter open.

Their eyes clashed. Her gaze was dewy, sleepy, and Julian's muscles tensed as he waited for her to speak up, praying her first words weren't "Put me down!"

He tightened his grip as he waited for the inevitable, but instead of kicking or screaming and demanding he release her, Molly hugged him even tighter and buried her face into his neck, where she quietly started sobbing.

The words tumbled out of his throat in an anxious rush. "Molly. Molly, I'm sorry. Don't cry. I'm sorry for what I said."

"No, Jules, I'm s-sorry, too. I—I overreacted, I—I'm s-so stupid. I should've known you anywhere. I should've known it was *you*."

Julian might have been considered a daredevil among

his sports friends, but seeing Molly cry just now tore up his insides.

He didn't think about what he was doing, only followed his instincts and carried her to his bedroom. He sat on the edge of his bed and clutched her quaking body to the exact place where his heart spasmed like an open wound inside his chest.

"I'm sorry, Molly. I should've brought it up and at least apologized," he said, smoothing his hands down her shivering back.

Her chest heaved as she sighed and stayed buried against his throat. "No, no, it was me. How could I not have known...not have *realized?*" She sniffled and glanced up, her eyes wide and blue and glazed with emotion. "At first I thought it was you, but then I felt his ring pressing against my arm. Why were you wearing it? Why didn't you tell me?"

"Baby, I thought you knew it was me that night. I thought you responded because it was *me*. I was going to leave you alone, Molly, but you called me back onto the terrace and I couldn't stop myself."

He had a similar sensation now as he marveled at the incredible feel of her in his arms, warm and shivering and vulnerable, like she'd been that night, ravenous for his mouth and his touches. He wanted to protect her, possess her, claim her, love her, make her never ever think again of anyone but him.

Cradling her face, he wiped her tears with the pads of his thumbs. "Why would you think it was Garrett, Molly? Don't you see the way I look at you? The way I want you? Everyone around us has noticed but you. Do you believe I'd help another man, *any* man, get even a little piece of you, when I've been waiting all my life to claim you as mine?"

She looked into his face, and her eyes widened at his

words, as though she'd only just realized that he *wanted* her. Her hands trembled as she cupped the back of his head, and then she kissed him. Softly. Whispering against his lips, "I love you. I'd die if I lost you, Jules. I'd rather lose my arms and never paint again than lose you."

Her lips pressed lightly against his, the words, the touch sending a shock of awareness bolting through his system. He stiffened under her, his heart kicking full speed, pumping hard and loud as a jolt of arousal coursed through his bloodstream.

When she drew back, her eyes shone like beacons, and the blatant desire he saw in those blue, blue eyes could've toppled him to his knees.

He was having trouble getting a word out, his arms shaking as he palmed her face between his open hands. "Do you want me?" he finally rasped.

His lips tingled from her sweet kiss, and now his mouth burned with the hunger to plunder her lips. Ripe with innocence, wet and pink and waiting to unleash all her passion on him. He needed to make her his. Only his. He couldn't bear another night, another second, another moment of his life without this.

He splayed his fingers across her scalp and gazed into her eyes in the shadows, so intoxicated with her nearness, he could only murmur in a thick whisper, "Do you want me, Molly? Do you want to be with me?" He slid his fingers down her back to palm the round curves of her buttocks, gently pulling her closer.

She nodded, struggling for air.

He gripped her hair within his fists and pinned her in place as he swept down. "I need to kiss you, touch you, make love to you." He fitted his lips perfectly to hers. His tongue plowed, swift and fast, into the warmth of her open mouth, and the pleasure of connection was so intense, a riptide of sensations racked his entire body.

She felt familiar and at the same time exotic and intoxicating to him. She was marshmallows in fire, lollipops under the covers, the best memories of his youth…she was museums, Monaco, fine wine….

She was Molly.

His lovely, effervescent Molly.

And he'd loved her almost as long as he'd been alive.

His arms snaked out to guide her legs around his hips, and suddenly she was straddling him, almost weightless, but burning hot and moving in restless excitement against him, her hands gliding up the bare muscles of his torso, her mouth ravenous on his. "Jules," she murmured. "Jules, I'm sorry for what I said."

"Shh, I'm sorry, too. Let's just forgive each other. You're mine, Molly, and I can't wait to be inside you." He twirled his tongue around hers, her body eagerly rocking over his hardness. Agonizing pleasure ripped through him as her weight bounced seductively over his straining erection.

Things went from slow to urgent in a heartbeat.

He anxiously unbuttoned her shirt, and when she started doing it herself, his hands slid up to caress her face. Panting fast and hard, he stroked her reddened bottom lip with alternating thumbs, her lovely jaw cradled within his cupped palms. He'd never seen so much desire in a woman's eyes. So much emotion. Her lips were so luscious, plump and damp and so unbelievably swollen from his kiss.

Desire pumped, hot and heady, through his bloodstream as he laid her down on the bed and pushed off his drawstring pants, licking her calves, her knees, touching her, looking at her—he couldn't get enough, do it quick enough, couldn't see her naked fast enough.

He wanted to part her slim, white thighs and taste her

honey. He wanted to make her gasp and moan and thrash against him as he introduced her to the greatest pleasures in the world. He was cooking inside of his body and he hadn't even started to do everything he wanted to. He had never thought he could want a woman like this.

He wanted to revere her. Adore her.

Molly was just as desperate, her fingers somehow cramping on the last buttons of her shirt. "I can't get this thing off. Please get it off, get it off, Jules!"

He cursed under his breath and lunged forward. He was being ripped in two from so much desire, so much rapture. He could barely speak from the euphoria, his fingers working as fast as they could through the tremors already shaking him.

"Is this mine? Is this an old shirt of mine?"

She nodded, and he swiftly grabbed it in both fists and tore it open, buttons flying everywhere. His blood roared like a monster in his ears when he parted the material, revealing flawless creamy skin he wanted to devour until tomorrow.

"Is this what you want, Molly?" He ducked to put his mouth on a beaded nipple that thrust up in the air. He laved it thoroughly as he rolled her to her side and sprawled his body right next to her as his hands engulfed the round curves of her buttocks and he drew her tighter against him, enabling him to feast on her breast like a man possessed.

She arched up against him as he twirled his tongue around the protruding tip, her whispers tickling his hair, "Yes, oh, please!"

He groaned, because he could never deny her. *Never*. He wanted her to be certain she wanted him and only him, as a man and as a lover, but she felt so right, was hot and lusty in his arms, in his bed, where he'd spent many sleepless nights as he imagined her lying in her own bed just next door.

No. He couldn't stop if he'd wanted to. For the first time in his life, he would be truly making love with someone.

Heart pounding at what was about to happen, something irrevocable, monumental, something he'd thought about his whole life, Julian turned her onto her back, his hands roaming down her curvy body, squeezing her lovely thighs as he kissed her long and languorously. "I want you. I need you. You feel so perfect. It's like coming home."

Her red hair splayed over his white down pillows. Her chest rose and fell heavily with each breath, her eyes so trusting he could drown in them. "I'm still a virgin, Jules." She reached out to stroke his dampened lips with one fingertip.

He placed a kiss on the tip of that fingertip. "Sweet, sweet baby, you have no idea what knowing that does to me." He was so honored, so turned on that he would be her first, her only. His hands shook as he eased the shirt off her shoulders and helped her pull it off her arms. "I'll be extra careful, but you have to tell me if I ever go too fa— Oh, Molly, *look at you*."

His eyes blurred at the sight of her completely naked. Her slim legs, her tiny hips, the little thatch of red curls at the apex of her thighs, and the two perfect globes of her breasts staring back at him, large and round, with those perky pink nipples that begged to be laved and licked and loved until morning.

She drew his hand up to one large globe, her eyes holding his with such innocent seduction he could've wept. His body trembled with anticipation, excitement.

"Do you want me to kiss you here again?" he gruffly said, and cupped both her breasts in his big hands, gently squeezing. She shivered in pleasure when he began teasing the pink areolae with his thumbs.

He bent his head and took one firm bud between his lips. He flicked it with his tongue first, then drew it deeply into his mouth as his hand trailed down her stomach. She gasped under him. Her hips rolled enticingly as his fingers teased through her moistness.

"You're so damp," he rasped, watching her expression melt as he eased one finger gently inside her. "And so damned tight you're going to make me come before I even get started."

Her honey pooled in his hand as her entry snugly enclosed his penetrating finger. Restless and mewing softly, she arched up on the bed and pressed her breast to his mouth. He suckled her with a growl of pleasure and plunged a second finger inside her.

Her soft moan tumbled into the air, and her hips rocked against his hand in silent plea. He drew back, panting, and met her blue gaze, an ocean of arousal, her lashes heavy, her mouth red, her nipples red...

Undone, he slid down her body and buried his head between her legs, giving her a hungry kiss that penetrated her to her sweet, warm depths. She cried out and pulled helplessly on his hair. "Stop, oh, please stop or you'll make me..."

He lifted his head. Urgency thrummed through his body like a living, breathing thing. He was panting, drowning in ecstasy, in his need to make it special and memorable for her while at the same time trying to withhold his body's natural reactions to tonight. To being with her after wanting her for so long.

"I'll make you what?" he prodded softly, coming up and brushing his nose against hers. "Do you already want to come?"

She nodded, her breath fast and hot against his face.

He wanted to take those breaths and suck them into his body, to take this woman and mark her with his touch, every inch of her, for eternity. Catching her bottom lip between his and gently suckling, he caressed her between the legs again. "But that's a good thing…"

She plunged her hands into his hair and set a kiss on his lips, the tip of his nose, his square jaw. "Not alone—Jules, please. When it happens, I want to feel you inside me. I've always wondered what it… I've been dying to feel this…"

Her fingers delved between their bodies, and he almost yelped at the incredible feel, the amazing feel, of her hand curling around his hard length as if she owned him. "I want you," she breathed, her eyes wide in surprise at what she touched. "I…I want *this*…" She stroked his full length exploratively, and a barrage of pleasure raced through his system. He bit back an oath as his body instantly tensed for release.

He grabbed her wrists and playfully pinned her arms up over her head, then he dived to give her a hot, ravenous kiss on the lips. "If you do that again we won't get to the part of me actually entering you."

She writhed underneath him, her breasts beckoning another kiss. "Please, please."

He was unraveled by her desire, enchanted by her openness to him, his undeniable connection to her. His hands shook with male-hormone overload as he reached out to the nightstand.

He briskly rolled on a condom as fast as he could. Realizing she'd been watching in fascination, he pushed her back down with his weight and reached for both her creamy ankles. He couldn't wait to be inside her. Feel her heat.

Make her mine, mine, mine.

"Do you want me inside you…?" he urged as he hooked her legs around his hips, his pulse fluttering like crazy.

"Please, yes. Oh…" She gasped as he penetrated her, firm and slow, pushing in inch by inch, her tender body fighting him. The effort it took to hold back made his every muscle quiver in restraint.

"Ahh, I'm sorry, this is going to hurt you…"

She'd gone motionless beneath him, those trusting, wide eyes clawing at his heart as she clasped his shoulders in a death grip. "Don't tense against me, don't fight me," he cooed, easing back to let her breathe, then carefully guiding himself back in, caressing her nipple tips to incite her relaxation as he gently rocked his hips. "Give yourself to me, Molly. Be mine."

He thumbed the little pearl above the entry of her sex, and he felt her give him another inch, and another, until he was almost buried to the hilt. Suddenly, with fierce determination, Molly thrust her pelvis up against him and they both cried out in surprise—he barked in pleasure, and she moaned in sudden pain, and they both went utterly still, completely joined, his length pulsing inside her, her body snugly wrapped around him.

He took her breathless little mouth and kissed her fiercely as the compact heat of her body adjusted to his length. Struggling to hold back, his heart thundering in his chest, he threw his head back in ecstasy and finally started to withdraw, enjoying every sliding inch. "So good. You feel so. *Good.*" He bent down and kissed her, a hot, wild kiss. "Please stay still, baby, I don't want to hurt you."

He went back in, and she moaned in pleasure, her fingers clenching his buttocks, urging him on. "It's okay now. It's okay. Don't hold back, Julian."

"Oh, Molly…you have no idea what you've been doing to me…." He rocked his hips gently against hers, the motion slow but deep and incredibly erotic. Excruciating pleasure shot through his system as he continued his rhythmic thrusting, waiting to feel her shudder, waiting for her to come apart in his arms.

Suddenly, their eyes locked, and Molly released an out-of-control moan, her nails biting into his skin as she arched up in pleasure.

She watched him watch her.

She felt like crying, dying, flying.

She thought she'd break when he first entered her, and now the pleasure had overridden anything else.

Julian's eyes were an inferno of passion, eating her up alive. His hands slid like satin on her skin, over her hips, her rib cage, caressing her breasts. Then he ducked his head once more and his velvet tongue branded every inch of her body until every cell and atom felt alive and fevered.

A sheen of perspiration clung to his forehead, and she ached to lick it up and get drunk on him. High on him. She thrashed under his eyes when their gazes met, glorying in the ravaged way he looked at her, the tender words that tumbled off his lips as he took her, words like *adore* and *want you* and *killing me*.

Inside her being, she overflowed with love for him. Him. She wanted all of him, all of Julian John Gage, as she watched his muscles flexing hard with each move of his powerful body against hers.

And when his rhythm turned erratic, her eyes drifted shut and the passion overtook her. She clutched his bulging shoulders with a soft cry of pure, unrefined bliss, hearing him let loose a growl of his own, and they snapped and twisted together, clutching each other, tense and shaking, and then…seconds later…slumping, relaxed and entwined, they felt as if they were one, at last.

* * *

They couldn't get enough of each other.

After less than two hours of sleep, Molly awakened to find Julian's tousled blond head trailing suspiciously down her tummy and heading south, his fingertips sensuously playing between her splayed thighs. Drawing out her wetness, he made her mew in her throat and toss her head back helplessly against the pillow.

When he buried his face in the damp, warm place where his fingers had been, she gripped the sheets at her sides as each hot flick of his knowing tongue set a rampage of sensations loose in her body. She arched and twisted. "Jules, please..." she gasped in the dark. He pushed her to a climax with his tongue, and then he wrapped her legs around his hips and rode her until she was crying out to him in ecstasy.

Less than an hour later, she stirred in bed and searched for his warmth, having somehow been separated from him during sleep. She hooked one leg around his narrow hips and draped her arm around his waist, and as she wiggled to get comfortable, she became aware of the large, prominent erection biting into her hip bone. She stilled, but Julian had already awakened. He groaned and dropped his head in search of her lips in the shadows, and she gave her mouth up to his. Lying on their sides on the bed, he entered her slowly, whispering sweet little nothings in her ears that drove her to a climax that left her gasping for breath and blushing over all the things he said.

They showered together and laughed over "bun-buns" and "JJ," then returned to bed. Then, at 5:00 a.m., while a tiny stream of light filtered through the closed drapes, Molly once again woke up to find herself entangled in Julian's muscled limbs and his Egyptian cotton bedsheets. She couldn't seem go back to sleep. She throbbed all over in such a delicious way. Adrenaline and excitement continued coursing through her system, and she couldn't stop touching him. Kissing him. Smelling his skin, which smelled clean and of his sandalwood soap.

"Jules," she whispered, going breathless at the excitement of waking up with him. "Are you asleep?"

"Not anymore." With an arm draped over his eyes as he lay sprawled on the bed, Julian's chest rose and fell with each breath, his voice groggy and sexy.

Molly sat up and edged closer, waiting for him to stir to action. "I'm still naked," she said, dropping her voice to a seductive purr.

Dropping his arm and cracking his eyes open, Julian stroked his thumb down the length of her arm, his expression deadly serious. "I know what you're begging for, Molls."

Before she could even blink, he'd rolled her over with a lionlike "rawr" that made her squeal and laugh her heart out as he gave her the tickle torture of her life. "Oh, I hate it when you do this, stop it, *stop!*" she squealed in between hysterical laughs, but he didn't pause for a whole half a minute—because it wasn't called torture for nothing. They ended up breathless and grinning from ear to ear when it was finally over.

He turned somber as he gazed down at her flushed features, then he reached out to cup her naked breast and manipulate it as though it were his property to play with. When her nipple responded eagerly, his smile turned wolfish, and a devilish glint appeared in his gaze.

"You sure you can take me?" he said, and bent his head to give her a leisurely good-morning kiss, his seductive lips stirring her senses. "I don't want you hurting all day."

She was still breathless from his torture. "Well, I do."

He laughed. "What an insatiable little devil my little

Molls is turning out to be." He smiled that wolf's smile again, his eyes spelling mischief, then he ducked his blond head and playfully nipped the beaded points of her nipples, and the stimulus was almost too much to bear.

"Thank you for the gift you've given me," he whispered against her flesh, switching from one nipple to the other. "My entire life I worried someone else would take what I wanted."

That husky, unexpected confession turned her on like flicking on a light switch, and together with the nibbles he was giving her? It was a winning combo. Her muscles stiffened as the blissful sensations rippled through her. She clung to his shoulders, squirming as red-hot desire took her over and his warm, wet tongue tortured her beyond measure.

"Oh, Jules," she sighed. "Don't do that unless you... you know."

"Yeah, I know," he said, coming up to her ear, murmuring, "I got you, baby, you know I do."

Molly turned her head, opened her mouth and kissed him, lazily at first, then vigorously. "No. Now it's my turn to torture you," she said sheepishly.

She pushed him under her and he obediently lay on his back as she greedily took in his magnificent body with her eyes. From head to toe, Julian was a masterpiece she wanted to memorize.

Eyes narrowed, he crossed his hands behind his head and let her touch him, like a pasha being pampered and tended to. She bit her bottom lip while her breasts throbbed for his touch and the place between her legs pricked with wanting. Her hands stroked his abs and pectorals and round, hard biceps, and then trailed downward to cup his mesmerizing hardness....

He sucked in a harsh breath through his teeth. Molly's

eyes blurred as she seized his hard length—so big she could not grip him with only one hand. He was so aroused and powerful that she could feel him pulsing underneath her palms and fingers. She wanted to lick him there, lick him everywhere, like a lollipop. "I want to kiss you here, Jules." She patted him gently, her insides clenching with pure, unadulterated lust.

His nostrils flared, his eyes almost black. "Then stop teasing and kiss me."

Molly watched his face as she bent her head, and she would never forget the flaming, pulse-pounding lust in his eyes, as if he could eat her up and not want anything else for the rest of his life. "Like this?" she asked tentatively as she dipped her puckered lips and placed a kiss right on the tip.

His hips bucked wildly, his biceps bulging as he fought to keep his arms back.

"Do you like it, Jules, or—?"

"Baby, I've dreamed of this," he murmured in a coarse, thick voice, his torso rising and falling with each soughing breath. "Morning, noon and night, I've dreamed of this…."

Molly bent her head and watched him, melting in heat at the harsh look of ecstasy on his face. His eyes burned into the top of her head as she snaked out her tongue to lick him in a slow circle around the tip, savoring his taste and the incredible feel of his hardness sliding into her mouth. She opened wider and took the first couple of inches inside of her. His hands rounded over the back of her head and his fingertips delved gently into her hair as he eased her head back so their gazes locked. Her eyes felt heavy with arousal, and his gaze was thick-lashed and stormy.

"Did you think of me, too, baby?" he said in a guttural whisper, and Molly released him, then climbed on top of him and straddled his hips, bending to press her lips hungrily to his.

"So much I've never even looked at another man, Jules," she whispered into his mouth.

She felt the powerful tremor that rushed through his body at her words. Then he took charge and twirled his tongue around hers while his hands slid down her back to grip her buttocks. He squeezed the plump flesh, moving her so their hips aligned and his rigid erection pressed right into the part where she was soaked.

"I've thought of this every day for so damned long. I won't even begin to tell you how many times during the night."

"I want you in me, Jules." She rocked her hips enticingly against his length. She was wonderfully sore and yet needed to feel him again, only to be sure this was real. This was happening. She was his, and he was hers.

Hard and strong, he easily rolled her over and loomed above her now, and the sight of him poised at her entry drove her to the edge. His golden skin glowed with a thin sheen of perspiration, and his shoulders and arms bulged with straining muscles, corded with pumping veins. She couldn't believe that this wonderful creature would want her like he did. Would look at her in the way he was looking down at her now. That her hero and friend and favorite person in the world could also be her lover.

Clutching him closer, she whispered, "I want you, but slowly so it won't hurt."

"I'll be careful with you. Come here, Moo." He gathered her closer, holding her firmly against him as he slowly eased inside her.

"Yes!" she cried out, squeezing her eyes shut against the onslaught of sensation—a deluge of love and passion and everything she'd always wanted. Right here in her arms, after years of being so close to it.

A sound tore from his straining body as he began a hard, thorough pace, his lips dragging wildly over her face, her lips, her cheeks, her temple as his hips rammed against hers and she held on to him for dear life. He drove her to the precipice and made her gasp out his name, and then he followed her with one last thrust, her body clutching his in a long, tight orgasm.

For an hour afterward they lay entangled in bed and remembered their little adventures as teenagers. As Molly drifted off to sleep, she felt so content, so genuinely happy, she thought at last her life was as it should be.

Nothing would come between her and her soul mate any longer.

Eight

Full sunlight streamed through the windows of Julian's bedroom as Molly cracked open one eye, and then the other. Noticing it was past 10:00 a.m., she moaned languorously and rolled and stretched on the bed, anxious to feel the warm contours of the body she'd snuggled against all night long. But Julian wasn't in bed with her.

Disappointment swept through her as she sat up. Then she spotted the note over his pillow, and she instantly relaxed.

Good morning, Picasso. Meet me upstairs? Business
is ready to open Monday and I'm giving it a thorough
check. Hope you don't mind I left another message
for you somewhere.
Yours,
Julian

The other message, it turned out, was right on her left buttock. Molly gasped when she caught sight of it as she passed by the mirror. It consisted of three red letters, perfectly curved, perfectly marking her fanny like a cattle brand, except he'd used her paint: *JJG.*

She laughed so hard that tears popped into her eyes. She'd never imagined she could wake up feeling so content, so full, so complete, so happy. How could she have spent all these years next to this man she would give her life for, and miss out on all of *this?*

It was as though last night Jules had opened the little box where she'd hidden away entire decades of special, secret feelings for him, and now that those feelings were out, Molly feared she'd burst from the love in her chest.

Scrambling to catch up with him, she showered and found herself drifting off to last night as she shampooed. They'd lain awake remembering stuff about their childhood, then they'd laughed, then their laughter had faded into heat once more, and they'd kissed and made out and made love until they'd exploded.

Hot and bothered by the memory alone, she jumped out of the shower, wrapped herself in a towel and rushed to the walk-in closet to survey her clothes. She settled on a short white jean skirt and a lacy white blouse. Then she fixed coffee and folded two warm croissants she'd heated in the oven into a pair of napkins. She carried the croissants and the two coffee mugs up in the elevator, watching them steam with a smile.

She could too easily picture doing this every day, too easily imagine having her husband's offices in the same building as her apartment. He could come and go as he pleased—take a few moments in his busy day to steal away between meetings and come home and kiss her. Kiss her heart out like at that masquerade, like last night, like, hopefully, later this morning. Her cheeks flamed at the prospect.

The elevator chimed and she stepped out, impressed by the sight that greeted her.

Wow.

The place had undergone a huge transformation. She hadn't noticed all this last night when she'd been painting like a fiend. But now full sunlight streamed through the windows, and every inch of the marble floor sparkled clean. Chrome chandeliers hung from the rafters, brand-new computers sat proudly atop their shiny new desks. A main reception desk stood before her, and behind it, the wall of her partly finished mural said a cheery good morning.

Just looking at that explosion of colors made her anxious to work on it some more. But the truth was, she was feverish to see Julian. Her breasts pricked at the thought of kissing his silken lips and wrapping herself around his big, hard body again....

She heard voices then. Angry voices.

Frowning, she went around the wall through a set of glass doors. And that was when she spotted Julian. Beautiful in khaki slacks and a white polo short, his casual weekend clothes. But there was nothing casual in his wide stance, in his massively tense shoulders, the arms that strained at his sides.

And then she saw the second man, his stance as menacing as Julian's.

Garrett.

Molly's heart stopped.

Her eyes wildly searched Julian's profile for clues. He looked more than furious. His nostrils were flaring, and though the movements were almost imperceptible, he kept flexing his fingers as though they were cramping. Or as though he was just aching to throttle someone.

O-oookay. This might just not be the morning she had envisioned while she was taking a shower. What were they arguing about anyway? And why was Garrett here if he didn't know about Julian's new—

Oh, no.

No, no, no.

All of a sudden it hit her. And she feared that she knew exactly what the two men were arguing about.

Her own words came back to haunt her like a curse.

"Who the hell can even work in peace with this sort of constant criticism? I'm glad he's ready to move on!"

Oh, no, please no.

Garrett had sounded less than thrilled when he'd demanded to know if Julian was leaving. She swayed nervously on her feet and a wash of hot coffee spilled across her left wrist. Pain shot up her arm, and when she gasped, both men turned.

She locked gazes with Garrett first, somehow avoiding Julian's gaze out of dread. She didn't want to know if he was angry. Not after the incredible, mesmerizing night they had spent together. But really, how angry could he be? He was naturally an easygoing man and would probably take it well and laugh about it later. It wasn't as if she had revealed super top secret information, had she? *Had she?*

She breathed out slowly and smiled at the window behind their shoulders. "I didn't know we had company, Jules."

"I find that hard to believe, somehow, since you issued the invitation."

Her heart skipped a beat when she heard his voice; it was low and silky as a ribbon, but it was the winter coolness of the tone that made the hairs on the back of her neck stand up in alarm. Her eyes jerked to lock with his, and for a moment she needed to recover from the utter slamming force of his accusing gaze.

"Jules," she said, slowly tossing her hair from side to side. "I didn't invite him here. I did not mean for him to… Uh, here, you can take my coffee, Garrett, if you'd like."

She extended a mug, trying once again to turn this crazy morning around to the morning she wanted. The one she'd dreamed of. If Garrett took the hospitable offering, Julian would have to take the second one and maybe after the croissants they'd all—

"Already bringing coffee to the love of your life, Molly? Too bad he was just leaving. Aren't you, brother?"

Once again, Molly's eyebrows furrowed in confusion over Julian's frigid tone. For a dazed moment, she almost expected Julian to chuckle and admit he was teasing her. Like he did when he dared her to wear that wench costume or asked her to kiss his six-pack and go as low as she would go in the darkened office at Landon's house.

But no laughter followed his words.

"What the hell are you talking about?" Garrett burst out.

Molly realized in dawning horror that Julian had referred to Garrett as the love of her life. She glanced down at the mugs both men had refused and the sticky residue of coffee on her wrist, growing numb in disbelief. Had he been making fun of her having stupidly thought she loved Garrett once upon a time, or did he actually believe it to be *true?*

Drawing in a steadying breath, she walked around and shakily set the mugs and croissants on a nearby desk. A little part of her already wanted to get hysterical, but she tried reminding herself that, although she'd spoken out impulsively, the last thing she'd intended was to harm Julian.

She would have time to explain all of this in a couple of minutes, just a few minutes more….

"Please tell me you're having someone check your goddamned head because you're not making any sense," Garrett thundered, then he turned to her. "Thanks for your visit yesterday, Molly," he said. "And for keeping us in the loop of this development."

Molly froze. She could not even believe he would say that to her in front of Julian. Seriously, she'd never expected things to go south so fast. Suddenly, she trembled with the fantastical urge to fling the coffee mugs at Garrett's face for ruining what should've been a perfect morning, for now there was no doubt whatsoever that Julian would believe she had been a little snitch who had betrayed his confidence and trust.

God. It sounded so bad now that she reflected on it, and yet she wouldn't have even said it at all if they hadn't infuriated her so on Julian's behalf!

Instead of giving Garrett any sort of answer, she pursed her lips and pretended to be super busy sucking the spilled coffee from her left wrist. Garrett had spoken the words in true gratitude, maybe even with a bit of tenderness, but she still loathed the fact that Julian had found out that her mouth had apparently gotten ahead of her brain yesterday.

Garrett sighed and turned to Julian, his timbre hardening. "Think about it, before you do something even stupider," he said, and walked toward the reception area and out to the elevators.

Molly finished sucking up the coffee and suddenly felt too energetic, as if she needed to do something. Parachute, river raft, hike Mount Everest? Artists were solitary people by nature, too emotional, too vulnerable, too incapable of handling awfulness like this. Fighting to stand still, she frantically counted the seconds after Garrett left that Julian remained silent. Just watching her. So very, very silent.

Fifty.

Fifty hellish seconds.

While Molly wanted to hide under the chair, blend with her mural or just scream.

Because she was just coming to realize how big a mistake she'd made. She'd done something very wrong to him. Very, very wrong.

Jules didn't trust anyone. Anyone but *her*. Oh, God, now his family would be riding him hard about coming back. Maybe they couldn't send him away like they used to when they were displeased with him, but did she dare wonder how they could pressure him to bend to their united wills?

What had she just *done* to him?

With a pounding heart, she waited for him to speak, every second eternal, miserable. The top two buttons of his polo shirt were unbuttoned. He wore the masquerade ring on his hand. His fingers were curling and uncurling into fists at his sides.

She wanted to die.

"You ratted me out to my brother."

He spoke softly. Too softly. Way too softly.

She sucked in a breath, surprised by the pain cutting through her rib cage. If he'd said, *You suck. You're a liar. Last night was a mistake,* it might have hurt less. Shame spread through her like wildfire. Because how had she not seen this coming? "It's not how it looks, Jules," she told him, but his expression was so harsh and scary her gaze dipped once more to the floor.

His shoes were so polished and shiny. Were they advancing toward her?

He turned her face up to his with his thumb and forefinger, forcing her to look into his piercing eyes. "You ratted me out to my brother, Molly. How the hell could you do this to me?"

Just to stand there under the searing heat of his reproachful green stare made her empty stomach churn. "I didn't mean to! It slipped. *It slipped.* What? Are you going to hate me now, is that it?"

"Hate? Molly, I freaking *love* you! I can't believe you'd line up with them against me." He raked his hands through his hair and then backed away, as though she had a rash he needed to distance himself from. "You want to know why I would leave a thriving, billion-dollar business, Molly? Fine, let me tell you why. Because as long as I'm under my family's thumb, I'll never be able to be with you."

His expression was grim as he watched her, his eyebrows drawn sharp and sullen over his eyes; eyes that killed her with emotion as he looked at her.

"That day you came to me begging me to help you get another man...I thought to *hell* with my family. I wasn't going to let them ruin my life anymore and let them keep me away from you, Moo."

Molly incongruously wondered why Julian could say *Moo* and make it sound revered and womanly, sexy and beautiful, but she was so distraught over the rest of what he said that she didn't wonder for long. Julian's face had hardened with pain and his voice felt like icicles on her skin. Molly's eyes had blurred with tears because each and every one of the words he'd said was eating her up inside.

"They've sent me away dozens of times, they've threatened to disown me, they've tried every twisted plot to keep me in line. And I'm sick and tired of dancing to their tune. I just want to be with *you*." His green eyes clawed her like talons as he spread his arms out, his jaw clenched so tight she feared it would crack like her heart was cracking. "So this was the plan. This was my plan. With my

full financial independence, I'll need no one—no one—
to tell me what to do, or tell me if I can or can't love you,
Molly. Dammit, I can't freaking believe you'd crucify me
for them—*for him*."

He pulled at the collar of his polo shirt as if he wanted to
rip it off him and then stalked to the floor-to-ceiling window. Molly mourned his affection already. No more sparkling green eyes. There were only tornadoes and storms
now.

And she'd put them there.

A tear slipped down her cheek as her brain replayed his
words over and over in her head, then a second tear followed, and a third, and they wouldn't stop. Julian *loved*
her. Oh, God. To know that he'd cared for her all this time,
had wanted her like she'd secretly wanted him and had
been actually doing something so he could be with her...

To know the truest kind of love could have been hers
all along...

This should have been the happiest day of her life. But
instead it had morphed into the worst.

Because to learn that you had something on the same
day you lost it *sucked*.

Molly wanted to tear her skin off with her nails, her
heart out with her hands so she could show him all she
wanted was to give it to him. "I'm sorry, Jules," she said,
clutching her stomach. "I didn't know it was so important.
I swear I would have watched my mouth better—"

"I trusted you, Molly," he interrupted, shaking his head
over and over again. "You know me better than my family, better than anyone. I've trusted you with everything.
Everything I think and want, and... Jesus, I just can't do
this right now."

He put even more distance between them and jammed his
fingers into his hair as each step carried him farther away.

"You can still trust me, Jules! I was careless, that's all. I mean…you're not going to let Garrett push you into anything you don't want to do. Are you?"

He halted. And she trembled at the expression on his face, so…vacant, as if not only would he never, ever trust her again, but neither would he care to try.

This steely detachment on his part was so new and alarming, when he turned to face the window and gave her a view of his broad, impenetrable back, she actually wanted to flee to her studio and lock herself up the rest of her life in a sanctuary of paint, brushes and blank canvases.

But her life would never be the same without him, would never be the same if she didn't stay here and work things out. Julian was, quite simply, the most valuable and treasured thing in the world to her.

He *had* to forgive her.

So she remained. She remained glued to the floor, to this present, this horrible alternate reality where Julian looked at her as a…fraud.

"Jules?" she prodded when he remained staring silently out the window for too long.

He ran a hand all the way through his hair and gripped the back of his neck, then stared down at the floor. "Was I your consolation prize, Molly? Do you still have…an idea of you and Garrett in your head?"

She opened her mouth to deny it, but only heard a shocked gasp, the question so terribly painful to hear. Did he not realize she *adored* him? Did he think she would spend a night like last night just for the *fun* of it?

"If it had been Garrett kissing you that night at the masquerade, for real, would you even be here with me, Molly? Or would you have left here with him?" he asked, and when he dropped his arm and turned slightly, his empty stare slashed her to bits.

How could he think that?

She wanted to hit him for even thinking it, but she felt shattered inside.

The magic she'd felt in that kiss could never have been there with Garrett or anyone else. It was him, Julian, it always had been, no matter how much she'd tried to fight it. He was The One.

Him and only him.

But she couldn't speak. To her frustration, she was crying now, and with her throat so tight, it was really hard to get a word out.

She'd never imagined she could ever hurt anyone. She loved to laugh, to enjoy life, to paint. She was young at heart and had never seen herself as a threat to anyone—not even to a bug, because she had a habit of escorting them out to the yard and never squashing a single one. She would cut out her eyes for Julian if he needed them, her hands so she could never paint again. She'd give him two kidneys, her liver, and her pancreas and lungs, too! She wouldn't even mention her heart because she'd never really had it to herself in the first place.

She'd given it along with her lollipop to a six-year-old boy a long, long time ago.

"Julian, don't be ridiculous, please. I love you," she said as she wiped her tears, rushing after him when he'd got tired of waiting for her to reply. But he was already boarding the elevator, as proud and stubborn as all the Gage men she'd ever known.

"Get your stuff, Molly. I'm taking you back home. Consider the mural done."

Nine

For exactly twelve days, eleven hours, forty-seven minutes and thirty-two seconds, Julian buried himself in work, sweat and sports. He hadn't set foot at the *San Antonio Daily* in almost two weeks. Not even to present his damned brothers with his resignation letter.

No. Since then, JJG Enterprises had officially opened for business, so instead he'd buried himself in work from 6:00 a.m. to 6:00 p.m. each day, and after that he had been rowing, paddling, kayaking, running, climbing and sky-diving his freaking heart out.

He would come home at midnight, soaked in sweat, to feed his body, bathe himself and drop down dead on the bed. But it was no use. His head continued swimming with memories of making love to Molly, kissing her sweet lips. Memories of her betrayal.

He'd never thought that a casual, collected guy like

him, with everything under control, would ever get to feel that way.

And every day when he saw her mural upstairs, he wanted to tear that wall down. It was so bright and vivid, so sassy, so Molly. He could bulldoze it to the ground if he didn't have millions invested up there. Millions. Hell, his whole damned heart, since he'd imagined sharing that future with Molly.

Now he didn't even want to wake up.

Even his home, once his sanctuary, seemed to assault him with memories at every turn.

Her scent lingered in the pillows. He kept finding her stuff around the house. Fashion magazines. A random paintbrush. In the kitchen pantry he'd find the artificial sweetener she claimed was the best sitting right next to the honey he liked to gobble. And those damned Sleepy-time Teas.

He hadn't realized until the glaring emptiness of life without Molly stared him in the face every day how deeply she had infiltrated his life. She had been involved, in little and big ways, in every part of his day. From the cookies he'd snack on at the office or at home, provided by Molly from Kate's delicious kitchen, to the text messages reminding him of a family gathering to her calls—*Forget to say hi yesterday, moron? Call me. Or else!*

He wanted to forget he'd ever met this woman, forget he'd ever wanted her, forget he'd been prepared to change his whole life around for her....

But he couldn't.

He couldn't forgive her. If only he could just forget her. Forget the way she laughed with him, at him, and poked and prodded him and made his body feel alive in a way nobody else did. He'd had strings of lovers but had never enjoyed sex so much, cherished the moment so fiercely as that night he'd spent with her.

He'd replayed it in his head dozens of times, groaning and suffering like a masochist, but the reality had been so sweet he didn't want to forget that time with her. Ever. To have finally seen her, sprawled and wanting him in his bed, that red hair fanning across his sheets, could still give a grown man wet dreams.

She'd said she loved him a thousand times in her life. He knew she did. As a friend. As a "brother." But did she *love* him? Julian had been inside her, knew every secret of her body, knew where to press her, how to make her moan, what she ate, what she feared, where to tickle her. Would she rather have spent that night with Garrett?

Garrett.

His blood boiled at the thought of his brother. Even though he knew Molly's feelings for Garrett had been based on a kiss that Julian himself had given her, he continued to feel so jealous he couldn't even see straight. He couldn't believe that she would betray him to his brother like she had. So *why* had she?

Had two decades of pure, raw friendship meant nothing to her?

He desperately tried fishing his memories for clues of her and his brother together. Looks he could've missed. Touches that had more weight to them than they should have. But he came up with nothing. Every memory of Molly was tied to one man, and that man was *him*. Maybe he had not always been a man. But when he had been a boy, he had been *her* boy.

Jules, Jules, gimme a piggyback ride.

And when Kate had tried to patch her up after a good scrape and would coo down at Molly in a maternal way, "I'm going to kiss your boo-boo better," little Molly would point at Julian across the room and grin. "No, I want him to do it."

And later, as teens: *Teach me to surf, Jules. Will you drive me over to art class, Jules?*

And as an adult: *Coffee? Tea? Call me! I'm still alive, you know, just been painting!*

But now he was alone.

So damned alone.

Yeah, that was him.

The careless playboy with a broken heart.

The sun shone overhead so bright, Molly was surprised she didn't disintegrate like a vampire under its glare. After being locked in her studio for weeks, it was almost a miracle her skin did not instantly peel off from sunlight exposure. She might even deserve such a fate.

At least if you asked Julian, who, she assumed, wanted her dead.

Eyes narrowed to shield herself from some of the sun's brightness, she gazed down at the envelope she gripped in her clammy hands, recognizing the handwriting as that of Julian's assistant, Ms. Watts.

So. This is what their friendship and one-night stand—because truly, that was all they'd managed to have together—had come to.

Communicating through the post office.

She closed her mailbox and had to sit down on the grass next to the sidewalk and just stare down at that white envelope.

Her texts had not been answered.

Her calls went straight to voice mail.

She wanted to kill the jerk for being so silly and dramatic, and at the same time she wanted to slap herself for opening her big mouth to Garrett without thinking.

Julian was, and had always been, an extremely private man. He showed his cool and aloof side to everyone but only showed his true self to a select few. Molly knew, deep down, that no one knew Julian better than she did.

He couldn't stand to talk about politics but oh, he sure loved to steal her Lucky Charms marshmallows. He was a sports and sports-memorabilia fanatic, and if he was not a businessman, he'd probably spend all day doing water sports at the lake surfer, with his suntan and lazy charm and a wakeboard under him. He'd never felt as if he belonged in his family—never really felt as if he belonged anywhere.

And that was why she couldn't stand to remember what she'd unwittingly done to him.

He'd longed for freedom in his life, and instead she'd blown the whistle on him to his family so they could tie him back up and keep him from flying. She had done that. To the man she had constantly, throughout her life, loved in every way a woman could love a man.

The worst part of it was that Julian never let anyone in.

But Molly had always come in through the back door.

And he'd let her. Enjoyed it, even. Cared for her, protected her, coddled her.

And she'd accidentally betrayed him to a man whom he'd believed she wanted over him.

How could she ever make things right if he didn't even want to talk to her?

It had been fifteen days since she'd seen him now, and each day she'd tried to make amends. Her last attempt had been returning every penny of the money he'd wired to her for her unfinished mural. With a note that read, I've never left a work unfinished until now. Please give me a chance—I'd like to finish this.

She'd written a thousand notes before settling on that

one. Some had said, *I love you* and *please* and *forgive me*. But she'd been too much of a chicken to send any of those, and so she'd settled on the most businesslike one, thinking it was probably her best chance of getting an entry with him.

She drew a deep breath and peeled the envelope open with shaky fingers. The check she had written to him for the $150,000 fell into her open palm, shredded to pieces. There was no note. Except her own note. Shredded to pieces, as well.

She thought she heard her heart crack.

Her eyes welled with tears and she ducked her face when a car approached. Tires screeched, a motor shut down and doors opened.

Kate and Beth stepped out of the Catering, Canapés and Curry van. "Molly?" Kate said, alarmed.

Molly used her hair to shield her profile from view and jammed the pieces of the check and note back into the envelope, rising to her feet and quickly wiping at her cheeks. "Hey. I'll help you." She didn't look at them as she went to the back of the van and began unloading their empty trays, but she could feel their eyes on her as she headed inside the house.

Beth caught up with her in the kitchen. "Molly?"

Molly prayed to God her eyes weren't red, and even smiled as she set the trays down on the kitchen counter. "Hey, Beth."

She could see the concern in Beth's expression, and she feared that there was even a little pity there, too. "You know, Julian came by the house the other day. To speak to Landon. He resigned from the *Daily*."

Molly nodded as her airway constricted. "Good for him."

Beth studied her. Molly knew she was a good woman.

She had known heartache and a horrid divorce before she had found true love in her life, and suddenly Molly wanted to wail her heart out to her. Because surely this woman would understand how it felt when you were ripped apart, shredded like your notes and broken. But then Kate's heart would break for Molly if she saw her like this, and Molly didn't want to break her sister's heart.

It was her own fault that all this had happened. Kate had warned her so many times, so, so many times, about Julian. Maybe Molly had even had it coming.

"You know—" Beth grasped her hand and gave her an encouraging squeeze "—if it makes you feel any better, he's not doing too good, either."

Molly looked down at her bare toes, her chest heavy as if it were carrying the weight of a whole country. "It doesn't," she admitted, feeling like a bug as she remembered Julian's anger, his disappointment. The last thing she'd wanted was to make him suffer. "But thanks anyway, Beth."

That afternoon she went back to finishing the two canvases she had left for her exhibit at the Blackstone Gallery in New York. They ended up awful, tenebrous and depressing, reflecting her mood. But she still owed the gallery these two works, and because she had no time to start anew, they would have to do.

At night she lay in bed, her eyes dry as she heard Kate on the phone: "Not doing well… What are we going to do?"

Molly wanted to make a humble suggestion and tell her, and whomever she was talking to, to stay the hell away from her life, but then she just put her pillow over her face and groaned.

"Molly," Kate said from the door, a shaft of light entering with her.

"I heard you, Kate. I have ears, you know, and we don't

live in a mansion," she grumbled angrily, flinging the pillow aside.

The mattress squeaked as her sister sat by her side and took her hand. "I'm sorry, Moo. I think we've made a terrible mistake. With you and Julian, I mean."

"No. You were right all along." Molly rolled to her side and pulled her hand free to stick it under her cheek, suddenly rejecting any physical contact that didn't come from where she most craved it.

"Molly, we're planning something. Garrett, Landon, Beth and I. If I tell you what it is, will you go with it?"

"If it involves me lying again to anyone or pretending to be something I'm not, count me out."

"No, Moo, this is actually a good plan," Kate said, a smile in her voice. "All you'd really need to do is follow some instructions in a note that I'm going to give you this weekend. The note will lead you to Julian."

"I hate him."

"You do?"

"I've never met such a frustrating bastard in my life!"

"All right, then." The bed squeaked again as Kate got up to leave.

Molly sprang back up on the bed, her heart picking up speed as she switched on the lamp, and frantically blurted, "I was never really with him, Kate. It was all a lie. I was confused and thought that Garrett was the one who kissed me that night at the masquerade. I foolishly thought Julian could help me make Garrett jealous so he'd come around, but then I realized all along…"

Kate cocked her head from the doorway, her eyes brimming with understanding. "I know," she said. Coming back, she sat down and ran her hand down the length of Molly's hair. "Do you really think I believed that little act?

You two were so obviously not lovers I could've laughed if I hadn't been so very worried."

"But it was actually Julian who kissed me at the masquerade and I...I got mixed up. It was like my soul recognized him, but my brain *couldn't* or maybe didn't want to. All I know is that I needed to find this man and I needed to be with Julian while I did... It's his fault I can never look at other men, never want to be with anyone else. I even think I was pretending to want to make Garrett jealous but really wanted to make Julian jealous instead."

"I know, I know. Relax. That man is your rock, Molly. And you're his soil. You have to *be* with him. We made a grave mistake keeping you two apart for so long. Garrett is worried sick about him. He's been running himself to death. Not eating. Not opening up to anyone. His family feels responsible for this, even his mother is trying to apologize for all her earlier threats, and he won't hear anything from anyone. He's really hurting, Molly. You want him, don't you?"

"You have no idea," she gasped brokenly, nodding so fast she was almost dizzy. The mere idea of being able to see him again was electrifying. Of talking to him. Touching him, even if only with the merest tip of her littlest finger. Oh, God, it hurt so much to love him from afar, reminding her of all the misery of growing up without him.

She had always dreamed of having a family, because hers had been broken before she'd even gotten to know her own parents. She'd just never tried for one of her own because she'd believed Julian would never be a part of it. Now a little kernel of hope sprang in her center, and she opened her eyes.

But she feared to hope too much and end up wretched. "Why?" she asked Kate. "Why is everyone going to help us, after all this time?"

"Because I love you, Molly. And you love him. And *he* loves you. And we all love you both."

Molly coiled her arms around Kate's waist and squeezed her sister as tight as possible, sighing when Kate squeezed her back just as hard. "I miss him so much, Kate."

"I know, Moo. I know you do."

<u>Ten</u>

It was a good day to be at the lake house. Sunny and breezy days on the cusp of summer were hard to come by in Texas. But that was just what the Gage family got when they visited their Canyon Lake home on the last Saturday of the month.

Julian had not planned to set foot here, but Landon had insisted, and he'd grudgingly agreed merely because he would be able to water-ski, swim and do the WaveRunner thing. After a day of that, the only thing that would be aching would be his goddamned muscles rather than his heart.

Now the wind slapped him as he roared across the lake on the WaveRunner, racing Garrett on his right and Landon on his left. He squinted in the direction of the mansion, which stood white and regal by the lake, with a small dock and bright pink bougainvillea hanging from the terrace columns. He could see his mother already seated at the long terrace table, calmly pouring glasses of lemonade for the two figures seated with her—Landon's wife, Beth, and his stepson, David.

Julian swerved and spewed water behind him as he jolted the machine to a stop right beside the dock. He tied up the WaveRunner and jumped out, wet suit soaked, dripping a path up the wood planks as he ambled toward the terrace. When he arrived, he plopped down on a chair and took a glass of lemonade from his mother.

"Landon tells me you're not coming back to the *Daily*," his mother said without preamble. "Are you certain about that?"

Julian nodded, not up to explaining the deal he'd made with Landon and his reasons for it. The point was, he would continue to support the *Daily* with JJG Enterprises' services, personally making sure the *Daily*'s client base thrived. But he was riding solo now.

Eleanor patted her bun absently with one hand, making a puppy-dog plea with her eyes until he groaned. "I've got 1,210 businesses already signed up for the services of JJG Enterprises. *No,* Mother. The *Daily* is my past. I'm a free agent from now on."

She relented quickly, and Julian knew it was due to the guilt that gnawed at her over the way she'd attempted to separate him from Molly over the years, and the pain it had ended up causing him now. In fact, she'd even relented about her threat of cutting off his trust fund because he'd quit the family business, though she was still trying to convince him to come back.

Now his brothers strolled over, wet suits soaked, and plopped down just as a redhead emerged from within the house, carrying a salad bowl.

Julian stiffened at the same time Garrett did.

It must have been the red hair, shining in the sun, flowing behind her in the wind. For a blind second, Julian thought it was Molly. He didn't even know how he felt about that, but his heart kicked in his chest like a wild thing. He was relieved when he realized that it was Kate.

He calmed back down while Garrett went over to take the bowl from her hands and whisper something in her ear.

"Hi, Julian," Kate said, spotting him. "You've been so busy all morning I haven't been able to say hi."

"You just did, so now you can sleep soundly," he said.

Then he realized how grumpy he sounded. Well, hell, he could still tackle some kayaks and hike this afternoon to let out some of his frustration. His every muscle ached, but there was still some juice in them, and he didn't want to have a drop left by the time he was finished. It wasn't enough; he needed to push harder. Push every single muscle to failure.

Servants brought out trays of canapés and wine. While the family chatted, Julian sat in silence, brooding when no second redhead came out of the house. Kate had been invited. So where the hell was Molly?

He wanted to ask, his tongue itching in his mouth. He wanted to ask where she was and how she'd been doing and why in the world she had betrayed him. He'd never gone twenty-three days, four hours, thirty-two minutes and about thirty seconds without talking to her. The time had dragged on so hellishly that it felt like years as far as he was concerned. However he measured it, this was proving to be the crappiest period of his life so far.

Kate kept her attention on him, and he could feel her gaze on his profile as she asked, "You're not going to eat anything?"

Julian stared at the salad bowl. Molly used to get all of his croutons and he'd eat all of her raisins.

He shook his head, not even hungry anymore.

Beth and Landon kept squeezing each other's hands tenderly as they nibbled salad and drank their lemonades, and the grenade inside Julian's stomach seemed to be ready to detonate. His oldest brother had a truly doting wife and a great kid, and he doted on them both in return. The family had been thrilled that Landon had been able to find love again after his first wife and their son had died. They thought he'd closed himself off for good, yet Beth had opened him up like a Christmas present and found gold.

Usually, the sight of them brought Julian immense cheer, but today he found it was…difficult. To see that connection.

Because the only person he'd ever had it with was not with him here.

"So how is dear Molly, Kate?" his mother asked, very politically bringing her up, damn her. "I'm so disappointed she couldn't come."

Lips compressed into a thin line, Julian stared at his empty glass of lemonade, wishing he'd gone for vodka.

"She was disappointed, too," Kate said, "but she had that exhibit in New York and had to fly over for the opening."

Julian refused to think about Molly flying all alone to her solo exhibit. Getting chatted up by someone next to her in first class. By her fans and collectors at the gallery. It was an important time in her career. And Molly had celebrated…alone.

He refused to think about how he should've been there, always had been there.

He restlessly shifted in his seat, trying to console himself with the thought that at least Josh Blackstone, her gallerist, would be there with her. Julian's old acquaintance was as ruthless as a hellhound, but fair with his artists and especially with Molly, whom he'd taken under his wing a long time ago when Julian urged her to submit her works for his consideration.

Blackstone had flipped, called it feisty and fresh, and the rest had been history.

"I've always loved her canvases, my dear. So bright and sunny. Like her. No wonder they do so well in the art market," his mother casually told Kate, and the topic only incensed Julian to a whole new level.

"Remember how she used to save all those wrappers," Garrett added in lingering disbelief. "And twine them around the tree trunks to make some weird..."

"Oh, yeah, the candy tree," Landon said, lifting up his glass. "I think she has one in this exhibition. It's considered to be her 'early work.'"

"Remember that one review?" Beth said, turning to Landon. "You know the one, Lan... Where the reviewer said Molly was the kind of artist who could draw a simple sketch on a paper napkin and sign it and with that, not only pay for her dinner tab, but for the entire restaurant's? Like it was rumored Picasso once did."

The chair legs screeched like angry banshees as Julian pushed back his seat and rose, his face black with rage. With a shove-it-where-it-hurts look, he grabbed his drink to leave.

"Oh, Julian, dear," Eleanor said, "Could you tell one of the servants to bring out the pies?"

He realized his drink was empty and slammed it back down. "Tell them yourself."

Ready to call it quits on family time, he marched toward the dry clothes he'd left on a wood bench by the dock, angrily unzipping and yanking the top part of his wet suit down to his hips. His family kept talking of Molly's artworks, how special they were, and yes, they were incredible pieces, amazing. But it was Molly whom he'd always considered the masterpiece. Living and breathing, coloring his world with passion and liveliness, making his every moment…worthwhile. God, he hated to remember how she used to make him feel.

Stopping in his tracks, he scowled at the wood bench. His clothes were nowhere to be found.

He stormed back to the group. "Where the hell is my stuff?"

Kate covered her cheeks with both hands, eyes wide. "Oh, I'm sorry! I hung everything in the closet at the cottage so it wouldn't get wet or wrinkled."

He rolled his eyes and stomped down the path to the spare cottage a good distance from the main house. Once he got there, he slammed the door shut behind him to keep the AC inside and went to the closet.

That was when he caught a shadow moving out of the corner of his eye.

He did a forty-five-degree turn and saw Molly. She stood by the window, like a virgin fire princess ready for the sacrifice of her life, her hair molten lava running down her rounded shoulders, wearing a sexy little strapless dress and glittery sandals, big earrings, big bangles and a big smile.

His body, traitorous, jumped to life at the sight of her as though *twenty-three* miserable, endless days of continual physical exertion were not enough to keep it numb. Oh, no, not around her. Her mere presence had flicked on his power switch. Now his blood rushed through his veins and his mind sparked to awareness, taking in every detail of her porcelain skin, her pale blue eyes, her shiny hair, her sweet, white, tiny little teeth she'd used to bite him lovingly. He took in every detail now only to torture himself with them later.

His palms itched, his breath hitched, and he said, "You."

He heard shuffling outside the door, and then the sound of a bolt sliding into place.

Plunk.

And he realized too late, that his family had just locked him in with her.

"Me," Molly agreed calmly.

And suddenly it didn't matter that Julian obviously didn't want to be here, that he didn't want to see her. It didn't matter that his eyes flashed reproachfully at her, that his stance was wide and defensive, that his lips were hard and pressed together in anger. The sight of him after all these painful days made her lungs throb and her head spin with the sheer joy of being able to look at him.

And he looked extremely good.

His torso was damp with lake water and tanned by the sun. His chest looked wider, his athletic form so incredibly sexy in the way the wet suit hung halfway down his body, emphasizing his narrow hips and waist. The shiny black fabric clung seductively to his thighs and to the prominent part of him that had once joined him with her. His hair was damp and slicked back from his face, revealing every inch of his formidable features. The features of a playboy, a Greek god, the man she loved—and the man who wanted nothing to do with her.

Molly trembled with nervousness, desire, regret.

She noticed his hair, still streaked enticingly by the sun, was growing a bit longer, to his nape, and she could smell the woods on him, the oaks and the cedars on the property.

"I thought you had a show," he said, his tone indicating that he didn't really care about her answer.

She still wanted to tell him—because he used to be the only one who truly listened—that it had gone well, that the reviews were excellent and everyone thought she was the luckiest person on earth to have succeeded so young. They thought she had it all.

But she didn't.

She didn't have what she wanted most. Had always wanted.

"I got back from the opening yesterday," she said slowly, her hands restless at her sides, fiddling with the skirt of her dress. "Everyone seemed to like my paintings, except for my two most depressing ones." *The ones that suck because of you.*

"You have no depressing works," he said, pointing at her.

He pursed his lips as he once again scanned his surroundings. Then he shook his head in disgust, marched back to the closet, yanked open the doors and began to pull out his clothes briskly from the hangers.

She felt an unwelcome rush of desire when he began to change right before her eyes. He pulled off his wet suit with a snap, and when he peeled it from his thighs and kicked it off, she saw his nude backside. Glorious muscles rippled and clenched as he put on his Boss underwear and khaki pants. He slipped on a polo shirt and buttoned the two top buttons, then crossed the room toward the cottage door and tried to force the knob. He cursed under his breath when it didn't open and angrily swung around to her.

"So you're into kidnapping now, Molls? Is that your new kick?"

"Yes, as a matter of fact, I'm into spanking, kidnapping and robbing unsuspecting clients of their money while I fail to complete their murals."

Jaw clamped, he stormed to one of the windows and attempted to open it so forcibly the glass rattled in its frame. He acted as if he was in prison and eager to be set free, which just made Molly sigh in despair.

"Look, this wasn't my idea, but I think the plan is brilliant," she said.

"Except for one flaw," he said wickedly, unlocking a second window with a surprising click. He cocked a devil-may-care brow at her and grinned as he pushed upward, only to realize there was another lock on the outside and the glass stayed right in place, no matter how hard he tried to get it open. *"Damn."*

"You don't want to talk to me, Julian, that's fine," Molly said softly. "But I need to talk to you. So now you're going to have to hear me out. Even if you *break* one of those windows, Jules, what are you planning to do? Let in some fresh air?"

He scowled as she pointed at the forged-iron bars on the outside.

"Your mother had that design made specially to keep the drunk teenagers from getting in like they've been doing at other lake houses, and if they can't come in through those bars, I doubt even *you* can go out through them."

The glare he shot her could've been Lucifer's. "I can't believe this idiocy. First they don't want me near you, now they lock me up with you?"

Shaking his head, he paced like a caged lion.

His tumultuous energy spun through the room like a whirlwind, making her want to go over there, wrap her arms around him and calm him down like she had many times before when he was irritated about other things.

But now he saw her as untrustworthy, and he wouldn't want to open up. Now his irritation was caused by the fact that he was locked in the same room as Molly.

"Your family has realized we're miserable and they're trying to make amends. Well, *I* have been miserable," she added, watching him pace. "Jules, will you please look at me so I can talk to you? Or do I need to call you JJ to make you react?"

He stopped in his tracks, his hands curling at his sides, fingers clenching. Although his face was a mask of cold indifference, his eyes blazed with intensity. "Don't even think about provoking me."

"Or you'll what? Kiss me?"

His glare was as bleak as a cemetery. "I'll spank the hell out of you, how about that? I'm *through* with kissing you, Molls."

The decisiveness in his words summoned a fresh wave of outrage from her. "Really? And who says I even *want* you to?"

"A closed door with a lock on it, that's who!" His teeth were clenched so tight, she could see a muscle twitch in the back of his jaw.

She glowered at him, but feared in the innermost part of her, where a candle of hope flickered its last lights, that this battle was already lost. Apparently, not only was her presence not wanted, her kiss was worth nothing to him, either. But she, on the other hand, remembered perfectly all the things she had done as a result of *his* masquerade kiss. "So are you going to listen to me, *JJ*? God, I'm trying to fix things here!" she cried.

He looked up at the ceiling and pinched his eyes shut as though supremely tested. She thought she heard him counting under his breath, stopping at thirty-eight, his hands still clenching and unclenching.

Gradually, he turned around to plant his hands on the wall, then stared out the window with his forehead almost touching the glass pane. His voice was a coarsened whisper. "I'm damned well listening. So talk."

Molly dragged in a breath as she watched his hands splay wider on the wall. She longed to feel those fingers again, feel him touch her, caress her, hold her. "Garrett wanted to talk to me that day I went to his office. He wanted to discuss our relationship."

His hands fisted against the window frame. "Whose?" he asked, his knuckles white. "His and yours?"

"Yours and mine, Jules." She flung her hands up in exasperation. "Obviously! So I told him—"

He spun around like a cyclone. "You told him that I was leaving the *Daily,* and my family could have ruined everything I've planned for years. What *else* did you tell him? You were fishing for his approval by ratting me out, weren't you?"

The hurt that exploded in Molly's chest was so massive that she almost staggered. "Do you really believe that? *Do you?*" Her voice sounded panicked, but she didn't care.

The look he shot back at her was so raw and stark it all but extinguished her candle of hope.

Her voice broke, and she opened her hands out in silent plea. "Look, I'm sorry, Jules. It wasn't on purpose. I was angry about the way they tried to warn me off you and wasn't even thinking clearly. Please, please help me out here. I'm so in love with you I just can't bear this anymore."

"That information wasn't yours to share and *especially* not with them, Moo!" He shook his head and plunged a hand into his damp hair. "Look, I just can't talk to you now. I can't. I'm too goddamned pissed that you would…" A halting hand shot up in the air when she started forward, and she abruptly stopped, her heart in her throat.

He sighed and backed away from her, and every step he took felt like a mile she would never be able to recover. He took a seat on the window bench, and Molly eased back and ended up alone on a floral couch, silent and hurt.

He didn't say he loves me back was all she could think. *God, please, doesn't he care for me just a little bit anymore?*

She thought of how easily he had jumped between lovers and beds his entire life and she wondered if there had been women warming his bed all this time, comforting him while she'd been pining for him alone, producing the worst artworks of her life because of him.

Seduce him, a little voice whispered. *Make him forgive you.*

But the thought made her feel cheap and as fake as he thought her to be. How could she go through with a seduction? First of all, he wasn't even giving any indication that he still *wanted* her. And it had never been just about sex between them. It had been about friendship and fun and sharing and trust....

Trust.

Once long ago, Molly had been careless and had broken Eleanor Gage's prized crystal figurine, one up on display over the chimney mantel. No matter how Julian tried to help her fix it, the thing could never be properly glued back together without looking pitifully disfigured. Now the thought that she could have shattered Julian's trust just like that dolphin figurine, a figurine they'd ended up *throwing away,* terrified her.

Despair made her sink deeper into her own personal bubble. She'd always felt strong in her life, plunging into adventures without thinking too much about their consequences. But now the source of her strength was gone, and she felt totally lost without him.

The sun began to set outside, the lights of dusk bathing the room in a golden glow. She wondered if some woman had been stroking Julian's Beckham-blond hair a day before. If a woman with model legs and bigger breasts had been feeling his beautiful hands on her skin and sighing under his searing kisses. His beautiful kisses.

"Have you been sleeping around again?" she blurted

out, unable to stand the torment of wondering about it any longer. The jealousy was ripping her insides into shreds.

"I don't feel like sex ever since you and I—" He glared, as though furious he'd revealed as much. Eyebrows pulled downward, he then growled, *"No."*

The relief she felt made her sag back against the couch.

"Have *you?*" he shot back.

"Of course not!" she cried.

His narrowed gaze held hers with magnetic force, and they both fell so quiet that Molly could've heard a pin drop across the room. Unable to bear the strength of his stare, she broke eye contact and surveyed her sandaled feet, her stomach roiling. God, how she missed his oak leaf–green eyes.

"So do they plan to leave us here all night?" Sounding just as thrilled as he had minutes ago—which was not thrilled *at all*—Julian looked around the cozy cottage as though he still hoped to find an escape route.

It made Molly feel about as wanted as an abandoned rug. She nodded dejectedly. "I think they left some food in the kitchenette and water and…champagne."

How foolish to even mention that last item.

As if they would both have something to celebrate. *Uh-huh. Right.*

She had totally underestimated the size of Julian's pride, and the size of her own, and now she just wanted to stop begging and curl up on a pillow and never wake up until the Earth spun the way it was supposed to. The way it used to.

Her eyes blurred as she glanced up at him, but he was looking out the window, still unapproachable, and though she trembled with the urge to feel his arms around her, she curled up on the sofa and grabbed a pillow embroidered with *Home Is Where the Heart Is*. Shutting her eyes tiredly, she cuddled on one corner and strove to pretend Julian wasn't here with her. It was easy. Because she'd never before felt so broken, so somber and so lonely when she was with him.

But then his voice flicked through her, soft and husky enough that she could almost pretend it was a caress.

"Do you remember when you flunked your second driving test, Molly?"

She nodded, throat tightening. He had to bring that up.

"Do you remember taking out Landon's car for a little practice drive and crashing the hell out of it?"

She nodded faster, her throat tightening even more.

"You pulled me out of a damn Spurs game in the final period. And I fixed things. Fixed them so that you'd never be caught, gladly taking the super-fun lecture from my brother and mother for you. I never ratted you out. Never."

Throat burning thick now, she kept her eyes closed and prayed he didn't notice the dampness in her lashes, the tears stealing from between her eyelids to slide down her cheeks and to the pillow. "I'm sorry," she gritted out helplessly, opening her eyes to see the blurry vision of him. "You've always been my hero. I'm *sorry* I turned out to be the villain in *your* plot!"

He laughed, a sarcastic sound that said he didn't even care, and then he said no more and leaned a shoulder on the window and stared outside, probably wishing he was anywhere but here. With her.

"If we hadn't slept together," she asked his profile, "would you still be my best friend and talk to me?"

He rubbed one of his arms absently over his chest as he continued staring out the window. "Ask Garrett to be your bud," he said quietly.

Her eyebrows furrowed, and the anger and injustice that had been building up in her for days overtook her in an explosion. She jumped to her feet, shaking in fury. "You know what, Jules? Go to hell! If you want to hang on to the one thing I've done wrong to you in my life, that's your call. But you know I've been there for you every single second of your life like your own private cheerleader. If you had a fan club you know damned well I'd be the *president*. I happen to think that there's no one in the world as perfectly wonderful and special and incredible as you. But if you think that I would willingly hurt you in any way, for *anyone* else, even your brothers, then you're an idiot. And you don't deserve me *or* my friendship, much less my *love!*"

She was just too hurt and too tired to beg anymore. She'd thought what Julian and she had would survive anything. That they were invincible and powerful.

And now here they were, strangers and almost enemies, as if they hadn't once meant everything to each other.

He didn't reply to her words, but kept staring stiffly out the window, his profile taut.

Molly sighed and dropped back to the sofa, tired from her trip, from twenty-three days without sleep, weeks of wishing to find love and losing everything precious in her life in the process. Tired and frustrated, she tossed and turned on the couch, and she did that until finally sleep took over.

During the night her eyes fluttered open to see him still sitting by the window. Every time she looked, she found those green eyes watching her in the darkness.

The last time she woke up shivering and confused, and when she saw him still sitting there, alone and watching her with eyes that were almost as shadowed as the room, she curled herself into a ball and groggily said, "You should get some sleep, Jules. You can keep on hating me tomorrow."

He started coming over with something in his hands. "People with insomnia don't sleep, Molls," he murmured, and covered her with a blanket.

And that was as close as he got to her.

Eleven

It was past 7:00 a.m. when Julian heard someone fiddling with the outside bolt, and he stalked across the room like a man chasing a diabolical fiend. He'd slept exactly zero hours, had been torn between taking Molly in his arms and breaking a freaking window with his fist, but he would be damned if he gave his family the satisfaction of doing either.

No. He was through doing whatever they wanted him to do.

They thought he and Molly would have something to celebrate? The only thing Julian was going to celebrate today was ramming his fist into his brothers' jaws.

And that was exactly what he did as soon as the bolt was removed and he pushed the cottage door open to find Garrett outside, turning to leave.

"Good morning," Julian said to make his brother turn back around. He did.

And the force Julian put into his punch was so heavy it floored him instantly. Garrett smacked the ground with a loud thump.

Inside the cottage, Molly jumped to her feet with a start, her eyes wide and startled as she came over and saw the middle Gage brother sprawled at Julian's feet. She whipped her face up to him and fiercely scowled. "Oh, you were just itching to do that, weren't you? You've been talking about your guns for months!"

Frowning, Julian stretched out his fingers in confusion, because damn, that had hurt. Apparently, Garrett was too hardheaded to punch without getting a bit of a jolt in his knuckles, too.

"Yeah," Julian admitted to her. Then he glowered down at his brother and nudged him with his foot. "That felt real good, you son of a bitch!"

Coming up to a sitting position, Garrett wiped the blood off his mouth with the sleeve of his polo shirt and spat out the rest. "We have the same mother, you *moron*."

"I'm going home," he heard Molly mutter under her breath as she stormed toward the terrace, where Julian watched her grab some keys from Kate's purse. A minute later the catering van was pulling out of the driveway.

He wanted to chase her, yell and fight with her, the adrenaline was so off the charts in his body. But his instinct to spare her his rage was still too strong, and he was more bloodthirsty to make his brother his outlet for his rage.

Garrett was pushing to his feet, but Julian didn't let him. He shoved him back down by bracing one knee on his shoulder. "Stop meddling in our lives! We're not your responsibility, or Mother's or anyone else's. And if we wanted to be together, we sure as hell have never needed your idiotic help!"

Garrett pushed him aside and shuffled to his feet, rubbing his sore jaw. "She loves you, Jules. You're being an ass."

"Make that a headline in the paper tomorrow, brother. See if I buy a copy." Julian stalked away and flipped Garrett his two middle fingers without even glancing backward.

"Argh, you hardheaded bastard." Garrett pounced, scowling as he blocked his path. "You're going to make me fight you, aren't you?" Gritting his teeth in obvious frustration, his older brother began rolling up his sleeves.

"Get out of my way," Julian warned.

"Molly didn't betray you, you imbecile! She was furious because we were warning her away from you. She didn't *know* we've been riding you about her for years and she was trying to defend you. Why can you not *see* that?"

Julian wasn't listening. He was still restless, reckless, seething.

All night. All night, watching inches and inches of goose-bump-covered, creamy white skin, lustrous red hair and parted pink lips. All night, torturing himself with wanting her so damned much. He'd had a hard-on for hours. Hours.

"You know that girl loves you more than anyone or anything in this world. Don't you? *Don't you, Julian?*" Garrett demanded.

He glared at his brother. Goddammit, he wished he was sure of her. That she did not want anyone else. That she would never put any other man before him, ever again, before *Julian.*

"And you love her so bad you were ready to dump your whole family just to be with her," Garrett insisted.

Julian was suddenly incensed. "Because she's mine. Mine. Always has been. Always will be. She gave me her damned lollipop, and I took it, and right then and there—she was mine, Garrett. *Mine*."

"Well, then. Why are you here arguing with me while she's on her way home?"

Julian dropped his face with a grimace of pain, remembering her words as he rubbed his throbbing temples. *Please, please help me out here. I'm so in love with you I can't bear this anymore.*

If only he could be absolutely sure that she truly loved him. *Him*.

Not…his brother.

"Well? Are you going to let her get away now that you have her?" Garrett pressed as he signaled at the empty driveway. "Do you think a good girl like Molly would be with you if she wasn't all for you, man?"

Julian stared off to where she'd disappeared. "She was never with me."

"Come again?"

"Molly. It was a lie. Our relationship. She was never really with me. She wanted…you."

Just saying that to Garrett made him feel sick to his empty stomach. He didn't even know how he could have gone along with her foolish plan in the first place.

"Sooooo…*that's* what this is about." Garrett threw his head back and released one of his few real laughs, the sound booming across the landscape. "Molly doesn't want me, Jules. Hell, I sure as hell would know when a woman does." His gaze strayed over to Kate. She was speaking to their mother by the docks, and Garrett watched her for a long, long moment, his eyes on fire with emotion.

He jerked back when he realized he was being watched and growled, "Molly's loved you her whole life, jerk. She wanted to marry you when she was younger. She thought when it was time for her prom, she would be taking *you*.

Kate had to tell her once and for all that she should see you as a brother and start thinking of another boy to invite to prom. She cried for days because she'd never be able to marry you. She even packed her bags and that feisty little girl actually tried to *leave*—said she didn't want to grow up with us and have you as a brother. Our mother forced her to stay, but can you please understand how Mother would remain concerned about this development?"

It took a moment for him to absorb this. He imagined Molly in all her stages. Never once had any man featured in any of them—except for Julian. While he'd known he could never have her and had sought to fill in the void with a thousand different women, she had done the opposite and had wanted no man.

Until one kiss from Julian had awakened her.

God, if he had known that all this time… All. This. Time. She'd wanted to go to *prom* with him? Had wanted to *marry* him?

She'd been his friend, and he'd been hers, and neither had realized that they had truly ever only loved and wanted each other.

His heart soared at the realization, and for the first time in days, he felt as if he could take a normal breath again. But he still glared at his brother for having made his life a living hell where Molly was concerned. "Clearly what you all failed to see is that I *loved* her. I always have, you morons."

Brow rising in interest, Garrett stopped pretending to roll up his sleeves and now began to roll them down. "Oh, well, then. So what are you doing here?"

Julian stared out at the placid lake, and then once again noticed how Garrett kept glancing at Kate on the docks. "You plan to give me advice, old man," Julian dared, pointing at her. "And yet I don't see you following your own. I know you want her, Garrett, I'm not blind. Why don't you freaking do something?"

Garrett stiffened, his face harsh and pained. "The difference between you and me is that you've always known you deserve Molly. And I'll never deserve Kate."

Every muscle tense with longing, Julian thought of Molly as she'd been last night, how vulnerable she'd looked as she slept, how she'd shivered and how he'd watched her, covered her with a blanket while he'd wanted to cover her with his body instead. All night. All night he'd spent memorizing her face, wanting to pretend this little beauty had not hurt him like she had.

If you had a fan club you know damned well I'd be the president!

How adorable she'd looked, ranting at him. And he'd been an ass. Unreasonable and closed off to her, not even listening, letting his anger and that damned feeling of jealousy overcome him.

His heart began to race at the thought of losing her, really losing her, for life. No. Never. Because Molly was smarter than he was, and she would not cling to the one thing he'd done wrong in his life. She was better than that.

And he was getting her back. He had to, and this time it would be for life. His heart swelled as he thought of her. His little Moo, his Mo-Po, his Mopey, his Molls, his Picasso, his *Molly*. The one he'd always wanted, with all her paint-streaked skin, frilly skirt and sassy attitude that got her into trouble.

No, Molly had not betrayed him to Garrett intentionally, or out of preference for the other man. She'd been too innocent for her own damn good, which was why she'd always needed Julian in the first place. He'd be damned if his pride and anger and jealousy would keep her away from him now.

"You're right," he said, resolute. "I do deserve Molly, or at least I did."

He started across the gravel path, suddenly wanting to get his favorite pair of Nikes and run like the wind to her home. But then, his Aston Martin was probably faster.

"I'll just go and put some ice on this," Garrett called after him sarcastically, rubbing his jaw.

"I have a better idea. Why don't you let Kate do it," Julian yelled in return, and began sprinting to his car, his heart galloping. He would tear her clothes off when he saw her. He would nibble, lick and kiss her until she couldn't stand it and begged for him to stop. And then he'd stop, only to do it all over again.

His heart pounded as he drove, his mind homing in on one thing, just one thing.

He could barely feel the pain in his muscles now, the synapses in his brain all firing on one word, one thought, one girl.

Outside her place, he grabbed the key they hid in the planter, opened the front door and slammed it shut. He could hear his own footsteps echo as he charged down the hallway to her room.

Her door was open a crack, and he stopped. All of a sudden his system was ready to go haywire, and he wanted to do everything at once.

When he entered her room, he saw her lying facedown on her bed, as if she'd been crying or just tired or—God, he hoped she hadn't been crying.

As he quietly backed out of the room, she sat upright with a start.

Then she saw him and leaped to her feet, her gaze throwing daggers at him. Gone were her earrings, her bangles and her smile. Despite her obvious anger, he was about to detonate with hunger and love for this passionate little redhead. He reversed course and advanced on her with slow purpose, like that night at the masquerade, with the single-minded determination of a man truly possessed. By love, by desire, by a woman. By *his* woman.

She continued to look fiercely at him. "Go back to fight with your brother, Julian," she snapped.

Julian paused in the middle of the hall and spread out his arms in a gesture of pure innocence. "I'd much rather fight with you, Moo."

"Well, I *wouldn't*. I don't plan to fight with you anymore."

He smiled the smile he knew to be irresistible to her, his hands up in the air as if she'd trained a loaded gun on him. "All right, then. Let's make up. What do you say?"

She opened her mouth to answer, then shut it.

At the first sign of her hesitation, Julian dropped his arms and started forward. "I'm so sorry, baby."

She shook her head. "You don't say you're sorry, Julian John. You bring flowers and say, 'Here are your flowers and look outside, there's another truckful for you.'"

"Damn, you're greedy, Moo. I'll get you a whole flower shop as soon as I get my hands off you."

Lines of confusion settled across her features, and suddenly her lips quirked at the ends. "You can't get them off me if you don't have them *on* me, Jules."

"Count to three." He could literally *see* her lovely baby blues start to glow for him once more.

"One," she suddenly whispered.

His heart turned over in his chest, and he almost fell to his knees from his gratitude to her. Struggling to find words, his voice came out rough and uneven. "I'm sorry I was so damned jealous and unreasonable, but please understand there's not a woman in the world who drives me as crazy as you do. I couldn't stand the thought of you siding with them, of you putting my brother before me in any way. The thought of you responding to him like you respond to me—"

"Jules, no one has ever come before you. It wasn't *him* I responded to that first night you kissed me, it was *you*. I realized right away that I was kissing my soul mate."

He charged toward her. "I want to spend the rest of my life with you, Molly, and I want to know that I will always be your first and foremost, because you're sure as hell mine."

She lunged forward. "Two, three!"

He laughed in pure male thrill when he opened his arms at the same time Molly leaped and curled herself around him. *"I love you,"* she murmured, open-lipped against him.

He slanted his head and fitted his mouth to hers, a sound of desperation and hunger rumbling up from his throat. Molly met this sound with her own breathless gasp, her fingers delving into his hair until he could feel the delicious bite of her nails on his scalp.

Oh, baby, yeah.

He could feel her kiss in his every living cell, she kissed him so thoroughly, so completely. He hungrily squeezed her buttocks as he suckled her tongue and almost drowned in the taste of mint and apples and Mopey.

"I missed you so bad I haven't even been myself," he growled. Ducking his head to her breasts, he pulled down her strapless dress to find them bare and waiting for him. He suctioned a nipple between his teeth and closed his eyes as bliss pummeled him from the inside.

"Jules, I could've killed you for being such a hard-headed, moronic—"

"Shh." His head came up and he silenced her with a fingertip. "Be nice to me or I won't do this, hmm." He stuck his finger into her mouth and she suckled it greedily while he watched, his eyes feeling heavy.

She mewed in protest when he retrieved his finger, so then he used his lips to part hers wider and thrust his hot, wet tongue inside her. "Please tell me I didn't make you cry, baby," he desperately whispered as he broke their kiss for a moment to slant his head and get a better angle.

She nodded, speaking into his mouth as she gloried in the taste of him. "Like eleven times."

"Now I'll have to make it up to my girl with an hour of this for every time I made her cry." He cupped her breasts lovingly and kissed each one with care.

Molly panted, quivering with arousal as his skillful hands gripped the fabric of her dress at her hips and pulled it over her head, leaving her in her lacy black panties.

"It was really more like thirty-five times. I just didn't want to sound desperate," she confessed, her voice full of yearning as she fondled his dampened lips with her fingertips.

"Poor baby." He drew back to take a good look at her, his eyelids heavy as he caressed her lovely curves with his fingers. "Let me get my math straight…how many times?"

"A hundred times," she concluded, her breasts jerking up and down with her laboring breaths as she tightened her legs around his hips.

"A hundred times that I made my baby cry… I have a lot of making up to do."

Molly shuddered at the words, at the way he muttered them against her swollen breast, the way he laved her nipples and then breathed on them until she thought she would burst.

She'd been waiting for him, praying and plotting and planning to get him back. The one and only man for her.

A little hardheaded, true. But to her, Julian John Gage was still the bomb. The *bomb*.

Now he was here, in her arms, and she never wanted him to leave.

She held her breath as she frantically pulled his shirt over his head, and when he sent it flying across the room, his magnificent muscles bulged.

"I was about to call Garrett and ask him to pretend to love me." She rubbed his hard, square shoulders and delighted over the satin feel of his skin. "Just to see if you came back around."

"Oh, yeah?"

His smile was all cocky as he set her on her feet, then he hooked a finger in her panties and pulled them down, off one leg, then the other. "The difference is," he said as he undid his belt buckle and sent it clattering to the floor, "that he would be pretending. While I never was."

Once he was naked, he kicked the door shut and boosted her up against the wall, guiding her legs around his hips. Molly locked her ankles at the small of his back, clenching him tight between her arms and thighs and never planning to let go. His eyes glowed so bright and tender on her face, the light warmed her to the very depths of her being.

"Make love with me?" he murmured.

She jerked her head breathlessly as he held her hips between his big hands, and then, as sunlight streamed in through her bedroom window and their eyes locked, he thrust inside of her. She cried out with the joy of being physically his again. She'd been so ready to settle for friendship, if that was all she'd get. But in the deepest, most secret parts of her, she had ached for so much more.

"Jules, love me. Say you love me."

"I love you like crazy." He framed her face and looked

into her eyes. "Never doubt it. I love you, I worship you, I adore you, Molly. You and you alone."

His passionate words drove her to the precipice. They came together with tempestuous force, and once their endless shudders subsided, Molly gasped and turned her face into his neck, struggling to catch her breath. She'd felt his warmth spill into her, had felt the powerful contractions that seized his body, and now her heart soared in the sheer joy of being entwined with Julian again.

Panting and sweaty, she lifted her head just as he was ducking to kiss her. Their lips met in a languorous, loving, lazy kiss that left her weak and buzzing. "Every time you kiss me," she said softly, stroking his face as he carried her to the bed, "it feels like the first time." A dreamy sigh escaped her as she remembered that masquerade. "I should've *known* I was being kissed by a playboy."

"Get used to it, Mopey." He set her down on the mattress with a kiss on her forehead, then stretched out beside her and rumpled her hair. "Because I promise you'll never see a playboy more into his wife than I."

Her heart stuttered at the word *wife,* then it just completely stopped beating.

"What do you mean?"

At the sight of her wide eyes, his wolfish smile appeared, and he took her left hand within his. She watched in disbelief as he slid the matte platinum ring, large and masculine, onto her ring finger.

The ring from the masquerade.

"I'll get you a real one tomorrow. One with a white diamond—a big one. This is just so you know my intentions are pure."

"Oh, I have no doubt your intentions are squeaky clean," she laughed as she pointedly glanced down at their nakedness, and then she fell somber as the magnitude of what was happening struck her. Settling her hands on his shoulders, she gazed at the ring, then into those oak leaf-green eyes. She could see his pulse fluttering rapidly at the base of his throat, could see the love and need in his eyes.

"You were meant to be my wife, Molly," he rasped, brushing her hair back, his hands, his tenderness undoing her. "Will you marry me?"

She held his caressing green gaze and nodded, her eyes mirroring the loving way that Julian looked down at her now. Stroking his strong jaw affectionately, she simply said, "As you wish."

* * * * *

HER ACCIDENTAL
ENGAGEMENT

MICHELLE MAJOR

To Mom and Dad: for your love, support and
the years of off-key harmonies

Chapter One

Julia Morgan lit the final match, determined to destroy the letter clenched in her fingers. She was well aware of the mistakes she'd made in her life, but seeing them typed on fancy letterhead was more than she could take at the moment. She drew the flickering flame toward the paper but another gust of damp wind blew it out.

The mountains surrounding her hometown of Brevia, North Carolina, were notoriously wet in late winter. Even though it hadn't rained for several days, moisture clung to the frigid March air this afternoon, producing a cold she felt right to her bones.

With a frustrated groan, she crumpled the letter into a tiny ball. Add the inability to burn a single piece of paper to her colossal list of failures. Sinking to her knees on the soggy ground, she dropped the used matchstick into a trash bag with all the others.

She ignored the wail of a siren from the highway above

her. She'd pulled off the road minutes earlier and climbed down the steep embankment, needing a moment to stop the panic welling inside her.

For a few seconds she focused her attention on the canopy of pine trees below the ridge where she stood, her heartbeat settling to a normal rhythm.

Since she'd returned to her hometown almost two years ago, this love of the forest had surprised her. She'd never been a nature girl, her gypsy existence taking her from one big city to another. Thanks to her beautiful son, Julia was now rooted in Brevia, and the dense woods that enveloped the town gave her the sense of peace she hadn't known she'd missed for years.

The makeshift fire hadn't been much of a plan, but flying by the seat of her pants was nothing new for Julia. With a deep breath, she smoothed the wrinkled letter against the grass. She'd read it compulsively over the past week until the urge to destroy it had overtaken her. She knew the words by heart but needed the satisfaction of watching them go up in flames.

Unfit mother. Seeking custody. Better options.

Tears pricked the backs of her eyes. Burning the letter wouldn't change the potential it had to ruin her life. She'd tried to dismiss the contents as lies and conjecture. In a corner of her heart, she worried they were true and she wouldn't be able to defend herself against them.

Suddenly she was hauled to her feet. "Are you hurt? What happened?" A pair of large hands ran along her bare arms, then down her waist toward...

Whoa, there. "Back off, Andy Griffith," Julia sputtered as parts of her body she thought were in permanent hibernation sprang to life.

As if realizing how tightly he held her, Sam Callahan, Brevia's police chief, pushed away. He stalked several yards up the hill toward the road, then turned and came at her again. Muscles bunched under the shoulders of his police uniform.

She had to work hard to ignore the quick pull of awareness that pulsed through her. Darn good thing Julia had sworn off men. Even better that big, strong alpha men were *so* not her type.

Julia gave herself a mental headshake. "What do you want, Sam? I'm sort of busy here."

She could have sworn his eye twitched under his aviator sunglasses. He jabbed one arm toward the top of the hill. "What I *want* is to know what the hell you're doing off the side of the road. *Again.*"

Right. She'd forgotten that the last time Sam had found her, she'd been eight months pregnant and had wrapped her ancient Honda around a tree trunk. He'd taken her to the hospital where her son, Charlie, had been born.

That day a year and a half ago had been the start of a new life for her. One she'd protect at any cost.

Sam had been new to Brevia and the role of police chief then. He'd also been a whole lot nicer. At least, to Julia. He'd made the rounds of the single ladies in town, but ever since Charlie's birth Sam had avoided her as though he thought he might be the first man in history to catch a pregnancy. Which was fine, especially given some of the details she'd heard about his history with women.

"Julia."

At the sound of her name, she focused on his words.

"There are skid marks where your car pulled off."

"I was in a hurry," she said and swiped at her still-moist cheeks.

His hands bunched at his sides as he eyed her bag. "Do I smell smoke?"

"I lit a match. Lots of them." Her chin hitched. "Wanna call Smokey Bear for backup?"

He muttered something under his breath at the same time a semi roared by on the road above.

"I didn't quite catch that."

Sam removed his sunglasses and tucked them into the front pocket of his shirt. He was almost *too* good-looking, his blond hair short but a little messy, as if he needed a trim. The effect softened his classically handsome features and a square jaw that fell just short of comic-book chiseled. His gaze slammed into hers, and Julia knew if ice could turn molten, it would be the exact color of Sam's blue eyes.

"You were on your knees," he said slowly.

Julia swallowed. "I lost a contact."

"You don't wear contacts."

"How do you…? Never mind." She bent to retrieve the bag of worthless matches.

His finger brushed the back of her arm. "What are you doing out here, Jules?"

Something about the sound of her name soft as a whisper broke through her defenses. She straightened and waved the letter at him. "I have a meeting in town and needed some fresh air to collect my thoughts."

"At the salon?"

She shook her head. "No. Hair dye doesn't require much mental fortitude. I have a real meeting, with an attorney."

He didn't ask for details but continued to watch her.

"It's about Charlie," she offered after a minute. "About my custody." To add to her humiliation, she choked on the last word.

"You're his mother. Of course you have custody."

"I know." She lifted the letter. "But Jeff and his parents think—"

"Who's Jeff?"

"My ex-boyfriend." She sighed. "Charlie's father."

Sam's eyes narrowed. "The one who's never set eyes on him?"

"He's a college professor and travels the world doing research. His dad runs an investment firm in Columbus, Ohio, and his mom is a retired cardiologist. They're rich, powerful and very intellectual. The whole family is off-the-charts smart. I guess they have…concerns. For Charlie's future and my ability to provide the right environment. Jeff wants a new custody arrangement."

"Have Jeff's parents met Charlie?"

"No. They called a couple of times after he was born. They didn't approve of me when I was with Jeff, and since he didn't want anything to do with the baby…" She paused then added, "I let my mom deal with them."

That made him smile. "In my opinion, Vera is also off-the-charts smart."

Julia ignored the shiver in her legs at his slow grin. Her mother, Vera Morgan, was a pit bull. But also keenly intelligent. Everyone in her family was smart. Everyone but her.

"Jeff's mother is here with their family attorney to meet me. To make sure everything's okay—that Charlie is in good hands."

"Of course he's in good hands." Sam's voice gentled as he repeated, "You're his mother."

"I've done a lot of stupid things in my life, made a lot of mistakes. Jeff knows the sordid details and I'm sure his parents do, too." Emotion clogged her throat.

Sam was not the man she wanted to have see her like this. She made a show of checking her watch. "What I could use is some damage control for my reputation. White picket fence, doting husband, pillar of the community stuff. It's a little late for me to join the Junior League." She shook her head. "Anyway, thanks for your concern today, but as you can see, I'm peachy keen."

"You shouldn't talk to anyone until you get an attorney of your own."

"Frank Davis said he would help me, but I hope it won't come to that. I'm sure the Johnsons want what's best for Charlie. I should at least hear them out. That boy deserves everything this world has to offer." She gave a humorless laugh and started back toward the road. "What he's got is me."

As she moved past Sam, his hand reached out, but she jerked away. If he touched her right now she'd be a goner, and she needed to keep it together. For Charlie.

"You're more than enough," he called after her.

"From your lips to God's ears, Chief," she whispered and climbed up to her car.

"Who are you and what have you done with my father?"

Sam shifted in his chair at Carl's, Brevia's most popular restaurant, still reeling from his unbelievable afternoon. From the bizarre encounter with Julia he'd been called to a domestic disturbance that ended up being a chicken loose in Bobby Royall's kitchen. It had made him almost thirty minutes late to dinner with his dad. Now he wished the bird hadn't been so easy to catch.

Joe Callahan adjusted his Patriots baseball cap and chuckled. "It's me, son. Only better."

Said who?

His father had been a police officer in Boston for almost forty years, most of which had been spent working homicide. Joe Callahan had dedicated his life to his career, and his family had suffered from the on-the-job stress and risks he took daily. Although it wasn't intentional, Sam had modeled his own life after his father's. Sam had put his job before everything and everyone in his life—just like Joe.

Recently, though, Joe had begun conducting programs for police departments on emotional awareness. Sam had resisted his father's repeated attempts to help him "get in touch" with his feelings. But now Joe was here and impossible to ignore.

"The boys down at the precinct loved my seminar. At least four of 'em were in tears by the end. I got thank-you notes from a half-dozen wives."

"That's great, Dad." Sam took a long drink of iced tea, wishing he wasn't on duty. A cold one would be mighty helpful tonight. "I don't see what that has to do with me or your unexpected visit to Brevia."

His father pulled a flyer out of the briefcase at his feet and pushed it across the table. "While I'm down here, I thought we could organize a workshop."

Sam glanced at the pamphlet. His stomach gave a hearty gurgle. *Law with Love, Presented by Retired Police Captain Joseph Callahan.* A picture of Joe hugging a group of uniformed officers filled the front page. Sam couldn't remember ever being hugged by his craggy, hard-nosed father. Holy mother of…

"I don't know. It's only me and one deputy on the force."

Joe tapped the sheet of paper. "It's for firefighters and paramedics, too. We could bring in neighboring towns— make it a regional event. Plus civil servants, city council. You're looking at a long-term reappointment, right? This could make quite an impression as far as your potential."

At the mention of his possible future in Brevia, Sam lost the battle with his temper. "My potential as what? I'm the chief of police, not the hug-it-out type."

His father's sharp intake of breath made Sam regret

his outburst. "Sorry. You know what a small town this is and—"

Joe held up a hand. "Don't apologize." He removed his bifocals and dabbed at his eyes with a napkin.

"You aren't going to cry," Sam muttered, disbelieving. "You don't cry."

"Yes. I *am* going to cry. To take a moment and *feel* my pain."

Great. This was the second time today he'd brought someone to tears.

After a loud nose blow, Joe's watery gaze met his. "I feel my pain, and I feel yours."

"I'm not in pain." Sam let his eyes drift shut. "Other than a raging headache."

Joe ignored him and continued, "I did this to you, Sammy."

Sammy? His father hadn't called him Sammy since—

"When your mother died my whole world collapsed. I didn't think I could live without her. I didn't want to. It broke me a little more every day to see you and your brother that sad. I did the only thing I could to survive. I shut off my heart, and I made you do the same. I was wrong. I'm here to make it right again."

Sam saw customers from the surrounding tables begin to stare. "It's okay. Let's go outside for a minute."

Joe followed Sam's gaze and shook his head. "I'm not embarrassed to show my feelings. Not anymore." He took another breath, this one steadier. "Ever since the incident with my ole ticker." He thumped his sweatshirt. "They say facing death can make you reevaluate your whole life."

"It was indigestion, Dad. Not a real heart attack. Remember?"

"Doesn't matter. The change to my heart was real. The

effect on my life was real." He readjusted his glasses. "I want the same change for you. I want you to be happy."

"I'm fine." Sam gulped a mouthful of ice and crunched. "Happy as a clam."

"Are you seeing anyone?"

Alarm bells went off in Sam's head. "I…sure…am actually. She's great." He looked away from his father's expectant face, unable to lie to him directly. He glanced around the crowded restaurant and his gaze landed on Julia at a booth in the back. He hadn't noticed her when he'd first walked in, but now he couldn't pull his eyes away.

This must be the meeting with her ex-boyfriend's family she'd told him about. The faces of the two women seated across from her were blocked, but Julia's cheeks flamed pink. Her palm smacked the table as if she was about to lose control.

Easy there, sweetheart, he counseled silently.

As if she'd heard him, her eyes met his and held for several moments. His pulse hammered against his throat. Then she squared her shoulders and folded her hands in her lap.

He turned back to his father. "You'd like her. She's a real spitfire."

Joe smiled. "Like your mother."

Sam forced himself not to look at Julia again. "I was ten when she died. I don't remember that much."

"This one's different than your other girls?"

Sam caught the waitress's attention and signaled for the check.

"Because I think you need a new perspective. After what happened with…"

"I don't want to rehash my relationship history."

Joe reached across the table and clasped Sam's hand in his. "I know you want to find love and settle down."

Sam heard a loud cough behind him and found the young waitress staring. Her look could only be described as predatory. *Fantastic.* Sam had dated some when he'd first come to town but had kept to himself recently, finding it easier and less complicated to be alone. The way gossip went viral in Brevia, he'd have a fresh line of eligible women in front of his office by morning.

"I told you," Sam said, loud enough for the waitress to hear. "I've got a girlfriend. We're very happy."

The waitress dropped the check on the table with a *humph* and stalked away.

"It's serious?" Joe asked.

Sam's gaze wandered to Julia again. "Very," he muttered as she jabbed a finger across the table. This time his mental warning to not lose control didn't reach her. Her voice grew so loud that people at surrounding tables turned.

"I want to meet her," his dad said, rubbing his palms together, oblivious to the commotion behind him. "Why don't you give her a call and see if she can meet us for dessert? If she's so wonderful, I can help make sure you don't blow it."

At the moment, Sam wasn't worried about screwing up anything himself or producing a nonexistent girlfriend for his dad to fawn over. Instead he felt the need to avert someone else's disaster. "I'll be right back."

Joe grabbed his arm as he started past. "Don't be sore, Sammy. I was joking. You're a great catch."

Sam shrugged out of his father's grasp. "I need a minute. Stay here."

He darted around a passing waiter as he made his way to Julia, who now stood in front of the booth.

"You have no idea what I'm capable of," she shouted. All eyes on this side of the restaurant were glued to her.

Just as he reached her, Julia picked up a glass of water from the table. Sam leaned in and wrapped his fingers around hers before she could hurl it at anyone.

"Hey there, sugar," he said as he pulled her tense body tight to his side. "I didn't realize your meeting was at Carl's tonight. You doing okay?"

"Let go of me," she said on a hiss of breath. "This is none of your concern."

"Well, I *am* concerned," he whispered then plastered on a wide smile. "I haven't met your new friends yet."

She squirmed against him. "They aren't my—"

"Howdy, folks," Sam interrupted, turning his attention to the two strangers staring at him. "I'm Sam Callahan. A...uh...friend of Julia's."

The woman in the corner practically screamed "old money," from her sophisticated haircut to her tailored suit. A thick strand of pearls hung around her neck and a massive diamond sparkled on her left hand. The way her gaze narrowed, she must be Charlie's paternal grandmother. Next to her was a younger woman, tiny and bookish. Her big owl eyes blinked from behind retro glasses. Faint streaks of color stole up her neck from the collar of her starched oxford shirt as she watched the two of them.

"Friend?" The older woman scoffed. "Latest conquest, no doubt." She nudged the woman beside her. "Are you taking notes on this? She's now flaunting her boy toy in front of us."

Boy toy? Sam's smile vanished and he worked to keep his voice pleasant. "Excuse me, ma'am, you have the wrong idea—"

She continued as if he hadn't spoken. "Can you imagine what my grandson's been subjected to when his mother is obviously a tramp? When the judge hears—"

Sam held up a hand. "Wait just one minute, lady. If you think you can waltz in here—"

Julia's fingernails dug into his arm. "I *don't* need your help. Walk away."

He glanced down at her and saw embarrassment shimmering along with anger in her expression. And fear. At the mention of the word *judge,* he'd felt some of the fight go out of her. He wished he hadn't interrupted, that he'd let her handle her own problems, the way she'd wanted to in the first place. But a part of Sam needed to be the hero just so he could feel something. It was what he was used to, one of the few things he could count on. That part of him couldn't walk away.

He released Julia and leveled his best law-enforcement stare at the grandmother. As he expected, she shrank back and darted a nervous glance at her companion. "I'm Sam Callahan, Brevia's police chief." Hands on hips, he held her gaze. "To be clear, I am *no one's* boy toy and would appreciate if you'd conduct yourself in a more civilized manner in my town. We don't take kindly to strangers spreading malicious rumors about our own. Do I make myself clear?"

Several beats passed before the studious-looking woman cleared her throat. "Mr. Callahan—"

Sam squared his shoulders. "You can call me Chief."

The attorney swallowed. "Chief Callahan, I'm Lexi Preston. I represent the interests of Charlie Morgan's father, Jeff Johnson, and grandparents, Dennis and Maria Johnson. My father is the Johnsons' family attorney and he asked me—"

"Get to the point."

"Yes, well…" Lexi mumbled as she shuffled papers around the table. "I was simply explaining to Ms. Morgan the facts of her case, or lack thereof, when she became hostile and confrontational. My client is not to blame for this unfortunate disturbance. We have statements from a number of Ms. Morgan's former acquaintances as to her character, so Dr. Johnson's assertion, while ill-advised, is not without foundation."

He heard Julia suck in a breath but kept his attention on the two women. "I don't care what your so-called statements allege. You're not going to drag Julia's name through the mud."

Preston collected the rest of the papers. "Why is Ms. Morgan's reputation your business? Is she under investigation by local law enforcement?"

"This can't get any worse," Julia whispered so low only he could here. "Go away, Sam. Now."

From the corner of his eye, Sam saw his father standing a few feet away, watching him intently. Sam was a good cop and he played things by the book, having learned the hard way not to bite off more than he could chew.

But some lessons didn't stick.

He peeled Julia's hand from its death grip around his upper arm and laced her fingers with his. "It's my business, Counselor, because I'm not going to let you or anyone hurt the woman I intend to marry."

Chapter Two

Julia thought things couldn't get worse.

Until they did.

She glanced around the restaurant, as dumbfounded as the people who stared at her from the surrounding tables. She recognized a lot of them; Carl's was a popular spot for Brevia locals.

Yanking Sam away from the table a few steps, she smiled up into his face, well aware of their audience. It took all her willpower to resist the urge to slap him silly. "Have you lost your mind?" she said, keeping her voice low.

The corners of his mouth were tight as he returned her smile. "Apparently."

"Fix this. You have to fix this."

"That's what I'm trying to do." He smoothed a stray hair from her cheek. "Trust me."

No way. Julia didn't trust men. She had a long line of

heartbreak in her past. Mountains of collateral damage that made her sure she was the only person she could trust to take care of her and Charlie. "Don't touch me," she whispered through gritted teeth.

His hand dropped from her face. "I'm going to help you. But you can't fight me. Not here."

She glanced over his shoulder at the attorney and Charlie's grandmother. For a fraction of a second, worry marred Maria Johnson's perfect features. Julia didn't understand the break in the ice queen's armor, but it must have had something to do with Sam.

"Fine." She reached forward and clasped both of his rock-solid arms, as if she could make him understand the gravity of her situation through a simple squeeze. "You better make it count. Charlie's future is on the line."

He searched her gaze for a long moment, then bent onto one knee. He took her fingers in his, tugging softly when she would have pulled away.

"I didn't mean..."

"Julia Morgan," he said, and his deep, clear voice rang out in the restaurant. "We've kept this quiet—no easy task in Brevia—but it's long past time to make things official." He cleared his throat, adjusting the collar of his starched uniform shirt. "Would you do me the honor of becoming my wife?"

Julia blinked back sudden tears. A marriage proposal was what she'd wanted, once upon a time. She'd wanted Jeff to see they could build a real life together. Foolishly sure he was the one, she'd been reckless and selfish. Then the universe had blessed her with a beautiful son. She was working day and night to make a good life for Charlie. Now that she wanted to do the right thing, she risked losing him.

Not for the first time, she wondered if he'd be better off

with the Johnsons and the privileged life filled with opportunities they could provide.

She squeezed her eyes shut to clear her thoughts. She
was Charlie's mother, no matter what, and wouldn't ever
stop fighting for him.

Sam ran his finger along the inside of her wrist. "Are
you going to answer the question? My leg is cramping."

"Oh, no. Sorry."

"No?" he asked over the collective gasp.

"I mean yes. Get up, you big oaf." Heat flooded her
face and her stomach churned. What was she doing? She'd
learned not to rely on a man for anything and now she was
putting her entire future in Sam's hands. Impulsive as ever,
she repeated, "Yes. My answer is yes."

He stood, rubbing one knee. "Cool it on the name-calling.
We're in love, remember."

"You betcha, honey-bunny."

That produced a genuine grin from him, and she was
again caught off guard by her body's reaction as tiny butterflies did a fast samba across her belly. Oblivious to his
effect on her, Sam turned to the booth.

Before he could speak, an older man wrapped them
both in a tight hug. "This is amazing."

Amazing? Not quite.

Sam caught her gaze, his eyes dark and unreadable. "I
forgot to tell you earlier. My dad came to town today. Meet
Joe Callahan, your future father-in-law."

Uh-oh.

Joe cupped her face between his large hands. "You're
just what he needed. I can already tell." Tears shimmered
in eyes the same color as Sam's, only sweeter and looking
at her with such kindness a lump formed in Julia's throat.
"You remind me of my Lorraine, rest her soul."

"Okay, Dad." Sam tugged her out of Joe's embrace. She took a step back but Sam pulled her against his side.

Joe turned to the booth. "I'll buy a round to celebrate. Any friends of…"

"Julia," Sam supplied with a sigh.

"Any friends of my future daughter-in-law are friends of mine."

"We're *not* friends," Lexi Preston ground out. "As I said earlier, I represent her son's biological father and his parents. They're interested in exploring a more viable custody arrangement. The Johnsons want what's best for the child. They can give him opportunities—"

"They want to take my baby," Julia mumbled. Sam's arm tightened around her waist.

If Joe was surprised to hear she had a child, he didn't let on. His posture went rigid. "That's ridiculous. She's the boy's mother."

"Dad, this isn't the time or place—" Sam began.

Joe wagged a finger at Lexi Preston and Maria Johnson. "Now listen here. I don't know what all this nonsense is about, but I can tell you my son will take care of that child and Julia. He's the law around here, for heaven's sake." He leaned closer and Lexi's nervous swallow mimicked Julia's. Joe Callahan might look like a teddy bear but he had a backbone of steel. "You'll have to come through both of us if you try to hurt her. We protect our own."

"I've had quite enough of this town for tonight." Maria pushed at the attorney, who stood quickly. "I don't care who you've got in your backwater little corner of the world, we're going to—"

Lexi put a hand on Maria's shoulder to silence her. "The less said tonight, the better. We have a court date next week." She gave Julia a curt nod. "Ms. Morgan, we'll see you then."

"Take care of the check, Lexi." Maria Johnson barked the order at her attorney before stalking out of the restaurant.

"Does that mean she's leaving Brevia?" Julia asked.

"For now. I'll stay for the duration of the process. The Johnsons will fly back and forth." Lexi leaned toward Julia. "I don't want to get your hopes up, but a stable home environment could change the situation." She clapped a hand over her mouth as if she'd said too much, then nodded to the group and scurried away.

Julia reached forward to hug Joe. "Thank you, Mr. Callahan. For what you said."

"I meant it. Sam isn't going to let anything happen to you."

Sam.

Julia turned, but focused her attention on the badge pinned to Sam's beige shirt, unable to make eye contact with him. Instead she looked out at the tables surrounding them. "Sorry for the commotion. Go back to dinner, and we'll get out of your way."

"Wait a minute." Sam's voice cut through the quiet.

Julia held her breath.

"As most of you heard tonight, Julia and I have something to celebrate." He grabbed her hand and drew her back to him. Her fingers spread across his broad chest of their own accord. "We need to make this believable for the gossip mill," he whispered against her ear.

A round of applause rang out in the restaurant followed by several clinks on glasses. "Kiss. Kiss. Kiss," came the call from the bar.

Julia froze as Sam gazed down at her, his expression heated. "Better give them what they want."

"It's totally unbelievable and I had garlic for dinner," she muttered, squirming in his arms.

"I'll take my chances," he answered with a laugh.

"Have it your way." Cheeks burning, she raised her head and pressed her mouth to his, a chaste peck fit for the balcony at Buckingham Palace. When she would have ended the kiss, Sam caught hold of her neck and dipped her low. She let out a startled gasp and he slid his tongue against the seam of her lips. Ever so gently he molded his mouth to hers.

A fire sparked low in her belly as she breathed in the scent of him, warm and woodsy and completely male. Lost in her reaction, her arms wound around his neck and her fingers played in the short hair along his collar. She heard his sharp intake of breath and suddenly he righted them both to a chorus of catcalls and stomping feet.

"That's what I'm talking about," someone yelled.

"Okay, folks." Sam's gaze swept across the restaurant and he smiled broadly. "Show's over. I'm going to see my lovely bride-to-be home."

Julia pressed her fingers to her lips and looked at Sam. The smile didn't reach his eyes.

When she turned, Joe watched her. "You're a breath of fresh air if I ever saw one," he said and gave her trembling hand a squeeze.

She led the group into the night but not before she noticed several members of the ladies' auxiliary huddled in the corner. They'd have a field day with this one. The salon would be buzzing with the news by morning. Her chest tightened as she felt Sam behind her, frustration pouring off him like a late-winter rainstorm. Maybe he'd already come to regret his stupid proposal.

This entire situation was his fault. She'd told him she didn't need a hero, and that was the truth.

Still, his announcement had rattled Maria Johnson and

her attorney. She couldn't figure out how a fake engagement would benefit Sam, but he wasn't her problem.

Charlie was Julia's only priority. She'd do anything for her son.

Right now she needed time to think, to figure out how to make this bizarre predicament work in her favor. "It's been a long day, boys," she said quickly. "Joe, it was nice to meet you. How long will you be—"

"We need to talk," Sam interrupted, gripping her arm when she tried to break away.

"I thought I'd be around for a while. Give my boy some lessons in tapping into his feelings, finding his passion and all that." Joe gave Sam a hearty thump on the back. "After that little display, I think he may have wised up on his own. You're good for him, Julia. Real good."

Sam's hold on her loosened. He studied his father. "You mean one kiss convinced you I can do without a dose of your emotional mumbo jumbo?"

Julia swatted his arm. "That's your father. Show some respect."

Sam shot her a withering look. "I'll remember that the next time your mom's around."

Joe laughed and wrapped them in another hug. "Not just any kiss. It's different when you kiss *the one*. Trust me, I know. I bet they could see the sparks flying between the two of you clear down to the coast."

Looking into Joe's trusting face, she couldn't let Sam's father pin his hopes on her. She had to tell him the truth.

"Mr. Callahan, I don't—"

"You're right, Dad," Sam agreed. "It's different with Julia. I'm different, and I don't want you to worry about me anymore." He pinched the tip of Julia's nose, a little harder than necessary if you asked her.

"Ouch."

"Such a delicate flower." He laughed and dropped a quick kiss on her forehead. "What would I do without you?"

"Troll for women over in Charlotte?" she offered.

"See why I need her by my side?"

Joe nodded. "I do."

Sam turned to Julia and rubbed his warm hands down her arms. "Where are you parked?"

Julia pointed to the blue Jetta a few spaces down from where they stood, her mind still reeling.

"Perfect. I'm going to walk Dad back to the hotel and we'll talk tomorrow."

She didn't like the look in his eye. "I'm kind of busy at the salon tomorrow."

"Never too busy for your one true love."

Julia stifled the urge to gag. "I guess not."

"Get going, then, sugar." He pinched her bottom, making her yelp. She rounded on him but, at the calculating gleam in his eye, turned back toward her car. Sam and his dad watched until she'd pulled out.

Despite this peculiar evening, his announcement had served its purpose. Lexi Preston had said having Sam in the picture might change things. That could be the understatement of the year, but if it kept Charlie safe, Julia would make it work.

No matter what.

Sam took a fortifying drink of coffee and watched as another woman walked through the door of The Best Little Hairhouse. He knew Julia had worked at the salon since her return to Brevia two years ago, but that wasn't why he avoided this place like the plague. It was too girlie for him. The bottles of hair product and little rows of nail polish on the shelves gave him the heebie-jeebies.

The one time he'd ventured into the Hairhouse, after the owner had reported a man lurking in the back alley, he'd felt like a prize steer come up for auction.

He adjusted the brim of his hat, buttoned his jacket against the late-morning rain and started across the street. He'd put the visit off until almost lunchtime, irritated with himself at how much he wanted to see Julia again. Part of him wanted to blame her for making him crazy, but another piece, the part he tried to ignore, wanted to get close enough to her to smell the scent of sunshine on her hair.

He scrubbed a hand across his face. Sunshine on her hair? What the hell was that about? Women didn't smell like sunshine. She worked at a salon and probably had a ton of gunk in her hair at any given moment. Although the way the strands had felt soft on his fingers when he'd bent to kiss her last night told another story.

One he wasn't interested in reading. Or so he told himself.

Sam opened the front door and heard a blood-curdling scream from behind the wall at the reception desk. He jerked to attention. He might not spend a lot of time in beauty salons but could guarantee that sound wasn't typical.

"I'm going to choke the life out of her," a woman yelled, "as soon as my nails dry."

Nope. Something wasn't right.

He glanced at the empty reception desk then stepped through the oversized doorway that led to the main room.

A pack of women huddled around one of the chairs, Julia in the center of the mix.

"Is there a problem here, ladies?"

Seven pairs of eyes, ranging from angry to horrified, turned to him.

"Sam, thank the Lord you're here."

"You would not believe what happened."

"Congrats on your engagement, Chief."

The last comment produced silence from the group. He met Julia's exasperated gaze. "Not a good time," she mouthed and turned back to the center of the cluster, only to be pushed aside by a woman with a black smock draped around her considerable girth. Sam tried not to gape at her head, where the neat curls framing her face glowed an iridescent pink.

"There will be time for celebrating later. I want that woman arrested," Ida Garvey announced. Sam was used to Ida issuing dictatorial commands. She was the wealthiest woman in town, thanks to a generous inheritance from her late husband. Other than the clown hair, she looked like a picture-perfect grandma, albeit one with a sharp tongue and a belief that she ruled the world.

For an instant, he thought she was pointing at Julia. Then he noticed the young woman hunched in the corner, furiously wiping tears from her cheeks.

"Ida, don't be a drama queen." Julia shook her head. "No one is being arrested. Accidents happen. We'll fix it, but—"

"She turned my hair pink!" With a screech, Ida vaulted from the chair and grabbed a curling iron from a stand. "I'm going to kill her!" Ida lunged toward the cowering woman, but Julia stepped into her path. The curling iron dropped, the barrel landing on Julia's arm before clattering to the floor.

Julia bit out an oath and Ida screamed again. "Look what you made me do," she bellowed at the now-sobbing stylist. "I burned her."

Sam strode forward with a new appreciation for the simplicity of breaking up a drunken bar brawl. Ida looked into his face then staggered back, one hand fluttering to her chest. "Are you gonna arrest me, Chief?"

"Sit down, Mrs. Garvey." He waved at the group of women. "All of you, back off. Now."

Ida plopped back into the chair as the group fell silent again.

Julia winced as he took her arm in his hands. A crimson mark slashed across her wrist, the skin already raised and angry. "Where's a faucet?"

"I'm fine," she said through gritted teeth. "Happens all the time."

"I sure as hell hope not."

"Not exactly like this. I can use the sink in back." She tugged her arm but he didn't let go.

"Don't anyone move," he ordered the women. "That means you, Ida."

"I don't need your help," Julia ground out as he followed her to the back of the salon.

"You aren't leaving me alone with that crowd."

"Not so brave now." Julia fumbled with the tap.

He nudged her out of the way. "I'll do it. Nice ring. I have good taste."

"I had it from… Well, it doesn't matter." Her cheeks flamed as she glanced at the diamond sparkling on her left hand. "I thought I should wear something until we had a chance to figure things out. Fewer questions that way. You know how nosy people are, especially in the salon."

They needed to talk, but Sam couldn't get beyond Julia being hurt, even by a curling iron. "Tell me what happened."

"Crystal, the one in the corner, is our newest stylist. Ida came in without an appointment and she was the only one available. When she went to mix the color, Ida started barking orders. Crystal got so nervous, she mixed it wrong.

Instead of a fluffy white cotton ball, Mrs. Garvey's head is now glowing neon pink."

Sam hid a smile as he drew her arm under the faucet and adjusted the temperature. She closed her eyes and sighed as cold water washed over the burn. He drew small circles on her palm, amazed at the softness of her skin under the pad of his thumb.

After a moment he asked, "Do you want to press charges?"

Her eyes flew open, and then she smiled at his expression. "Assault with a deadly styling tool? No, thanks."

Her smile softened the angles of her face, made her beauty less ethereal and more earthy. God help him, he loved earthy.

She must have read something in his eyes because she yanked her hand away and flipped off the water. "I need to get out there before Ida goes after Crystal again."

"Did you hire Crystal?"

"About three weeks ago. She came over from Memphis right out of school to stay with her aunt and needs a break…" She paused, her eyes narrowing. "You think I'm an idiot for hiring a girl with so little experience."

"I didn't say that."

"Everyone thinks Val's a fool to leave me in charge. They're waiting for me to mess up." She wrapped her arms around her waist then flinched when the burn touched her sweater. "And here I am."

Sam knew Val Dupree, the Hairhouse's longtime owner, was planning to retire, and Julia was working to secure a loan to buy the business. She was acting as the salon's manager while Val spent the winter in Florida. "No one expects you to mess up."

"You've been in town long enough to know what people think of me."

The words held no malice, but she said them with a

quiet conviction. Sam wanted to take her in his arms to soothe her worry and at the same time shake some sense into her. "Was it a mistake to hire Crystal?"

"No." She looked at him as though she expected an argument. When he offered none she continued, "She's good. Or she will be. I know it."

"Then we'd better make sure Ida Garvey doesn't attack your future star again."

"Right." She led him back into the main salon, where Ida still pinned Crystal to the wall with her angry stare. Everyone else's attention was fixed on Julia and Sam.

Julia glanced over her shoulder. "It's been twenty questions about our relationship all morning."

He nodded. "Let's take on one disaster at a time."

She squared her shoulders and approached Mrs. Garvey, no trace of self-doubt evident. "Ida, I'm sorry." She bent in front of the chair and took the older woman's hands in hers. "I'm going to clear my schedule for the afternoon and make your hair better than before. You'll get three months' worth of free services for your trouble."

Mrs. Garvey patted her pink hair. "That would help."

"Lizzy?" Julia called. A young woman peeked around the doorway from the front of the salon. "Would you reschedule the rest of my clients? Everyone else, back to work."

"I'm sorry," Crystal said from the corner, taking a step toward Julia.

Ida shifted in the chair. "Don't you come near me."

Sam moved forward but Julia simply patted Ida's fleshy arm. "Take the rest of the day off, Crystal. I'll see you back here in the morning."

"Day off?" Ida screeched. "You're going to fire her, aren't you? Val would have fired her on the spot!"

Color rose in Julia's cheeks but she held her ground. "No, Mrs. Garvey. Crystal made a mistake."

"She's a menace. I knew she was doing it wrong from the start."

"She made a mistake," Julia repeated. "In part because you didn't let her do her job." She looked at Crystal. "Go on, hon. We'll talk in the morning."

"I have half a mind to call Val Dupree this minute and tell her how you're going to run her business into the ground."

"I'd watch what you say right now, Mrs. Garvey." Sam pointed to her hair. "Julia may leave you pink if you're not careful."

"She wouldn't dare." But Ida shut her mouth, chewing furiously on her bottom lip.

"Get comfortable," Julia told her. "We'll be here for a while."

She turned to Sam. "I think your work here is done, Chief."

He leveled a steely look at her. "We're not finished."

"Unless you want to pull up a chair next to Ida we are. The longer that color sits on her hair, the harder time I'll have getting it out."

"You don't play fair."

Her eyes glinted. "I never have."

Chapter Three

Julia rubbed her nose against Charlie's dimpled neck and was rewarded by a soft belly laugh. "Who's my best boy?" she asked and kissed the top of his head.

"Charlie," he answered in his sweet toddler voice.

"Thanks for keeping him today, Lainey." Julia's younger sister and their mother, Vera, took turns watching Charlie on the days when his normal babysitter was unavailable. "Things were crazy today at work."

She couldn't imagine balancing everything without her family's help. Two years ago, Julia's relationship with Lainey had been almost nonexistent. Thanks in large part to Charlie, she now felt a sisterly bond she hadn't realized was missing from her life.

"Crazy, how?" Lainey asked from where she stirred a pot of soup at the stove.

"Ida Garvey ended up with hair so pink it looked like cotton candy."

Lainey's mouth dropped open.

"She freaked out, as you can imagine." Charlie scrambled off her lap to play with a toy fire truck on the kitchen floor. "It took the whole afternoon to make it better."

"I thought you meant crazy like telling people about your secret boyfriend and his public proposal." Lainey turned and pointed a wooden spoon at Julia as if it were a weapon. "I can't believe I didn't even know you two were dating."

Julia groaned at the accusation in her sister's tone and the hurt that shadowed her green eyes. When she'd gone along with Sam's fake proposal last night, Julia hadn't thought about the repercussions of people believing them. Thinking things through wasn't her strong suit.

She didn't talk about her years away from Brevia with Lainey or their mother. They had some inkling of her penchant for dating losers and changing cities at the end of each bad relationship. When the going got tough, it had always seemed easier to move on than stick it out.

From the outside, Julia knew she appeared to have it together. She was quick with a sarcastic retort that made people believe life's little setbacks didn't affect her. She'd painted herself as the free spirit who wouldn't be tied to anyone or any place.

But her devil-may-care mask hid a deeply rooted insecurity that, if someone really got to know her, she wouldn't measure up. Because of her learning disabilities and in so many other ways.

Her struggles to read and process numbers at the most basic level had defined who she was for years. The shame she felt, as a result, was part of the very fiber of her being. She'd been labeled stupid and lazy, and despite what anyone told her to the contrary, she couldn't shake the belief that it was true.

Maybe that was why she picked men who were obviously bad bets. Maybe that was why she'd been a mean girl in high school—to keep people at arm's length so she wouldn't have a chance of being rejected.

She wondered for a moment how it would feel to confide the entire complicated situation to Lainey. For one person to truly understand her problem. She ached to lean in for support as fear weighed on her heart. But as much as they'd worked to repair their fractured relationship, Julia still couldn't tell her sister how scared she was of failing at what meant the most to her in life: being a mother to Charlie.

"I'm sorry. I didn't mean for half the town to find out at Carl's." No one in her family even knew about Jeff's interest in a new custody arrangement.

She stood, trying to come up with a plausible reason she wouldn't have shared big boyfriend news. "My track record with guys is common knowledge, and I didn't want Sam to have people beating down his door to warn him away from me."

Lainey's gaze turned sympathetic. "Oh, Jules. When Ethan and I first got back together I didn't want anyone to know, either. I felt like the town would hold my past mistakes against me and you were back and... Never mind now. I'm going to forgive you because it's so wonderful." She threw her arms around Julia. "Everyone loves Sam, so..." Lainey's voice trailed off.

Julia's stomach turned with frustration. "So, what? By default people are suddenly going to open their arms to me?"

Lainey shrugged. "It can't hurt. Do you have a date?"

"For what?"

Lainey pushed away. "The wedding, silly. You'll get married in Brevia, right?"

Julia blinked. "I suppose so. We're taking the planning slowly. I want a long engagement. It'll be better for Charlie."

"Sure." Lainey frowned but went back to the stove.

"Just enjoying each other and all that," Julia added quickly, guilt building with every lie she told. "So in love. You know."

"I want to be involved in the planning."

"Of course. We can have a girls' day out to look for dresses and stuff." With each detail, the difficulty of deceiving her family became more apparent.

She reminded herself that it was only for a short time, and she was protecting everyone from the stress of the custody fight. "I should go. Thanks to the commotion today, I'm late on the product order I should have sent. If Charlie goes down early enough, I'll be able to get it in tomorrow morning. A night full of numbers, lucky me."

"Do you want some help?"

Julia tensed. "I can handle it. I'm not a total idiot, despite rumors to the contrary." She saw hurt flash again in her sister's gaze and regretted her defensive tone.

She did most of the paperwork for the salon when Charlie went to bed to minimize her hours away from him. She spent many late nights pouring over the accounts and payroll information, terrified she'd make a mistake or miss an important detail. She was determined no one would ever see how unqualified she was to run her own business.

"No one thinks you're an idiot," Lainey said quietly. "You're doing an amazing job with the salon, but I know how things get when you're tired. I'm offering another set of eyes if you need them."

"I'm sorry I snapped." Julia rubbed two fingers against each temple, trying to ward off an impending headache.

"I'll take it slow. It's routine paperwork, not splitting the atom."

"Could you delegate some of this to the receptionist or one of the part-time girls? Why does it all have to fall on you? If you'd only tell them—"

"They can't know. No one can. What if Val found out? The deal isn't final. She could change her mind about selling to me."

"She wouldn't do that," Lainey argued.

"Someone could take advantage, mix things up without me understanding until it's too late." Julia gathered Charlie's sippy cup and extra snacks into the diaper bag.

Lainey shook her head, frustration evident as she fisted her hands at her sides. "Learning disabilities don't make you stupid, Julia. When are you going to realize that? Your brain processes information differently. It has nothing to do with your IQ, and you have the best intuition of anyone I know. No one could take advantage of you—"

"Have you seen my list of ex-boyfriends?"

"—without you letting them," Lainey finished.

"Point taken." Even as much as Julia had wanted her relationship with Jeff to work out, she should have known it was doomed. He'd been the opposite of most guys she'd dated, and she should have known someone so academic and cultured wouldn't truly want her. They'd gone to museums and gallery openings, his interest in her giving her hope that someone would finally see her for more than a pretty face.

She'd craved his approval and made the mistake of sharing her secret with him. None of the men before him had known about the severe learning disabilities that had plagued her since grade school. She'd managed for years to keep her LD hidden from almost everyone.

Only her family and certain trusted teachers had known

the struggles she'd faced in learning to read and process both words and numbers. She wasn't sure any of them understood how deep her problems were. The embarrassment and frustrations she'd felt as a kid had prevented her from letting teachers, interventionists or even her parents truly help her.

It had been easier to play the part of being too cool for school or, as she got older, not wanting to be tied down to a real job or responsibilities. Only for Charlie was she finally willing to put her best effort forward, constantly worried it wouldn't be enough.

"Are you still working with the literacy specialist?"

"Every week. It's a slow process, though. Between my visual and auditory learning deficiencies, I feel like a lost cause. Sometimes I wonder if it's even worth it."

"It's worth it," Lainey said as she lifted Charlie from the floor and gave him a hug before depositing him into Julia's arms. "LD is complex and I'm proud of you for everything you've accomplished despite it. I'm here if you need me. Ethan and Mom can take Charlie, so—"

"Mom's back?" Julia swallowed. She'd assumed her sister hadn't heard about the engagement. But their mother had her finger on the pulse of every snippet of gossip from Brevia to the state line. "She wasn't scheduled back until next week." Long enough for Julia to get a handle on her mess of a life.

"She flew in this morning. I can help contain her, you know. You'll need reinforcements for damage control on that front."

Julia stopped in her tracks. Even though she'd worried about her mother finding out, hearing Lainey say it made her knees quiver the tiniest bit. "Mom knows? I thought she just got back."

"She knows," Lainey answered with an eye roll. "I think she's waiting for you to call and explain yourself."

Another layer of dread curled in the pit of Julia's stomach. Her mother would support her. Vera was a big part of Charlie's life and would fight tooth and nail to protect him. But she understood Julia's limitations better than anyone. Julia didn't want to know if her mom had any doubts about her ability to give Charlie a good life on her own.

Now was the time to come clean, but with Charlie in her arms, she couldn't bring herself to voice her fears. It might make them too real.

"I'll call her. She'll understand. I'll make her understand."

Lainey only smiled. "Good luck."

Julia needed a lot more than luck.

She tried to ignore the persistent knocking at her apartment door later that night. She hadn't called her mother and silently debated whether Vera would make the twenty-minute drive to Julia's apartment to rake her over the coals in person.

But Charlie had just fallen asleep after six verses of "The Wheels on the Bus," and Julia wasn't going to risk the noise waking him, so she opened the door, prepared for the mother–daughter smackdown of the century.

Sam stood in the hallway watching her.

Even better.

"Long day, Chief. I'll call you tomorrow." She tried to close the door but he shoved his foot into the opening. Blast those steel-toed boots.

He held up a white cardboard box and a six-pack of beer. "It's been a long day for both of us. We eat first and then dig ourselves out of this mess."

She sniffed the air. "Pepperoni?"

"With extra cheese."

She took a step back and he eased around her into the tiny apartment. It actually didn't feel so small with just her and Charlie in it. Somehow, Sam not only filled the room but used more than his fair share of the oxygen in it. Julia drew a shaky breath and led the way to the small dining area.

"Sorry," she apologized automatically as she picked macaroni noodles from the maple tabletop. "Charlie's been practicing his QB skills at mealtime."

"Nothing wrong with starting early. Where's the little guy?"

"Asleep. Finally."

Sam put the box on the table and handed her a beer as he cocked his head. "Is that classical music?"

"Beethoven."

"Sounds different than I remember. More animated."

She picked up a remote and pointed it at the television on the other side of the room. "It's a Junior Genius DVD."

"Come again?"

"A program designed to increase a young child's brain activity." She clicked off the television. "They have research to show that it works."

His brows rose. "I still hear music."

She felt color creep into her cheeks. "I play a Mozart disc as he falls asleep." She walked past him to the kitchen and pulled two plates from a cabinet.

"Are you a classical-music fan?"

She spun around and stalked back to the table. "Why? Do you think classical is too highbrow for someone like me? Would it make more sense if I was a Toby Keith groupie?"

He took a step back and studied her. "First off, don't hate on Toby Keith. Secondly, it was a question." He waved one hand in the direction of the bookcases that flanked the television. "You have more classical CDs on your shelves than I've seen in my entire life. It's a logical assumption."

"Sorry." She sighed. "I like some composers but it's mainly for Charlie. I figure he needs all the help he can get, living with me. You may have heard I'm not the sharpest knife in the drawer."

"Is that so?"

"It's a well-known fact in town. My mom will tell you I have 'street smarts.'" She met his gaze with a wry smile. "I'm sure any number of my former friends would be happy to tell you how I skated through school by charming teachers or bullying other students into helping me." She broke off as Sam watched her, worrying that she'd somehow given him a clue into her defective inner self. She plastered on a saucy smile and stretched up her arms in an exaggerated pose. "At that point my life's ambition was to be a supermodel."

"Personally, I wanted to be Eddie Van Halen." He shrugged. "Were you really a bully?"

"I like to remember it as a benevolent dictatorship. I had my reasons, but have discovered that the kids I ordered around back in the day have become adults who are more than happy to see the golden girl taken down a few pegs." She opened the pizza box and pulled out a slice, embarrassed at her silly adolescent dream. "I was the ring leader and the 'pretty one' in Brevia, but couldn't cut it in the big leagues."

"You started over. There's nothing wrong with that. People do it all the time."

"Right. I went to beauty school, dated a string of losers, partied too much and tried to live below my potential." She tipped her beer in a mock toast. "And that's pretty low."

"Somebody did a number on you, sweetheart. Because

the way you handled that mess at the salon today took some clever negotiation skills. Not the work of a fool."

"We'll see what Val thinks once Ida spins it." She slid a piece of pizza onto his plate. "Sit down and eat. Unless the pizza was a ruse to get in the door so you could rip my head off without the neighbors hearing. Might be easier than going through with your *grand proposal*."

His knee brushed against her bare leg as he folded himself into the chair across from her. It occurred to Julia that she was wearing only boxer shorts and a faded Red Hot Chili Peppers T-shirt with no bra. Bad choice for tonight.

"Such violent thoughts," he said, sprinkling a packet of cheese flakes on his pizza.

She sat back and crossed her arms over her chest. As soon as she'd realized she was braless, her nipples had sprung to attention as if to yell "over here, look at us." Not something she wanted Sam to notice in a million years.

"Why did you do it? This crazy situation is your fault."

He frowned. "You weren't exactly convincing as the levelheaded, responsible parent. You were about to dive across the table and take out the grandma."

"She deserved it." Julia popped out of her chair and grabbed a fleece sweatshirt from a hook near the hallway, trying not to let her belly show as she pulled it over her head. "But I didn't need to be rescued. Especially not by Three Strikes Sam." She sat back in her chair and picked up the pizza. "We're quite a pair. Do you really think anyone is going to believe you're engaged, given your reputation?"

"What reputation, and who is Three Strikes Sam?"

She finished her bite. "You don't know? Brevia is a small town. But we've got more than our share of single ladies. Apparently the long line of women you've dated since you arrived has banded together. The story is that you don't go on more than three dates with one woman. You've got your own fan club here in town. The ladies blog, tweet and keep track of you on Facebook. They call you Three Strikes Sam."

Sam felt as though he'd been kneed in the family jewels. Never mind the social-media insanity, what shocked him more was that Julia acted as if she knew the details of his dating history. That possibility was fright-night scary.

"You're making it up."

"I'm not that creative. You can log on to my computer and see for yourself. I only found out a couple of weeks ago, when Jean Hawkins was in the salon."

Sam swallowed hard. Jean was the dispatcher for the county sheriff's office. They'd had a couple of casual dinners last month but had agreed not to take it further. Or so he'd thought.

"She got a blowout and a bang trim. A 'wash that man right out of her hair' afternoon." Julia wrinkled her pert nose. "You know how it is—stylists are like therapists for some people. Get a woman in the chair and she has to spill her secrets."

"And *she* told you about this fan club?"

Julia nodded and took a drink of beer. "Three seems to be the magic number for you. You're a serial get-to-know-you dater."

Sam pushed away from the table and paced to the end of the narrow living room. "That's ridiculous." He ran a hand through his hair. "There's no arbitrary limit on the number of dates I'll go on with one woman."

"A dozen ladies claim there is," she countered. "They say you've more than made the rounds."

"I haven't dated a *dozen* ladies in Brevia. Besides, why would anyone gossip about dating me?"

"You've been in Brevia long enough to know how it

works." She laughed, but he found no humor in the situation. Sure, he'd been on dates with a few different women. When he'd first come to town, it had sort of happened that way. He'd always been a gentleman. If things led to the bedroom he didn't complain, but he also didn't push it. No one had grumbled at the time.

He wasn't a serial dater. The way she said it made him sound like a scumbag. So what if he was a little gun-shy? Walking in on your fiancée with her legs wrapped around another guy would do that to a man. It had been almost three years now since he'd had his heart crushed, and he wasn't itching to repeat that particular form of hell. "You're telling me I'm a joke with these women because I'm not in a relationship?" His voice started to rise. "In case they haven't noticed, I have a serious job. One that's more important to me than my damned social life."

"It's not like that," she said quickly, reaching out to place her cool fingers on his arm. A light touch that was oddly comforting. "No one is laughing at you. It's more like a challenge. Scary as it may sound, you have a town full of women who are determined to see you settle down. According to my sources, you're quite the catch."

He dropped back into the chair. "I came to Brevia because I wanted a fresh start."

"As Mick Jagger would say, 'you can't always get what you want.'"

"You think this fake engagement is what I need?"

"It was your idea to start. Plus, it's quieted the gossips, and your dad seemed to approve."

He nodded and took a long drink of beer. "My father loved you."

"Who can blame him?" she asked with a hair toss.

Sam smiled despite himself. "He wants to help me tap into my emotions."

She studied him as she took another bite. "Is that so bad?"

"I don't need to be more emotional."

"Your fans beg to differ."

"Don't remind me," he muttered.

A tiny cry came from the corner of the table and Julia adjusted a baby monitor. "I'm going to check on him." She padded down the hall, leaving Sam alone with his thoughts. Something he didn't need right now.

He preferred his emotions tightly bottled. It wasn't as if he didn't have feelings. Hell, he'd felt awful after calling off his engagement. He would have made a decent husband: loyal, faithful...

Maybe those were better attributes in a family pet, but he managed okay.

In Sam's opinion, there was no use wearing his heart on his sleeve. The scraps of memory he had from the months after his mother died were awful, his dad too often passed out drunk on the couch. Neighbors shuttling Sam and his brother to school and a steady diet of peanut butter and jelly sandwiches. When Joe finally got a handle on his emotions, it had saved their family.

Sam would never risk caring for someone like that. Feeling too much, connecting to the feelings he'd locked up tight, might spiral him back into that uncontrolled chaos.

He looked around the apartment, taking in more details with Julia out of the room. The dining area opened directly onto the living room, which was filled with comfortable, oversized furniture covered in a creamy fabric. Several fuzzy blankets fell over the arm of one chair. A wicker box overflowed with various toys, most of which looked far more complex than he remembered from childhood.

In addition to the classical CDs, framed pictures of Charlie with Julia, Vera, Lainey and Ethan sat on the bookshelves. Sam had also noticed an impressive collection of books—several classics by Hemingway, Dickens, even Ayn Rand. For someone who clearly didn't see her own intelligence, Julia had sophisticated taste in reading material.

The baby monitor crackled, drawing his attention. He heard Julia's voice through the static. "Did you have a dream, Charlie-boy?" she cooed. "Can Mommy sing you back to sleep?"

Charlie gave another sleepy cry as an answer and a moment later Sam heard a familiar James Taylor song in a soft soprano.

He smiled as he listened to Julia sing. Classical for Charlie, Sweet Baby James for his mother.

Sam felt a thread of unfamiliar connection fill his heart. At the same time there was a release of pressure he hadn't realized he'd held. In the quiet of the moment, listening to her sweet and slightly off-key voice, the day's stress slipped away. He took a deep breath as his shoulders relaxed.

"I love you, sweetie," he heard her whisper, her tone so full of tenderness it made his heart ache all the more.

He understood in an instant how much it meant for Julia to keep her son. Knew that she'd do anything to keep Charlie safe.

Suddenly Sam wanted that for her more than he cared about his own future. But he was a man who'd made it through life taking care of himself, protecting number one at all costs. No matter how he felt about one spirited single mother, he couldn't afford to change that now.

Hearing footsteps, he quickly stood to clear the dishes from the table.

"I think he's back down," she said as she came into the kitchen.

Sam rounded on her, needing to get to the crux of the matter before he completely lost control. "You're right," he told her. "This deal was my idea and I'll play the part of doting fiancé because it helps us both."

"Doting may be pushing it," she said, fumbling with the pizza box, clearly wary of his change in mood. "We don't need to go overboard."

He propped one hip on the counter. "We need to make it believable." He kept his tone all business. "Whatever it takes."

"Fine. We'll make people believe we're totally in love. I'm in. Whatever it takes to convince Jeff to drop the custody suit."

"Will he?"

"He still hasn't even seen Charlie. I get the impression his parents are pushing for the new custody deal. The attorney is really here to figure out if they have a viable case or not before they go public. Jeff didn't want kids in the first place. He'd even talked about getting the big snip. They probably think Charlie is their only shot at a grandchild, someone to mold and shape in their likeness."

"I don't think that's how kids work."

She shook her head. "I don't think they care. If we can convince Lexi that Charlie has a happy, stable home and that he's better off here than with Jeff and his family, that's the report she'll give to them. It will be enough. It has to. Once I get the custody agreement—"

"You'll dump my sorry butt," Sam supplied.

"Or you can break it off with me." She rinsed a plate and put it into the dishwasher. "People will expect it. You're up for reappointment soon. It should earn extra points with some of the council members. Everyone around here knows I'm a bad bet."

"I thought you and Ethan had been the town's golden couple back in the day."

"He was the golden boy," she corrected. "I was the eye

candy on his arm. But I messed that up. My first in a series of epic fails in the relationship department."

"Does it bother you that he's with Lainey?" Sam asked, not willing to admit how much her answer meant to him.

She smiled. "They're perfect together in a way he and I never were. She completes him and all that."

"Do you think there's someone out there who'd complete you?"

"Absolutely." She nodded. "At this moment, he's drooling in the crib at the end of the hall."

He took a step closer to her and tucked a lock of hair behind her ear. "We're going to make sure he stays there."

Her lips parted as she looked up at him. Instinctively he eased toward her.

She blinked and raised her hands to his chest, almost pushing him away but not quite. "We have to establish some ground rules," she said, sounding as breathless as he felt.

"I'm the law around these parts, ma'am," he said in his best Southern drawl. "I make the rules."

"Nice try." She laughed and a thrill ran through him. "First off, no touching or kissing of any kind."

It was his turn to throw back his head and laugh. "We're supposed to be in love. You think people will believe you could keep your hands off me?"

She smacked his chest lightly. "I'm surprised your ego made it through the front door. Okay, if the situation calls for it you can kiss me. A little." Her eyes narrowed. "But no tongue."

He tried to keep a straight face. "Where's the fun in that?"

"My best offer," she whispered.

He traced her lips with the tip of one finger and felt

himself grow heavy when they parted again. "I think we'd better practice to see if I'll be able to manage it."

He leaned in, but instead of claiming her mouth he tilted his head to reach the smooth column of her neck. He trailed delicate kisses up to her ear and was rewarded with a soft moan. Pushing her hair back, he cradled her face between his palms.

Her breath tingled against his skin and she looked at him, desire and self-control warring in the depths of her eyes. He wanted to keep this arrangement business but couldn't stop his overwhelming need. As out of control as a runaway train, he captured her lips with his.

Chapter Four

It should be illegal for a kiss to feel so good. The thought registered in Julia's dizzy brain. Followed quickly by her body's silent demand for more…more…more. Her arms wound around Sam's neck and she pressed into him, the heat from his body stoking a fire deep within her. His mouth melded to hers as he drew his hands up underneath her shirt.

A man hadn't kissed her like this in so long. As though he meant it, his mouth a promise of so much more.

A familiar voice cut through her lust-filled haze. "So, the rumors are true. Doesn't seem right your mother should be the last to know."

Sam's eyes flew open as he stepped away from her. Julia let out a soft groan.

"Ever think of knocking?" she asked, pressing her hands over her eyes.

"No" was her mother's succinct answer.

"Nice to see you, Mrs. Morgan." Although Sam's voice sounded a little shaky, Julia had to admire his courage in holding her mother's gaze.

Almost unwillingly, Julia turned and met her mom's steely glare. "I'm sorry, Mom. We wanted to keep things quiet a bit longer."

Vera Morgan was a tiny blonde dynamo of a woman. Her hair pulled back into a neat bun, she retained the beauty of her youth mixed with the maturity of decades spent overseeing her life and everyone in it. She crossed her arms over her chest. "Until you could announce your engagement in the middle of a crowded restaurant?"

Julia cringed. "Not the exact plan."

"I don't understand what this is about. It sounds like one of your typical impetuous decisions. Your father and I raised you to be more careful with how you act. I thought you'd have learned to be more responsible about the choices you make. Have you thought of Charlie? What's best for him?"

"He's all I think about and of course I want what's best for him. You have no idea…" Julia wanted to lay it all on the line for her mother—Jeff's family, the attorney, her fear of losing Charlie. She paused and glanced at Sam. He nodded slightly as if to encourage her.

How could she admit her years of bad choices could jeopardize Charlie's future? She knew her mother thought she was irresponsible, fickle and flighty. For most of her life, Julia had been all of those things and worse.

Her mother waited for an answer while the toe of one shoe tapped out a disapproving rhythm. Julia could measure the milestone moments of her life by her mother's slow toe tap. She swore sometimes she could hear it in her sleep.

"I don't expect you to understand, but this is good for Charlie. For both of us."

Vera's gaze slanted between Julia and Sam. "Having the hots for a guy isn't the same as love. From what I just witnessed, you two have chemistry, but marriage is a lot more than physical attraction."

Julia felt a blush rise to her cheeks. "I'm not a teenager anymore," she mumbled. "I get that."

"I worry about you rushing into something." Vera paused and pinned Sam with a look before continuing. "Especially with a man who has a reputation around town. I don't want you to be hurt."

"I know what I'm doing. Trust me. For once trust that I'm making the right decision." She hated that her voice cracked. She'd made some stupid choices in her life. So what? Lots of people did and they lived through it. Did she have to be raked over the coals for every indiscretion?

Sam's hand pressed into the small of her back, surprisingly comforting. "Mrs. Morgan," he began, his voice strong and confident. Julia wished she felt either right now. "Your daughter is the most amazing woman I've ever met."

Julia glanced over her shoulder, for a moment wondering if he was talking about her sister.

The corner of his mouth turned up as he looked at her. "*You* are amazing. You're honest and brave and willing to fight for what you want."

Charlie's sweet face flashed in Julia's mind, and she gave a slight nod.

"You're a lot stronger and smarter than you give yourself credit for." His gaze switched to Vera. "Than most people give her credit for. But that's going to change. I want people to see the woman I do. Maybe we shouldn't have hidden our relationship, but it wasn't anyone's business. To hell with my reputation and Julia's, too."

"I hear a couple town-council members are making a big deal about your single status as they're starting to review your contract. They think only a family man can impart the kind of values and leadership Brevia needs."

"Another reason we were quiet. I don't want to use Julia and Charlie to get reappointed. The job I've done as police chief should be enough."

He sounded so convincing, Julia almost believed him. At the very least, his conviction gave her the courage to stand up for herself a little more. "Sam's right. We're not looking for anyone's approval. This is about us."

"Have you set a date yet?" Vera asked, her tone hard again.

"We're working on that."

Sam cleared his throat. "I'm going to head home." He dropped a quick kiss on Julia's cheek. "I'll talk to you tomorrow."

"Coward," she whispered.

"Sticks and stones," he said softly before turning to Vera.

"Mrs. Morgan, I'm sorry you found out this way. I hope you know I have Julia and Charlie's best interests at heart."

Her mother's eyes narrowed.

"That's my cue." Sam scooted around Vera and let himself out the front door.

"I only want what's best for you." Vera stepped forward. "Your father and I didn't do enough to help you when you were younger. I won't make that mistake again." She wrapped one arm around Julia's waist. "I don't understand how this happened and I don't trust Sam Callahan. But I know Charlie is your number one priority. That's what counts."

Julia didn't want her mother to feel guilty. As a child, she'd tried to hide the extent of her problems from her parents, as well as everyone else. They weren't to blame. She let out a slow breath. "I'm doing this for Charlie."

"You love him?"

"He's my entire life."

"I meant, do you love Sam? Enough to marry him."

"Sam is a wonderful man," Julia answered quickly. "I'd be a fool not to want to marry him." Not exactly a declaration of deep and abiding love but it was as much as she could offer tonight. "I'm sorry you had to come over."

Her mother watched her for several moments before releasing her hold. "You're my daughter. I'll do anything to protect you. You know that, right?"

Julia nodded. Once again, she had the urge to share the whole sordid mess with her mother. She swallowed back her emotions. "It's late. I'll bring Charlie by in the morning before I drop him at the sitter's."

Vera patted her cheek. "Get some sleep. You look like you could use it. You can't keep up this pace. You're no spring chicken."

"Thanks for the reminder." That was the reason Julia wanted to handle this on her own. Vera couldn't help but judge her. It was in her mother's nature to point out all the ways Julia needed improvement. She'd have a field day with the custody situation. Julia had enough trouble without adding her mother's opinion into the mix.

She closed and locked the door behind her mother then sagged against it. She'd done a lot of reckless things in her life but wondered if this time she'd gone off the deep end.

The baby monitor made a noise. Charlie gave a short cry before silence descended once more. Her gaze caught on a framed photo on one end table, taken minutes after his birth. She'd known as soon as the nurse had placed him in her arms that Charlie was the best part of her. She'd vowed that day to make something of her life, to become worthy of the gift she'd been given. While she had a difficult time tamping down her self-doubt, she never questioned how far she would go to protect her son. She'd do whatever it took to keep him safe, even this ridiculous charade with Sam. If it helped her custody case in the least, Julia would become the most devoted fiancée Brevia had ever seen.

That commitment was put to the test the next morning when a posse of angry women descended on the salon. Two to be exact, but it felt like a mob.

She'd swung by her mother's after breakfast then dropped Charlie with Mavis Donnelly, the older woman who watched him and one other toddler in her home. She'd gotten into town by eight-thirty, thanks to Charlie's propensity to wake with the sun. She wanted time to look over the monthly billing spreadsheets before anyone else arrived.

No one outside her immediate family knew about her condition, and she intended to keep it that way, afraid of being taken advantage of or thought too stupid to handle her own business. She put in the extra time she needed to get each financial piece right. Sometimes she studied the numbers until she felt almost physically ill.

When the knocking started, she straightened from her desk in the back, assuming it was one of the stylists who'd forgotten her key. Instead the front door swung open to reveal two pairs of angry eyes glaring at her.

"How'd you do it?" Annabeth Sullivan asked, pushing past her into the salon without an invitation. Annabeth had been in the same high-school class as Julia, a girl Julia would have referred to as a "band geek" back in the day. She hadn't been kind, and Annabeth, who now managed the bank reviewing Julia's loan application, hadn't let her forget it. Annabeth's younger sister, Diane, followed her inside.

"Morning to you, ladies."

"He never goes on more than three dates." Annabeth held up three plump fingers. "Never."

"Can I see the ring?" Diane asked, her tone gentler.

Reluctantly, Julia held out her hand. "It's perfect," Diane gushed.

"Kind of small," Annabeth said, peering at it from the corner of one eye. "I figured you'd go for the gaudy flash."

Julia felt her temper flare. "You don't know me, then."

Annabeth took a step closer. "I know you, Julia Morgan. I know you had your minions stuff my locker with Twinkies the first day of freshman year. And made my life hell every day after that. I spent four years trying to stay off your radar and still you'd hunt me down."

The truth of the accusation made Julia cringe. "I'm sorry. I tried to make amends when I came back. I was awful and I'm truly sorry. I offered you free services for a year to try to repay a tiny portion of my debt."

"A year?" Diane turned to her sister. "You never told me that."

"Be quiet, Diane. That doesn't matter now. What I want to know is how you cast your evil spell over Sam Callahan."

"I'm not a witch. No spells, no magic." She paused then added, "We fell in love. Simple enough. Is there something else you need?" She took a step toward the front door but Annabeth held up a hand.

"Nothing is simple with you. Sam is a good man. He went on three dates with Diane."

"Almost four," Diane added. "I thought I'd made it past the cutoff. But he got called to a fire and had to cancel our last dinner. After that, he told me he wanted to be just friends."

"So, how come you two are all of a sudden engaged when no one even knew you were dating?"

"Even Abby was surprised and she knows *everything* about Sam." Diane clamped a hand over her mouth as Annabeth leveled a scowl at her.

As Julia understood it, Abby Brighton had moved to Brevia to take care of her elderly grandfather. She was the police chief's secretary and dispatcher. She didn't know about Abby's relationship with Sam, but the way Annabeth was looking at her sister, there was more to the story.

"Plus, you're a little long in the tooth for Sam," Annabeth stated, getting back to the business at hand.

Her mom had just said she was no spring chicken and now this. Lucky thing she'd chucked her ego to the curb years ago. "I'm thirty-two, the same age as you, Annabeth. We're not quite over the hill."

Annabeth pulled a small notebook out of her purse. "That's old for Sam. He usually dates women at least four years younger than him."

"And how old is that?"

"Don't you know how old he is?" Diane asked.

Julia met Annabeth's shrewd gaze. Calculated error on her part. "Of course. What I don't understand is why you carry a notebook with Sam's dating stats in it."

Annabeth snapped the notebook shut. "I don't have his dating stats, just a few pertinent facts. He and Diane seemed closer than any of the other women he dated. I want my sister to be happy. She had a chance before you came into the picture."

Julia studied Diane and couldn't begin to picture the dainty woman and Sam as a couple. "Did Sam break your heart?"

Diane scrunched up her nose. "No," she admitted after a moment. "Don't get me wrong, he's supercute and such a gentleman. But he's a little um…big…for me."

Julia's mouth dropped open. "Big?"

"Not like that," Diane amended. "He's just…with the uniform, all those muscles and he's so tall. It's kind of intimidating."

"I know what you mean," Julia agreed, although Sam's size appealed to her. She was five-nine, so it took a lot of guy to make Julia feel petite, but Sam did it in a way that also made her feel safe.

"You have real feelings for him." Annabeth interrupted her musings.

"I… We're engaged. I'd better have real feelings."

"Frankly, I thought this was another one of your stunts to show up the other single women in town. Prove that you're still the leader of the pack and all that." She glanced at Diane. "I didn't want my sister to fall prey to you the way I did."

"I'm *not* the same person I was. I can apologize but you'll need to choose whether to forgive me. I don't blame you if the answer is no, but it's your decision. My priority is Charlie. I want to live a life that will make him proud. I don't intend to re-create the past. You're married now, right?"

The other woman nodded. "Five years to my college sweetheart. He's my best friend."

"Why is it so strange to believe that I might want that for myself? My parents had a great marriage and you probably remember my sister recently married the love of her life, who just happened to be *my* high-school sweetheart. They're happy and I want to be happy. Last time I checked, that wasn't a crime in this town."

Julia pointed a finger at Diane. "If your sister wants to find a man, she will without you hunting down potential suitors for her or tallying lists of how far ahead of other women she is in the dating pool. Sam is a real person, too. I don't think he intended to become such a hot topic of gos-

sip. He's living his life the best way he can. We both are."
She stopped for breath and noticed Annabeth and Diane
staring at her, eyebrows raised.

She realized how much she'd revealed with her little
tirade and tried to calm her panic. Maybe she didn't want
to be known as the town's head mean girl anymore, but
she had a reputation to protect. She made people think
she didn't take things seriously so that they'd never notice when she got hurt. She plastered a smile on her face.
"What? Was that a little too mama grizzly for you?"

Annabeth shook her head, looking dazed. "I didn't realize that's how you felt about things. Sam is lucky to
have you."

"I'm not sure—"

"I'm sure."

The three women turned to see Sam standing in the
doorway. Julia's face burned. "How much did you hear?"

"Enough to know that I agree with Annabeth. I'm
damned lucky to have you."

Annabeth and Diane scooted toward the front door. "If
you'll excuse us. We'll leave you two alone."

He didn't move. "Is this going to hit the gossip train or
however it works?"

Diane shook her head. "We weren't the ones who started
analyzing you. It was—"

Annabeth gave her sister a hard pinch on the arm. "It
doesn't matter anymore. It's clear you're not the person
everyone thought."

Sam eased to the side of the doorway. "I think that could
be said for more than just me."

Annabeth threw a glance at Julia and nodded.

"Maybe you should spread that news around."

"I'll get on it, Chief." The two women hurried out of the
salon, and Sam pulled the door shut behind them.

"I'm a real man?" he said, repeating Julia's earlier comment. "I'm glad you think so, Ms. Morgan."

Julia slumped into a chair, breathing as if she'd just finished a marathon run. Her eyes were bleak as they met his. "It's pointless, Sam. This is never going to work."

Chapter Five

Sam stared at Julia. Her blond hair curled around her shoulders and fell forward, covering one high cheekbone. His fingers itched to smooth it back from her face, to touch her skin and wipe the pain from those large gray eyes. She looked so alone sitting in the oversized stylist's chair.

Sam knew what it felt like to be alone. Hell, he'd courted solitude for most of his life. He'd learned early on only to depend on himself, because when he relied on other people for his happiness he got hurt. First when his mother died and his dad had almost lost it. Then, later, in the relationship that had ended with his fiancée cheating on him.

He'd come to believe that happiness was overrated. He wanted to work hard and make a difference—the only way he knew to chase the demons away for a little peace.

When he'd heard Julia defending his character, something tight in his gut unwound. He was used to making things happen and having people depend on him. He prided himself on not needing anyone. It bothered him to know that women were spreading rumors about him, but he would have soldiered through with his head held high. Hearing Julia take on those ladies had made him realize he liked not feeling totally alone.

Her declaration that they couldn't make it work made no sense. "Why the change of heart?" He moved closer to her. "You convinced Annabeth and Diane."

"How old are you?"

"Thirty-three."

"Why do you only date younger women?"

He stopped short. "I don't."

"Are you sure? I've heard you average women at least four years younger. I'm thirty-two. My birthday's in two months."

"I don't ask a woman about her age before we go out. If there's a connection, that's what I go on."

"You never asked me out."

"I asked you to marry me," he said, blowing out a frustrated breath. "Doesn't that count?"

She shook her head. "I mean when you first came to town. When you were making the rounds."

"I didn't make the rounds. Besides, you were pregnant."

"I haven't been pregnant for a while."

"Did you want me to ask you out?" The attraction he'd denied since the first time he saw her roared to life again.

She shook her head again. "I'm just curious, like most of the town is now. We've barely spoken to each other in the last two years."

"I thought the idea was that we were keeping the relationship under wraps."

"What's your favorite color?"

"Green," he answered automatically then held up a hand. "What's going on? I don't understand why you think this won't work. You made a believer of Annabeth Sullivan, the town's main gossip funnel."

Julia stood and glanced at her watch. "The girls will start coming in any minute. I don't know, Sam. This is complicated."

"Only if you make it complicated."

"What's my favorite food?"

"How the heck am I supposed to know?"

"If we were in love, you'd know."

Sam thought about his ex-fiancée and tried to conjure a memory of what she'd like to eat. "Salad?" he guessed.

Julia rolled her eyes. "Nobody's favorite food is salad. Mine is lobster bisque."

Sam tapped one finger on the side of his head. "Got it."

"There's more to it than that."

"Come to dinner tonight," he countered.

"Where?"

"My place. Five-thirty. I talked to my dad this morning. He didn't mention delving into my emotions once. Huge progress as far as I'm concerned. He can't wait to spend more time with you."

"That's a bad idea, and I have Charlie."

"The invitation is for both of you." He took her shoulders between his hands. "We're going to make this work, Julia. Bring your list of questions tonight—favorite color, food, movie, whatever."

"There's more to it than—"

"I know but it's going to work." As if by their own accord, his fingers strayed to her hair and he sifted the golden strands between them. "For both of us."

At the sound of voices in the salon, Julia's back stiffened and her eyes widened a fraction. "You need to go."

"We're engaged," he reminded her. "We want people to see us together."

"Not here."

He wanted to question her but she looked so panicked, he decided to give her a break. "Dinner tonight," he repeated, and as three women emerged from the hallway behind the salon's main room, he bent forward and pressed his lips against hers.

Her sharp intake of breath made him smile. "Lasagna," he whispered against her mouth.

"What?" she said, her voice as dazed as he felt.

"My favorite food is lasagna."

She nodded and he kissed her again. "See you later, sweetheart," he said and pulled back, leaving Julia and the three stylists staring at him.

"Abby, how old are you?" Sam stepped out of his office into the lobby of the police station.

Abby Brighton, who'd started as the receptionist shortly after he'd been hired, looked up from her computer. "I'll be twenty-eight in the fall."

"That's young."

"Not really," she answered. "Maggie Betric is twenty-six and Suzanne over at the courthouse in Jefferson just turned twenty-five."

"Twenty-five?" Sam swallowed. He'd gone out to dinner with both women and had no idea they'd been that much younger than him. When did he become a small-town cradle robber? Jeez. He needed to watch himself.

"Julia's in her thirties, right?" Abby asked.

"Thirty-two."

"When's her birthday?"

"Uh…" Wait, he knew this. "It's in May."

Abby turned her chair around to face him. "I still can't believe I didn't know you two were dating."

"No one knew."

"But I know everything about you." She looked away. "Not everything, of course. But a lot. Because I make the schedule and we work so closely together."

He studied Abby another minute. She was cute, in a girl-next-door sort of way. Her short pixie cut framed a small face, her dark eyes as big as saucers. They'd worked together for almost two years now, and he supposed she did know him better than most people. But what did he know about her? What did he know about anyone, outside his dad and brother?

Sure, Sam had friends, a Friday-night poker game, fishing with the boys. He knew who was married and which guys were confirmed bachelors. Did knowing the kind of beer his buddies drank count as being close?

"Do you have a boyfriend, Abby?"

Her eyes widened farther. "Not at the moment."

"And your only family in town is your granddad?"

She nodded.

Okay, that was good. He knew something about the woman he saw every day at work. He looked around her brightly colored workspace. "I'm guessing your favorite color is yellow."

She smiled. "Yours is hunter green."

How did she know that?

"Does Julia make you happy?" she asked after a moment.

"Yes," he answered automatically. "Why?"

"I just wouldn't have pictured her as your type." Abby fidgeted with a paper clip. "She's beautiful and everything, but I always saw you with someone more…"

"More?"

"Someone nicer, I suppose."

"You don't think Julia's nice? Has she been unkind to you?"

Abby shook her head. "No, but I hear stories from when she was in high school. I'm in a book club with some ladies who knew her then."

"People change."

"You deserve someone who will take care of you."

"I'm a grown man, Abby. I can take care of myself."

"I know but you need—" She stopped midsentence when the phone rang. She answered and, after a moment, cupped her hand over the receiver. "Someone ran into a telephone pole out at the county line. No injuries but a live wire might be down."

Sam nodded and headed for the front door. "Call it in to the utility company. I'm on my way."

He drove toward the edge of town, grateful to get out and clear his head. He'd done more talking about himself and what he needed and felt in the past twenty-four hours than he had in the previous five years. His dad's fault, for sure.

This engagement was supposed to help Sam dodge his father's attempts to make him more in touch with his feelings. Hopefully, this dinner would smooth things over enough so life could return to normal. Other than the pretend engagement.

It wouldn't be as difficult as Julia thought to fool people. They'd hold hands, be seen around town together for a few PDAs and everyone would believe them. Kissing Julia was one of the perks of this arrangement. He loved her moment of surprise each time he leaned in. Sam hadn't been with a woman for a long time, which must explain why her touch affected him so much.

He understood the importance of making this work. Tonight, they'd come to an understanding of how to get what they both wanted.

* * *

Julia lifted Charlie out of his car seat and turned to face the quaint house tucked onto one of the tree-lined streets near downtown Brevia.

"He even has a picket fence," she said to her son, who answered her with a hearty laugh and a slew of indecipherable words.

"My sentiments exactly." She kissed the top of Charlie's head.

"Do you need a hand?"

Joe Callahan stepped off the porch and headed toward her.

"I've got it, Mr. Callahan. Thank you."

He met her halfway up the walk. "Call me Joe. And you—" he held out his hands for Charlie "—can call me Papa."

"Pap-y," Charlie repeated in his singsong voice and leaned forward for Joe to scoop him up. Her son, the extrovert.

"You don't have to do that."

Joe was already swinging Charlie above his head, much to the boy's delight. "What a handsome fellow," he said. He smiled at Julia. "He favors his beautiful mother."

Julia couldn't help but return his grin. "Are you always this charming?"

Joe gave an easy laugh. "For decades I was a real hard—" He lifted Charlie again. "I was hard-nosed. A walking grim reaper. Sam and his brother got the brunt of that. I've learned a lot since then."

"Wisdom you want to impart to your son?"

"If he'll let me." Joe tucked Charlie into the crook of his arm and the boy shoved his fist into his mouth, sucking contently. "You've already helped him start."

It was Julia's turn to laugh. "I don't have much wisdom to share with anyone."

Joe started toward the house. "Mothers have inherent wisdom. My late wife was the smartest, most insightful woman I've ever met."

"How old was Sam when she died?"

"Ten and Scott was seven. It was a dark period for our family."

"Was it a long illness?"

Joe turned and immediately Julia realized her mistake. "Sam hasn't told you about his mother?"

She shook her head, unable to hide her lack of knowledge. "It's difficult for him to speak about."

Joe sighed as if he understood. "That's my fault. After Lorraine passed, I was so overcome with grief that I shut down and made the boys do the same. Looking back, it was selfish and cowardly. They were kids and they needed me."

Julia patted his arm. "How did she die?"

"A car accident," he said quietly. Charlie rested his small head on Joe's shoulder as if sensing the older man needed comfort.

"How tragic. I'm so sorry for all of you."

"The tragic part was that it was my fault. I'd been on the force over ten years. I became obsessed with being the most dedicated cop Boston had ever seen. Like a bone-head, I took on the most dangerous assignments they'd give me—whatever I could do to prove that I was the baddest dude on the block. Lorraine couldn't handle the stress. She begged me to slow down. I wouldn't listen, brushed aside her worries and only focused on what I wanted."

He ran his hands through his hair, so much like Sam, then continued, "She'd started drinking at night—not so much that she was falling-down drunk, but enough to numb her. I was tuned out and didn't realize how bad it had gotten. I got home late one night and we fought. She went for a drive after the boys were in bed—to cool off. She wasn't even a half mile from the house when she ran the red light. She swerved to avoid another car. Wrapped her car around a telephone pole. She was gone instantly."

Julia sucked in a breath. The first time she'd met Sam had been when he'd found her after she'd hydroplaned on a wet road and gone over an embankment, her car slamming into a tree. She'd been pregnant at the time, and thinking the accident might have hurt her baby had been the scariest moment of her life. Sam had gotten her to the hospital and stayed with her until Lainey had arrived. She wondered if he'd thought about his mother during that time, or if it had just been another day on the job.

"How devastating for all of you." She leaned forward and wrapped her arms around Joe. Charlie squealed with delight then wriggled to be let down.

"Okay." She lifted him from Joe's arms and deposited him on the porch.

Joe swiped at his eyes. "I would have followed her in a minute. I could barely function and had two boys at home who needed me more than ever. Instead, I threw myself into the job like I was tempting fate. If they gave awards for stupidity and selfishness, I would have been a top candidate."

"Nothing can prepare you for something like that. I'm sure you did the best you could. Sam and his brother must know that."

Joe held open the screen door and Charlie headed into the house. "It should have been a wake-up call but it took me another twenty years to get my priorities straight. I want to make it right by Sam."

She looked into Joe Callahan's kind eyes and her stomach twisted. Julia didn't have much luck making things right by anyone, and if Joe knew the details of their arrangement, it would break his heart.

"Mama, come." Charlie peered around the doorway to the kitchen. Charlie. He was the reason she'd entered into this deal in the first place.

"Where's Sam?" She held out her hand to her son, who ran toward her to take it.

Joe smiled. "Grilling out back."

She scooped Charlie into her arms and followed Joe down the hall. She'd guess Sam's house had been built in the early 1900s, and he'd obviously renovated, drawing inspiration from the Craftsman tradition with hardwood floors throughout. In the open kitchen, beautiful maple cabinets hung on each wall. The colors were neutral but not boring, a mix of classic and modern traditions.

Joe led her through one of the French doors that opened to the back patio. It hadn't rained for a couple of days, and while it was cool, the evening air held the unmistakable scent of spring, with the elms and oaks surrounding the green yard beginning to bud.

Sam stood in front of a stainless-steel grill, enveloped in smoke. He turned and smiled at her and her chest caught again. He wore a dark T-shirt, faded jeans and flip-flops. Julia hadn't often seen him out of uniform, and while the casual outfit should have made him less intimidating, certain parts of her body responded differently.

"Ball," Charlie shouted and squirmed in her arms. When Julia put him down, he ran toward an oversized bouncy ball and several plastic trucks stacked near the wrought-iron table.

Sam closed the grill's lid and met her questioning gaze. "I thought he'd like some toys to play with over here."

She nodded, a little dumbfounded at the impact the small gesture had on her.

"Sammy said you two are mainly at your place."

"It's easier that way."

"Have you given any thought to where you'll live once you're married?"

"Here," Sam answered at the same time Julia said, "Not really."

Joe's brows furrowed, so she added, "My apartment is a rental, so I assumed we'd move in with Sam."

Sam came to her side and placed a quick kiss on her forehead. "We're going to make the spare bedroom into Charlie's room."

Julia coughed wildly.

"Can I get you a glass of water?" Sam asked.

"I'll grab it," Joe said and disappeared into the house.

Sam clapped her on the back. "Are you okay?"

"Not at all." She drew in a breath. "Charlie's room?"

"We're engaged, remember. It's going to seem strange enough that the kid barely knows me. I didn't have any of his stuff or toys in the house and my dad started asking questions."

At that moment, the bouncy ball knocked against Julia's leg.

"Ball, Mama. Ball." Charlie squealed with delight.

Sam handed Julia a pair of tongs. "Will you pull the steaks off the grill?" He picked up the ball and tucked it under his arm. "I'm going in for some male bonding."

Julia watched, fascinated as Sam walked over to Charlie and held out a hand. Without hesitation, Charlie took it and Sam led him into the yard to roll the ball back and forth.

The only man in Charlie's life was Ethan. Julia tried not to depend too much on him. Lainey, Ethan and Julia had a long history between them, and Julia didn't want to push the limits of their relationship.

Charlie did his best to mimic Sam's motions as he rolled

and threw the ball, and Julia realized how important it was for her son to have a father figure.

"I knew he'd be great with kids," Joe said as he handed her a tall glass of water. "Scott is a wild one, but Sam…"

"Why do you think Sam never married?" Julia asked, tapping one finger against her lips. Annabeth's story about Sam's record as a three-dates-and-done serial dater came back to her.

"It's not for lack of trying," Joe answered candidly then amended. "But I can tell you're a better fit for him than Jenny."

Julia tried not to look startled. "Jenny?"

Joe studied her. "His ex-fiancée. He *did* tell you about her?"

"He was really hurt when it ended," she offered, not an outright lie but enough to cover her lack of knowledge. She and Sam had a lot they needed to get clear about each other if this charade was going to work.

Joe nodded. "Not that he would have told anyone. He bottled up his emotions just like I'd done when his mom passed. But Jenny's infidelity was a huge blow to him."

"I can understand why." Julia's mind reeled at this new information. Sam had been previously engaged and his fiancée had cheated on him. That might explain a little about his commitment issues.

"She wasn't a good match even before that. Sure, she was perfect on paper—a schoolteacher, sweet and popular with his friends, but she didn't get him. They were marrying what they thought they wanted without paying attention to what they needed."

Julia understood that line of thinking better than most. It was what had led her to believe her ex-boyfriend could make her happy. She'd thought she loved Jeff but realized what she loved was the image she'd had of him, not who he truly was. Was that what Sam had thought about his ex, as well, or had this Jenny been the love of his life? The thought gave Julia a sick feeling in the pit of her stomach.

Sam looked up from where he was currently chasing Charlie across the backyard. "How about those steaks, sweetie?"

"I'm on it," she called and headed for the grill.

Much to Joe's delight, Charlie insisted on sitting on Sam's lap during dinner. Sam looked vaguely uncomfortable as the toddler fed him bites of meat but dutifully ate each one.

In addition to the steak, Sam had roasted vegetables and made a salad. She'd brought a loaf of bread from the bakery next to the salon, along with a bottle of red wine. The dinner was surprisingly fun and Julia found herself relaxing. Joe did most of the talking, regaling her with stories, of his years with the force and more recently of the workshops he facilitated around the region.

"Someone needs a diaper change," she said as they finished the meal. At the look of horror on Sam's face, she laughed. "I'll take it from here."

"Good idea," he agreed.

"You'd better get used to stinky bottoms," his father chided.

Sam's eyes widened and Julia laughed again. "All in good time, Joe. For now, I'll take the poop duty."

Sam stood quickly and handed Charlie to her. "I'll clear the dishes." To her surprise, he placed a soft kiss on her mouth. Charlie giggled and Julia felt her world tilt the tiniest bit.

"Right," she said around a gulp of air. She met Joe's gaze as she turned for the house and he winked at her. Right. Sam was her fake fiancé. Of course he was going to kiss her sometimes. They'd discussed that it was all part of the act. It didn't mean anything.

At least, not to her.

Right.

She changed Charlie's diaper on the floor of Sam's living room. Unlike her cozy apartment filled with well-worn flea-market finds and hand-me-downs from her mother, the furnishings in this room appeared very new and hardly used.

A sleek leather couch faced an entertainment center with an enormous flat-screen television and several pieces of stereo equipment. He had a few books scattered on the shelves, mainly fly-fishing manuals and guidebooks for the North Carolina mountains. A couple of pieces of abstract art hung on the walls. Unlike her family room, there wasn't a single framed photo of any of Sam's family or friends.

Julia loved the reminders of each stage in Charlie's life on display around her house. It was as though Sam didn't have a personal life. Maybe it was just a guy thing, she thought, but then remembered how Jeff had documented each of his research trips with photos spread around their condo in Columbus.

Maybe not.

She pulled on Charlie's sweatpants and watched as he scrambled to his feet and headed back toward the kitchen.

"Hey, little man, where are you headed in such a rush?"

Joe picked him up as Charlie answered, "Ou-side," and he planted a raspberry on the boy's belly, making him laugh out loud.

"I'll see you later, gator." Joe put Charlie on the ground and he made a beeline for the back of the house.

"It was nice to spend time with you." Julia gave the older man a quick hug.

"I hope it's the first of many dinners. I'd love to meet

your family while I'm in town. Sammy said your mom is famous around here for the animal shelter she runs."

"It was a labor of love after my dad died." The thought of Joe Callahan and her mother getting together made her want to squirm. Keeping their respective families separate would make the summer much simpler. The complications of this arrangement were almost more than she could handle.

"I meant what I said at the restaurant," Joe told her. "Sam will protect you and Charlie. I don't know the details of your custody arrangement, but I believe that boy is better off with you than anyone else in the world."

Julia blinked back sudden tears. "Thank you. I better go track him down."

Joe nodded. "Good night, Julia. I'll see you soon."

The front door shut behind him, and Julia thought about Joe's last words. Charlie was better off with her. She had to believe that. He belonged to her and she to him. Nothing and no one was going to change that.

She turned for the kitchen just as Charlie's high-pitched scream came from the backyard.

Chapter Six

Julia raced onto the patio, following the sounds of her son's cries, her heart pounding in her chest.

Sam stood in the backyard, cradling Charlie against his chest with one arm. With his free hand he waved the tongs she'd used for the meat. A large gray dog hopped up and down in front of him.

"What happened?" Julia yelled as she sprinted down the back steps. "Is Charlie hurt?"

At the sound of his mother's voice, the boy lifted his tear-streaked face from Sam's shoulder. "Ball, Mama. No doggy." He pointed a slobbery finger at the Weimaraner running circles in the yard, the deflated bouncy ball clamped in his jaws.

His eyes never leaving the dog, Sam scooted closer to Julia. "Charlie's fine. Take him back to the house. I've never seen this animal before. He could be rabid."

Charlie shook his head. "No doggy," he repeated. "Charlie ball."

Julia looked from her son to Sam to the dog bounding and leaping, his stubby tail wagging, clearly relishing this impromptu game of keep-away. Rabid? Overenthusiastic and in need of some training. Not rabid.

Julia had grown up with a variety of animals underfoot. Her dad had been Brevia's vet for years, and the shelter her mother had built and run after his death attracted animals from all over the South. Her mom's ability to rehabilitate strays was legendary—Vera had even written a dog-behavior book that had become a bestseller a few years ago. Julia might not be the expert her mother was, but she had a fairly good sense for reading canine energy. And every inch of the Weimaraner was shouting "let's play."

"Sam, the dog isn't going to hurt you."

"It bared its teeth. It's a lunatic."

"You've never seen it before?" Julia moved slowly forward.

"No. I told you to get back on the porch. I don't want you or Charlie hurt."

She gave a quick whistle. The dog stopped and looked at her, its tail still wagging.

"Julia, you can't—"

"Drop it," she commanded, her finger pointed to the ground.

"Dop." Charlie mimicked her. "Charlie ball."

The dog waited a moment then lowered the lump of plastic to the ground.

"Sit."

The dog's bottom plopped to the ground.

She held out her palm. "Stay."

She took a step toward the dog. His bottom lifted but she gave a stern "No," and he sank back down.

"I'm sorry about your ball, sweetie," she told Charlie.

"Bad," he said with a whine.

"Not bad, but he needs someone to help him learn."

As she got nearer, the animal trembled with excitement.

"You shouldn't be that close."

"Do you have any rope?"

"I'm not leaving you out here. I'm serious. Back off from the dog."

"What is your problem? This dog isn't a threat."

"You don't know—"

As if sensing that her attention was divided, the dog stood and bounded the few feet toward her. The skin around its mouth drew back and wrinkled, exposing a row of shiny teeth.

"Get back, Julia. It's snarling." Sam lunged forward, but before he got the animal, the dog flopped at Julia's feet and flipped onto his back, writhing in apparent ecstasy as she bent to rub his belly.

Sam stopped in his tracks. "What the…?"

"He's a smiler."

"Dogs don't smile."

"Some do."

Charlie wriggled out of Sam's arms and, before either of them could stop him, headed for the dog. "Good doggy. No ball."

Julia put an arm around Charlie, holding him back, as Sam's breath hitched. "You shouldn't let him so near that thing."

She offered what she hoped was a reassuring smile. "My mom runs an animal shelter, remember? Charlie's been around dogs since he was born. I'm careful to supervise him and make sure he's safe." She tickled her fingers under the dog's ear and got a soft lick on her arm for the effort. "This boy is gorgeous."

"A good-looking animal can still be crazy."

Julia's shoulders stiffened. "What makes you think he's crazy?" Before he'd left for good, Jeff had said something similar to her. He'd told her she was beautiful but a nut job. He'd thrown in a dig about her intelligence as icing on the cake.

Her mother was the expert on stray animals, but Julia knew a thing or two about being damaged on the inside. Her gut told her this dog had a heart of gold.

"He snarled at me."

"He *smiled* at you," she insisted. "Pet him. He's a real sweetie."

"I don't like dogs," Sam said simply.

"I wouldn't have guessed it." She ran her hand along the length of the dog's side. "He's way underweight. No collar and he's dirty. I'd guess he's been on his own for a while now. You haven't seen him around?"

Sam shook his head. "A section of the fenced yard came loose in the storm a few nights ago. He must have smelled the grill and come in that way."

She straightened. "Would you take Charlie for a minute? I have a leash in the trunk of my car."

"You don't have a dog."

"Mom makes everyone keep an extra in case we come across a stray." The Weimaraner jumped to his feet and nudged at Julia's pants leg.

"Mama doggy," Charlie said as Julia shifted him into Sam's arms.

"No, honey, not mine. We'll take him to Grandma in the morning and she'll find a good home for him."

Charlie frowned. "Mama doggy."

Julia noticed Sam tense as the dog trotted over to sniff him. "Are you scared of dogs, Chief Callahan?"

"Wary, not scared." He held Charlie a little higher in his arms.

"If you say so." She headed up the steps toward the house and the dog followed.

"What if he runs away?"

"I have a feeling he'll stick close by. Weims are usually Velcro dogs."

"Are you going to keep him overnight?"

She nodded. "It won't be the first time. Mom says the strays have a knack for finding me. The scrappier they are, the harder I work to bring them in. I've rescued dogs from Dumpsters, highway ditches—"

"Stop!" Sam shook his head. "The thought of you luring in unknown dogs from who knows where makes my head pound."

"What can I tell you?" She laughed. "I have a soft spot for lost causes."

Sam met her gaze then, and for an instant she saw the kind of longing and vulnerability in his eyes she'd never imagined from a man as tough and strong as he seemed. "Lucky dogs," he whispered.

The hair on her arms stood on end and her mouth went dry. He blinked, closing off his feelings from her.

"Add this one to the lucky list," she said, her voice a little breathy. Quickly, she led the dog through the house, grabbing a piece of bread off the counter for good measure. But she didn't need it. The dog walked by her side, his early rambunctiousness tempered because he had her attention.

She pulled the leash out of her trunk and looped it over his head. He shook his head, as if he wasn't used to a collar. "Easy there, boy," Julia crooned and knelt to pet him. The dog nuzzled into her chest. "I bet you've had a rough time of it. If anyone can find you a good home, it's my mom."

She walked the dog back onto the porch, where she could hear the sound of the television coming through the open screen door.

"Is it okay if I bring him in the house?"

"As long as he doesn't lift his leg on the furniture," came the hushed reply.

She leveled a look at the dog, who cocked his head at her. "Keep it together," she told him, and his stubby tail wagged again.

"I should get Charlie home and to bed," she said as she walked into the family room then stopped short. Sam sat on the couch, Charlie nestled into the crook of his arm, their attention riveted to the television. An IndyCar race was on the big set, and Sam was quietly explaining the details of the scene to Charlie.

"Lubock thinks he's got this one in the bag. He's in the blue-and-yellow car out front."

"Blue," Charlie said, his fist popping out of his mouth to point to the screen.

"That's right, but watch out for Eckhard in the red and white. See where he's coming around the outside?"

Charlie nodded drowsily then snuggled in deeper.

"I thought you didn't like kids," Julia said quietly, as Charlie's eyes drifted shut.

Sam glanced at the boy then tucked a blanket from the back of the couch around him. "I like kids. Everyone likes kids."

Julia scoffed. "Hardly. Most people like dogs. You don't."

"That's different."

She watched the pair for several seconds then added, "Charlie's father doesn't like kids."

Sam met her gaze. "His loss."

"You've never even said hello to Charlie before this week."

"He and I don't run in the same circles," he countered.

"You know what I mean."

Sam picked up the remote and hit the mute button. He knew what she meant. Ever since he'd found Julia after her car crashed, he'd avoided both her and her son. That moment had terrified him more than it should someone in his position. He didn't know whether it was the memory of losing his mother, or the strange way his body reacted to the woman sitting across from him. Or a combination of both. But when he'd lifted her out of that car and carried her to his cruiser, his instinct for danger had been on high alert.

Sam was used to saving people from mishaps. It was part of the job. But she'd looked at him as if she'd put all her faith in him. That had made it feel different. More real, and scary as hell. Charlie had been born that same day, and Sam had decided it was better for both of them if he stayed away. He had nothing to offer a single mom and her child. His heart had shut down a long time ago.

Holding Charlie in his arms, he felt something fierce and protective roar to life inside him. If he wasn't careful, he could easily fall for this boy and his mother. He had to keep his distance but still play the part. His dad had spent most of the evening fawning over Julia and her son, leaving Sam blessedly alone.

He wanted to keep up the charade long enough for his father to leave town satisfied. When the eventual breakup came, Sam was sure he'd have a better chance of convincing Joe how heartbroken he was over the phone than in person.

"We should go over a few things before you leave," he

said, trying to make his tone all business but soft enough that he didn't wake Charlie.

Julia nodded. "I can take him from you first."

Sam shook his head and adjusted the blanket. "He's fine. Thanks for bringing him. You saw how happy it made my dad."

"He's going to be devastated when this doesn't work out."

Sam shrugged. "He'll get over it. You've given him hope that I'm not a total lost cause in the commitment department. That should hold him over for a while."

Julia adjusted in her chair as the dog settled at her feet with a contented sigh. Sam had heard a lot about Vera Morgan's exceptional skills with animals. It appeared the gift was genetic.

"He mentioned your ex-girlfriend."

Sam flinched. If he didn't have Charlie sleeping against him, he would have gotten up to pace the room. "Leave it to dear old dad to knock the skeleton from my closet."

"We're engaged. He assumed I already knew."

"And you thought knowing my favorite color was going to be a big deal."

"We need to understand the details about each other if this is going to work. Otherwise, no one is going to believe we're legitimate."

"Why not?" he countered. "People run off to Vegas all the time. Maybe you fell so head over heels for me that you didn't care about the details."

"Highly unlikely. You're not that irresistible."

Her comeback made him smile, which he realized was her intention. It was strange that this woman he knew so little could read him so well. "I was engaged for six months. She cheated on me a month before the wedding."

"That's awful."

"I caught her with my brother."

Julia's jaw dropped. "Wow."

"That's an understatement."

"What happened? Do you still speak to your brother? Are they together? What kind of awful people would do that to someone they both loved?"

"The way Scott explained it, before I kicked him out of my house, was that she was bad news and he was saving me from making a mistake. The way Jenny spun it before she followed him out the door was that he'd seduced her." He expected to feel the familiar pain of betrayal but only emptiness washed over him. "They aren't together and weren't again as far as I know. Turns out he was right. I found out later it wasn't the first time she'd cheated. She'd also been with one of the guys on the squad. Made me look like a fool."

"She's the fool." Julia came to stand before him. She lifted Charlie from his arms and sat down, laying her son beside her on the soft leather. "And your brother?"

"Scott was in the army for several years. Now he works out of D.C. for the U.S. Marshals."

She squeezed his arm and the warmth of her hand relaxed him a little. "I'm not interested in his job. What about your relationship?"

"My dad had a health scare almost two years ago. I passed my brother in the hall at the hospital. That's the extent of it."

"Oh, Sam."

"We were never close. My dad didn't encourage family bonding."

"Still—"

"This isn't helping our arrangement." Sam took her hand in his. "How long have we been dating?"

"Four months," Julia answered automatically.

"Favorite color?"

"Blue."

"Where we going on a honeymoon?"

"A Disney cruise."

"You can't be serious."

"Because of Charlie."

He laughed. "Fine." Some of the tension eased out of his shoulders and he asked, "Big or small wedding?"

"Small, close friends and immediate family."

"Who are your close friends?"

Her eyes darted away and she took several beats to answer. "The girls from the salon, I guess. A few of them, anyway. My sister."

"What about your friends from high school?"

"I didn't really have friends. Followers was more like it, and most of them have outgrown me."

"Their loss," he said, using his earlier phrase, and was rewarded with a smile. "What about your ex-boyfriend? Do you still have feelings for him? Should I be jealous?"

"Of Jeff? No. We were over long before he left me."

An interesting way to phrase it. Sam couldn't help but ask, "Could I kick his butt?"

She smiled. "Absolutely."

"Good. When is your next court date?"

"Friday."

"Do you want me to come?"

She shook her head and Sam felt a surprising rush of disappointment. "I might be able to help."

"You already are."

"You can't believe the judge will award custody to Jeff and his family. Is he even going to be here?"

"I don't know. But I can't take any chances. Even if he gets joint custody, they could take Charlie from me for extended periods of time. I won't risk it. Jeff made it clear he didn't want to be a father, so I don't understand why he's letting this happen. He was never close to his family."

"Have you talked to him directly?"

"I left a message on his cell phone right after the letter came. I might have sounded hysterical. He hasn't returned my call."

"You're going to have to tell your family what's going on before it goes too much further."

She nodded. "I realized that tonight. If my mom finds out your dad knew before her… It's all too much. I'm finally starting to get my life on track, with the salon and Charlie. For the first time in as long as I can remember, my mother isn't looking at me with disappointment in her eyes. When she finds out…"

"Vera will want to help. This isn't your fault."

"It sure feels like it is." She sank back against the couch and scrubbed her hands across her face. Sam saw pain and fear etched in her features. It gnawed away at him until he couldn't stand it. Why was she so afraid of her mother's judgment? Why did she think so little of herself, to believe her son was at risk of being taken away? Maybe she'd made some mistakes in her past but Sam didn't know anyone who hadn't. She couldn't be punished forever.

He might not be willing to give his heart again, but he needed to give her some comfort. He wasn't great with words and knew that if he got sentimental, she'd only use her dry wit to turn it into a joke. Instead, he placed a soft kiss on the inside of her palm.

She tugged on her hand but he didn't let go. "You don't need to do that now," she whispered, her voice no more than a breath in the quiet. "There's no one watching."

One side of his mouth quirked. "It's a good thing, too, because what I want to do to you is best kept in private."

Her mouth formed a round *oh* and he lifted a finger to trace the soft flesh of her lips.

"Charlie."

"I know." He leaned closer. "You're safe tonight. Almost."

"We shouldn't…"

"I know," he repeated. "But I can't think of anything I want more."

"Me, too." She sat up and brought both of her hands to the sides of his face, cupping his jaw. "This isn't going to get complicated, right?"

"Other than planning a pretend wedding, a custody battle, my meddling father and a town filled with nosy neighbors? I think we can keep it fairly simple."

She smoothed her thumbs along his cheeks and her scent filled his head again. "I mean you and me. We're on the same page. It's all part of the show, the time spent together, pretending like we're in love. It ends when we both get what we want."

He agreed in theory, but at the moment all Sam wanted was her. He knew telling her that would make her more skittish than she already was. He didn't want this night to end quite yet, even if her sleeping son was going to keep the evening G-rated. So he answered, "That's the plan."

She nodded then licked her lips, and he suppressed a groan. "Then it won't matter if I do this…" She brought her mouth to his and they melted together. When her tongue mixed with his, he did groan. Or maybe Julia did. Her fingers wound through his hair and down his neck, pressing him closer, right where he wanted to be.

He deepened the kiss as his hands found their way underneath her blouse, his palms spread across the smooth skin on her back.

"Stop." Julia's breathing sounded ragged.

His hands stilled and he drew back enough to look into her big gray eyes, now hazy with desire.

A small smile played on the corners of her mouth. "I want to make sure we both stay in control. No getting carried away."

Like to his bedroom, Sam thought. All the wonderful, devilish, naked things he could do to her there ran through his brain. He wanted to know this woman—every inch of her—with a passion he hadn't thought himself capable of feeling.

He didn't answer, not sure his brain could manage a coherent sentence at the moment. They stared at each other and he wondered if Julia's heart was pounding as hard as his.

He heard Charlie snore softly and let his eyes drift closed for a few seconds. He counted to ten in his head, thought about the pile of work waiting in his office and tried like hell to rein in his desire and emotions.

He withdrew his hands, smoothed her shirt back down and forced a casual smile.

"My middle name is control, sweetheart."

She cocked her head. "That's a good point," she said and didn't sound at all as affected as Sam felt. "What *is* your middle name?"

He shook his head slightly. "Matthew."

"Mine's Christine," she told him, as if she had no memory of a minute earlier when she'd been kissing him as if her life depended on it. "I'm going to get Charlie home." She stood and picked up the sleeping boy. The Weimaraner jumped to attention and stayed close by her side.

Sam felt off balance at her switch in mood but didn't want to admit it. "I'll walk you to your car," he said, keeping the frustration out of his voice. This *was* a business arrangement, after all, passionate kissing aside. Maybe Julia had the right of it.

She nodded and grabbed the diaper bag, pushing it at Sam. "If you could carry that," she said, as if she didn't trust him with his hands free.

The night had cooled at least ten degrees and she shivered as she hurried down the front walk. "Do you want a jacket?" he asked, taking large strides to keep up with her.

"I'm fine."

While it might be true that Sam hadn't had any long-term relationships since moving to Brevia, and had stayed out of the dating pool totally for the past few months, his evenings never ended like this.

Usually he was the one who put the brakes on, sexually. More than once, he'd been invited back to a woman's house—or she'd asked to see his place—on the first date and gotten a clear signal that she'd been eager to take things to the next level. Sam was cautious and tried to not let an evening go there if he thought someone wanted more than he could give.

Never, until tonight, could he remember a woman literally running out of his house when he so badly wanted her to stay.

Julia opened the back door and placed Charlie in his car seat then gave the dog a little tug. The Weim jumped up without a sound, as if he knew enough not to wake the sleeping boy.

Turning, Julia held out her hand for the diaper bag.

"Are we good?" Sam asked.

"Yep," she said, again not meeting his gaze. "I'll talk to you in a few days."

A few days? They were engaged. He told himself it wouldn't look good to the town, but the truth was he couldn't wait a few days. Before he could respond, she'd scurried to the driver's side, climbing in with one last wave and "Thanks" thrown over her shoulder.

Sam was left standing alone at the curb, wondering what had gone so wrong so quickly. He headed back to the house, hoping a cold shower would help him make some sense of things.

Chapter Seven

Julia swiped under her eyes and focused her attention on her mug of lukewarm coffee, unable to make eye contact with her mother or sister.

Lainey paced the length of Vera's office in the All Creatures Great and Small animal shelter. By contrast, their mother sat stock-still behind her desk.

"That's the whole story," Julia finished. "The judge ordered us into mediation and that meeting is tomorrow morning. I don't think it will do any good. I know what I want and Jeff's parents know what they want. If we can't come to an agreement with the mediator, there will be a final hearing where the judge makes a ruling."

"Is Jeff going to be there?" Vera asked, her tone both soft and razor-sharp.

"I guess so, but it will be better if he isn't, if it looks like it's his parents who want this." Her breath hitched. "The latest document I got from their attorney asks for an every-other-year joint-custody arrangement. There's an opportunity for it to be amended if Charlie's well-being is in jeopardy with one of the parties."

"Every other year?" Lainey stopped pacing. "How can they think of taking him away from you for that long? You should have told us this as soon as you knew, Jules. Maybe we could have done something—"

"What, Lainey?" Julia snapped then sighed. "I'm sorry. I don't mean to take it out on you. But what could have been done? I hoped if I made it difficult for them, they might give up. The first letter said they wanted full custody and offered a hefty payment for the expenses I've already incurred in raising Charlie."

"They thought you'd sell them your son?" Lainey's voice was incredulous.

"That's one way of looking at it. The last Jeff knew, I'd gotten pregnant as a way to keep him. He could have told his parents I didn't really want to be a mother or wouldn't be able to handle it on my own."

"You're not on your own." Vera tapped one finger on the desk. "You have us. And Sam."

Conflicting emotions welled in Julia's chest again as she thought of Sam. He'd told her to talk to her mom and sister. She knew it was inevitable, so she'd called them both on the way home last night and asked them to meet her at the shelter before work. At the time, it had been a good way to distract herself from Sam and the way he made her feel.

He must have been baffled by her behavior after they'd kissed. Most women he knew could probably handle a simple kiss. Not Julia. Maybe it had been too long since she'd been in a man's arms. It had taken every ounce of her willpower not to beg him to take her to bed. His touch had rocked her to her core and she'd had to beat a quick retreat so she wouldn't do or say something she'd later regret.

When he'd proposed the pretend engagement, she'd had no idea how much her emotions would get in the way. She'd had no idea how it would affect her to see Sam cuddling Charlie against his broad chest. How much her body and heart would react to his arms around her. How quickly she'd come to depend on the comfort he gave her and how he made her feel strong by believing in her.

"I'm the one they're going after," she told her mom. "And Charlie." A sob escaped her lips and she clamped her hand over her mouth.

Lainey rushed to her side and Julia let herself be cradled in her sister's warm embrace. Silence descended over the trio. This was the time Julia would normally make a joke or sarcastic remark about her propensity to ruin her own life. But, right now, she was just struggling to not break down completely.

This was the reason she hadn't told her family. Their sympathy and the disappointment she felt from them brought back too many memories of the past and the feelings that went with it. Her LD and the shame that went with it had made her put up walls against everyone around her. She'd gotten used to getting by, keeping secrets, not letting on how bad things really were. It was a difficult pattern to break.

From the time she'd been younger, Julia had made an unintentional habit of disappointing the people she loved. She'd let other people's judgments guide the way she lived her life. The belief that she was lazy and stupid had stopped her from getting help so many times. It was easier not to open up to her family about her emotions. She was too afraid of being exposed as weak and lacking in their eyes.

Even when she'd shown up on her mother's doorstep, pregnant, broke and alone, she hadn't cried or offered long explanations or excuses. She just kept moving. Now she felt stuck in quicksand, as though nothing could save her.

Vera's palm slammed onto the desk. "We won't let this happen. Have you consulted Frank?"

Julia nodded. Frank Davis had been practicing law in Brevia for as long as she could remember and was a friend of her mother's. After Sam's suggestion that she see an attorney, she'd hired him to represent her. "He's helping with the case."

Vera nodded. "That's a good start. You need to talk to Jeff. To understand why he's doing this now when he had no previous interest in being a dad. Surely you'll be awarded sole custody. You're Charlie's mother and you do a wonderful job with him."

"I don't know, Mom. Jeff's family is arguing that they can give Charlie opportunities he'll never have with me."

"A child doesn't need anything more than a loving family. Let them set up a college trust if they're so concerned with opportunities."

"What do you want to see happen?" Lainey asked.

That question had kept Julia up many nights. "I'll support them having a relationship with Charlie. I'm sure as he gets older he'll have questions about his father's family. I want him to be surrounded by all the people who love him." She paused and took a breath. "I'm afraid he'll eventually choose them."

"He won't," Lainey said softly.

"You can't know that. But he needs to live with me now. Full-time. Swapping him back and forth is ludicrous."

"I'm going to the mediation," Vera announced.

Julia's stomach lurched. As much as she appreciated and needed her family's support, she was afraid it would only make her more nervous to have her mother with her.

"That's not a good idea. I appreciate the offer but I need to handle this on my own."

Lainey squeezed her shoulder and asked, "Has Jeff contacted you directly or tried to see Charlie?"

Julia shook her head. "No. Neither have his parents, other than when I got messages about discussing the custody arrangement."

"When did that start?" Vera came around the side of the desk.

"About a month ago. I ignored them until the certified letter arrived last week."

"Ignoring your problems doesn't make them go away."

Funny, it had always worked for Julia in the past. She'd taken the easy way out of every difficult situation that came her way before Charlie. And thanks to the complexity of her difficulties processing both words and numbers, problems seemed to plague her. From bad rental agreements to unfair terms on a car loan, her inability to manage the details of her life took its toll in a variety of ways. Still, nothing had prepared her for this.

A knock at the door interrupted them.

"Come in," Vera said.

A member of the shelter staff entered, leading in a gray dog. Or more accurately, the gray dog led her. Upon seeing Julia, the animal pulled at the leash, his stubby tail wagging. His lips drew back to expose his teeth.

"That's quite a greeting," Lainey said with a laugh.

"Sam thought it was a snarl when the dog first came at him." Julia bent to pet him. The dog wiggled and tried to put his front paws on her chest. She body blocked him. "Down."

"What's the report?" Vera asked the young woman.

"We've done his blood work and tested him for heartworm and parasites. Surprisingly, he got a clean bill of health."

"That's great." Julia felt relief wash over her. "Have you had any calls about a lost Weim?"

The young woman shook her head. "Not yet."

"We'll do a three-day hold before he moves onto the available-dog list." Vera dropped to her knees next to Julia. The dog lunged for her, teeth gleaming, but Vera held up a hand and gave a firm "No." The dog's rear end hit the carpet, although one corner of his mouth still curled.

Julia met her mother's gaze. "The smile's not good for him, is it?"

Vera shrugged. "It depends on the potential adopter, but a lot of people might think the same thing Sam did. We'll find a place for him. We always do."

Julia stroked the dog's silky ear. She'd planned on leaving the Weimaraner at the shelter this morning. "Can I foster him? Until the waiting period is over or someone shows interest. I'll work on basic training commands to help offset the shock of the smile."

Vera hesitated. "You've got a lot going on right now, honey. Weims aren't easy dogs. They can have separation anxiety and get destructive."

Frustration crept across Julia's neck and shoulders. "You know being in a foster home is better for a dog's well-being." She couldn't believe her mother would insinuate the dog would be better in the shelter than with her.

"Of course," Vera agreed, as if she realized she'd crossed some imaginary line. "If you're willing to, it would help him immensely."

"Have they named him yet?" Julia knew the shelter staff named each animal that came in to make their care more personal.

The young woman shook her head.

"Call him Casper," Julia said.

"The friendly gray ghost?" Lainey asked, referring to the breed's well-known nickname.

Julia nodded. "It fits him and will give people a sense of his personality."

"Perfect," her mother said then asked the young woman, "They've done a temperament test?"

She nodded. "He's a big sweetie." The walkie-talkie clipped to her belt hissed. "I'll finish the paperwork with Julia as the foster." When Vera nodded, the woman smiled and walked out of the office.

"It's settled." Julia was going to make sure this dog found the perfect home. She straightened. "Charlie will be thrilled."

She turned to her mother. "I need to get Charlie from Ethan and drop him to the sitter before heading to the salon."

"I'll take him today," her mother said, in the same no-argument tone she'd used earlier.

"Really? I'm sure your schedule is packed after your trip."

"I'd love to."

Julia gave her mother a quick hug. "Thank you." She turned to Lainey. "Both of you. It helps to know I'm not alone."

"You never have been," Vera told her.

"And never will be," Lainey added.

As she gave Charlie a bath later that night, Julia had to admit Sam had been right. Talking about the situation with Lainey and her mother had made her feel more hopeful. She might have flitted from job to job and through a number of cities during her twenties, but now she'd settled in Brevia. She was close to the point where she could make an offer to buy the salon, assuming this custody battle didn't wipe out her meager savings.

She wrapped Charlie in a fluffy towel, put on a fresh diaper and his pajamas, Casper at her side the whole time. She didn't mind the company. She'd taken him for a walk with Charlie in the stroller earlier, after the dog had spent the day with her in the salon.

A few of the clients had been shocked at his wide grin, but his affectionate nature had quickly won them over. It also made Julia feel more confident about his chances for adoption.

When the doorbell rang, Casper ran for it and began a steady bark. Carrying Charlie with her, she put a leash on the dog. A part of her hoped Sam was making another unexpected evening call.

Instead, Jeff Johnson stood on the other side of the door. Casper lunged for him but Julia held tight to the leash. She stumbled forward when the shock of seeing her ex-boyfriend combined with the dog's strength threw her off balance.

"Watch it," Jeff snapped as he righted her.

Casper smiled.

"What the...? Is that thing dangerous?" Jeff stepped back. "He looks rabid. You shouldn't have it near the baby. Are you crazy?"

"Casper, sit." Julia gave the command as she straightened. The dog sat, the skin around his mouth quivering. "Be careful, or I may give the attack command." She made her voice flip despite the flood of emotions roaring through her.

For a satisfying moment, Jeff looked as if he might make a run for it. Then his own lip curled. "Very funny."

"Good doggy." Charlie pointed at the canine.

"He talks," Jeff said, surprise clear.

"He does a lot of things," Julia answered, her eyes narrowed. "Not that you'd know or care since you beat a fast escape as soon as you found out I was pregnant."

Jeff flashed his most disarming smile, a little sheepish with his big chocolate eyes warm behind his square glasses. That exact smile had initially charmed her when he'd come in for a haircut at the salon where she'd worked in Columbus, Ohio.

For several months dating Jeff had been magical for her. He'd taken her to the theater and ballet, using his family's tickets. They'd gone to poetry readings and talks by famous authors on campus. Some of what she heard was difficult to process, and in a moment of vulnerability, she'd told Jeff about the extent of her learning disabilities. He'd been sympathetic and supportive, taking time over long evenings to read articles and stories to her, discussing them as if her opinion mattered. It was the first time in her life Julia felt valued for her intelligence, and she became committed to making their relationship work at any cost.

Soon she realized what a fool she'd been to think a well-respected professor would be truly interested in someone like her. It was clear that Jeff liked how his friends reacted when he'd shown up at dinner parties with a leggy blonde on his arm. He'd also gotten a lot of use out of the way she'd bent over backward cooking and cleaning to his exacting standards when she'd moved in with him. If she couldn't be on his level intellectually, she'd fulfill the other roles of a doting girlfriend. She'd wanted to believe that a baby would make him see how good their life together could be. She'd been dead wrong. Once she wasn't useful to him, he'd thrown her off like yesterday's news.

"Come on, Julia," he said softly, his grin holding steady. "Don't act like you aren't glad to see me." She'd been fooled by that smile once and wasn't going to make the same mistake again.

She flashed a smile of her own. "I don't see anyone throwing a ticker-tape parade. You can turn right around. I've got no use for you here."

"I'm here to see my son," Jeff said, as any trace of charm vanished.

Charlie met his biological father's gaze then buried his face in Julia's shoulder, suddenly shy.

"Why now, Jeff?" She rubbed a hand against Charlie's back when he began to fidget. "Why all of this now?"

He sighed. "The custody request, you mean."

Jeff's IQ was in the genius range, but sometimes he could be purposefully obtuse. "Of course the custody request. Do you know the hell you and your parents have put me through? We've barely scratched the surface."

"Invite me in, Jules," he said, coaxing, "and we can talk about it. I have an offer that may make this whole mess go away."

It had felt different when Sam stood at her door waiting to be invited through. Her stomach had danced with awareness and her only doubt had been worrying about her heart's exhilarated reaction to him. Still, Julia relented. If she had a chance to make this better, she couldn't refuse it.

Jeff stepped into her apartment but froze when Casper greeted him by sticking his snout into Jeff's crotch. "Get away, you stupid mutt." Jeff kicked out his foot, hitting Casper in the ribs. The dog growled.

"Casper, no." She pulled him back to her side with the leash then leveled a look at Jeff. "Don't kick my dog."

"It was going for my balls. What do you expect?"

"I wouldn't worry too much. As I remember, your mother keeps them on her mantel."

Jeff gave a humorless laugh. "Always one for the quick retort. I miss that about you."

"Good doggy. Charlie doggy." The boy wiggled in her arms and Julia put him on the floor. His chubby finger pulled the leash from her hand and he led the dog toward the kitchen. "Doggy nice." Casper followed willingly.

"You trust that beast with him?"

"More than I trust you." Julia folded her arms across her chest. "For the record, there's nothing I miss about you."

Jeff's eyes narrowed. "He's still my son. Whether you like it or not, I deserve to be a part of his life. There's no judge in the world who will deny me access."

"I never wanted to deny you access. I called you after he was born, emailed pictures and never heard one word back. You haven't answered my question. Why now?"

His gaze shifted to the floor. "Change of heart."

"You need a heart for it to change. You made it clear you never wanted to be a dad. What's the real story?" Before he could answer, Charlie led the dog back into the family room. He pulled a blanket off the couch and spread it on the floor. "Mama, doggy bed." She smiled as her son took a board book from the coffee table and sat on the blanket with Casper, making up words to an imaginary story.

Her gaze caught on Jeff, who yawned and looked around her apartment, obvious distaste written on his face for the kid-friendly decorating style. He didn't pay a bit of attention to his son. Since she'd opened the door, he'd barely looked at Charlie. It was the first time he'd laid eyes on his own flesh and blood. She realized he couldn't care less.

Unable to resist testing her theory, she said, "He's about to go to sleep. Do you want to read him a story? He loves books."

Jeff held up his palms as if she'd offered him a venomous snake. "No, thanks."

"I've got paperwork that says you want joint custody of my son. You act like you'd rather be dipped in boiling oil than have any interaction with him."

"I told you. I've got a proposition for you."

"What?"

"Marry me."

Julia stared at him, disbelief coursing through her. He couldn't have shocked her more if he'd offered her a million bucks. "Is that a joke? It's sick and wrong, but it must be a joke."

"I'm serious, Jules. You're right—I have no interest in being a father in any sense of the word. Ever. In fact—" he paused and ran his fingers through his hair "—I got a vasectomy."

"Excuse me?"

"After you, I was determined no woman would try to trap me again."

"It takes two. I'm sorry, Jeff, that I ever believed we could be a family. I know how wrong I was. But I don't understand why you've changed your mind now?"

"Are you kidding? I love my life. I've been on two research expeditions in the past year. I make my own schedule and can teach whatever classes I want. Why would I want to be tied down to a woman or a baby?"

"Then why are you suddenly proposing? Why the custody suit?"

Jeff had the grace to look embarrassed. "My parents found out about my surgery. It made them interested in our kid. You know I'm an only child. They expected me to marry and 'carry on the family line.'" He rolled his eyes. "Whatever. But my dad's company is a big funder of my grants. If he wants a grandchild, I need to give him one."

Julia's gaze strayed to Charlie, who was snuggled against Casper's back, sucking on his thumb. His eyes drifted closed. She felt a wave of nausea roll through her. "You need to *give* him one? And you think you're going to give him mine?"

Jeff shrugged. "Technically, he's *ours*. When my parents want something, they don't stop until they get it."

"How is anything you're saying good news for me? Why don't you get the hell out of my house and out of my son's life?"

"Not going to happen."

"When the judge finds out your plan…"

"No one is going to find out. I'm the father. You can't keep him from me."

"I want to keep him safe and protected."

"That's why you should marry me. Oh, I heard all about your engagement to the cop. He's not for you. I know you. You want someone who's going to make you look smart."

Julia sucked in a breath. "You have no idea what you're talking about."

"Does he know about your problem?"

When she didn't answer, Jeff smiled. "I thought so. I'm guessing you don't want him to. It hasn't come up in the court proceedings, either, but that can change. Here's my proposal. Marry me, move to Ohio. My parents' property is huge. They have a guesthouse where you can live with the boy. All of your expenses will be covered."

"Why would I agree to that, and what does it have to do with us being married?"

"A marriage will seem more legit to my parents' precious social circle. They'll get off my back with someone to shape and mold into their own image."

"Like they did you?"

"My parents are proud of me."

"I thought your father wanted you to give up the university and take over his business."

"Not going to happen."

"Instead, Charlie and I should spend our lives at their beck and call?"

"They'll keep fighting until they take him away from you. We all will."

Her temper about to blow, Julia yanked open the front door. "Get out, Jeff."

"On second thought, maybe I should read the kid a story. Get to know him before he comes to live with us."

"Get out!"

Jeff must have read something in her eyes that told him she would die before she let him touch her son tonight. He hesitated then turned for the door.

She slammed it behind him. The noise startled the dog and woke Charlie, who began to cry. She rushed over and cradled him in her arms.

"It's okay, sweetie. Mama's here." Tears streamed down her face as she hugged Charlie close. "No one's going to take you away from me. No one." She made the promise as much to herself as to him, wanting to believe the words were true.

Chapter Eight

Julia stepped into the afternoon light and put on her sunglasses, more to hide the unshed tears welling in her eyes than for sun protection.

Frank Davis, her attorney, took her elbow to guide her down the steps of the county courthouse. They'd spent the past two hours in a heated session with Jeff, his parents and their lawyer. She couldn't believe how much information they'd dug up, from the details of her finances, including the business loan that had yet to be approved, to her credit history. Thanks to a loser boyfriend who'd stolen her bank-account information, her credit was spotty, at best.

They knew all of the dead-end jobs she'd had over the years, including those she'd been fired from or quit without notice, and had a detailed record of her habit of moving from city to city for short periods of time.

They'd brought in statements from one of her ex-boyfriends and a former employer stating she was flighty and irresponsible. Her old boss even said that she'd threatened to set fire to her hair salon. No one mentioned the woman had skimmed Julia's paycheck without her knowledge for over nine months after she'd discovered Julia's learning disabilities. Torching the place had been an idle threat, of course, but it hadn't sounded that way today.

"They made me seem crazy," she muttered.

Frank clucked softly. "It's all right, darlin'. A lot of mamas in the South are a bit touched. No one around here's gonna hold that against you." He checked his watch. "I got a tee time with some of the boys at one. Give me a call tomorrow and we'll plan our next move." He leaned in and planted a fatherly kiss on her cheek, then moved toward his vintage Cadillac parked at the curb.

Frank had known her since she'd been in diapers. He'd been one of her father's fraternity brothers in college. Not for the first time, she questioned the wisdom of hiring him to represent her. It was no secret Frank was close to retirement, and from what Julia could tell, he spent more time on the golf course and fishing with his friends than in his office or working on cases.

Lexi Preston might look like a pussycat, but she was an absolute shark. From her guilty expression every time they made eye contact, Julia knew Lexi was the one who'd researched her so thoroughly. Julia would have admired her skills if they hadn't been directed at her.

She glanced toward the courthouse entrance. Jeff and his parents could come out at any minute and she didn't want them to see her alone and on the verge of a breakdown. She wished now that she'd let her mother or Lainey come with her today.

She turned to make her way to her car and came face-to-face with Sam.

"Hey," he said softly and drew the sunglasses off her

nose, his eyes studying hers as if he could read what she was thinking. "How did things go today?"

"I told you not to come," she said on a shaky breath.

"I don't take direction well." He folded her glasses and pulled her into a tight embrace. "It's okay, honey. Whatever happened, we can make it better."

She tried to pull away but he didn't let her go. After a moment, she sagged against him, burying her face in the fabric of his uniform shirt.

As his palm drew circles on her back, her tears flowed freely. She gulped in ragged breaths. "So awful," she said around sobs. "They made me seem so awful."

"I don't believe that," he said against her ear. "Anyone who knows you knows you're a fantastic mother."

"What if they take him from me?"

"We're not going to let that happen. Not a snowball's chance."

Julia wiped her eyes. "They're going to come out any minute. Jeff can't see me like this."

"My truck's right here." Sam looped one arm around her shoulders, leading her away from the courthouse steps. He opened the passenger door of his truck then came around and climbed in himself. He started the engine but didn't make a move to drive off.

Julia kept her face covered with her hands and worked to control her breathing.

"Is that him?" Sam asked after a minute.

Julia peeked through her fingers as Jeff, his parents and the attorney walked out of the courthouse. Shading his eyes with one hand, Jeff scanned the area.

"He's looking for me so he can gloat." Julia sank down lower in the seat. "Jerk," she mumbled.

The group came down the steps.

"They're heading right for us."

"Sit up," Sam ordered, and she immediately straightened. "Smile and lean over to kiss me when they come by."

The urge to duck was huge, but Julia made her mouth turn up at the ends. "Here goes," she whispered as Jeff led the group closer, his father clapping him hard on the back. She waited until he noticed her through the windshield then leaned over and cupped Sam's jaw between her hands. She gave him a gentle kiss and pressed her forehead against his.

"That a girl," he told her. "Don't give him the satisfaction of seeing you upset."

"I can do this," she said, and Sam kissed her again.

"They've passed."

Julia stayed pressed against him for another moment before moving away. She leaned against the seat back in order to see out the side-view mirror. Jeff and his parents headed away, but Lexi trailed behind the group, looking over her shoulder every few steps.

"This isn't going to work."

"Yes, it is."

She shook her head. "I told you before, I made a lot of stupid decisions in my life. It's like they've uncovered every single one of them to use against me."

"Did you kill someone?"

Her head whipped toward him. "Of course not."

"Armed robbery?"

"No."

"Do you know how many people I meet in the course of my job who do bad things every day? Their kids are rarely taken away."

"Maybe they should be," she suggested, too unsettled to be comforted. "Maybe if they had people with buckets of money and tons of power going after them, they'd lose their babies."

He wrapped his fingers around hers. "You aren't going to lose Charlie. Stop thinking like that."

"You don't know, Sam. You weren't in that room."

"A mistake I don't intend to repeat. I should have been there with you. For you."

The tenderness in his voice touched a place deep within her: an intimate, open well of emotion she'd locked the lid to many years ago. She wanted to believe in him, to trust that he could protect her the way she'd never been willing to protect herself or even believed she deserved. The part of her who'd been hurt too many times in the past wanted to run.

She excelled at running away. She'd practically perfected it as an art.

That was what she'd been thinking in the courthouse. People disappeared all the time with no trace. She'd wanted to slip out of that room, gather up Charlie and whatever would fit in her trunk and drive away from the threat looming over her. She could cut hair anywhere. Why not start over in a place where no one knew her or her insecurities or all the ways she didn't measure up? She had friends around the country who'd help her if she asked.

The weight of trying to make a new life in a place that was as familiar to her as a worn blanket seemed too heavy. Of course trouble had followed her to Brevia. This was where it had started in the first place.

Sam's faith had made her feel as though things could work out, the same way Charlie's birth had renewed her hope in herself and her desire to really try.

What was the use? This morning was a cold, harsh dose of reality and she didn't like it.

"Stop it," he said quietly. "Whatever's going through your mind right now, put it out. It's not going to do you or Charlie any good for you to give up."

Because she couldn't help it, she met his gaze again. "I'm scared, Sam." A miserable groan escaped her lips. "I'm terrified they're going to take my baby and I won't be able to stop them."

"We're going to stop them." He took her hand. "What did Frank say?"

"That all Southern women were crazy, so it wouldn't be an issue, and he needed to make his tee time and we'd talk tomorrow."

"Tell me what happened in there."

"I can't." She bit her lip again and tasted blood on her tongue. "I put my mistakes behind me. Or I thought I did. Their attorney knew things about my past I hadn't even told Jeff. They went after my character and I had nothing to offer in my defense. Nothing as bad as me killing someone, although the urge to wipe the smug smile off of Maria Johnson's face was almost overwhelming. They made me seem unstable and irresponsible. Two things I can't afford if I'm going to keep sole custody of Charlie."

"Then we'll come up with something."

"This isn't your problem, Sam."

"Hell, yes, it's my problem. You're my fiancée."

The lunacy of that statement actually made her laugh. "Your fake fiancée. Not the same thing."

"For the purposes of your custody case it is. You're not alone, Julia. We both get something out of this arrangement. My dad has talked about heading back home before the wedding. That's huge for me. Dinner was a big success. It's my turn to repay you."

Sam knew there was more to his interest in her case than wanting to repay her. Yes, his dad had backed off, but it was more than that. Sam cared about Julia and Charlie, about keeping them safe. No one should be able to make her feel this bad about herself. He also knew it was dangerous territory for him. He'd let his heart lead him before, with disastrous results.

His father might be the king of emotional diarrhea these days, but Sam remembered clearly the months after his mother's death. He'd fixed lunches for his little brother, made sure they both had baths at night and taken money out of his dad's wallet to buy groceries on his way home from school. He'd walked a mile out of his way once a week so no one at the local grocery would recognize him and be concerned. When he wasn't at work, his father had sat in the darkened living room, paging through photo albums, a glass of amber-colored liquid in his hand.

That was what loving someone too much could do to a man. Sam had learned early on he wasn't going to make that mistake. When he'd caught his brother, Scott, with his ex-fiancée, he'd been angry and embarrassed, but mainly numb.

When he'd broken off the engagement, Jenny had told him the entire situation was his fault. He'd been too cold and distant. She wanted to be with a man who could feel passion. She'd thought seeing her with someone else would awaken Sam's passion. Talk about crazy, and she wasn't even Southern.

He'd known he didn't have any more to give her or any woman. Even though his pattern of dating hadn't been deliberate, the look a woman sometimes got in her eye after a couple of dates scared him. The look said "I want something more." She wanted to talk about her feelings. Sam felt sick thinking about it.

As far as he was concerned, a pretend engagement suited him fine. He cared about Julia and he wanted to help her, but their arrangement was clear. He didn't have to give more of himself than he was able to, and she wasn't going to expect anything else.

"Jeff asked me to marry him," she said, breaking his reverie.

"During the mediation?" he asked, sure he must have heard her wrong.

She shook her head. "Last night. He came to my apartment."

Sam felt his blood pressure skyrocket. "You let him in? What were you thinking?" Especially since Sam had practically had to hold himself back from making the short drive to her apartment. He'd had a long day at work, and as he was pulling into his driveway, he'd realized how much he didn't want to be alone in his quiet house. He'd resisted the urge, telling himself that he shouldn't get too attached to Julia or her son. They had boundaries and he was a stickler for the rules. Now to find out that her creep of an ex-boyfriend had been there?

"He came crawling back." Sam kept his tone casual. Inside, his emotions were in turmoil. This was the guy she'd wanted to marry so badly. What if she still carried a torch for him? He'd obviously been an idiot to let her go once. If he came back now, trying to rekindle a romance and wanting to be a real family, would Julia consider taking him back? That thought hit Sam straight in the gut. "What did you say?"

She studied him for a moment. "He didn't quite come crawling. More like trumpeting his own horn. He told me the reason they're coming after Charlie is because his parents want an heir to the family business."

"They've got a son. Let him take over."

"Not his deal, and Jeff isn't going to have other children. He's made sure of that. Although it's crazy to think they could start grooming a mere toddler. No wonder Jeff has so many issues. If only I'd been smart enough to see it when we were together. You know what the strange part of this is? No one in Jeff's family has tried to get to know Charlie. It's like they want him on paper but they don't care about having a grandson. I want him to know their family if they have a real interest in him. But I saw how Jeff suffered from being a pawn in his parents' power games. I can't let the same thing happen to Charlie."

He held her hand, his brilliant blue eyes warm with emotion. "Your son needs you. He needs you to fight for him."

She nodded and wiped at her nose.

"What you need is a plan of defense. You flaked on some jobs. It happens."

"There's a reason," she mumbled, almost reluctantly.

"A reason that will explain it away?"

She shrugged and shook free from his hand, adjusting the vents to the air-conditioning as a way to keep her fingers occupied. "I have severe learning disabilities."

When he didn't respond she continued, "I've been keeping it a secret since I was a kid. It's a neurobiological disorder, both visual and auditory. Only my family and a few teachers knew, and I kept it from them for as long as I could. Everyone else assumed I was lazy or didn't care."

"Why would you hide that?"

"You have no idea what it's like, how much shame and embarrassment is involved. To people who've never dealt with it, it seems cut-and-dried. It's not." Her hands clenched into fists as she struggled with her next words. "I'm a good mimic and my bad attitude served me well as a way to keep everyone from digging too much. I got by okay, but I can barely read. Numbers on a page are a puzzle."

"All those books on your shelf…"

"I'm nothing if not determined. I'll get through them someday. Right now, I'm working with a literacy specialist. They have a lot of methods that weren't available when

I was in school. But it never gets easier. For years, I tried so hard in school but people thought I was a total slacker. Ditzy blonde cheerleader with no brain. A lot of the time that's how it felt. Once I was out on my own, I hid it as best I could. People can take advantage of me pretty easily when it comes to contracts or finances. And that's what happened. A number of times. It always seemed easier to just move on rather than to fight them."

"Every time someone got wind of it, you left."

She nodded. "It was cowardly but I don't want to be treated like I'm stupid. Although, looking back, I acted pretty dumb most of the time. Especially when it came to boyfriends. I trusted Jeff. He never let me forget it."

"That you had a learning disability?"

"That I'm just a pretty face. The blond hair and long legs. When I told him I was pregnant, he told me that once my looks faded I wouldn't have anything left to offer."

"He's a real piece of work." Sam couldn't believe how angry he was. At her idiot ex-boyfriend and all the others who took advantage of her. But also with Julia. Watching her, Sam could tell she believed the garbage people had fed her over the years. He threw the truck into gear, not wanting to lose his temper. "Where's your car?"

"Around the corner." She pointed then shifted in her seat. "Thanks for coming today, Sam. I was a mess after the mediation. You helped."

"I could have helped more if you'd let me be in there with you." He pulled out from the curb and turned onto the next street. Her car was parked a few spaces down.

"Maybe next time," she said quietly. She reached for the door handle but he took her arm.

"You have a lot more to offer than looks. Any guy who can't see that is either blind or an enormous jackass." He kept his gaze out the front window, afraid of giving away too much if he looked at her.

"Thanks."

He heard the catch in her voice and released her. After she'd shut the door, he rolled down the window. "The Mardi Gras Carnival is tonight. I'll pick you and Charlie up at five."

"I'm beat. I wasn't planning on going."

"I'll pick you up at five. You need to take your mind off this, and it's a good place for us to be seen together."

Her chest rose and fell. "Fine. We'll be ready."

After she'd gotten into her car, Sam pulled away. Although the air was hot for mid-March, he shut the windows. Julia's scent hovered in the truck's cab. Sam wanted to keep it with him as long as he could.

He'd meant what he said about taking her mind off today. As police chief, he was obligated to make an appearance at town events, but he looked forward to tonight knowing he'd have Julia and Charlie with him.

Chapter Nine

Julia dabbed on a bit of lip gloss just as the doorbell rang. She picked up Charlie, who was petting Casper through the wire crate.

"Let's go."

"'Bye, doggy."

Casper whined softly.

"We'll be back soon," Julia told him. The doorbell rang again. "Coming," she called.

She grabbed the diaper bag off the table and opened the front door, adjusting her short, flowing minidress as she did.

"We're ready."

"Sammy," Charlie said, bouncing up and down in her arms.

"Hey, bud." Sam held out his hands and Charlie dived forward.

Julia worried for a moment about Charlie bonding so

quickly with Sam. In a way it worked to their advantage, at least as their pretend engagement went. But she had concerns about Charlie's clear affection for Sam. She didn't want her son to be hurt once their time together ended.

"You don't have to take him."

"My pleasure." Sam looked her over from head to toe then whistled softly. "You look amazing."

Julia felt a blush creep up her cheeks. "You, too."

It was true. Tonight he wore a light polo shirt and dark blue jeans. His hair was still longer and her fingers pulsed as she thought about running them through the ends. He hadn't shaved, and the dusting of short whiskers along his jaw made him look wilder than he normally did as police chief.

It excited her more than she cared to admit. She hadn't been on a real date in over two years. This wasn't real, she reminded herself. This was showing off for the town, convincing people their relationship was genuine.

Not that being in this relationship had helped her earlier. She'd barely said two words in her own defense as the Johnsons' attorney had put forward more and more information about her deficiencies as a person and how they might be detrimental to raising her son.

The mediator, an older woman who was all business, hadn't said much, nodding as she took in everything and occasionally looking over her glasses to stare at Julia.

Sam was right. She needed to get her mind off the custody case. So what if this night wasn't a real date and Sam wasn't her real boyfriend? It wouldn't stop her from enjoying herself.

Because of Charlie's car seat, she drove. Once they were close to the high school, she could see the line of cars. Half the town was at the carnival. She knew Lainey and Ethan would be there along with her mother.

"Is your dad coming tonight?" she asked, a thought suddenly blasting across her mind.

Sam nodded. "I told him we'll meet him."

"My mom is, too."

Sam made a choking sound. "Okay, good. They can get to know each other. It'll be great."

"That's one word for it."

"Does your mom believe the engagement? I haven't seen her since she walked in on us."

"I think so." Julia slowed to turn into the lower parking lot. "It's not the first time she's seen me be impulsive."

Sam shook his head as she turned off the ignition. "You never give yourself a break."

"Why do I deserve one?" She paused then said, "It's fine. I'm repairing my reputation with my family. It's a long progress, but I'm getting there. What makes you ask about my mom?"

"I saw Ethan downtown yesterday and he gave me the third degree about my intentions toward you."

"Ethan?"

"His big-brother routine was going strong. Told me how special you are and that if I hurt you or Charlie I'd have him to answer to."

"I don't know why he'd care. He went through hell because of me, although it's ancient history now."

"There you go again with the self-flagellation. We're going to need to work on that."

"Whatever you say." She got out of the car and picked up Charlie from his car seat. As she turned, she took in her old high school. It looked the same as it had almost fifteen years ago.

She filled her lungs with the cool night air. This was her favorite time of year in the North Carolina mountains. It smelled fresh and clean, the scent of spring reminding her of new beginnings. Coming off of the cold, wet winter, the change of seasons gave her hope.

Just like Sam.

Julia knew hope was dangerous. She was a sucker for believing in things that would never come to pass. She'd been like that in high school, too—wanting to believe she'd be able to keep up. Or, at least, admit how deeply her problem ran.

For some reason, that never seemed an option. Sam could say what he wanted about her learning disabilities being beyond her control. She knew it was true. But by high school, when elementary-age kids read more clearly than she could, it felt like stupidity.

None of her teachers had understood what was going on in her head. She'd never truly opened up to anyone about how bad it was. It had been easier to act as though she didn't care, to limp through school with a lot of blustering attitude and paying smarter kids to write her papers.

Charlie tapped her on the cheek. "Hi, Mama."

She shook off the memories. Sam stood next to her, watching with his too-knowing eyes.

"I'm guessing you haven't been back here for a while?"

"Not since graduation." She adjusted Charlie and headed for the gymnasium entrance. "Remind me again why we're here."

Sam put his hand on the small of her back, the gentle touch oddly comforting. "The annual Kiwanis carnival not only celebrates Fat Tuesday but raises a lot of money each year for local kids. It's a great event for the town."

"Spoken like a true pillar of the community." She gave an involuntary shiver. "Which I'm not and never will be."

"You never know. Either way, I promise you'll have fun. Greasy food, games, dancing."

Since she'd been back, she hadn't attended any town

events. It was one thing to reconnect with people she'd known within the relative safety of the salon. No one was going to rehash old resentments while she wielded scissors. Here she was out of her element and not confident about the reception she'd get from the girls she once knew. Especially since she'd taken Brevia's most eligible bachelor off the market.

A memory niggled at the back of her mind. "Didn't you do a kissing booth last year or something like that?"

Sam's confident stride faltered. "They auctioned off dates with a couple local guys."

She flashed him a smile. "How much did you go for, Chief?"

In the fading light, she saw a distinct trail of red creep up his neck. "I don't remember."

"Liar." She stood in one spot until he turned to look at her. "Tell me."

"A thousand," he mumbled.

"Dollars?" She gasped. "Who in the world paid that much money for you?" When he leveled a look at her, she added, "Not that I don't think you're worth it. But not a lot of people around here have that kind of cash."

"It was for a good cause" was his only answer.

Another thought struck. "Unless...it was Ida Garvey!"

He turned and she trotted to catch up with him, Charlie bouncing on her hip. "Let me take him." Sam slid his arms around Charlie and scooped him up.

"It was Ida, wasn't it? She's the only one around here rich enough to pay that amount."

He gave a reluctant nod. "I got the most money."

"What kind of date did you take her on?"

"Would you believe I escorted her to her fiftieth high-school reunion over in Asheville? She had me wait on her hand and foot. Kept calling me her 'boy toy' in front of her old friends." He shook his head. "I swear my butt had bruises from being pinched so often."

Julia laughed harder than she had in ages. "You really are a hero, you know?"

"It's not funny."

"Yes, it is." She looked at him and saw humor shining in his eyes, as well. Then she noticed they were at the gym entrance, light spilling out into the darkening night. She studied Sam for another moment, wondering if he'd told her that story to ease her nerves.

He really was a good guy, she thought. He should be with someone like him—a woman who was smart and sweet.

Someone nothing like her.

He smoothed the skin between her eyebrows. "Stop frowning," he said gently. "We're going to have fun."

He dropped his hand, intertwined his fingers with hers and led her into the gymnasium. He greeted the two women working the ticket counter, neither of whom Julia recognized. Sam made introductions, and both women gave her a genuine smile and shook her hand, offering congratulations on their engagement. She flashed her ring but noticed Sam stiffen when one of the ladies complimented him on it.

Charlie became suddenly shy and buried his face in the crook of Sam's neck, something Julia would have loved to do, as well.

"Come on, buddy," Sam coaxed. "Let's find some cotton candy."

"I don't think so," Julia said. "He hasn't had dinner yet."

Charlie gave Sam a wide grin. "Can-ee."

"We'll get a hot dog first," Sam promised her and moved into the crowd.

"Kids can always count on their dad for a good time," one of the women said with a laugh.

"While Mom cleans up the sick stomach," the other added.

"He's not…" Julia began, wanting to explain that Sam wasn't her son's father. Then she realized they already knew that, although Sam was certainly acting like the doting dad.

"He's quite a catch." The blonder of the two women winked at her.

Julia's stomach flipped because she knew how right the woman's statement was. "I'd better stick with them," she said and hurried after the two, emotions already at war in her mind and heart.

"Julia!" Lainey's voice carried over the crowd, and a moment later, she was surrounded by her sister, Ethan and their mother. Lainey gave her a long hug. "Sam said today was rough. Are you feeling any better?"

"I knew I should have come with you." Vera shook her head. "I'd like to get ahold of that family and talk some sense into them."

"When did you see Sam?" The thought of Sam giving information about her to her family made her more than a little uncomfortable.

"I ran into him downtown," Lainey said. "What's the big deal?"

"He shouldn't have said anything."

"He's going to be your husband," Vera corrected. "He has a right to worry."

"We all do," Lainey echoed. "Jules, you've got to let us help you. You're not alone."

"Where's the little man?" Ethan asked, his internal radar about conflict between the three Morgan women practically glowing bright red through his T-shirt.

"Right here," Sam answered, balancing a huge cotton

candy and a paper plate with hot-dog chunks and small pieces of watermelon on it.

Charlie reached for a piece of fruit and babbled a few nonsense words.

"You cut up the hot dog," Julia said, stunned.

Sam's forehead wrinkled. "I thought you were supposed to cut up round food when kids are little."

"You are." Julia felt ridiculous that something so minor had such an effect on her emotions. "I didn't realize you'd know it."

"Don't be silly." Vera reached for Charlie and snuggled him against her. "He's spent enough time around you and Charlie to realize that."

Julia saw Lainey studying her, a thoughtful expression on her face. "That's right. Isn't it, Jules?"

Julia nodded and stepped next to Sam, leaning up to kiss him on the cheek. "Of course. Thanks, hon."

Lainey's features relaxed and Julia blew out a quiet breath of relief.

"There's my favorite son and future daughter-in-law." So much for her short-lived relief. Julia heard Sam groan.

She turned and was enveloped in one of Joe Callahan's bear hugs. He moved from her to Sam. "Look at you, Sammy. Surrounded by friends with the woman you love at your side." His meaty hands clasped either side of Sam's jaw. "I'm so proud of you, son. You're not a loner anymore. I thought my mistakes had cost you a chance at a real life. But you're making it happen."

"Dad, enough." Sam pulled Joe's hands away. "Not the time or the place."

"There's always time to say 'I love you.'"

Sam met Julia's gaze over his father's shoulders. His eyes screamed "help me," and as fascinating as everyone seemed to find the father-son interaction, she intervened.

"Joe, I'd like you to meet my family."

He turned, his smile a mile wide.

"This is my sister, Lainey, and her husband, Ethan Daniels."

Joe pumped their hands enthusiastically. "Pleasure to meet you both. I'm Joe Callahan."

"Are you in town for long, Mr. Callahan?" Lainey asked.

"As long as it takes," Joe said with a wink at Sam.

A muscle in Sam's jaw ticked and his eyes drifted shut as he muttered to himself. They flew open a moment later when Ethan added, "You, Sammy and I should do some fishing once the weather warms up."

"Don't call me Sammy."

"I'd love to."

Vera cleared her throat.

"Sorry. This is my mother, Vera Morgan. And you've met Charlie."

Joe's eyes widened as he looked at Vera. "Well, I certainly see where you two girls get your beauty. Ms. Morgan, you are a sight to behold."

Vera held out her hand like the Southern belle she'd once been. Joe bent over her fingers and kissed them lightly. "Why, Mr. Callahan," she said, her accent getting thicker with every syllable. "You are a silver-tongued devil, I believe."

"Shoot me now," Sam muttered.

Julia's eyes rolled. She was used to this routine with her mother. Vera had been a devoted wife to her late husband, but since his death, she'd reinvented herself not only as an animal-rescue expert but as a woman with a long list of admirers. Unlike Julia, her mother always made sure the men with whom she was acquainted treated her like a lady, fawning around her until Vera moved on to the next one in line.

"Here she goes," Lainey whispered, as Vera tucked her chin and fluttered her eyelashes. Charlie watched the two for a moment then reached for Sam.

"Can-ee," the boy demanded, and Joe took the cotton candy from Sam.

"Come here, Charlie," Joe said and lifted him from Vera's arms. At this rate, Charlie would be held by more people than the Stanley Cup.

"Why don't I take him," Julia suggested.

"Joe and I will take him to the carnival games," Vera said.

"That's right," Joe told them with a wink. "You young folks can head to the dance floor or grab a drink."

Before she could argue, Joe and Vera disappeared into the sea of people, Charlie waving over Joe's shoulder.

"I'm up for a beer." Ethan looked at Sam. "How about you, Sammy boy?"

"Don't go there," Sam warned.

"Stop—you're going to make me cry." Ethan laughed until Lainey socked him in the gut. "Hey," he said on a cough.

"I thought Sam's dad was sweet." Lainey grinned at Sam. "He obviously loves you." Her gaze switched to Julia. "You and Charlie, too. Mom's going to eat him up with a spoon."

"A terrifying thought." Julia'd known this night was a bad idea.

"Come on," Lainey said to all three of them. "Let's get something to eat. They had a pasta booth in the corner."

Ethan wrapped one long arm around Lainey and kissed the top of her head. "Yeah, like a double date."

Julia couldn't help it—she burst out laughing. "This is going to be great. We'll be besties." Who would have thought that she'd be double-dating with her first boyfriend and her sister? It was too crazy to imagine.

She looked at Sam, expecting him to be laughing right along with her. Instead, his brows were drawn low over his vivid blue eyes.

"Fine by me." He took her hand to follow Lainey and Ethan toward the back of the gym.

"What's wrong?" she whispered, pulling him to slow down so they were out of hearing range. "Is it my mom and Joe? She's harmless, I promise. Her former admirers still adore her. Whatever happens, she won't hurt your dad."

Sam's arm was solid as a rock as his muscles tensed. "Does it seem strange to be so chummy with your ex-boyfriend?"

Julia thought about Jeff, then realized that was not who Sam meant. "Ethan's married to my sister. We've been over more than a decade. He's so much like my brother, I barely remember he's seen me naked."

Sam stopped on a dime, causing her to bump into the length of him. "Is that a joke?"

She wrinkled her nose. "I thought it was funny."

"It's not."

"Come on, Sam. You see how he looks at Lainey. He never once looked at me in that way. He's different with her, and I couldn't be happier. For both of them. It's old news, even around Brevia. That's an accomplishment, given how gossip takes on a life of its own in this town." She flashed him a sassy grin. "Chief Callahan, is it possible you're jealous?"

"I don't want to look like a fool. I've been down the road of public humiliation and the scenery sucks. Why would I be jealous? You said yourself Ethan's like your brother."

Julia studied him then placed a soft kiss on his mouth.

"I'd never do something to make you look like a fool. Scout's honor."

"I can't imagine you as a Girl Scout." Sam forced his lips to curve into a smile, wondering at his odd reaction. He wasn't the jealous type, and he knew how happy Ethan and Lainey were together. "Let's find them." He took Julia's hand again.

A number of people waved or stopped to say hello as they made their way through the crowd. At first, Julia tensed at every new greeting. Eventually he felt her relax, but she never loosened her death grip on his hand. He wanted to protect her, he realized, and also to show her she could belong to this community again. The people of Brevia had welcomed him, and if Julia gave them a chance, he was sure they'd accept her.

They caught up with Ethan and Lainey and grabbed a table near the makeshift dance floor. The sisters bantered back and forth, making Sam wish for a better relationship with his own brother.

Even before Scott had cheated with Sam's fiancée, they hadn't been close. Sam had been the responsible brother, stoic and toeing the line, while Scott had been wild, always getting into trouble and constantly resenting his older brother's interference in his life.

"How are things around town these days?" Ethan asked as he set a second beer on the table next to Sam.

"Quiet for a change." Sam took another bite of pasta then swallowed hard as Julia tilted back her head to laugh at something Lainey said. The column of her neck was smooth and long. He ached to trail a line of kisses across her skin.

He pushed away the beer, realizing he was going to need his wits about him to remain in control tonight.

"Were you involved in the drug bust over in Tellet County a few nights back?"

Julia stopped midsentence as her eyes snapped to his. "What drug bust? Sounds dangerous. Why didn't I hear about a drug bust?"

Sam threw Ethan what he hoped was a *shut your mouth* look.

"Sorry, man," Ethan said quickly. "Hey, Lainey, let's hit the dance floor."

Lainey popped out of her chair. "Love to."

"Cowards," Julia muttered as she watched them go. She turned her angry gaze back to Sam. "You were saying?"

"A meth lab outside the county lines," he told her. It had been a long time since anyone had cared about what he was doing and whether it was dangerous or not. "It's been kept quiet so far because the sheriff thinks it's part of a bigger tristate operation. We want to see if we can flush out a couple of the bigger fish."

She tapped one finger on the table. "I don't like you being involved in something like that."

"It's my job, Julia."

"I need to know about these things. I bet Abby Brighton knew where you were during the drug bust."

"She's my secretary. Of course she knew."

"We're engaged."

"Is that so?"

To his great amusement, she squirmed in her chair. "As far as everyone around here thinks. I need to be kept informed."

"Why?"

"To know whether I should worry."

"One more reason I wouldn't be a good bet in a real relationship. Ask my ex. I don't like to report in. I don't like anyone worried about me." He blew out a frustrated breath. "My job is dangerous almost every day. I deal with it, but I don't expect you or anyone else to."

"No one's allowed to care about you?" Her eyes flashed, temper lighting them.

"I don't need anyone to care."

"The Lone Ranger rides again." Julia pushed away from the table. He grabbed her wrist so she couldn't escape.

"Why are you mad? This doesn't have anything to do with you. We have a business arrangement. That's what we both wanted. It's not going to help either of us to be emotionally involved with the other one's life."

"Some of us care, whether we want to or not."

Her eyes shone and his heart leaped in his chest. He pulled her tight against him, aware they were gathering stares from people standing nearby. "Thank you for caring. I'm not used to it, but it means a lot." He pressed his forehead to hers. "I'm sorry I'm bad at this. Even for pretend."

"You're not *so* bad," she whispered.

"Do you want to dance?"

"Do you?"

He grinned at her. "Hell, no. But I can make it work."

"Give me a minute. I need to catch up with my mom and Joe, make sure Charlie's okay."

He studied her. "If I didn't know better, I'd say you're avoiding me right now."

She shook her head. "I want to find Charlie."

"They headed back toward the game booths. I'm going to say hi to the mayor and I'll meet you over there."

The gym was full, and without Sam at her side, Julia got a little panicked by the crowd.

She moved toward the far end of the gymnasium where the carnival booths were set up, then veered off quickly when she saw two women from her high-school class standing together near one of the attractions. One was

Annabeth Sullivan, whom Julia felt friendlier toward after their conversation at the salon. The other was Lucy Peterson, their graduating class's valedictorian. Julia had always been uncomfortable around her. She'd made it clear during high school that Lucy was persona non grata and knew the slightly chubby teen had suffered because of it.

Lucy had gotten her revenge, though. Because of her work in the school office and her access to the files, she'd found out about Julia's learning disabilities. She hadn't told anyone outright, but had spread the rumor that Julia had only graduated because she'd slept with one of her teachers and he'd fixed her grade.

She'd told Julia that if she denied it, Lucy would tell people the real reason she had so much trouble in school. Having a reputation as a slut hadn't been half as bad as the school knowing about her LD.

She ducked out a door and into the cool night air, walking toward the football field situated next to the main building. Two streetlights glowed in the darkness as her eyes scanned the shadowy length of the field.

She'd spent so much time here in high school. If she'd been queen of her class, this was her royal court. She'd felt confident on the field in her cheerleading uniform or on the sidelines cheering for Ethan. She'd hated falling back on her looks, but the insecure girl who had nothing else to offer had exploited her one gift as best she could.

Now she breathed in the cool night air and closed her eyes, remembering the familiar smells and sounds.

Her memories here were a long time gone. She was no longer a scared teenager. She had Charlie to protect. She'd made mistakes and was trying her damnedest to make amends for them. There was no way of moving forward without finally confronting her past, once and for all.

Chapter Ten

She took another breath and headed toward the school, determined to hold her head high. She had as much right to return to her high school as anyone.

Once inside, she stopped at the girls' bathroom to sprinkle cold water on her face. When a stall opened and Lucy Peterson stepped out, Julia wondered if she'd actually conjured her.

"Hi, Lucy." The other woman's eyes widened in surprise.

Lucy hadn't changed much since high school. She was still short and full figured, her chest heaving as she adjusted the wire-rimmed glasses on her face.

"Hello, Julia. I didn't expect to see you here. I'm in town for the weekend for my parents' anniversary. Normally I wouldn't be caught dead back in this high school. I live in Chicago. I'm a doctor." Lucy paused for a breath. "I'm babbling."

"What kind of doctor?" Julia asked.

"Molecular biologist."

Julia nodded. Figured. Julia knew better than to compare herself to a genius like Lucy. "That's great."

The two women stared at each other for several long moments. At the same time they blurted, "I'm sorry."

Relief mixed with a healthy dose of confusion made Julia's shoulders sag. "I'm the one who should apologize. I know I was horrible in high school. You were on the top of my list. Not that it matters, but you should know I was jealous of you."

Lucy looked doubtful. "Of me? You were the homecoming queen, prom queen, head cheerleader, and you dated the football captain. I was nobody."

"You were smart."

"I shouldn't have spread that rumor about you." Lucy fiddled with the ring on her left finger. "You weren't a slut."

"There are worse things you could have said about me."

"You weren't stupid, either."

Julia made her voice light. "The grade record would beg to differ."

"I read your file," Lucy said slowly. "It was wrong, but I know you had significant learning disabilities, which means..."

"It means there's something wrong with my brain," Julia finished. "*Stupid* is a much clearer description of my basic problem."

"You must have been pretty clever to have hid it all those years. I'm guessing you still are."

"I cut hair for a living. It's not nuclear science. Or molecular biology."

"That's right. My mom told me you'd taken over the Hairhouse."

"I'm working on it. The loan still needs to go through."

"Are you going to keep the name?"

Julia relaxed a little as she smiled. "I don't think so. 'The Best Little Hairhouse in Brevia' is quite a mouthful."

Lucy returned the smile then pulled at the ends of her hair. "I'm in town until Tuesday. Could you fit me in?"

"You don't hate me?"

Lucy shook her head. "In high school, I thought I was the only one who was miserable. Once I got away from Brevia, I realized lots of kids had problems. We were all just too narcissistic to see it in each other. Some people can't let go of the past. I've moved on, Julia. I'm happy in Chicago. I have a great career and a fantastic husband. I don't even mind visiting my mom a couple times a year, although I avoid the old crowd. I know in my heart they can't hurt me because their opinions don't matter. I don't hate you. You probably did me a favor. You made me determined to escape. Now I can come back on my own terms."

"I'm glad for you, Lucy." Julia checked her mental calendar. She'd trained herself to keep her schedule in her head so she didn't have to rely on a planner or smartphone. "How about eleven on Monday?"

Lucy nodded. "Maybe we could grab lunch after. I may not care too much about certain ladies' opinions but I wouldn't mind seeing their faces if we showed up at Carl's."

"I'd love that."

"I'll see you Monday." With a quick, awkward hug, Lucy hurried out the door.

Julia studied herself in the hazy mirror above the row of bathroom sinks. She felt lighter than she had in years, the weight of her guilt over how she'd treated Lucy finally lifted. One past mistake vanquished, only a hundred more to go.

"She's right, you know." The door to one of the stalls swung open to reveal Lexi Preston.

Julia's shoulders went rigid again. "Eavesdrop much?" She took a step toward Lexi. "I don't suppose you're going to put that conversation on the official record? It didn't make me out to be the deadbeat you're trying to convince the court I am."

"I don't think you're a deadbeat," Lexi said, sounding almost contrite. "You're not stupid, either. But I have to do my job. The Johnsons—"

"They call the shots, right? You do the dirty work for them, digging up damaging information on me and probably countless other family enemies."

"It's not personal." Lexi's voice was a miserable whisper.

Julia felt a quick stab of sympathy before her temper began to boil over. She was always too gullible, wanting to believe people weren't as bad as they seemed. It led to her being taken advantage of on more than one occasion. Not this time, though.

She had to physically restrain herself from grabbing Lexi's crisp button-down and slamming the petite attorney into one of the metal stalls. "How can you say that? You're helping them take my son away from me. My son!" Tears flooded her eyes and she turned away, once again feeling helpless to stop the inevitable outcome.

"I don't want you to lose your son," Lexi said quietly. "If I had my way…" She paused then added, "Hiding who you are and the reasons you did things isn't going to help your case. You're not the one with the big secrets here."

Julia whirled around. "Are the Johnsons hiding something? Do you have information that could help me keep Charlie?"

Lexi shook her head. "I've said too much." She reached

for the door. "You're a good mother, Julia. But you have to believe it."

Julia followed Lexi into the hall, but before she could catch up a loud crash from down the hall distracted her. She heard a round of shouts and her first thought was of Charlie.

Chaos reigned in the gymnasium as people pushed toward the exits. Julia stood on her tiptoes and scanned the crowd, spotting Joe Callahan with his arm around her mother near the bleachers. Vera held Charlie, who was contentedly spooning ice cream into his mouth, oblivious to the commotion.

Julia elbowed her way through the throng of people to Vera and Joe. "Charlie," she said on a breath, and her son launched himself at her.

"Banilla, Mama."

"I see, sweetie." She hugged him tight against her.

"Why is everyone rushing out of here?" She noticed that many older folks, like Joe and Vera, hung back.

"Big fight outside," someone passing by called. "Eddie Kelton caught his wife in the back of their minivan with his best friend."

"He's going to kill him," the man's companion said with a sick laugh. "Someone said Eddie's got a knife."

Julia grimaced. She'd gone to school with Eddie's older brother. "The Keltons are not a stable bunch," she murmured.

Joe patted her shoulder. "Don't worry, hon. Sam will handle it. I'd be out there but I don't want to leave your mom."

"Such a gentleman."

"Sam?" Julia's heart rate quickened. "Why is Sam out there?"

"Because he's the police chief." Vera spoke slowly, as if Julia were a small child.

"He's not on duty. Shouldn't they call a deputy?"

"Cops are never truly off duty," Joe said with a sigh. "But Sammy can take care of himself."

"Eddie Kelton has a knife." Julia practically jumped up and down with agitation. Her palms were sweating and clammy. Sam could take care of himself, but she couldn't stop her anxiety from spilling over. "This isn't part of the evening's entertainment. It's real life."

Joe nodded. "Being the wife of a law-enforcement officer isn't easy." He patted her shoulder again and she wanted to rip his wrist out of the socket. He pulled his hand away as if he could read her mind. "If it will make you feel better, I'll check on him. I may be rusty but I could handle a couple troublemakers in my day."

Vera gave a dreamy sigh. A muscle above Julia's eye began to twitch.

"I bet you were quite a sight," Vera practically purred.

"You know what would make me feel better? If I go and check on him." She sat Charlie on the bleachers. "Stay here with Grandma, okay, buddy?"

"Gramma," Charlie said around a mouthful.

"I'll escort you," Joe said in the same cop tone Julia'd heard Sam use. "If you're okay for a few minutes on your own?" he asked Vera.

"Be a hero," Vera answered, batting her lashes.

Julia thought about arguing but figured he could be useful. "Can you get me to the front?"

"Yes, ma'am."

He took her elbow and, true to his word, guided her through the groups spilling into the parking lot. Was it some kind of police Jedi mind trick that enabled cops to manage throngs of people?

She poked her head through the row of spectators to see Sam between two men, arms out, a finger pointed at each of them.

Eddie Kelton, his wife, Stacey, and a man Julia didn't recognize stood in the parking lot under the lights. The unknown man had his shirt on inside out and his jeans were half zipped. Julia assumed he was the man Stacey had been with. Another telltale sign was the black eye forming above his cheek.

Stacey stood to one side, weeping loudly into her hands.

"For the last time, Eddie, put the knife down." Sam looked as if he'd grown several inches since Julia had seen him minutes earlier. He was broad and strong, every muscle in his body on full alert. A surge of pride flashed through her, along with the nail-biting fear of seeing him in action.

Eddie Kelton couldn't have been more than five foot seven, a wiry strip of a man, aged beyond his years thanks to working in the sun on a local construction crew. His face sported a bloody nose, busted lip and a large scratch above his left eye. Julia gathered he'd been on the losing end of the fight until he'd brandished the six-inch blade jiggling between his fingers.

"That's my woman, Chief." Eddie's arm trembled. "My wife. He's supposed to be my best friend and he had my wife." Eddie's wild gaze switched to Stacey. "How could you do this to me? I loved you."

She let out a wretched sob. "You don't act like you love me. Always down at the bar after work or passed out on the couch." Her eyes darted around the crowd. "I found the adult movies on the computer. I want someone who wants me. Who pays attention to me. Who makes me feel like a woman and not just the housekeeper."

"I loved you," Eddie screamed.

"It was only—" the half-dressed man began.

"Shut up, Jon-o," Eddie and Stacey yelled at the same time.

Eddie slashed the air with his knife.

Sam held his ground.

Julia held her breath.

"Eddie, I know what you're feeling." Sam's voice was a soothing murmur.

"You don't know squat," Eddie spat out, dancing back and forth on the balls of his feet. "I'm going to cut off his junk here and now."

"Don't you threaten my junk," the other man yelled back. "If you were a real man—"

Sam's head whipped around. "Jon Dallas, shut your mouth or I'm going to arrest you for public indecency." He turned back to Eddie. "I do know. A few years ago I walked in on my brother and my fiancée getting busy on the kitchen table."

A collective gasp went up from the crowd and several heads turned toward Julia. "Not me," she whispered impatiently. "His ex."

Sam's gaze never left Eddie, so she had no idea if he realized she was there.

Eddie's bloodshot eyes brimmed with tears. "It gets you right here," he said, thumping his chest with the hand not gripping the knife. "Like she reached in and cut out your heart."

Sam nodded. "You're not going to make anything better with the knife. Drop it and we'll talk about what's next."

"I'm sorry, Eddie." Stacey's voice was so filled with anguish Julia almost felt sorry for her. Except for the small matter that she'd been caught cheating on her husband. "I made a horrible mistake. It didn't mean anything."

"Hey—" Jon-o sputtered.

"I love you, Eddie." Stacey sobbed.

Eddie lowered the knife but Sam didn't relax. "Drop it and kick it to me," he ordered. "She loves you, Eddie."

"I love her, too." Eddie's voice was miserable. "But she cheated."

"We didn't even do it," Stacey called, and Julia wished the woman understood the concept of *too much information*. "He was drunk. Couldn't get it—"

Jon-o took an angry step toward her. "Shut your fat mouth, you liar. I was the best—"

For a second, Sam's attention switched to Jon-o and Stacey. In that instant, Eddie launched himself forward.

He lunged for Jon-o but Sam grabbed his arm. Julia screamed as Eddie stabbed wildly at Sam, who knocked the blade out of the man's hand then slammed him to the ground. Pete Butler, Sam's deputy, rushed forward and tossed Sam a pair of handcuffs before turning his attention to Jon-o, pushing him away from the action.

Stacey melted into a puddle on the ground. "Eddie, no," she whimpered. "Don't put handcuffs on my husband."

Sam got Eddie to his feet.

"Don't worry, honey." Stacey took a step forward. "I'll bail you out. I love you so much."

Tears ran down Eddie's face. "I love you, sugar-buns."

Stacey would have wrapped herself around her husband but Sam held up a hand. "Later, Stacey." Jon-o disappeared into the crowd and Sam yanked Eddie toward Pete. "Put him in the holding cell overnight. He can sober up."

Pete pointed to Sam's shoulder. Sam shook his head, so the deputy led Eddie toward the waiting squad car.

"We're done out here," Sam announced to the crowd. "Everyone head inside. There's a lot more money to be raised tonight."

After a quiet round of applause, people drifted toward

the gymnasium. A couple of men approached Sam, slapping him on the back.

"I told you he'd handle it," Joe said proudly from Julia's side.

"You did." Julia felt rooted to the spot where she stood. Her body felt as though it weighed a thousand pounds. She couldn't explain what she'd felt when Eddie had rushed at Sam with the knife. She'd swear she'd aged ten years in those few seconds.

"Nice going, son," Joe called.

Sam looked up and his gaze met Julia's. He gave her a small smile and her whole body began to shake. She walked toward him and threw her arms around his neck, burying her face in his shirt collar. He smelled sweet, like leftover cotton candy, and felt so undeniably strong, she could have wept. She wouldn't cry. She wasn't that much of an emotional basket case, but she squeezed her eyes shut for good measure.

She willed the trembling to stop. It started to as he rubbed his palm against her back.

"Hey," he said into her hair. "Not that I'm complaining about you wrapped around me, but it's okay. It was nothing. Eddie was too drunk to do any real damage, even if he'd wanted to."

She didn't know how long he held her. She was vaguely aware of people milling about, of Joe watching from nearby. Sam didn't seem in any hurry to let her go. She needed the strength of his body around hers to reassure her that he was truly all right.

When she was finally in control enough to open her eyes, she was shocked to see blood staining his shirt near the shoulder. "You're hurt." Her voice came out a croak.

He shook his head. "The blade nicked me. It's a scratch.

I'll stop by the hospital after we finish the paperwork to have it cleaned. Nothing more."

"He could have hurt you," she whispered, unable to take her eyes off his shoulder.

He tipped up her chin. His eyes were warm on hers, kind and understanding. "I'm okay. Nothing happened."

"It could have. Every day something *could* happen to you, Sam. Drug busts, drunken fights and who knows what else."

"I'm fine."

"I'm not. I can't stand knowing you're always at risk."

He looked over her shoulder to where Joe stood. When his eyes met hers again, they were cold and unreadable. He leaned in close to her ear. "Then it's a good thing this is a fake engagement. I'm not giving up my life for a woman."

Julia felt the air rush from her lungs. "I didn't say I wanted you to." She grabbed on to the front of his shirt as he moved to pull away. "I know this is fake. Sue me, but I was worried. Heaven forbid someone cares about you, Sam. Expects something from you. Maybe I shouldn't have—"

"Forget it." Sam kissed her cheek, but she knew it was because his father was still watching. "I have to go into the station and then to the hospital, so I'll be a while. Take Charlie home. We'll talk tomorrow."

"Don't do this," she whispered as he walked away, climbing into the police cruiser without looking back.

She knew this was fake. Because she'd never be stupid enough to fall in love with a man so irritating, annoying and unwilling to have a meaningful conversation about his feelings.

She turned to Joe. "At least he's okay. That's most important, right?"

"It's hard for him to be needed by someone," Joe said,

taking her arm and leading her back toward the high school.

Julia snorted. "Ya think?"

Rotating his shoulder where the nurse had cleaned his wound, Sam stepped out of the E.R. into the darkness. His father's car wasn't in front, so he sat on the bench near the entrance to wait.

He scrubbed his palms against his face, wondering how he'd made such a colossal mess of a night that had started off so well. Julia had looked beautiful, as always, and they'd had fun with Charlie at the carnival. He'd even survived his dad and her mother meeting and almost felt okay about her relationship with Ethan.

Then he'd put his foot in his mouth in a thousand different ways when she'd been concerned about his job. Hell, he couldn't name a cop's wife who didn't worry. He'd liked that she'd been worried, liked the feeling of being needed. It had also scared him and he'd pushed her away.

Like he pushed everyone away.

He was alone. Again. As always.

"Need a lift, Chief?"

He turned to see her standing a few feet away, the light from the hospital's entrance making her glow like an angel. Not that he knew whether angels glowed. He imagined they'd want to, if it meant they'd look like Julia Morgan.

"My dad's coming to get me. Where's Charlie?"

"He's having a sleepover with Grandma." She walked to the bench and sat next to him. "How's your shoulder?"

He shrugged, finding it difficult to concentrate with her thigh pressed against his leg. "Hurts worse after the nurse messed with it than when the knife grazed me."

She bit her lip when he said the word *knife*. "You're lucky it wasn't worse."

"I guess."

"Joe's not coming to get you."

"I may want to reconsider that ride."

"You may."

"Why are you here, Julia?"

She rocked back far enough to stuff her fingers under her legs. Lucky fingers. He'd give anything to trade places with her hands.

"Just because our engagement isn't real doesn't mean I can't worry about you. I'm human. I like you. Caring about friends is what people do."

"We're friends." He tried the word out in his mind and decided he liked it. Sam didn't have many real friends.

"I think so."

He couldn't resist asking, "With benefits?"

She continued to stare straight ahead but one side of her mouth kicked up. "That remains to be seen. You're not moving in the right direction with the bad 'tude earlier."

"Would it help if I said I was sorry?"

"Are you?"

With one finger, he traced a path down her arm, gently tugging on her wrist until she lifted her hand. He intertwined his fingers with hers. "Yes, I'm sorry. I'm sorry you were scared. I'm sorry I was a jerk."

"I know you don't owe me anything."

"I do owe you. So far, I'm the only one who's benefited from our arrangement. You wouldn't let me go to court with you. I made an enormous mess of trying to get your mind off the case and now you're here picking me up. What have I done to help you? Nothing."

"That's not true."

"It is. I want to help. I'm going to the final hearing with you."

"I—"

"No arguments."

She nodded. That was a start. "We can get people to submit affidavits on your behalf," he continued. "Character references for you. The girls from the salon will do it. I bet Ida Garvey would, too, now that her hair isn't bright pink. I want to hear you agree. I can help. You have to let me."

"My LD changes everything." She looked at him, her eyes fierce. He knew this moment meant something big.

"You have trouble reading," he said slowly. "And with numbers. It caused a lot of problems but you told me you're working with a specialist."

"My brain doesn't work right." She made the statement with conviction, as if daring him to disagree.

"Is that the clinical diagnosis? Your brain doesn't work right? I don't think so, sweetie."

"Don't 'sweetie' me. I'm stupid, and Jeff and his family know it. My brain is broken. It takes me twice as long as it should to read a simple letter. Why do you think I bring paperwork home from the salon so often? I spend all night checking and rechecking my work so I don't make mistakes."

"Everyone makes mistakes."

"You don't understand. But Jeff does. He knows how badly I want this to stay a secret." She bolted up from the bench, pacing back and forth in front of him. "So much of what the attorney is talking about stems from my LD. I've hidden it for years and now they're using it against me."

"Why keep it a secret?"

"Because—" she dragged out the word on a ragged breath "—if the people around me knew how dumb I am, they could and would take advantage of me. In Brevia, I can hide it. If I really get into a bind, my mom or Lainey can help. I don't want the whole town talking about it."

Something struck a chord deep within Sam. He knew

what it was like to put on a mask so people couldn't really see what was inside of you. He knew how it felt to be afraid you wouldn't measure up. But his demons were more easily buried than Julia's. The thought of how much time and energy she'd put into hiding this piece of herself made his heart ache.

She was smart, proud and brave. She'd spent years making everyone believe she didn't care, when the reality was that she cared more than she could admit. He could see it on her face, see the tension radiating through her body as she waited for him to judge her the way she'd been judging herself for years.

He stood and cupped her face between his hands. "You're not stupid."

She searched his eyes, as if willing the words to be true. "They're trying to use it against me, Sam. To prove that Charlie would be better off with them. Not only are they ready to lavish him with their version of lifestyles of the rich and famous, they're saying that if he has the same disorder…" Her voice caught and she bit her lip before continuing, "If I've given this to him, they have the resources to get him the best help."

"*You* are what's best for him." He used his thumb to wipe away a lone tear that trailed down her cheek then brought his lips to the spot, tasting the salt on her skin.

The automatic doors slid open and a hospital worker pushed a wheelchair into the night.

"Let's get out of here," Sam whispered.

Julia nodded, and he cradled her against him as they walked to her car.

"Let me drive," he said when she reached into her purse for the keys.

"You're the injured one." But when he took the keys from her hand, she didn't argue.

The streets were quiet. Julia didn't speak, but she held on to the hand he placed in her lap. He could imagine the thoughts running through her mind as she realized the secret she'd held close for so long was about to become public. She was wrung out emotionally, and he hated seeing it. All he wanted was to make her feel better, if only for a few moments.

He pulled into his driveway and turned off the ignition.

"I should go home," she said, releasing his fingers. "You need to rest."

Rest was the last thing on Sam's mind. He might not be a master with words but he knew he wasn't going to let her go tonight. If he couldn't tell her how amazing she was and have her believe it, he could damn well show her.

He came around to open her car door and draw her out, lacing his fingers with hers once again.

"I need to go," she repeated, her voice small.

Without a word, he led her up onto the porch and unlocked his front door. He turned and pulled her to him, slanting his mouth over hers. For a moment she froze, then she melted against him, the spark between them flaring into an incendiary fire.

He kissed her jaw and the creamy skin of her throat, whispering, "Stay with me."

She nodded as he nipped at her earlobe and, not letting her go, reached back to push open the door and drag them both through. He kicked it shut and tugged on the hem of her T-shirt.

"This. Off. Now."

"Bossy," she said breathlessly. Through his desire, he heard the confidence return to her tone and was so glad for it, he could have laughed out loud.

Just as suddenly, he couldn't make a sound as she pulled the soft cotton over her head and was left bathed in moonlight wearing only a lacy black bra and jeans slung low on her hips.

Sweet mercy.

He knew she was beautiful, but he'd been with beautiful women before. Watching her watch him, though, her eyes smoky and wanting, was almost his undoing.

He flicked one thin strap off her shoulder, then the other, not quite exposing her completely but giving him a view of more creamy flesh. He traced the line of fabric across the tops of her breasts and his body grew heavy at her intake of breath.

She wrapped her hand around his finger and lifted it to her mouth, kissing the tip softly. "You, now," she commanded, her voice husky.

Sam was happy to comply, and he threw his shirt onto the nearby couch. She stepped forward and, in one fluid motion, reached behind her to unhook her bra. It fell to the floor between them. Then she pressed herself against his chest and trailed her lips over his wounded shoulder.

"If it matters," he said, his voice hoarse, "that's not the part that hurts."

He felt her smile against him. "We'll get to that. All in good time, Chief. All in good time."

From Sam's point of view, that time was now. He bent his head and took her mouth, kissing her as he reached between them to unfasten her jeans. He dropped to his knees in front of her, kissing the curve of her belly. She smelled like sin and sunshine, and the mix made him dizzy with need.

"I want you, Julia Morgan." He lifted his head so he could look into her eyes. "I want you," he repeated. "All of you. Just the way you are."

Her lips parted, and he saw trust and vulnerability flash in her eyes. He wanted that, wanted all of this. For the first time in his life, he wanted to be a man someone could depend on for the long haul.

He wanted to be a real hero.

"I'm going to take care of you," he whispered.

She smiled at him and shimmied her hips so that her jeans slipped off them.

"What are you waiting for?" she asked, and he straightened, capturing her mouth again.

Sam broke the kiss long enough to lead her the few steps to the couch. He stripped off his jeans then eased his body over hers, relishing the feel of skin on skin. She fit perfectly under him, as he'd guessed she would.

He savored every touch, taking the time to explore her body with his fingers and mouth. Her answering passion filled him with a desire he'd never imagined before tonight. He finally made her his, entering her with an exquisite slowness before his need for her took over and they moved together in a perfect rhythm.

"You are amazing," he whispered as he held her gaze.

"You're not so bad yourself," she answered, but her eyes were cloudy with passion.

"I'm going to prove how very good I am." He smiled then nipped at the soft skin of her earlobe. "All night long."

Chapter Eleven

Wow.

Hours later, Julia's brain registered that one syllable.

"Wow," Sam murmured against her hair, clearly still trying to catch his breath.

She knew the feeling. She'd had good sex in her life—maybe even great a couple of times. This night had blown away her every expectation about what intimacy felt like when it was exactly right. She wanted to believe it was because she'd been on a long hiatus.

If she admitted the truth, Sam had been worth a two-year wait. Her body felt boneless, as if she never wanted to move from where she lay stretched across him, the short hair on his chest tickling her bare skin.

The unfamiliar feeling of contentment jolted her back into reality. Their relationship was precarious enough, sometimes hot and often cold enough to give her frost-bite. He challenged her, irritated her and filled her with such incredible need, she wondered how she'd walk away when the business part of their arrangement was over.

That sobering thought in mind, she rolled off him. He automatically tucked the light duvet in around her. They'd made it to his bedroom.

Eventually.

After the couch in his living room. And the stairs. The stairs? She hadn't even known that was possible, let alone that it would be downright amazing.

It was still dark and she couldn't make out much more than the outlines of furniture around the room and the fact that his bed was enormous. It suited him.

She glanced at the glowing numbers of the digital clock on the nightstand next to the bed. He shifted, propping himself on one elbow and wrapping the other arm around her waist.

"Don't go."

She tilted her head away, his face in shadow from the moonlight slanting through the bedroom window. She couldn't see his eyes and hoped hers were hidden, as well.

How did he know she was getting ready to bolt? Julia had never been much of a cuddler. The emotional boundaries she put around herself often manifested in physical limits, as well.

She looked at the ceiling. Even if she couldn't see his eyes, she knew his gaze was intense. "As fun as this was…"

His soft chuckle rumbled in the quiet, making her insides tingle again. She'd done a lot of tingling tonight.

"Fun," he repeated.

"We've got chemistry."

He laughed again.

"This isn't funny." She didn't want to make more of this than it was. She'd start talking and end up embarrassing herself with romantic declarations about how much she liked—more than liked, if she admitted the truth—being with Sam, both in the bedroom and out of it. He was the first man she felt wanted her for her, not what she looked like or an image she portrayed. It was both liberating and frightening to reveal her true self to someone.

"*You're* funny." He kissed the tip of her nose and pulled her tighter against the length of him. "And smart." He kissed one cheek. "And sexy as hell." Then the other. "I want you to spend the night." His lips met hers.

She broke the kiss. "I think we've about wrapped things up here."

He traced the seam of her mouth with his tongue. "We've only gotten started."

Julia felt her resolve disappear. She knew it was a mistake but she couldn't make her body move an inch. "Are you sure?"

"I've never been more sure."

It had been ages since Julia'd wanted to be with someone as much as she did Sam. "I guess that would be okay."

"Okay?" He tickled her belly and she wriggled in response.

"More than okay."

"That's what I thought."

She expected him to kiss her again, but instead he snuggled in behind her, smoothing her hair across the pillow.

"Sleep," he told her.

"Oh. I thought you wanted to…"

"I do. Later."

Her spine stiffened. "I've never been much for spooning."

"I can tell." His finger drew circles along her back until she began to relax. "Why did you pick me up tonight?"

"I don't like pillow talk, either," she muttered, and he laughed again.

He didn't press her for more, just continued to trace patterns along her skin. The silence was companionable, the room still and soft in the night. She stretched her head against the pillow, relishing the feeling of being surrounded by Sam. His scent lingered in the sheets, the combination of outdoors and spice that continued to make her head spin.

"Okay," she said after a few minutes, "I kind of get why all those women were hung up on you."

"What women?"

She lightly jabbed her elbow into his stomach. "Your Three Strikes Sam fan club. You're pretty good at this stuff."

"Only with you."

"I don't believe that."

"No changing the subject. I was a jerk tonight. You gave me another chance. Thank you."

She took a deep breath. "I can use all the help I can get. There's no use hiding it."

"You shouldn't hide anything," he said softly.

"I saw Lexi Preston at the carnival."

"Your ex's attorney?"

"She was there checking up on me, I think. Lots of stories to be dished from my former frenemies." She gave a sad laugh. "Lexi thinks they wouldn't be so hard on me now if they'd known what I was dealing with back then."

"Maybe you wouldn't be so hard on yourself if you told the truth," Sam suggested.

"Could be," she said with a yawn. It had been a long day. A light shiver ran through her and he pulled her closer. "Good Lord, you're a furnace." She snuggled in closer. "My own personal space heater."

"Whatever you need me to be," Sam agreed.

That was the last thing Julia heard him say before she drifted off to sleep.

She woke a few hours later and they made love again in the hazy predawn light. His eyes never left hers as they moved together, and Julia knew this night changed what was between them, even if they both acted as though it didn't.

She'd wanted him since the first time she'd laid eyes on him, no matter how much she tried to deny it. Now that she knew how good it could be, she wasn't sure how she'd ever adjust back to real life. She had to, she reminded herself, even as she snuggled in closer to him. This night was a fringe benefit of their business arrangement, and if she let herself forget that, she knew she'd lose her heart along the way.

"You're finally ready to get back into action?"

Sam ripped open a sugar packet and dumped it into his coffee. "I haven't been sitting on a beach sipping fruity drinks for the past couple of years."

"You know what I mean."

He watched his brother shovel another bite of pancakes into his mouth. Scott always could eat like a horse. Not that Scott was a kid anymore. He was twenty-nine and a good two inches taller than Sam's six feet. They both had the Callahan blue eyes and linebacker build, but Scott had their mother's olive coloring and dark hair. Sometimes a look or gesture from Scott could bring back a memory of their mom so vividly it was as if she was still with them.

"I'm glad you called me." Scott downed the rest of his orange juice and signaled the waitress for another. "I felt real bad about what happened."

"About having sex with my fiancée?"

Scott flinched. "Pretty much. Although you have to know by now I wasn't the first."

Sam gave a curt nod. "I'm still not going to thank you, if that's what you're getting at."

"I'm not."

"I didn't come here to talk about Jenny or rehash the past."

"Dad called last week. He told me you're engaged again."

Sam looked out the window of the café into the sunny morning. He'd met Scott in a town halfway between Brevia and D.C., far enough away that he wouldn't see any familiar faces. It had been almost a week since the night of the carnival. He'd seen Julia and Charlie almost every day. Sometimes it was under the guise of making their relationship look real. He'd taken them to lunch and to a neighboring playground, stopped by the salon when he had a break during the day.

He was happiest when it was just the three of them. He'd pick up dinner after his shift, or she'd cook and they'd take the dog for a walk, and then he'd help get Charlie ready for bed. They agreed if he was going to be a presence at the mediation or future court dates, it would be smart for Charlie to feel comfortable with him.

Sam hadn't expected how much playing family would fill up the empty parts of him. He counted the hours each day until he could lift Charlie in his arms and even more the moments until he could pull Julia to him.

He took another drink of coffee then answered, "It's complicated. But I'm engaged."

Complicated might be the understatement of the century where Julia was concerned. She'd opened up to him and shared her deepest secret. She trusted him with her son, her dreams for the future, and it scared him to death. He steered their conversations away from the topic of his work, no matter how often she asked about details of his day.

After the scene at the carnival, he didn't want to see

worry in her gaze or argue about the risks he took. It reminded him too much of his parents. Even so, he knew he was going to go through hell when their arrangement was finished. He'd called Scott last week and set up this meeting to talk about a new job away from Brevia, but now his purpose was twofold.

"I need some information on a family from Ohio, very prominent in the area. Dennis and Maria Johnson."

"What kind of information?" Scott asked.

"Whatever you've got. My fiancée, Julia, has a kid with their son and they're making waves with the current custody arrangement. They've got a lot of money and influence and are pulling out the stops to make her life hell. From my experience, people who want to throw their weight around like that have done it before. I'm guessing they have some skeletons from past skirmishes. I want to know what they are."

Scott nodded. "I've got a couple of friends up there. I'll make a call, see what I can find out." He stabbed another bite of pancake then pointed his fork at Sam. "This Julia must be special. You always play by the rule book. It's not like you to fight dirty."

"I'm fighting to win. There's too much at stake not to."

"I'd like to meet her."

Sam felt his whole body tense. His voice lowered to a controlled growl. "Stay away from her, Scott. She isn't like Jenny."

Scott held up his hands, palms up. "I get it. I get it."

The waitress brought a second juice and refilled Sam's coffee. Scott winked at her and she practically tripped backing away from the table.

Sam wanted to roll his eyes. "I see you haven't changed. Still chasing tail all over the place?"

"Why mess with a system that works so damn well? I'm

happy. The ladies are happy. All good. I wasn't cut out for commitment." He lifted one eyebrow. "Until I got Dad's call, I would have guessed you weren't, either."

"Dad thinks love makes the world go round."

"Dad's gone soft and it gives me the creeps."

"Amen to that."

"When you texted, you asked about openings at headquarters." Scott had worked for the U.S. Marshals Service since he'd gotten out of the army.

Sam took a drink of coffee. "You got anything?" It had been easy to imagine a future in Brevia when he'd only been the police chief, before it had started to really feel like home. Before Julia.

Scott nodded. "Maybe, but I don't get it. Why do you want to look at a new job if you're getting married? Being a cop is tough enough on a relationship. The Marshals Service would be the kiss of death. What we do doesn't compute with the minivan lifestyle."

"I told you, it's complicated."

"You're gonna run," Scott said, his voice quiet.

"I'm not running anywhere." Sam felt pressure build behind his eyes. Despite being younger, wild and reckless, Scott always had an uncanny ability to read Sam. It drove him nuts. "You said yourself the Callahans aren't meant for commitment. It may be a matter of time before she sees that. It'll be easier on us both if I'm not around for the fallout."

Scott nodded. "That's more like the brother I know and love. For a minute I thought Dad had brainwashed you with all his hug-it-out bull. Do you know he called my boss to see if he could do a seminar on using emotional intelligence in the field?"

"What's emotional intelligence?"

"Beats me," Scott said with a shrug. "But I'm sure as

hell not interested in finding out. Did you fill out the paperwork I sent you?"

Sam slid an envelope across the table. "It's got my résumé with it."

"We'd be lucky to have you," Scott said solemnly. "I'd be honored to work together."

Sam's phone buzzed, alerting him that he had a voicemail message. Coverage was spotty in this area, so he wasn't sure when the call had come in. He looked at his phone and saw six messages waiting.

"We did have some good times," he admitted as he punched the keypad to retrieve them. He wasn't on duty, so he couldn't imagine why anyone would need him so urgently.

"Here's to many more." Scott lifted his juice glass in a toast.

Sam listened to the first message and felt the blood drain from his face. He stood, tossing a twenty on the table. "I need to go."

"Everything okay?" Scott asked, mopping up syrup with his last bite of pancake.

Sam was already out the door.

Chapter Twelve

Sam was about forty-five minutes from Brevia. He made it to the hospital in less than thirty.

"Charlie Morgan," he said to the woman at the front desk of the E.R., and she pointed to a room halfway down the hall. He stopped to catch his breath then pushed open the door.

A nurse stood talking to Julia as Vera held Charlie in her lap on the bed. A bright blue cast covered the boy's left wrist.

All three women looked up as Sam walked in. Julia stood so stiff he imagined she might crack in half if he touched her. The urge to ease some of her worry engulfed him.

"Sam," Charlie said, a little groggily, waving his casted arm.

"Hey, buddy." Sam came forward and bent down in front of the boy. "I like your new super arm."

Charlie giggled softly and reached out for Sam to hold him. Vera's eyes widened but she let Sam scoop him up. With Charlie in his arms, he turned to Julia.

"Are you okay?" he asked, wrapping his free arm around her shoulders.

She nodded but remained tense. "The nurse is giving me discharge papers. We've been here for over two hours." Her eyes searched his. "I couldn't reach you."

"I'm sorry," he said simply. "I was out of cell range."

She looked as if she wanted to say more but the nurse cleared her throat. "I've got instructions on bathing him with the cast," she said, holding out a slip of paper. "Take a look and let me know if you have questions."

Gingerly, Julia took the piece of paper. She stared at it, her forehead puckering as her mouth tightened into a thin, frustrated line.

Vera rose to stand beside him. Julia looked up and met his gaze, her eyes miserable. He tugged the paper from her fingers. "Why don't you go over what we need to do?" he said to the nurse. "Just to be on the safe side. We'll take the instructions home, too."

As the woman explained the procedure, Sam felt Vera squeeze his shoulder. "Thank you," she whispered then slipped out of the room.

When the nurse finished her explanation, Julia asked a couple of questions, and then the woman left them alone. Charlie's head drooped on Sam's shoulder and his eyes drifted shut.

"I can take him," Julia said, holding out her hands but keeping her gaze focused on her son.

"I've got him." Sam tipped her chin up so she had to look him in the eye. "I'm sorry, Jules. I'm sorry I wasn't here."

"You don't owe us anything." She picked up the diaper bag from the chair next to the bed. "I want to go home."

Sam followed her into the hall and toward the elevator. She didn't say a word until they were in the parking lot. "I shouldn't have called you. We're not your problem." She took Charlie and settled him in the car seat.

"I'm sorry," Sam said again. A warm breeze played with the ends of her hair. Spring was in full swing in the Smoky Mountains. He wondered how old Charlie needed to be to hold a tiny fishing rod. There were so many things he wanted to do with her and Charlie before their time together ended. Before she figured out she should have never depended on him in the first place. He couldn't stand the thought that today might be the first nail in his coffin. "I know you were scared. I wish I had been here earlier."

She jerked her head in response and he saw tears fill her eyes. "I put the toy car together—one of those ones a toddler pushes around." She swiped at her cheeks. "I swear I followed the directions, but when he knocked it against the kitchen table, it fell apart. Charlie went down over it and landed on his arm. His scream was the worst sound I've ever heard."

Sam wrapped his arms around her. "It was an accident. Not your fault."

She let him hold her but stayed ramrod straight, obviously trying to manage her fear and anxiety. "It *was* my fault. I'm sure I read the directions wrong and Charlie got hurt because of it. Because of me!"

She yanked away from him, pacing next to the car. "Maybe the Johnsons are doing the right thing." Her eyes searched his. "I felt like an idiot when the nurse gave me his discharge papers. Do you know how long it takes me to figure out the right dose of medicine for him? How many things I have to memorize and hope I don't mess up? He's still a baby, Sam. What's going to happen when he gets into school and needs help with his homework? When he wants me to read real books to him? He's going to know his mother is stupid."

"Stop it." Sam grabbed her wrists and pulled her to him, forcing her to look up at him. "Learning disabilities don't make you stupid."

"You don't know how people have looked at me my whole life. It will kill me if Charlie someday looks at me like that." She took a deep, shuddering breath and Sam felt the fight go out of her.

"He's not going to, Julia. He's going to see you like I do. Like your family does. Like a brave, intelligent, fearless woman who doesn't let anything hold her back."

"Really?" She gave him a sad smile. "Because I don't see anyone around here who fits your description." She shrugged out of his embrace and opened the door of her car. "I need to get him home. Thanks for coming, Sam."

"I'll meet you at your apartment."

"You don't need to—"

"I'm going to pick up dinner and a change of clothes and I'll be there within the hour. For once, don't argue with me. Please."

She nodded. "Nice touch with the *please*."

He watched her drive away then headed to his own car. He had to make Julia see how much she had to offer her son. That was the key to her winning the custody battle, no matter what crazy accusations her ex-boyfriend's family threw out. If he could make her believe in herself, he knew she was strong enough to overcome any odds.

She'd win and he'd get the hell out of her life. His heart was lacking what it took to give her the life she deserved. He knew for certain that if she got too close to him, he'd only hurt her and Charlie. Just like he had today.

Sam was like a tin man, without a real heart. He might have been born with one but it had shriveled into nothing when his mother died. He couldn't risk loving and being hurt like that again.

Julia was standing over Charlie's crib when the doorbell rang. Casper growled softly from his place next to her.

"No bark," she whispered, amazed at how the dog seemed to know to keep quiet while Charlie was asleep.

She padded to the door.

"How's Charlie?" Sam asked when she opened it.

She nodded and stepped back. "Sleeping soundly."

Casper gave Sam a full-tooth grin and wagged his stubby tail. "No home for this guy yet?" Sam asked, reaching down to scratch behind the dog's ears. "You need to learn to keep your choppers hidden, buddy."

"I'm adopting him."

Sam's eyebrows rose. "Kind of a small place for a big dog."

"Charlie loves him." She didn't want to admit how much of her decision was based on her need to make something work, even if it was rescuing a stray animal. She took the carryout bag from his hand and turned for the kitchen.

Sam grabbed her around the waist and pulled her against him. "You've got a sharp tongue but a soft heart," he whispered against her ear.

"Wicked elbow, too," she said and jabbed him in the stomach.

He grunted a laugh and released her. "Why is it you don't want people to see how much you care?"

She busied herself pulling plates out of the cabinet. "I care about Charlie. That's enough for me."

"Ida Garvey told me you volunteered to do hair for the middle-school dance team's competition next month."

"Did you see those girls last year? It was updo à la light socket. I know Southerners love big hair but jeez." She set the table and took out the food. "Is this from Carl's?"

"Double burgers with cheese. Hope you approve."

"Perfect."

"I also heard you go to the retirement home once a week and do the ladies' hair."

She shrugged. "A lot of those gals were once customers at the Hairhouse, and their daughters and granddaughters still are. It's good for my business."

"It's because you care."

Why was Sam giving her the third degree on her volunteer hours? "You're making too much of it. I do things that benefit me. Ask anyone around here. I have a long history of being in it for myself."

"That's what you want people to believe."

"That *is* what they believe." She picked up a fry and pointed it at him, feeling her temper starting to rise. "What does it matter?"

He folded himself into the seat across from her. "I want you to understand you're not alone. You have a community here that would rally around you if you gave them a chance."

She took a bite of burger, her eyes narrowing. What the hell did Sam Callahan know about her part in this community? "Are you seriously giving me a lecture on letting people in, Mr. I-am-a-rock-I-am-an-island? You could take your own advice."

He frowned. "I'm a part of this community."

"No, you're not. You circle around the perimeter and insert yourself when someone needs a helping hand. No one really understands how much you give or the toll it takes on you. You're always 'on.' You're terrified of being alone with your empty soul, so you spend a little time with a woman. You get her to fall in love with you so you can hold on to the affection without having to offer any in return. People know what kind of cookies you like, so their single daughters can bake you a batch. But you're as closed off as I am in your own way."

He got up from the table so quickly she thought he was going to storm out. Instead, he grabbed two beers from her fridge, opened them and handed one to her. "We're quite a pair," he said softly, clinking the top of his bottle against hers. "Both so damned independent we'd rather fake an engagement than actually deal with real feelings."

"It's better that way," she answered and took a long drink.

"I used to think so," he said, and his eyes were so intense on hers she lost her breath for a moment. "Do you ever wonder what it would feel like to let someone in?"

She didn't need to because she already had, with him.

Oh, no. Where had that thought come from?

It was true. Without realizing it or intending to, Julia had let Sam not only into her life but into her heart, as well.

She was in love with him.

She stood, gripping the edge of the counter as if it was the only solid thing in her world. She'd called him today when Charlie had gotten hurt before she'd even called her mother. She loved him and she needed him. Julia didn't know which scared her more.

They had a deal, and she was pretty sure Sam was the type of guy who kept his word. He'd help her get through the custody battle as much as he could, but that didn't mean… It didn't mean what her heart wanted it to.

"I don't have room to let anyone in but Charlie," she said in the most casual tone she could muster. "There's not enough of me left for anyone else to hold on to. Everything I can give belongs to him."

"I never had that much to begin with," Sam said from the table.

When Julia felt as if she could turn around without revealing her true emotions, she smiled at him. "That's why we're a perfect match. Hollow to the core."

Sam tossed her a sexy smile. "I know a good way to fill the void."

She tried to ignore the flash of electricity that raced along her spine at the suggestion in his words. "It's been a long day."

He stood and she wrapped her arms around her waist. "Really long."

"It could be an even longer night if you play your cards right."

She couldn't help the grin that spread across her face. "The only game I play is Old Maid."

"I'll teach you."

"No, thanks."

He reached out his hand, palm up, but didn't touch her. "You want to be alone tonight? Say the word and I'll go. I'm not going to push you." One side of his mouth quirked. "No matter how much you want me to."

She shut her eyes, a war raging inside of her. Letting him go was the smart thing to do, the best way to protect what little hold she still had on her heart.

"Tell me to go, Julia."

"Stay," she whispered and found herself enveloped in his arms, his mouth pressed hard on hers. Their tongues mingled and she let her hands slide up his back, underneath his shirt, reveling in the corded muscles that tightened at her touch.

"You feel like heaven," he said as he trailed kisses along her throat, her skin igniting hotter at every touch.

"Bedroom," she said on a ragged breath. "Now."

She gave a small squeak as he lifted her into his arms as if she weighed nothing. It felt good to be swept off her feet, even for the few moments he carried her down the hall.

She glanced at the door to Charlie's room. She hadn't had a man in her bed since she'd gotten pregnant with her son. It felt new and strange.

"It's going to be a challenge," Sam whispered.

"What?"

"Keeping you quiet with what I have planned."

"Oh." Her heart skipped a beat at the promise in his voice.

He laid her across the bed then followed her down, kissing her until her senses spun with desire.

"Too many clothes." She tugged on his shirt.

He stood, pulling the T-shirt over his head and shrugging out of his faded cargo shorts. Julia's breath caught again. His body was perfect, muscles rippling—actually rippling—as he bent forward and caught the waistband of her shorts with two fingers. She lifted herself to meet him as he undressed her, sliding his soft fingers across her skin.

She tried to speed their pace but Sam wouldn't have it, taking his time to explore every inch of her. He murmured endearments against her flesh, making it impossible for her to keep her emotions out of the equation.

When he finally entered her, Julia practically hummed with desire. They moved together, climbing to the highest peaks of ecstasy.

Later, as he held her, she tried to convince herself that it was only a physical connection, but her heart burned for him as much as her body did.

When she finally woke, light poured through the curtains. Julia glanced at the clock then bounded out of bed and across the hall. Charlie never slept past seven and it was already nine-thirty. Panic gripped her.

Her son's crib was empty. She heard voices in the kitchen and took a deep breath. Sam sat at the table next to Charlie's high chair, giving him spoonfuls of oatmeal.

Charlie waved his sippy cup when he saw her, squealing with delight. Casper trotted up, another big grin spread across his face.

Julia noticed the two paper coffee cups on the counter.

Sam followed her gaze. "We took the dog out to do his business and grabbed coffee and muffins. Charlie picked blueberry for you."

She dropped a kiss on Charlie's forehead. "How do you feel, sweet boy?" she asked, and he babbled a response to her. Her fingers brushed over the cast on his arm, but he didn't seem bothered by it. She sent up a silent prayer of thanks that he was okay.

She turned to Sam, who looked rumpled, sleepy and absolutely irresistible as he stirred the soupy oatmeal with a plastic spoon. "What time did he get up?"

"I heard him talking to himself around sunrise-thirty," he said with a smile.

Julia grimaced. "He's an early riser. You should have woken me."

"You were sleeping soundly. I figure you don't get too many mornings off, so…"

"Thanks." She leaned down to kiss him, and he pulled her between his thighs into a quick hug. "For everything. This morning and last night."

"More," Charlie yelled, and Sam shifted so he could give the boy another bite.

Julia stepped to the counter and took a long drink of coffee, and then she dug in the bag for a muffin.

This was too easy, she thought, as she watched Sam make faces at Charlie while he fed him, her son laughing and playing peekaboo with his cup. It felt too right. This was what she wanted, for Charlie and for herself. A family. This was what she'd never have with Sam. He'd made it clear to her that he didn't want a family. Now or ever. The thought was like a swift kick to her gut.

"I should get ready," she said, realizing her tone must have been too harsh when he glanced at her, a question in his eyes.

"I can stay while you shower," he offered.

She wanted to refuse. She knew she should push him out of her house and her life before it became harder to think of letting him go. But that would give too much away. Whether it was Old Maid or some other game, Julia did one thing well: playing her cards close to the vest.

"That would be great." She headed for the bathroom. By the time she was out, Sam had dressed, made her bed and cleaned up the kitchen. Charlie sat watching *Sesame Street,* cuddled with Casper on the couch as Sam leaned against the back of it.

"When is the next meeting?"

She sighed. "Two days from now."

"I'll drive with you."

She nodded, unable to put into words what that meant to her.

"My dad left a message this morning. He wants to take us to dinner tonight."

"I can do that."

"Along with your mom."

"Uh-oh."

"You can say that again. If those two are plotting…"

"Do you think they suspect anything?"

He shook his head. "They want to talk about wedding plans."

Julia's stomach lurched. "That's bad."

Sam pushed away from the couch. "We'll make it work. We've come this far."

He brushed his lips against hers, a soft touch but it still made her stomach quiver. "Five-thirty. Do you want me to pick you up?"

"I'll have to get Charlie from the sitter's first. I'll meet you there."

He kissed her again. "Have a good day, Julia."

He made those five little words sound like a caress.

"You, too," she muttered and stepped back.

"I'll see you later, buddy." Sam bent and ruffled Charlie's hair, the gesture so natural Julia felt herself melt all over again.

Charlie's fist popped out of his mouth. "'Bye, Dada," he said, not taking his eyes from the television.

Sam straightened slowly.

"He didn't mean anything," Julia said with a forced laugh, not wanting to reveal how disconcerted she felt.

"I know," Sam said softly.

"He knows you're not his dad. He doesn't even understand what that word means. It's something he sees on TV. A word for men. It isn't—"

"Julia." He cut her off, his hand chopping through the air. "It's okay."

But it wasn't okay. Sam was spooked. She knew by the way he didn't turn to her again. He lifted his hand to wave, and with a stilted "See you later," he was gone.

Chapter Thirteen

Sam was freaked out. He took another drink of his beer and glanced around the crowd at Carl's, reliving the pure terror he'd felt this morning.

In his career as a police officer, he'd had guns and knives pulled on him, dealt with drug dealers, prostitutes and an assortment of random losers. He didn't lose his cool or let his guard down. The danger and risk of the job never rattled him.

But one word from a toddler had shaken him to his core. Charlie'd called him Dada. Although Julia had tried to play it off, he knew that she was affected by it, too. He'd heard it in her tone. Not that he'd been able to do much talking, afraid his voice would crack under the weight of the conflicting emotions warring inside him.

Sam had never planned on being a father. Even when he'd been engaged to Jenny, neither of them had wanted kids. That was one of the things that had made him propose, even when he'd had the nagging sense something wasn't right in their relationship. It wasn't every day a guy found a woman who wasn't itching to have babies.

Sam liked kids, but he knew he didn't have what it took to be a decent father. He lacked the emotional depth to put someone else's needs before his own. He believed he was incapable of feeling something, much like his own father had been after his mother's death.

Charlie made him want to change, to be a better man.

He loved the feeling of that boy cuddled against him, his small head nestled in the crook of Sam's neck. He loved watching him follow the silly dog around and vice versa. He especially loved seeing Julia with Charlie, how happy it made her to be with her son.

He hadn't understood that bond when Charlie was a newborn. When he'd seen Julia with the small bundle after the boy's birth, Sam had run the other way. Part of him might have known instinctively how much he'd want to be a part of their world.

That was impossible. He could help her fight for her son, but he didn't have any more to give. He understood the look in her eyes when she'd thought he was in danger. He remembered the same fear in his mother's eyes each time the phone rang while his father was on duty. Her fear and worry had eventually turned into resentment.

He wouldn't give up who he was and he couldn't ask Julia to be a part of his life. He wouldn't risk what it could do to her. He knew Julia was stronger than his mother had ever been, but the life of cop's wife could wreck the strongest woman, no two ways about it.

He'd miss her like crazy, though. Already he could feel the loss of the two of them and he wasn't even gone.

"Okay, let's do this." Julia sat down at the table, her

posture rigid. Her eyes darted around as if scoping escape routes. "They're not here yet?"

Sam shook his head. "Did you have a good day?" He reached across the table to take her hand but she snatched it away.

"No use for the small talk. Save it for the audience."

Despite the fact she'd never truly been his, Sam wished for the way it had been before this morning, when she'd been unguarded and happy to be with him. He glanced around at the crowded restaurant. "There's always an audience in Brevia. Where's Charlie?"

"His sitter had an appointment, so I had him at the salon this afternoon. Lainey is watching him tonight. I thought…it's simpler without him here. We should limit the amount of time he spends with you. So that he doesn't get too attached and all." Her eyes flashed, daring him to argue with her. She was in full mama-bear mode tonight. It made him want her all the more.

Sam's gut twisted at the thought of not spending time with Charlie. "He's an amazing boy, Julia."

"He's great," she agreed distractedly. Her fingers played with the napkin on the table.

He gave a short laugh. "I didn't realize how quiet my life was until you came along."

She glanced toward the front of the restaurant. "Where do you think they are? I want to get this over with."

"My dad and your mom are coming to discuss wedding plans. You look like you can't stand to be in the same room as me." He extended his ankle and pressed it against her shin. "Relax."

She snatched her leg away, her knee banging on the underside of the table. She grabbed the water glass before it tumbled over. "I can't relax," she said between clenched teeth. "This whole thing was a mistake. You're in our lives temporarily, and now Charlie is developing feelings for you. It has to end, Sam."

He swallowed the panic rising in his throat. "You don't mean tonight?"

"Why not?" she countered. "The sooner the better."

Hell, no, he screamed inside his head.

"I don't think that's prudent at this time, Julia," he told her, his voice calm and measured. "I don't want Charlie hurt, but our business arrangement is helping all of us in the long run. You're so close to a ruling, and my dad should be heading back to Boston within the week. Stick it out, Jules. I promise it'll be worth it."

"Business arrangement," she repeated softly. "You still consider this a business arrangement?"

Something in the way she looked at him made him uneasy, but she had to know what he meant. He was doing this for her benefit—at least that was what he tried to tell himself.

"We talked about it last night. You and I are built the same way, and it isn't for emotional connections. But you can't deny our chemistry, and Charlie is a great kid. We're friends and that doesn't have to change. I provide the stability you need. Don't throw it away now."

She bit down on her lip and studied him, as if trying to gain control of her emotions. "I can't believe…" she began, but she was cut off when Sam's dad came up behind her.

"Sorry we're late," he boomed, taking Julia's hand and placing a loud kiss on her fingers. "You're looking fantastic as usual, my dear. So good to see you again."

Vera's gaze traveled between the two of them. "Is everything okay?" she asked, studying Julia.

The color had drained from Julia's face. Her eyes had grown large and shadowed. Sam wished he could pull her aside and finish their conversation. He got the feeling he'd made a huge misstep.

"We're fine," Julia said, taking a sip of water. She stood and hugged Joe then her mother. "Just working out details. You know."

Sam watched her gaze travel up and down her mother. "Are you all right, Mom?" she asked slowly.

"Never better," Vera said, smoothing her blouse.

"Why is your shirt buttoned wrong?"

Sam looked at his father, who had the decency to turn a bright shade of pink. Joe and Vera broke into a fit of giggles. Sam didn't know Vera well, but she'd never struck him as much of a giggler.

"I'll head to the little girls' room and adjust this." She swatted Joe playfully on the arm as she passed. "You old devil."

"You've got to be kidding." Julia followed her mother toward the back of the restaurant.

Joe took the seat across from Sam and gave him a hearty pat on the back. "How's it going, Sammy? Wedding stress getting to your girl?"

Sam's temper flared. "Finding out her mother is having sex with you might be getting to her."

Joe looked genuinely confused. "Really? I thought you two would be happy for us." A grin spread across his face. "Who knows, maybe we'll beat you to the altar."

"You've known Vera about a minute, Dad. That's not funny."

"Who's joking?" Joe opened his arms, lifting them toward the ceiling. "Some things are destined to be."

Sam needed a bigger supply of aspirin if he was going to continue to spend time with his dad. He pushed his fingers through his hair and took a breath. "Dad, tell me you aren't serious. I swear I'll throw you in the cruiser and deposit you at the state line if you keep talking like this. If you have an itch you want to scratch with Vera, that's one thing. But marriage? No way."

"Let me tell you something." His father leaned forward. "I'm not a young man anymore, in case you haven't noticed. I spent a lot of years sad and lonely after your mother died. Vera knows what it's like to lose a spouse. She knows what it feels like to be alone and crave something more."

"Vera is hardly ever alone." Sam shook his head. "She dates, Dad. A lot."

"From what I understand, you dated a lot before Julia. Did it make you feel less lonely?"

Sam opened his mouth then snapped it shut again. His father was right. All the women he'd dated when he first got to Brevia had just been passing time. He'd never felt connected to any of them. He'd always been on his own.

Until Julia.

"I'm going to ask her to marry me," Joe said. "It was love at first sight, and I'm smart enough not to let her get away."

"Do you think she'll say yes? I'd hope to hell she's smart enough to know not to be swept off her feet."

"What's wrong with being swept away? But don't worry. We won't plan a wedding until after you and Julia are settled. Neither of us wants to take anything away from you kids."

"That's so reassuring," Sam ground out. He scrubbed his hand over his face. "You don't have to marry her. Date for a little while. Take your time. Why rush into anything?"

"Life is short. It can turn on a dime. I'm taking every opportunity for happiness I can get. Just like you and Julia."

Nothing like him and Julia, Sam thought. This was a

disaster. His father's gushing romanticism made him look like an emotional robot.

He had to believe they were on the same page. She didn't want anything more from him than he was able to give.

Let his father rush blindly into marriage for love. It wasn't going to make him happy. If Joe hadn't learned that lesson from Sam's mother, Sam definitely had.

His plan was far more prudent. Enjoy each other but still protect his heart. It would be better for everyone in the long run.

The next day Julia cradled the phone between her cheek and shoulder as she sat in her office at the salon. She'd spent an hour staring blindly at the figures dancing before her on the computer and had made a call to an old friend to give herself a break.

"It's okay, Derek," she said with a sigh. "I'll figure it out."

"If those Southern belles get too much for you, I can always find a place for you in Phoenix. Everything's hotter out West, jewel-eyed Julia." Derek laughed at his own joke then said, "I've got to run, darlin'. My last appointment for the day just came in."

"Thanks, sweetie," Julia said, "I'll keep that offer in mind."

She hung up with Derek, a stylist she'd met years ago in Columbus. They'd both moved on from Ohio, but she still considered him one of her few true friends. For a brief moment she entertained the thought of taking Charlie and running away to Arizona. Not that it would solve her myriad of problems, but it sure seemed easier than facing everything head-on.

Julia drummed her fingers on the top of her desk, wishing she were out in the warm sun instead of stuck in the salon on such a gorgeous spring day. She needed to clear her head, and computer work wasn't cutting it.

What had started as a simple plan with Sam had gotten too complicated. She'd been stupid to think she could keep her heart out of the equation. If Julia were better at leading with her mind, she wouldn't have gotten into most of the trouble she'd had during her life. She wanted to be in control of her emotions. To be more like Sam, who could make every decision in his life based on rational thinking.

Not Julia. She was more a leap-first-then-look kind of person.

The only time that had worked in her favor was with Charlie. Now she'd even managed to mess up that.

Sam wanted to stay with her for the right reasons, at least on paper, but it felt wrong. His father and her mother were heading in that same direction on the express train. It had been torture to watch them last night at dinner, making googly eyes and barely able to keep their hands off each other.

She didn't realize it was possible to ache for a man's touch, but that was how she felt around Sam. Other than enough touching to make their fake arrangement seem real, they'd both kept their distance. Except when they were alone. In the bedroom, Sam was sweet and attentive and Julia had made the mistake of believing that meant something.

She pushed away from the desk and stalked toward the main salon. They were busy today, with every chair filled. She hoped to get the final approval on her business loan next week, needed to prove to herself and to the town and Jeff's family that she could stand on her own two feet.

Lizzy, the salon's longtime receptionist, stopped her in the doorway.

"Julia, could you take a look at this product order and make sure I didn't miss anything?" She shoved a piece of paper filled with numbers into Julia's hand.

Julia looked down as the figures on the page swam in front of her eyes. "Leave it on my desk. I'll check it over the weekend."

"I need to get it in before month end, which is today. It'll only take a minute. Please."

"I can't," Julia snapped with more force than she'd meant.

Lizzy took a quick step back and Julia noticed several customers and stylists glance her way. "Fine," she stammered. "But if we run out of anything, don't blame me." She turned away, ripping the paper from Julia's fingers.

"I'm sorry." Julia reached out to touch the woman's arm. "Lizzy, wait. I need to tell you something."

"That you're too dang important to be bothered by little details?"

Julia glanced around the crowded salon, her gaze landing on Lexi Preston, who watched her from where she sat with a head full of coloring foils. What was Jeff's attorney doing in her salon? Lexi blinked then raised one brow, as if in an odd challenge.

"I'm waiting," Lizzy muttered.

Fine. She was sick of hiding who she was, tired of working so hard to live up to her own unattainable expectations. She squared her shoulders and took a deep breath. "I have a learning disability."

"Come again?" A little of the anger went out of Lizzy's posture.

"I need time to look over the figures because I can't read them well."

"Since when?"

A hush had fallen over the salon and Julia realized everyone was waiting for her answer.

"Forever," she said, making her voice loud and clear. "I was officially diagnosed in third grade."

Lizzy looked confused. "I think I would have heard that before now. I was only a few years behind you in school."

Julia shrugged. "It wasn't public knowledge."

"Is that why you were always cutting class and getting kids to write your papers for you?"

Julia nodded. "I'm not proud of it. I was embarrassed and it made me feel stupid." She took a breath. "It still does. But I'm working on that. I hid behind a bad attitude and unkindness for a lot of years. I've changed. I don't want you to think I don't value what you're asking me to do. It just may take me longer to get it done." She swallowed down the lump of emotion crowding her throat. "That's my big secret."

Lizzy offered her a genuine smile. "My cousin was bulimic for most of her teenage years. She tried to hide that, too."

One of the customers tipped her head in Julia's direction. "My husband's addicted to internet porn."

"Oh." Julia didn't quite know how that related to her learning disability. "Well, I'll take these figures." She gently tugged the paper from Lizzy's hand. "I'll see if I can get through them this afternoon. If not, first thing Monday morning."

She looked around the salon one last time, her gaze catching again on Lexi's, and the lawyer gave her a surprisingly genuine smile. Head held high, Julia closed the door to her office. Once safely by herself, she leaned against it, bending her knees until she sank to the floor.

Her whole body trembled from the adrenaline rush that followed sharing her deepest, darkest secret with the ladies in the salon. Julia knew how the gossip mill worked in Brevia. Within hours, everyone to the county line and back would know about her learning disability.

The truth was that she no longer cared. Now that she'd talked about her disorder, its hold over her had loosened the tiniest bit. If people wanted to judge her or tried to take advantage of her, she'd deal with that. She realized she could handle a lot more when she used the truth to her advantage than when she tried to cover it up.

A little voice inside her head piped up, saying she might take that advice when it came to dealing with the custody case and Charlie's future. She quickly put it aside. Public humiliation she could risk—her son's fate she couldn't. Whether that meant keeping up the charade with Sam, or fighting tooth and nail with the Johnsons, Julia would do whatever she had to to keep Charlie safe.

Chapter Fourteen

"The Callahan brothers ride again."

Sam slanted Scott a look. "Who are you supposed to be, Billy the Kid?"

Scott grinned. "It's about time you stopped hiding in this backwater town and did some real work."

"I'm police chief, idiot. That is real work."

"If you say so. But it's nothing like being a marshal. You're going to love it, Sam. You won't have time to think about anything else."

That was a plus, Sam thought. He'd gotten the job offer early this morning. Scott had shown up at the station soon after to offer his congratulations. Sam was on duty, so they had coffee and a breakfast burrito in the car as Sam went out on an early-morning call.

His father was going to hit the roof. Joe had taken Vera down to the coast for a couple of days, so at least Sam would have time to formulate a plan before he had to explain what he was doing.

He had no idea what to say to Julia. He figured she'd understand. She'd tried to break it off last night. He knew their time together was at an end. After the custody ruling came through, she wouldn't need him anymore. Not that she ever really had. Despite her self-doubt, Julia was going to have a great life. He was the one who was hopeless.

Although he hadn't even thought himself capable of it, he felt his heart literally expanding every day with love for her and Charlie, but he couldn't make it work. He felt vulnerable, as if he was a moving target with no cover. He couldn't offer her anything more because he was too afraid of being hurt.

He'd spent most of yesterday working with Julia's attorney to file several affidavits on behalf of people around town attesting to Julia's character, her contributions to the local community and what they'd observed as far as her being a great mother was concerned. He knew she would never ask for help from anyone, let alone believe she deserved it. Once he'd explained what she was facing, people had come forward in droves to stand behind her.

He hoped that would be enough, would make up for what he wanted to tell her but couldn't find the guts to say. Instead, he was going to move on. Leave Brevia and cut his ties because that was easier than letting someone in.

"Before you go all bro-mance on me, you need to know I still think you're a jerk for what you did to me."

"You'll thank me eventually."

"I doubt that." Sam turned onto the long dirt road that led to the house he'd received the call about earlier. Strange noises, the neighbor had said. Here on the outskirts of town, Sam knew the parties could go on all through the night. He figured someone hadn't known when to let it go.

He shifted the cruiser into Park and turned to his brother. "If we're going to work together, there need to be some ground rules. The first is you stay the hell out of my personal life. It's none of your business. Even if you think you've got my best interests at heart."

"What are you going to do about the fiancée when you leave town?" Scott asked.

"I'm going to do her a favor."

"That's cold, Sam. Even for you. And I thought I was the heartbreaker. You're giving me a run for my money in the love-'em-and-leave-'em department."

"Don't make it a bigger issue than it is, Scott. She's better off without me. It's not going to work out. I'm not what she needs, after all."

"I can see why she'd be what *you* need, though. Her legs must be a mile long."

The hair on the back of Sam's neck stood on end.

"When did you see Julia?"

Scott gave him a hesitant smile. "Probably shouldn't have mentioned that."

"When did you see her?" Sam repeated, his knuckles tightening around the steering wheel.

"I drove down to have lunch with Dad last week. I needed a trim, so I checked out her salon."

"And her," Sam said between clenched teeth.

"After what Dad told me about how in love you are and the way you skipped out of breakfast to go running to her, it had me worried. I wanted to see what could be so flippin' amazing about this woman to make you all whipped."

"I'm not whipped."

"I was worried," Scott continued. "I put my butt on the line to get you this job. It wouldn't look good for you to flake before you even started. I have to admit, she'd be a big temptation. Her kid was there, too. Cute, if you're into the whole family-man scene. But I know you, Sam. That isn't who you are. Never was."

"Stay away from Julia."

"It's not like that. I told you that what happened with Jenny, I did it for your own good. Granted, I could have found a better way to handle things but…"

"You slept with her."

"I'm sorry, Sam."

Scott's voice was quiet, sincere. It made Sam's teeth hurt, because he knew his brother was sorry. He also knew that, in a warped way, Scott had done him a favor. At that point in his life, Sam had been so determined to prove that he wasn't like his father, that he could have both a career and a personal life, he'd ignored all the warning signs about how wrong he and Jenny had been for each other. She would have left him eventually. He would have driven her away.

Now he knew better, and he wasn't going to risk it again. Not his heart or his pride. He thought Julia understood him, but it was for the best that their relationship ended. As much as he didn't want to admit it, he was falling for her. He was close to feeling something he'd never felt before in his life, and it scared the hell out of him. What if he did let her in and she realized there was nothing inside him to hold on to? His heart had stopped working right the day his mother had died and he didn't know how to fix it.

Sam glanced at his brother. "Do you think about what would have happened if Mom hadn't been in the accident?"

"I used to," Scott said, a muscle ticking in his jaw. "But she would have divorced him, and the end result on us would have been the same."

"Yeah." Sam nodded. "I think Dad discovered his emotional self about two decades too late to make any difference in my life."

"You need to get out of here. Once you're working for the Marshals, you won't have time for all this thinking about your life. I'm telling you—"

Whatever Scott was going to say next was cut off when a stream of shots rang out from the house. "Stay here," Sam yelled as he jumped out of the car.

"Not a chance," Scott said, right on his heels, his gun in hand. "Call me your backup."

Sam gave a brief nod. "You go around the side," he whispered and headed toward the front of the house.

Julia dropped her cell phone back into her purse and took a deep breath. "I didn't get the loan," she said to her sister, the words sounding hollow to her own ears.

Lainey reached out a hand. The Tellett County court-house was crowded on a Tuesday morning, and they stood near the end of the hallway, in front of a window that looked out onto the street. Julia thought it odd that the people below went about their business so calmly as her life spun out of control.

"Why not? What did they say? Oh, Jules, there has to be another way."

Julia shook her head. "They don't think I'm a good investment. It's me, Lainey. Nothing is going to change that. Everyone in the salon yesterday heard me. I told Lizzy about my learning disabilities. Clearly, the bank doesn't think I'm the right person to own my own business." She tried to smile but couldn't make her mouth move that way. "I can't blame them."

"I can." Lainey's tone was severe. "It's the most outrageous thing I've ever heard."

"Annabeth Sullivan is a vice president at the bank. I thought we'd come to an understanding and she'd forgiven me. I guess she still wants revenge."

"How long are you going to have to pay for your past mistakes? You're not the same person you were in high school. You've changed and everyone who knows you can see that. You're a good person. It's about time people gave you credit for how much you've accomplished."

"I haven't accomplished anything. The salon was my chance to make something of my life, to become more than what anyone thought I could." She scrubbed her hands over her face. "There's a reason I kept the LD a secret for so many years. It's easier to talk my way out of people thinking I'm stupid than to deal with the truth."

Lainey sucked in a breath. "Don't say that. You'll find another way. Ethan and I—"

"No. I'm not taking charity from you and Ethan, or Mom for that matter. Some things weren't meant to be. I've had enough disappointment in my life to know that." She glanced down the hall and saw Frank Davis motioning to them. "The hearing is starting."

"I thought Sam was meeting you here."

Julia swallowed back the tears that clogged her throat. "Like I said, I'm used to disappointment."

"Don't be silly. He'll be here."

Julia gave her sister a small hug. "Whatever you say, Lain. Right now, wish me luck."

"You don't need luck. You're a wonderful mother and that's what's most important. I'll be here when you're finished. We'll have a celebratory lunch."

The elevator doors opened as Julia walked past and she paused, her chest tightening as she willed Sam to materialize. When an older woman walked out, Julia continued down the hall alone.

She took her seat across from Jeff, his parents and their attorney. A small smile played around the corners of Jeff's mother's mouth. Lexi Preston didn't make eye contact, her eyes glued to the stack of papers on the table. A pit of dread began to open in Julia's stomach.

She darted a glance toward her attorney, who appeared blissfully unaware. But Julia could feel the long tendrils of impending doom reaching for her. She'd been in their grip too many times before not to recognize it now.

"Frank, what's going on?"

He looked up, a big smile on his face. "Didn't Sam tell you? He got a bunch of folks to write testimonials about your character. Really good, too. All of them."

Sam did that. For her. Then why did the Johnson family look so smug?

"Where is Sam?" Frank asked. "I thought he was meeting us here."

"Me, too." Julia swallowed. "I don't know what's keeping him."

The judge came into the courtroom. "In light of the new information given to me by both parties, I'm going to need a few more days to render my decision."

"What new information did they give her?" Julia said in a frantic whisper.

"Your Honor," Frank said as he patted Julia's arm reassuringly, "we aren't aware of any new information brought forward by the other party."

The judge slowly removed her glasses and narrowed her eyes at him. "Mr. Davis, you do know about your client's recent professional setbacks."

Frank threw a glance at Julia. "I'm not sure—"

"I didn't get the loan," Julia said miserably.

"We've spoken to a reliable source that tells us Ms. Morgan is planning to move out of the area." Lexi's shoulders were stiff as she spoke. "A colleague of Ms. Morgan's, Derek Lamb, had a conversation with her last week in which she expressed interest in a job with him at his salon in Phoenix."

Julia knew Lexi had somehow gleaned that information, as well. "I wasn't serious. I was upset about…about a lot of things, and Derek is an old friend—"

"An old boyfriend," Lexi supplied.

Julia shook her head, panic threatening to overtake her. "Hardly. I don't have the right equipment."

Frank squeezed her arm. "Be quiet, Julia."

The judge pointed a finger at her. "Ms. Morgan, your petition for sole custody was based partially on the stability of your current circumstances. Your ties to the community and your family being close were something I took into account when looking at your request."

"Her ties to the community are highlighted in the affidavits I submitted." Frank's voice shook with frustration.

"There is also the matter of her engagement," Lexi said, reaching over to hand a piece of paper to Frank.

Blood roared in Julia's head. No one could have found out her relationship with Sam wasn't real. They'd done everything right and she hadn't told a soul, not even Lainey.

Unless Sam…

She snatched the paper from Frank Davis's fingers and tried to decipher the words on the page, willing them to stop moving in front of her eyes. When they did, she felt the whole room start to spin.

"Were you aware," the judge asked, "that Sam Callahan has accepted a position with the U.S. Marshals Service in Washington, D.C.?"

Julia looked at the woman, unable to speak. Finally, she whispered, "No."

The woman's mouth tightened. "May I ask, Ms. Morgan, if you're still engaged to be married to Sam Callahan?"

Julia stared at the piece of paper in her hand, her vision blurring as angry tears filled her eyes. She blinked several times, refusing to cry in front of Jeff and his family. Refusing to cry over any man. "No, ma'am," she answered quietly. "I don't believe we are still engaged."

Frank sucked in a quick breath next to her. "In light of these new findings, I'd ask for a recess to regroup with my client."

"Yes, Mr. Davis, I think that would be a good idea. Our time is valuable, though, so please, no more wasting it. Get your facts straight and come back to me with a new proposal in one week."

"Judge Williams—" Lexi Preston's voice was clear and confident in the silence "—on behalf of my client, I'd like to request that you make your ruling today. The information that's come to light this morning is another example of Julia Morgan's inability to successfully manage her own life. It speaks directly to Jeff Johnson's concerns for his son and the reason he is here seeking joint custody."

Julia's gaze met Jeff's and he nodded slightly, as if to say "I told you so." Which, of course, he had. And she hadn't listened, convinced that this time events would work out in her favor. In large part because of Sam's confidence in her.

Sam, who'd encouraged her to go public with her learning disorder.

Sam, who'd promised to stay by her side until her custody arrangement was secure.

Sam, who'd betrayed her today.

Lexi cleared her throat. "I motion that you award sole physical custody of Charles David Morgan to Jeff Johnson."

The attorney's words registered in Julia's brain. They wanted to take Charlie from her. Completely.

She saw Jeff lean over and speak into Lexi's ear. The younger woman shook her head then glanced at Julia.

Julia felt the walls of the room close in around her. She looked at the judge's impassive face, trying to find some clue as to what the woman was thinking.

"Don't let this happen," she whispered to Frank. She needed to get back to Brevia, to wrap her arms around her son.

"We request you stay with your decision to rule next week," Frank said, his voice steady. "My client has been blindsided by some of these new developments. That in no way decreases her dedication as a parent or her love for her son."

To Julia's immense relief, the judge nodded. "We'll meet next Tuesday morning." She pointed a finger at Frank Davis. "Before that, I expect you to submit a revised proposal for custody. Remember, we all want what's best for the child, not simply what's easiest for one of the parents."

What's best for Charlie, Julia wanted to scream, *is to stay with his mother.*

She'd come into this meeting so confident. How could things have gone to hell so quickly?

She pushed back from the table. "I need to get out of here," she told the attorney.

"Be in my office tomorrow morning, first thing." His frustration was clear as he watched her. "This was a clear-cut case," he mumbled. "What happened with Sam?"

She bit her lip. "I don't know." What she did know was that Sam had left her vulnerable to losing her son.

Julia would never forgive him.

Chapter Fifteen

Sam ran his hands through his still-wet hair and straightened his shirt before knocking on Julia's door.

He'd stopped home for a quick shower after the mess this morning had finally settled down. An all-night party had turned into a domestic disturbance that led to a four-hour standoff. The homeowner, high on an assortment of illegal drugs, wouldn't let his girlfriend or her two kids out of the house. The situation had eventually ended with no injuries, for which Sam was thankful. But he'd been tied up in logistics and paperwork for most of the day.

He felt awful about missing the hearing and had called and texted Julia at least a half-dozen times with no answer. He'd then called Lainey, but she hadn't picked up, either. As mad as she'd be about him missing the meeting, the character affidavits he'd helped compile had to make up for it.

Sam couldn't wait to see the joy on Julia's face now that

Charlie was safe. He wanted to hear how things went, take the two of them to dinner to celebrate her victory. Even if she didn't want to be with him anymore, he'd make her see how important it was to keep up appearances a little while longer. He told himself it was good for her reputation but knew he couldn't bear to let go of her quite yet.

Julia deserved all the happiness life could offer, and Sam wanted to have a hand in helping with that before they ended their relationship. The thought of leaving her and Charlie made his whole body go cold. But he knew it would be best for Julia and that was his priority now.

He knocked again, surprised when Lainey opened the door. Even more surprised at how angry she looked.

"You have a lot of nerve showing up here," she said through a hiss. "She doesn't want to see you. You've done enough damage already."

The confusion of not being able to get in touch with her turned to panic. "Where is she? What happened?"

Lainey went to shut the door in his face but he shoved one gym shoe into the doorway. Lainey kicked at his toe. "I mean it, Sam. You need to leave."

"I swear, Lainey," Sam ground out, "I'll push right through you if I have to but I'm going to see her. Now."

Casper came up behind Lainey, barking wildly. Sam could see the dog's teeth shining and wondered if the dog actually meant to bite him.

"Casper, quiet." The dog stopped barking but continued to growl low in his throat. Lainey studied Sam through the crack in the door. "I'd like to call the cops on you."

"I can give you the number."

She blew out a frustrated breath and opened the door. Sam went to push past. "Where is she?"

Lainey didn't move to let him by. "I'm warning you. She doesn't want to see you ever again. She's in bad shape."

He shook his head. "I don't understand. Everything was lined up. Didn't Frank Davis submit the affidavits? They were supposed to make everything better."

"Julia didn't mention any affidavits. What she did tell me, between sobs, is that you'd told her to go public with her learning disabilities. For whatever reason, Annabeth Sullivan convinced the bank that she was a bad investment for the loan."

Sam's breath caught. "No."

"The best part, " Lainey said and poked her finger into his chest, "the part that really made all the difference, was the little bombshell that you've taken a job with the U.S. Marshals Service."

Sam's whole body tensed. "How did they find out?"

"You don't deny it? How could you have done that to her?" Lainey turned on her heel and stalked several paces into the small apartment.

"No one was supposed to find out until after she got the custody ruling."

Lainey whirled back toward him, keeping her voice low. "And that makes it better? You were her fiancé. A stable father figure for Charlie."

"Did Julia—"

"Oh, yes." Lainey waved an angry hand toward him. "I know all about your *arrangement*. It's ridiculous."

"I didn't mean for it to be. I wanted to help."

"You've put her at risk, Sam. At real risk of losing custody of Charlie."

"Where is she?"

Lainey stared at him. "In the bedroom," she answered finally.

"I'm going to fix this." Sam tried for confidence but his voice cracked on the last word.

"I hope you can."

He walked past her, Casper at his heels. The dog no longer seemed to want to rip off his head. Julia, he imagined, was another matter.

"I can make this right," he muttered to the animal. "I have to."

He knocked softly on the door, but when there was no response, he opened it. The curtain was pulled back, the room bathed in early-evening sunlight. Julia sat on the bed, her knees curled up to her chin, arms hugging her legs tight against her.

Sam stepped into the room and the dog edged past him, silently hopping up on the bed and giving Julia's hand a gentle lick before curling into a ball at her side. Without acknowledging Sam, she reached out to stroke the dog's soft head.

"Jules?"

Her hand stilled. "Go away," she whispered, her voice awful.

"Julia, look at me." Sam took another step into the room.

"I said go away." She lifted her head, her eyes puffy from crying, tears dried on her cheeks. She looked as miserable as Sam felt. He waited for her to scream at him, to hurl insults and obscenities. He wanted her to let loose her temper but she only stared, her gaze filled with the pain of betrayal.

Knowing it was his betrayal that had caused her suffering almost killed him on the spot. "I'm sorry," he began but stopped when she scrambled back against the headboard. The dog jumped up and stood like a sentry in front of her.

"I could lose him." Her voice was dull and wooden, as if she was in a pit of despair so deep she couldn't even manage emotion.

"You won't lose him." Sam said the words with conviction, hoping they would be true.

"You don't know. You weren't there."

The accusation in her voice cut like a knife through his heart. "It was work, Jules. I meant to be there." He sat down on the edge of the bed gingerly, not wanting to spook her or the dog.

"You're leaving."

"I thought it was for the best," he lied. The best thing that ever happened to him was this woman, but he was too scared of being hurt to give her what she needed. "That when you didn't need me anymore, it would be easier for us both if I was gone."

"I needed you today and instead I found out from Jeff's lawyer that you were taking a new job. You made me look like a fool, Sam."

The truth of her words struck him to his core. She was right. He was supposed to be there for her and he'd let her down. In a big way. It was the reason he knew he was destined to be alone: the work always came first for him. He was the same as his dad had been. It had cost his mother her life and now it might cost Julia her future with Charlie. He had to make it better somehow. "What can I do?"

She shook her head. "Nothing. There's nothing anyone can do. I have one good thing in my life. Charlie was the one thing I did right. And I've ruined that, too."

"You haven't—"

"I trusted you, Sam." As much as the words hurt, her voice, still empty of emotion, was the worst. "My mistake. I should have learned by now I can't rely on anyone except myself." She gave a brittle laugh. "And I'm iffy at best."

"Where's Charlie?"

"He's with Ethan. I couldn't let him see me like this." She ran her fingers through her hair. "I'm going to pull it together. I have to. But I needed a little time."

"We can get through this."

"There's no *we*. There never really was. You proved that today."

"I didn't mean it to end like this." He reached out for her again and Casper growled like he meant it.

Julia went rigid. "Don't touch me. I never want to see you again. I don't know what's going to happen with the custody arrangement. But I'll find a way to keep my son. He's all that matters to me now."

Sam shook his head. "Don't say that," he whispered.

Her eyes blazed as she spoke. "I thought you were different. I wanted to depend on you. I wanted to love you. Hell, I was halfway there already. It's over. I don't care what you say to your father or anyone in town about why this is ending. Blame it on me."

"This isn't over and I'm not blaming anything on you. If you let me—"

"I did let you. I let you into my heart and into my son's life and you betrayed us." She took a shuddering breath. "We're over. Whatever I thought we had is done."

"You can't be serious."

"Please go, Sam. Please."

He stared at her as she turned to the dog, petting him until he lay down again beside her. Sam wanted to grab her and pull her to him, hold on until she melted into him. This couldn't be the end.

He'd wanted to leave her happy, to do the right thing by her. Maybe he couldn't be the man she wanted but he'd been determined to see her through. To be the hero when it really mattered.

Now he was nothing more than the jerk who'd put her at risk of losing her son.

He stood slowly, his eyes never leaving her. He prayed she would look at him, give him some small glimmer of hope. When she didn't, he turned and walked from the room.

Lainey hung up the phone as he came down the hallway. "How is she?"

He shook his head. "She should never have trusted me."

"But she did, Sam. What are you going to do now?"

He thought for a moment then answered the only way he could. "I'm going to do what I do best—disappoint someone I care about."

Lainey looked as if she'd expected him to give some white-knight answer. But Sam was only good at playing the hero when the stakes didn't matter to him personally. When his emotions were on the line, he had a knack for royally messing up everything around him.

He walked out the door and into the dark night knowing he'd just ruined his best opportunity at a happy ending in life.

The image of Julia so forlorn would haunt him for a long time. Her anger and hatred might be deserved, but it hurt the most to know that he couldn't take away the pain he'd caused her.

For that, he'd never forgive himself.

Julia pushed the stroller along the plush carpet of the retirement home until she got to the common room that also served as a makeshift salon for residents.

"Good morning, Julia."

"Hey, Charlie."

Several voices called out to greet them, and she was thankful the people here were unaware of her personal turmoil, unlike most of the town. Charlie waved as though he was in a parade, which made Julia smile a bit. Her first in several days. She took a small sip of her coffee then placed it in the cup holder attached to the stroller's handle. It had been a rough week.

She tried not to show her emotions in front of Charlie, so she had spent a few sleepless nights crying in the dark hours and worrying about her future. The days were just as difficult to get through, since everywhere she went someone had a comment on her recent struggles. To her surprise, most of what people said had been supportive. Old friends and other locals seemed to come out of the woodwork to offer her a word of encouragement or commiserate on her situation.

Even Val Dupree, the Hairhouse's owner, had called from Florida to tell Julia that she was still willing to work with her to find a way for Julia to buy the salon. Julia had thanked her, but at this point she was afraid it was too little, too late. The Johnsons had so much power and she wasn't sure there was anything she could do to keep her future with Charlie secure.

Nothing mattered except Charlie.

She hadn't seen or spoken to Sam, although a couple of ladies had come into the salon specifically to tell her how they'd given him an earful about his reprehensible behavior toward her. Apparently, being screwed over by a man made you an automatic member of a certain girls' club.

If it wasn't for her constant worry about Charlie, Julia might be happy right now. For the first time in as long as she could remember, she felt as if she was a true member of the Brevia community.

But everything else faded when she thought of her son and what she'd need to do to keep him with her.

Before moving forward with her plan, she had this one last loose end to tie up.

"Good morning, Mrs. Shilling," she said as she walked into the room.

"Well, hello, dear." A gray-haired woman, sitting at the games table with a deck of cards, lifted her head and smiled.

"Hi, Iris." Julia directed that greeting to the younger woman wiping down counters at the back of the room.

"Hey, Jules. Thanks for coming on such short notice." The younger woman waved at Charlie. "Hey there, Chuckie-boy. Do you want to check out the fish while your mommy helps Mrs. S.?"

Charlie bounced up and down in his seat. "Fishy," he squealed. "Charlie, fishy."

"Thanks, Iris." Julia picked up her coffee from the stroller and pushed the buggy toward Iris. She always brought Charlie when she came to Shady Acres. The residents and employees loved seeing him.

As Iris left with Charlie, Julia turned to the older woman. "Mrs. Shilling, where did you find the scissors?" She stepped forward and ran her fingers through the spiky tufts of hair on the top of the woman's head.

Mrs. Shilling placed her hand over Julia's and winked. "In the craft cabinet, dear. They forgot to lock it after our art class yesterday."

Julia opened her bag and pulled out a plastic apron, spray bottle, scissors and a comb. "What do you think if I clean it up a little? You've done a nice job here, but I can even up the sides a bit."

"I suppose," Mrs. Shilling answered with a shrug. "When I was a girl, I had the cutest haircut, just like Shirley Temple. I wanted to look that cute again." She met Julia's gaze, her hazy eyes filled with hope. "Can you make me look like Shirley Temple, dear?"

Julia patted Mrs. Shilling's soft, downy hair. "I'll do my best." She wrapped the apron around the woman's frail shoulders. "Next time, go easy with the scissors, Mrs. S. You're beautiful just the way you are."

She usually came to Shady Acres every other week to cut and shampoo the hair of a group of residents. But Iris had called her last night to say that Mrs. Shilling, one of her favorite ladies, had butchered her hair. Julia made time to come here before she needed to be at the salon.

She used the scissors to snip a few tendrils of hair as Mrs. Shilling hummed softly.

"Everything okay in here?"

Julia turned, shocked to see Ida Garvey walk into the room.

Mrs. Shilling's face lit up. "Ida, so nice to see you here this morning. This is my friend Julia. She's making me look like Shirley Temple." She glanced at Julia. "This is my daughter, Ida. She's a very good girl." Her voice lowered to a whisper. "She still wets the bed sometimes. Has nightmares, poor girl. I let her snuggle with me until she falls asleep."

Julia gave a small smile. "Nice to see you, Mrs. Garvey."

The older woman shook her head. "I haven't wet the bed since I was seven years old. The Alzheimer's has affected my mother's memory of time."

"I figured as much. I won't be long here."

"They called to tell me she'd cut her own hair again."

"If she ever wants a part-time job, we could use her skills at the Hairhouse." Julia continued trimming the woman's fluffy hair.

"She can't do any worse than some of those girls you've got working there."

"Play nice, Mrs. Garvey. I've got the scissors."

One side of Ida's mouth quirked. "She talks about you a lot."

Julia glanced up. "Really? Me?"

"In fact, I have a suspicion she might have done this just to get you out here again."

Mrs. Shilling pointed a bony finger at her daughter.

"Children are supposed to be seen and not heard, young lady."

"I'm almost seventy, Mom."

"Still holds true," the woman said with a humph. "Besides, she's going to make me look like Shirley Temple. Or maybe Carole Lombard."

Julia smiled, something about this woman's affection lifting her spirits the tiniest bit. She was grateful for every lift she could get right now. "I was thinking Katharine Hepburn, circa *Adam's Rib*. Gorgeous but spunky."

"I'll take spunky," Mrs. Shilling agreed and settled back into her chair.

"I heard about your recent troubles," Ida said, her gaze assessing. "What are you going to do about the salon?"

"My loan wasn't approved. What else can I do? I'm not sure if I'm going to be in town for much longer, actually." She squeezed Mrs. Shilling's shoulder. "I'll miss you when I go."

The woman heaved a sigh. "All the good ones move on." She gave a watery smile to her daughter. "Except Ida. She's my best girl. Always has been."

Julia's chest fluttered at the love in the older woman's gaze when she looked at her daughter. She suddenly saw crotchety Ida Garvey in a new light. Julia knew she'd look at Charlie like that one day. She'd do anything to keep him by her side so she'd have that chance. Nothing was more important to her.

Ida gave her mother an indulgent smile, and then with her customary bluntness she asked Julia, "How did the bank deal get messed up?"

Julia pulled in a deep breath and paused in her cutting. "They didn't think I was a good investment, I guess." She paused, squaring her shoulders, and then said, "As you've probably heard, my learning disabilities are severe. Not exactly the type of applicant you'd trust to run a business, even a small local salon. Too bad, though. I had big plans."

Mrs. Shilling clapped her hands. "She told me all about it, Ida. Getting rid of that horrid name. She's going to offer spa services. I want to bathe in a big tub of mud!"

"Is that so?" Mrs. Garvey asked, looking between her mother and Julia.

Julia gave a small laugh, embarrassed now that she'd confided so much in the older woman. "My idea was to make it a destination for people traveling in the area and the go-to place for a day of pampering for women around the region. There's really nothing like that unless you head over to Asheville or down to the coast."

Ida nodded. "Tell me about it. I've put most of the miles on my car driving back and forth for a monthly facial."

Julia felt color rise to her cheeks, embarrassed she'd shared her dream now that it wasn't going to come true. "That's probably more information than you wanted for a simple question." She used a comb to fluff Mrs. Shilling's white hair. "There you are, beautiful." She handed her a small mirror. "Katharine Hepburn, eat your heart out."

The woman smiled as she looked in the mirror then at her daughter. "Do you love it, Ida?"

"I do," she agreed.

Julia removed the apron and took a broom from the supply closet in the corner. "I'll have one of the girls come out to do your hair when I'm gone." She began to sweep up the hair from around the chair.

"Ida, give her some money," Mrs. Shilling ordered.

Mrs. Garvey pulled her wallet from her purse.

Julia shook her head. "I don't charge for my time here."

Ida took out a business card and handed it to Julia. "This is the firm that handles my financial portfolio. The president's contact information is there."

Julia took the card. "Oh." She knew Ida Garvey's late husband had left her a sizable inheritance.

"If you decide you want to stay in the area and are still interested in investors for your business, call him. I see the need for the type of spa you're describing. I assume you have a business plan our loan team could review?"

Julia nodded, dumbfounded by the offer.

"Good. I don't want to pressure you. I don't know why the bank here didn't approve your loan, but I'd guess it had something to do with Annabeth. That girl isn't the sharpest knife in the drawer. But I certainly hope it wasn't because of your learning disorder. It doesn't make you a bad bet for a loan."

"Thank you for saying that."

Mrs. Shilling reached out and took Julia's hand. "Ida is rich," she said in a loud whisper. "She takes good care of me."

"You're very lucky," Julia told the woman, feeling a tiny flicker of hope that her own luck had taken a turn for the better.

Chapter Sixteen

Sam hit the mute button on the television and jumped off the couch, throwing on an old T-shirt in the process.

His heart soared at the thought that Julia could be the person insistently knocking on his front door.

He groaned as he opened it to reveal his father and brother standing side by side on his front porch. "Not now, boys," he said and went to swing the door shut again.

His dad pushed it open and knocked him hard in the chest. "What the—" Sam muttered as he stumbled back into the house.

"That's what I'd like to know." Joe's voice was hard as he stalked past Sam. Gone was the gentle emotion of his recent visit and in its place the tough, take-no-prisoners Boston cop had returned. Sam wanted to be grateful but knew what it was like to be on the receiving end of his father's temper. His own fuse felt too short to deal with that right now.

He glanced at his brother, who shrugged and stepped into the house, closing the door behind him.

"What the hell were you thinking?" Joe bellowed, slamming his palm against the wall. "You took advantage of that girl. You used her to deceive me and now you've deserted her. That's not how I raised you. I've never been so angry and disappointed in all my years."

Angry and disappointed? Even in the midst of a full-blown tirade, Joe was talking about how he felt. Sam had damn near had enough of it.

"This is your fault," Sam countered. "If you had left me alone, none of this would have happened." He squared his shoulders, warming up to the subject, needing a place to vent his own anger. "You came in here, emotional guns a-blazin', and wanted me to turn into somebody I'm not. It's never going to happen, Dad. I'm never going to be some heart-on-my-sleeve kind of guy, spouting out my feelings and crying at sappy chick flicks." He pointed a finger at his father. "You raised me to ignore my emotions. It's what you made Scott and me into after Mom died. I can't change. The mess I made of things with Julia is proof of that."

"You faked an engagement," his father interrupted, hands on hips, matching Sam's anger.

"It was wrong. I know that now. The alternative was you following me around waiting for unicorns and rainbows to come spewing out of my mouth. It ain't going to happen. Ever. Julia and I had a business arrangement and I messed it up. If I could go back and change things, I would."

"No, you wouldn't."

Sam and his father both turned as Scott spoke for the first time.

"You don't know anything about me or what I would do," Sam spat out. "Neither of you do."

"I know you," Scott countered. "I know that girl got

too close. She got under your skin, and I bet it scared the hell out of you. It sure would have me. With her big eyes, long legs and cute baby. She made you feel things and the Callahans don't like to feel." He nodded toward Joe. "Another gift from you, Dad. I don't know what she wanted or expected from you, but it's a good thing you ended it when you did. We don't do love. We're not built that way."

How could his brother be so right and so wrong at the same time? Being with Julia and Charlie had scared him. But it was because he realized he did love her even though he'd tried to ignore, then bury, his emotions. He'd fallen hard and fast, and it had made him want things that could never be.

She wanted someone to be a father to Charlie. Sam's paternal relationship was so dysfunctional it was almost laughable. How could he be a decent father with the role model he'd had in Joe?

What if he tried and failed with Julia? He was capable of love, but not in the way a woman like Julia deserved.

Suddenly Joe fell back onto the couch, clutching at his chest.

"Dad!" Both Sam and Scott were at his side in a second.

"What is it, Dad?" Sam asked.

"It's his heart, you idiot."

Joe's eyes drifted closed, and Sam moved his head and legs so he was lying flat across the cushions. "Call 911," he ordered his brother.

Scott pulled his cell phone from his back pocket, but Joe's eyes flew open and he reached out a hand. "No, I don't need medical attention."

"The hell you don't," Sam said on a hiss. "Make the call, Scott."

"My heart hurts," Joe said, his voice trembling, "because of the pain I've caused the two of you." He lifted himself to his elbows and looked from Sam to Scott. "My sons, I've failed you and I'll never forgive myself for it." He covered his eyes with one hand as sobs racked his shoulders.

"Of all the…" Sam grumbled and sank to one arm of the sofa.

Scott threw his cell phone on the coffee table and stalked to the front window, grumbling under his breath.

"Scoot over, old man." Sam sank down on the couch next to him. "You just about gave *me* a heart attack there."

"I need a drink." Scott's voice was tense.

"Make it three," Sam told him. "There's a bottle of Scotch in the cabinet next to the stove."

Joe still sat motionless, other than an occasional moan.

Sam's headache spread until his entire body hurt. "Dad, pull it together. It's going to be okay."

"Do you believe that?" Joe asked finally, wiping his damp cheeks. "Do you feel like you're going to be all right without her?"

No. Sam knew his life was going to be dark and dim, that he could spend years chasing the adrenaline rush that came with his career and nothing would compare with the excitement of having Charlie call him Dada. He felt as though he could be a hero to hundreds of nameless people, and it would pale in comparison to coaxing a real smile out of Julia.

"What choice do I have?"

"You always have a choice. That's what I didn't realize until recently. I had a choice to let your mother's death practically kill me, too, or to keep living. I didn't do a very good job of making my life count until recently. But I'm learning from the mistakes I made and doing my damnedest to make them better. You have a real chance for love with Julia. Take it."

"What do I have to offer her?" Sam asked quietly, finally getting to the real heart of the matter. His own fear. "She deserves so much more."

"I know you think that, son. But if there's even a glimmer of hope, you've got to try. Hell, you've got to try even if there isn't. Because what you have to offer is everything you are. It may not feel like it's enough but that's for her to decide. If you never put it out there, you'll spend your whole life feeling empty and alone. Trust me, that's no way to live."

What if Sam opened himself up to try? He may not feel as if he had enough to offer, but he was certain he'd work harder than any other man alive to make her happy. He wanted to see Charlie grow up, to be there for every T-ball game and skinned knee. He wanted to watch Julia hold their babies and grow old with her and everything that came between.

She was everything he'd ever wanted but was too scared to believe he deserved. He nodded as resolve built deep within him. "I've got to talk to her."

"You'd better get moving, then. She's got a head start on you."

Scott walked back into the room, balancing three glasses of whiskey. "Turn on ESPN and let's drown your sorrows."

Sam ignored his brother. "What do you mean 'head start'?" he asked his father. "Where did she go?"

"According to Vera, Julia took Charlie and headed to Ohio this morning. They caught a flight out of Charlotte. She told her mother she had some kind of a plan and needed to talk to the ex-boyfriend before the final ruling."

Sam's head spun. All he could think of was that Jeff had offered to marry Julia—some sort of business deal where Julia would come to Ohio to raise Charlie near the grandparents and they'd pay all the living expenses. Not a real relationship, but it was no better than what Sam had offered. And it would end the custody battle once and for all.

How could he have been stupid enough to let her go? What if she wouldn't take him back? What if she figured Charlie's father was a better deal?

Sam had to stop her. He loved her with his heart and soul. His life would be incomplete without Julia and Charlie in it, and he'd fight as long and as hard as he could to win them back.

He jumped off the couch and grabbed his keys and wallet from the side table. "I've got to go," he yelled to his father. "Lock up behind you."

Scott grabbed his arm as he strode past. "Don't do this. No woman is worth running after like you're some cow-eyed schoolboy."

"You're wrong," Sam answered, shrugging him off. "Julia is everything to me. Someday I hope you'll find a woman who makes you want to risk your heart. You deserve that. We both do. Dad's right. He messed up after Mom died, but we don't have to repeat his mistakes. I've got a chance to make it work and you'd better believe I'm going to take it."

"What if it's too late?"

"I've got to try."

Scott shook his head, disgust obvious in his angry gaze. "You have to be in D.C. tomorrow at eight o'clock sharp. You're going to make it, right?"

"I sure as hell hope not."

Scott cursed under his breath. "Idiot," he mumbled and drained his glass of Scotch.

"Sam."

Sam turned to his father. "I'm going to make it work, Dad. You know how relentless we Callahans can be."

"Good luck, son." Joe smiled at him. "I'm proud of you."

Scott snorted and picked up a second drink. "You go turn in your man card. I'm getting drunk."

Sam wanted to shake his brother, to open his eyes the way Sam's had been, but he didn't have time. His only priority right now was Julia and getting to her before she made a deal with Jeff Johnson.

"Sam?"

He turned to his father, who threw a small, velvet box in his direction. Sam caught it in one hand. "Is this…?" His voice trailed off as emotion overtook him.

"I had it sent down from Boston. Your mother would want you to have it."

He nodded. "Thanks, Dad," he said on a hoarse whisper then sprinted out the door.

"You've got a lot of nerve coming into my home un-invited." Maria Johnson looked down her nose at Julia. "Watch your child," she barked suddenly. "That's an antique Tiffany vase."

Julia leaned forward to pick up Charlie, who had toddled over to a wooden table and reached up to rub his tiny fingers on a glass vase perched on top.

"Hi, Mama," he said. His gaze went to Maria, who scowled at him, causing him to bury his face in Julia's neck.

Julia looked around the formal sitting room where a housekeeper had led her. It was cold, sterile and, like the rest of the house, totally inappropriate for an energetic boy. Even now she heard Maria *tsk* softly when she noticed the fingerprints Charlie had left around the bottom of the vase.

She'd asked for Jeff, but he was on his way back from a round of golf with his father. Unwilling to be distracted from her mission, or maybe afraid she'd lose her nerve,

Julia had insisted on being let into the enormous house. She'd known Jeff's family had money when they'd dated, but the *Dynasty*-sized home gave her a much better perspective on how rich the Johnsons really were. They clearly had unlimited resources at their disposal to get what they wanted.

Which brought her back to the matter at hand.

"I still can't believe you have the nerve to try to take my son from me," she said with a dry smile. "I guess that makes us even."

"Your case is crumbling, and you lied about your relationship status. It's only a matter of time until they take him from you. It will be better in the end. We can give him so much more than you could ever dream of. Look at Jeffrey."

"Speaking of *Jeffrey,* he asked me to marry him."

Maria didn't speak but the anger in her eyes said it all. Her face remained as smooth as marble, her expression typically blank, thanks to one too many cosmetic procedures. "Why would he do that? We don't need you to raise the child properly."

"Maybe giving a kid every material thing they want doesn't cut it. Your son is a loser, truth be told."

"How dare you! He's a respected professor with—"

"Funny, I thought that, too, when I first met him. Turns out, Jeff is a bit of a joke around campus. He does his research expeditions, conveniently funded by your husband's corporation, but little else." Julia sat Charlie on the floor and gave him several plastic toys from the diaper bag to keep him occupied. She dug through her bag for a stack of papers. "I have written documentation from the university about the sexual-misconduct charges filed against Jeff by four different undergraduates. Apparently, when he was teaching, it took a bit of extra work to get an A from Professor Johnson." Julia didn't mention that three of the incidents had happened during the time she'd been dating Jeff.

Maria tried to narrow her eyes, but they only moved a fraction. "How did you get those?"

Julia wasn't going to say where because she honestly didn't know. She hadn't even known until this moment whether the information she'd been given was real or fake. She'd been desperate, racking her brain for a way to make the custody battle go away, even wondering if she actually should accept Jeff's horrible proposal for Charlie's sake.

Then, two days ago, a package had arrived for her at the salon, containing the information about Jeff and other sordid details regarding the Johnsons.

At that moment, Jeff and his father walked into the room.

"What's she doing here?" Dennis Johnson said through his teeth.

"Julia, have you finally realized my offer's the best you're going to get?" Jeff gave her a wink and a sneer. To think she'd once found him attractive. She'd been such a fool. Charlie threw the set of plastic keys then went to retrieve them. Both men looked at him as though he was some sort of flesh-eating alien. There was no way she was going to let this family get their hands on her son for one minute, no matter what she had to do to prevent it.

"Jeffrey, be quiet." This from Maria. "Thanks to your on-campus dalliances, Ms. Morgan thinks she has some hold over us."

Jeff's voice turned petulant. "Mom, I didn't—"

"Sit down, son." Maria's voice took on a dictator-like quality and Jeff's mouth clamped shut. "You were groomed for so much more. We gave you everything." She pointed to the damask-covered couch. "Sit down and let your father and I fix this problem like we have all your others.

You've messed up things for the last time. We've got another chance with your son. I won't let you get in the way."

A sick pit grew in Julia's stomach as Jeff's shoulders slumped and he threw himself onto the couch. She'd known he didn't get along with his parents and now she understood why. She wondered how many of his problems were thanks to being raised by Mommy Dearest's twin sister.

Julia might have problems, but she knew she'd always put Charlie's best interests first in her life. Which was why she straightened her shoulders and said, "Jeff's not the only one in the family who has trouble keeping his parts in his pants." She waved a few more papers toward Dennis. "Like father, like son, from what I've discovered."

Dennis swallowed visibly as Maria sucked in a harsh breath. "How do you know that? No one has that information. I paid good money to make sure of it."

"Not enough, apparently." Julia picked up Charlie, who was grabbing at her legs. "Now let's talk—"

The door to the sitting room opened and Sam burst through, followed closely by the Johnsons' housekeeper.

"I'm sorry, ma'am," the older woman said, gasping. "He barged right past me."

Sam stood in the entry for a moment, looking every bit the bull in a china shop. Oh, how she loved him, even now. Every part of him. Julia's heart seemed to stop for a second. Charlie squirmed in her arms at the sight of Sam, squealing with delight. Julia hated that her body had the exact same reaction.

"The fake fiancé?" Jeff drawled from the couch. "Really, Julia? This is a bit of a production, even for you."

Sam pointed at Jeff. "Shut your mouth, pretty boy, or I'll come over and do it for you."

"What are you doing here, Sam?" Julia asked, her voice hoarse with emotion. She didn't want to need him. She didn't want to need anyone but was so relieved to not be fighting this battle alone, she could barely hold it together.

He looked at her and she knew he saw it, saw everything about her. He knew she had a tough exterior but was soft and scared at the core. And she knew it was okay to be vulnerable around him, that he wouldn't judge her or use her weakness to his advantage. Even with all that had happened between them, she ached to trust him. To lean on him and use his strength as her own.

"I'm here because at your side is where I belong. Forever."

"Don't bother," Maria said with a sniff. "There's no audience. The judge isn't here. No use pretending now, Chief Callahan. It's too late."

"That's where you're wrong." Sam took a step forward. "At least I hope you're wrong. Is it too late, Jules?"

"For what?"

"For me to be the man you want and need me to be." He walked toward her then bent to his knee. "For this." He pulled a small box out of his pocket and opened it, a diamond flanked by two emeralds twinkling up at her.

Julia and Maria gasped at the same time.

"It was my mother's ring. I want you to have it." He smiled at her hopefully. "I want all of it, Julia. You and Charlie and me. I love you. I want to spend the rest of my life proving how much. Proving I can be the man you deserve."

"What about the U.S. Marshals job?"

"I called today and said I wouldn't be joining them. The Brevia town council has renewed my contract for another three years. I'm there for keeps, and I want it to be with you. We're going to make this work. I'll be at your side fighting for Charlie, for our family, as long and as hard as it takes. Just don't give up on me, Julia."

Confined to her arms long enough, Charlie practically dived forward toward Sam, who wrapped his arms around him. "Hey, buddy. I've missed you."

He took the box from Sam's hand. "Here, Mama." Perched on Sam's knee, Charlie held the ring up to Julia.

She held out her hand, and the two men she loved most in the world slipped the ring onto her finger. "I love you, Sam. Always have. You had me at the car wreck two years ago."

He straightened and wrapped both her and Charlie in a tight hug then kissed her softly, using the pad of his thumb to wipe away the tears that flowed down her cheeks.

"This doesn't change anything," Maria hissed. "We've got all the time and money in the world."

"But don't forget the information I still have. I don't want to use it but I will, Mrs. Johnson. I'll do anything to keep my son safe."

"That won't be necessary." Jeff stood, looking as thoughtful and serious as Julia could ever remember.

"Jeffrey, stay out of this."

"Not this time, Mother." He took a step toward Julia and Sam. "I don't want to be a father. I never did. But I can tell you that my son deserves better than what I had growing up."

"You had everything," Dennis argued, his face turning bright red.

"He deserves a family who loves and cherishes him." Jeff's gaze never left Julia. "Have your attorney draw up the paperwork for me to relinquish custody and send it to my office at the university. I'll sign whatever you want me to."

"No!" his mother screeched.

Julia felt a lump form in her throat as Sam placed a

calming hand on her back. "Thank you, Jeff. You won't regret it."

One side of his mouth kicked up. "When it comes to funding my next research trip, I may. But I'll take that risk. Good luck, Julia." And with that, he walked from the room, followed quickly by his parents, screaming at him the entire way.

"Too 'oud," Charlie said, covering his ears with his chubby hands.

Sam's arm was strong around her shoulders. "Let's take our son home," he whispered against her ear. "We've got a wedding to plan."

* * * * *

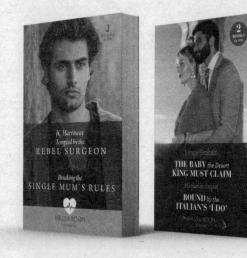

MILLS & BOON

HEROES

At Your Service

Experience all the excitement of a
gripping thriller, with an intense romance
at its heart. Resourceful, true-to-life
women and strong, fearless men face
danger and desire – a killer combination!

JOIN US ON SOCIAL MEDIA!

Stay up to date with our latest releases, author news and gossip, special offers and discounts, and all the behind-the-scenes action from Mills & Boon...

 @millsandboon

 @millsandboonuk

 facebook.com/millsandboon

 @millsandboonuk

It might just be true love...

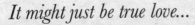

GET YOUR ROMANCE FIX!

Get the latest romance news, exclusive author interviews, story extracts and much more!